Iris Gower was born in Swansea. The mother
of four grown-up children, she now lives with
her husband in a house in Swansea overlooking
the sea she loves. She has written over fourteen
bestselling novels, and has recently been awarded
an MA in Creative Writing from the University
of Cardiff.

The Shoemaker's Daughter is the first title in her
Cordwainers series. *Sweet Rosie*, the third novel
in her latest series, the *Firebird* sequence, is
now available from Bantam Press.

Also by Iris Gower

THE LOVES OF CATRIN
THE OYSTER CATCHERS
HONEY'S FARM
ARIAN
SEA MISTRESS
THE WILD SEED
WHEN NIGHT CLOSES IN
FIREBIRD
DREAM CATCHER

and published by Corgi Books

THE
SHOEMAKER'S
DAUGHTER

Iris Gower

CORGI BOOKS

THE SHOEMAKER'S DAUGHTER
A CORGI BOOK : 0 552 13686 7

Originally published in Great Britain by Bantam Press,
a division of Transworld Publishers

PRINTING HISTORY
Bantam Press edition published 1991
Corgi edition published 1992

10

Set in 10/12pt Plantin by
County Typesetters, Margate, Kent.

Corgi Books are published by Transworld Publishers,
61–63 Uxbridge Road, London W5 5SA,
a division of The Random House Group Ltd,
in Australia by Random House Australia (Pty) Ltd,
20 Alfred Street, Milsons Point, Sydney, NSW 2061, Australia,
in New Zealand by Random House New Zealand Ltd,
18 Poland Road, Glenfield, Auckland 10, New Zealand
and in South Africa by Random House (Pty) Ltd,
Endulini, 5a Jubilee Road, Parktown 2193, South Africa.

Printed and bound in Great Britain by
Cox & Wyman Ltd, Reading, Berkshire.

For the two Joans
– in love and friendship

I

Hari Morgan sat near the fire grateful for its warmth; lighting the fire had been a long struggle, the sticks were damp and refused to catch, but at last the coals had blazed into life. Her arms ached, her fingers were blistered from the hard leather she had been working all day, her back ached from bending over the wooden last and the only thing she wanted was to fall asleep.

But from the bedroom above her the insistent hammering of a walking-stick against the boards was beating like a recurring pain in her head.

Hari sighed heavily and forcing herself to rise from the sagging armchair, stared out through the uncurtained window to where the shimmering gas lamp threw its pale light on the cobbled street.

World's End, that was what the locals called the small area beyond Wassail Square, a place of tall, decaying buildings, the slum area of Swansea according to the toffs. But Hari needed those toffs, they were her best customers. The richly dressed leather lords and the affluent copper barons in their fine houses on the open land above the town, it was they who paid her wages.

They all had a way of keeping her in her place, did her customers, only today Hari had been to Summer Lodge, the gracious house of the Grenfell family, perhaps the most influential family in Swansea.

In her basket, Hari had carried a pair of ladies' fine

riding boots, neatly soled and heeled and the leather lovingly polished.

Summer Lodge was a large, airy building facing the fresh breezes from the bay, and as Hari walked up the gracious sweeping drive, she heard the clatter of horses' hooves behind her. She glanced round to see Emily Grenfell ride past her without a glance.

The kitchen of Summer Lodge was the only part of the house Hari ever managed to see, it was huge and always smelled of succulent food. To Hari it underlined the difference in her own life and that of the rich Emily Grenfell.

But Hari had her pride, she earned her own living and though she did not bring in a fortune, she at least made enough to pay the rent and to keep herself and her mother in relative comfort. Though, worryingly, the work had been slow coming in of late.

The banging became more insistent. 'Angharad, what are you doing down there, have you gone deaf?'

Her mother never used the diminutive form of her name, but then Win Morgan was of the strong-minded Welsh stock that believed the old ways should be preserved for they had stood generations of her family in good stead. It was the sins of the present generation which would bring about the downfall of mankind, didn't the good book warn of such happenings?

As Hari entered the room, her mother looked up from her pillows. 'About time you brought me my medicine, *merchi*, I'm just about faint from the coughing that pains at my poor old lungs, mind.'

Hari resisted a smile, she was well aware that the gin in the glass did little to prevent the coughing that racked her mother's thin frame. But it did put mam in a better frame of mind and Hari obediently poured a good measure of the sweet scented liquid into the mug on the table.

'Angharad! You could at least get me a fresh mug, *duw*, the young people of today have no sense, mind.' Win Morgan warmed to her subject. 'In my young days we were expected to know how to raise a family by the time we were your age.'

'Yes, mam, you've told me all that many times before.' Hari sighed impatiently and her mother gave her a dark look.

'It's all right for you, my girl, you're young and strong, you can still get about, I'm stuck in my bed most of the time, remember.'

Hari tried to conceal her weariness. 'Can I get you something to eat, mam, a bit of egg custard tart or perhaps a little slice of bread and a bit of *cawse*?'

'No, not cheese again, Angharad, I'm not a mouse, can't you make me a bit of *cawl*, a nice hot bowl of soup would go down lovely now.'

Hari nodded wearily, there was a bit of mutton left from yesterday and if she cut the swede and carrots small enough it would not take long to cook her mother's supper.

Come to think of it she could do with something substantial herself, she'd given mam the last of the meat pie for dinner while she had made do with a slice of bread and honey.

She looked down at her figure, she was very thin, her small frame covered with a leather apron was almost boyishly slender, but since the death of her father Hari had worked harder than she had ever worked in her life.

Left to look after her mother, Hari had been determined to continue the trade of shoemaking that dad had taught her so painstakingly throughout the happy days of her childhood.

But now she was no longer a child, she was a woman of seventeen years and proud of the living, however poor, she carved out for herself in long hours and hard graft.

'Well, go on then, girl, don't stand there day dreaming, *duw*,' Win Morgan appealed to no-one in particular, her eyes raised heavenward. 'Did you ever see such a one as my daughter for gazing into thin air as if a thousand ghosts stood in her way.'

Hari moved down the rickety staircase, her feet tapping against the bare wood. It was very dark, the stock of candles was running low, she really must get out tomorrow and do a bit of shopping and yet could she spare the money?

She quickly cut up the few vegetables that were left in the basket in the larder and, after washing them in the cold darkness of the pump in the yard, threw them into the pot with the rest of yesterday's mutton.

The smell rose invitingly as the onions turned soft and simmered gently in the salted water.

What did her mother always say? A soup boiled was a soup spoiled. And it was true enough. 'But my stomach thinks my throat is cut, I'm that hungry.' Her voice fell into the silence of the kitchen and Hari felt suddenly so vulnerable. She sank into the old leather armchair that still bore the faint scent of her father's tobacco and tears shimmered on her lashes.

The light of the candles in the worn china holders flickered before her blurred vision like so many ghosts.

'Dad, why did you have to die?' It was a question she had asked many times but only in the silence of her own mind, it was a subject that her mother would not discuss, not after her angry outburst on the day of the funeral, her last foray from the sanctuary of her house.

She had loudly and bitterly blamed *Dewi* Morgan for leaving his sick wife alone in the world. As she had leaned heavily on Hari's arm, staring down into the black earth of her husband's grave, there had been the pain and grief but no tears.

Much as Hari felt for her mother, she could think of no words of comfort for her own grief was almost too much to bear. Fear of the future added to her sense of panic and Hari had bit her lip so hard that she'd drawn blood.

As she had led her mother back to the borrowed pony and trap, she was seized by a trembling that had nothing to do with the coldness of the wind blowing across the desolate cemetery.

But she could remember her father with pride, Dewi Morgan had been a strong man all his life, a big, genial man with a ready smile and a kind heart. Many a time he would tap the shoes of an out-of-work miner in exchange for a chicken or a rabbit ignoring the fact that the prize would have been come by illegally.

'*Duw*,' he would say, 'if a man can't take from the land that which is rightfully his, then things have come to a sorry pass.'

And now, Hari mused as she impatiently rubbed the back of her hand against her eyes, it was she and her mother who had come to a sorry pass for tomorrow the rent was due and only enough in the china teapot to pay for one more week.

The worst of it was that her mother had no idea of the difficulties that had beset Hari these past weeks, when the work had been slow to come in. Win Morgan had taken to her bed on the day of the funeral and seldom rose from it.

The renewed tapping on the ceiling roused Hari and she moved from the depths of her chair with a swiftness born of guilt; her mother was an invalid, she needed to be cared for and here was Hari mooning about feeling sorry for herself.

The soup was simmering nicely, exuding an aroma of mutton and herbs that made Hari's mouth water. She spooned out some of the liquid and it tasted like manna from heaven.

11

She moved to the larder and looked in the wooden bread basket and saw that there was only one thick crust left. Well, that would do for mam, especially if it was cut up into small pieces and arranged nicely on a china plate.

In spite of everything, mam had a hearty appetite and sometimes Hari felt she was dealing with a baby chick with its mouth constantly open waiting for sustenance which she was expected to provide.

She lifted the heavy wooden tray and placed the plate of bread upon it. The banging on the ceiling became more furious and Hari bit her lip in frustration.

'I'm coming, mam.' She deliberately kept her voice light; at any sign of irritation, mam would usually develop a fit of anger or worse, dissolve into tears. Hari recognized that the moods were the only outlet for Win Morgan's grief and tried to make allowances but sometimes it was very difficult.

Looking longingly at the generous helping of soup in the earthenware bowl, she felt like falling upon the meal and devouring it all but there was mam to see to first.

'About time too, Angharad, have you been growing the vegetables then?'

'No, mam,' Hari answered absent-mindedly, more concerned with settling the tray carefully over her mother's bad legs than listening to her grumbles. 'Come on now, eat up and I'll bring you a nice cup of hot milk after you've finished.'

Before her mother could say any more, Hari hurried from the room and clattered down the stairs anxious to have her own meal.

Her stomach ached with hunger and Hari sighed softly as she bent over the soup and began to eat. The mutton was a little tough but the vegetables were cooked perfectly, the flavour enhanced by the bay leaf and basil she had added to the stew.

She ate quickly and all too soon, the bowl was empty. Hari was tempted to have more of the rich-smelling soup, but she cautioned herself. 'Watch now, there's dinner tomorrow and nothing in the larder.'

She left the table and sank wearily into the hard-backed chair that stood beneath the window. She stared moodily out into the cobbled street, silent now but soon all that would change.

Once the night-time crowds flocked from their homes, World's End would be a different place, it would become a hub of activity, lights from the public bars would spill warmly on to the cobbles, voices would be raised in song and the street women would cajole the men into tasting the joys of the flesh.

While her father was alive, Hari was never allowed to look out into the night-time squalor of World's End, Dewi would hang his big apron over the window and all Hari could do was to imagine the scenes taking place in the street.

But now she saw it all, the drunken sailors greedily taking the first woman who came along and the men who had supped too long of the ale raising their fists to each other. The pickpockets would be having a fine old time, slipping expert fingers into coats and trousers extracting anything from money to a watch from some toff's waist-coat.

Hari had been surprised at first to see any of the rich patronizing the dangerous streets of World's End at night, but now she was used to the sight of a fine carriage bowling along the cobbles spilling out men, sometimes one alone but mostly groups of revellers, before rolling noisily away.

She moved from the chair and drew back from the window as two men paused outside the house, one of them carelessly unbuttoning his trousers swearing loudly as he urinated in the street. Some men, it seemed, were well drunk with ale before the night was half over.

The fire was dying low in the grate and, with a sigh, Hari thrust the poker into the embers riddling the ashes that fell like tiny stars of light to fade into the ash pan. She should have brought in a bowl of water and washed long before now, while the fire was full and threw out some light and warmth.

She fetched the chipped enamel basin from the scullery and took it into the kitchen. Tonight she would have what mam called a cow's lick, a quick wash over with a damp flannel rubbed on the cake of coarse soap that clung hard and cracked to the dish.

Hari placed the bowl on the floor before the spent fire and then quickly crossing the room, hung her father's apron over the window shutting out the night. She was a woman alone with no man to protect her, she must be careful.

She was so tired and it was with a sense of dismay that she saw the hem of her petticoat was muddied and slightly torn. When she had washed, she rubbed at the petticoat and then hung it over the warmth of the oven door.

It was time she locked up and went to bed. Hari moved to the door to slip home the bolt chiding herself for not doing it sooner.

Her hand was on the latch when suddenly the door was flung open. Startled and off balance, Hari stumbled back into the room crying out in fear. The candle flickered in the sudden draft and went out.

A tall figure stood over her, huge shoulders outlined against the flickering light from the street lamp.

Too frightened to speak, Hari tried to run but a hand grasped her shoulder, forcing her back against the wall and even in her terror, Hari noticed that the intruder was breathing heavily, as though he had been running for a long time.

The door was slammed shut and, in the darkness, the bolt shot home with a thud of finality and then Hari was aware of the huge shape moving about the room. The candle flickered into life once more and Hari stood blinking, forcing her eyes to focus on the man standing before her.

Her first impression was that he was a vagrant; he was wearing a torn coat and his hair was curling untidily about his forehead. His beard hung over his collarless shirt and yet direct, dark eyes looked into hers without fear.

'What do you want?' She tried to force some strength in to her tone but she was only too aware of the trembling thinness of her voice.

'I need somewhere to hide.' He spoke out strong and clear and his voice was the voice of a toff. 'I mean you no harm but please be quiet, I don't want to use force.'

He smiled, showing strong even teeth, 'And you are far too pretty for me to want to hurt you.'

Hari became aware that she was wearing only her under garments. 'Will you at least allow me to get dressed?' Hari felt the colour sweep into her face as he gave a mock bow and turned away.

Quickly, she slipped into her discarded clothes, her hands clumsy and slow as she struggled with the hooks and eyes of her damp petticoat. When she was dressed, she felt more composed and she turned to face the intruder more boldly.

'I need food,' he said before she could speak, 'will you fetch me something?'

Taken aback by his demand, she nodded. 'There's only a bit of soup in the pot but I suppose you can have that.' Warily she skirted round him and went over to the hob, ladling out what was left of the mutton soup and placing it on the table.

'It's cold, mind, and there's no bread.' She felt her fear ebbing away to be replaced by resentment. Why was she giving this stranger the last of her food? There was no sense in it.

As she retreated from the table, putting as much distance as she could between herself and the unkempt stranger, she almost laughed at her own foolish reasoning, she was in fear for her life and she was carping about giving a man a bit of soup.

He ate ravenously but his manners were impeccable. She watched him, hoping he would leave the house once he was finished but her hope was a vain one.

'I'll need to sleep here for tonight, are you alone in the house?' he asked. She glanced up to the ceiling and catching the look, he was on his feet in a moment, grasping her arm. 'Who lives here with you, you'd better tell me.'

She was tempted to lie and tell him she had a husband in bed but she didn't think he would believe her, from the sound of his voice he was an educated man.

'Only my mother and she's sick,' Hari said defensively. 'But who are you hiding from, what have you done?'

'Nothing,' he said quietly, 'but I am accused of taking money and the law in its wisdom, or lack of it, decided I was to go to prison.'

'The prison?' Hari said quickly. 'You've escaped from Swansea prison?'

'Quick witted as well as pretty.' She heard the laughter in his voice and she felt her colour rise.

'There's no need to make fun.' She drew away from him. 'All right, sleep down by here in the kitchen but you'd better be gone by the morning, mind.'

He moved towards the hearth without answering and began to mend the fire. Hari watched him, partly in fear but more in anger. There was no denying that he was a finely built man, his broad shoulders tapered into a slimness of hip that spoke of strength. His hair was thick and curly, hanging untidily round a narrow face, but clean and shaved, he would probably be quite presentable.

He glanced at her over his shoulder. 'You'll know me next time,' he said easily. Quickly Hari moved to the door aware that she had been staring at him.

'Go easy with the coal now,' she said, 'we haven't got any to waste, coal costs money don't forget. And put the candle out before you go to sleep, we don't want the place burning down.'

Hari had just climbed fully dressed into bed when a sudden sound of running footsteps sounded on the cobbles outside. She peered through the window and saw a group of men armed with truncheons going from house to house.

She was hurrying downstairs before she knew it. 'The constables,' she said, 'they're searching the houses.' The stranger nodded before moving swiftly through the scullery to disappear into the darkness.

Hari heard a hammering and for a moment she didn't know if it was in her head, because suddenly she felt dizzy. She forced herself to be calm and went back to the kitchen.

'What's that noise, who's disturbing decent people at this time of night?' she called and the door was banged again.

'Open up misses, there's a criminal about, let me in for to search the house, this man could be dangerous.'

Cautiously, Hari opened the door and saw the shining buttons of the police constable gleaming against the dark uniform.

'Well, there's no-one here but me and my mam,' Hari said quickly. 'Don't you think I'd be screaming my head

17

off if there was?' Why was she shielding the stranger, was she out of her mind?

'Well, I'll just take a look anyway, misses, righto?' The constable peered round the room and then moved to the scullery. Hari held her breath as he opened the back door.

'Do you think he might be hiding under the bed?' she asked quickly. 'I thought I heard a noise in the back bedroom a little while ago.'

'We'll have a look now, misses, don't you worry.' He hurried upstairs and sighing with relief, Hari followed him.

In the bedroom, Win Morgan was fast asleep, her pains eased by the gin, not even the flickering of the candle in the policeman's hand roused her.

Hari put her finger to her lips. 'Mam sleeps heavy, mind,' she said, 'if we don't make too much noise we won't wake her.'

She watched as the constable crouched on the floor peering beneath the sagging springs of the old bed. He straightened and shook his head without speaking.

As he moved to the backroom, Hari waited as he searched and then led the way downstairs to the kitchen. It was with a sense of relief she saw the constable shrug and move to the street door.

'Keep a sharp look out, mind,' the man said as he handed her the candle, 'the escaped criminal may be desperate.'

As Hari secured the door, she wondered why she wanted to protect the stranger from the law, but there was something about him she trusted.

She moved swiftly to the scullery and quietly opening the rear door, whispered into the darkness.

'You can come in, now.' She waited breathlessly but there was no reply from the shadows in the yard. With a mixture of disappointment and relief, Hari closed the back door and bolted it.

After a moment, she sighed heavily, her brief adventure was over and the intriguing stranger had gone from her life as abruptly as he had entered it.

2

Emily Grenfell clasped her hands together, sitting on the edge of her seat gazing through the small window of the coach as it rumbled along Mumbles Road in the fashionable area of Swansea. The journey from her home to the Assembly Rooms was a short one, but she was filled with excitement for she was at last being introduced into the social life of the town in a manner that befitted the daughter of one of Wales's leading leather lords.

Her father sat beside her and glancing at him she could see that he was quite puffed out with pride. His Albert gleamed rich gold against the fine cloth of his waistcoat, the fine watch lifted now from its hidden pocket to be scrutinized for the hundredth time, a sure sign that Thomas Grenfell was nervous. But then he didn't enjoy the hustle and bustle of Swansea's night-life, he preferred the warmth of his own fireside and the simple pleasures of a good cigar and a glass of brandy. It was simply out of duty to his only child that he was venturing out at all.

Emily glanced at her aunt; Sophie was half asleep against her seat, her hands quiet in her lap. Emily smiled, her aunt could be a holy terror but tonight she would be on her best behaviour because the élite of the Swansea gentry would be at the Race Ball and Aunt Sophie had not found herself invited into the social circles lately, not since Craig's arrest.

Emily pushed the unpleasant thought aside, she would

forget Craig and the trouble he was in, just for tonight, she promised herself.

Emily suddenly felt a surge of elation, she was eager for the new experience of being introduced into what she considered was the world of adulthood. She glanced down at her magnificent dress and the rich emerald jewellery glistening on her hands and throat, her mother's favourite gems.

There had been tears in her father's eyes as he'd handed her the satin-lined box containing the jewels and Emily, taking it, had felt a constriction in her throat for, with the gift, her father was recognizing she was now a woman.

As though reading her thoughts, Thomas reached out a large hand and covered Emily's cold fingers. 'You do an old man proud, *cariad*,' he said softly, 'I only wish your mother was here to see you today, she would have been so happy.'

'I know,' Emily said softly. She rested her head for a moment against his shoulder and then sat up straight, conscious that she must not ruffle her carefully coiffured hair.

Gloucester Place seemed awash with the carriages of other guests attending the ball and Emily chafed as she sat waiting impatiently to move on, watched by ladies' maids and servants of the lower orders who seemed to think that the spectacle was for their pleasure. Emily caught sight of the shoemaker's daughter, a basket over her arm, and for a moment their eyes locked and then Emily looked away. It was enough that the girl had made the shoes which she was wearing for this special occasion, she certainly had no place in this night of Emily's triumph.

A gentleman strolled casually past the carriage, staring at Emily with bold eyes much to her father's mixture of chagrin and pride.

'You see, *cariad*, the gentlemen can't keep their eyes off

you.' He laughed, 'I'll have no trouble finding you a good husband.'

Emily stared at him. 'But father, I'm going to marry Craig, it was all arranged years ago.'

'Hush, my dear, you don't want your aunt to hear us talk ill about her son. Now listen to me, all you feel for your cousin is only a childhood fancy.' His lip tightened. 'In any case, things are different now, you must see that. The man is a rogue, he stole from his own firm and now that he is serving time in Swansea Prison, I could never allow him near you, let alone marry you.'

Emily was suddenly cold. 'This is the first I've heard of your objection, father!' She could hardly believe her own ears. 'You know that Craig is innocent.'

Emily paused, angrily searching for the right words. 'I don't care what anyone says, Craig wouldn't stoop to thieving, I just know he wouldn't. How could you believe it of him?'

'The man is in prison, what further evidence do you need? Now be quiet, see the carriage is moving again.'

Emily remained silent, it was pointless arguing with her father. She'd better make the most of the occasion and put her views on marriage more forcibly once she returned home.

The coach drew to a jerky halt near the curbside. Aunt Sophie woke suddenly, eyes clear, as though she had never been asleep. She touched a hand to her hair and smiled at Emily, indicating she alight from the coach first.

Emily was being handed down to stand before the light-filled doorway of the Assembly Rooms and she took a deep breath of anticipation, this was her night, the night she was to be accepted as an adult and she would make the most of it.

In the main ballroom, the lights blazed from all sides and the many mirrors reflected the light a thousand-fold.

Emily gasped as she looked around her.

It seemed as if she was facing a sea of glittering gowns. Diamonds, emeralds, rubies and sapphires as well as a mixture of semi-precious stones glinted and sparkled at her from all directions. One woman seemed to drift in a sea of amethyst and diamonds, they were all about her, in her hair, on her gown, even her shoes were decorated with flowers made of amethyst with a huge diamond as a centre piece. She must have shoes just like that, Emily decided.

'Good thing I'm wearing mother's emeralds,' Emily whispered to her aunt, 'you won't see finer gems than mine anywhere in this room.'

She glanced at the backdrop of gentlemen, most of them in uniform, standing uncomfortably near the wall as though to divorce themselves from the proceedings and her heart sank as she thought of Craig, he should be here today, sharing in her adventure.

She had written to him while he was in prison but had received no reply, but then she had excused him in her own mind, telling herself he would be free soon, then he would come home to her and make her his bride.

Craig was a fine catch, a handsome man and one of action rather than words. She could not picture him behind the grim walls of Swansea Prison, instead she remembered him riding with her in the park, smiling down at her with his dark eyes, making her feel so small and helpless.

She glanced around the room, there wasn't a man here to come near to Craig for looks and presence.

Tomorrow she would ride in the park again but Craig would not be with her. But she would write and tell him how fine the flower-beds were and how across the road the sea rushed into the golden shore and she would tell him how much she missed him.

But no, she could not ride tomorrow, her boots had not

come back from the shoemaker's. Emily felt a flash of irritation, she had insisted that the shoemaker's daughter take the boots away to be soled and heeled and at the same time she'd had a fitting for some new slippers. The girl was a gifted shoemaker, but there was something insolent about her, perhaps it was the way she held her head high with her glorious abundant hair flowing free that somehow irritated Emily.

She had requested new riding boots but her father with unaccustomed frugality had told her bluntly she must be satisfied with having her old boots repaired.

The orchestra began to play, an air of excitement gripped Emily and she forgot the shoemaker's daughter, she even forgot Craig in the excitement of the occasion as some of the ladies swung like flowers on to the floor in the arms of the men. She sighed in anticipation, this would be an evening to remember for ever.

Hari was seated in the small shed at the side of the house bent industriously over the wooden last. She had soaked the leather to bend and shape it into the form of a small shoe, but her hands were sore and her back ached and she wondered briefly if there might be an easier way of making a living than the trade her father had chosen for her.

Dewi Morgan had disregarded the customs and brought up his daughter to do what folk considered a man's trade. Her hands, he had complained laughing, were a bit on the small side but they had learned strength and the skill was there already.

She paused for a moment remembering how from her earliest days she had sat with her father in the small shed working the leather. When she was older, he had paid for her to go to school, proud of her ability to read and write and work out figures. Dewi had wanted her to be independent, to fend for herself when he was no longer

24

there to take care of her, but he could not have known that his death would have come so suddenly, striking him down in the prime of his manhood.

Hari sighed and returned to her task, the shoes she was making were for Emily Grenfell. They were soft slippers, decorated with amethyst for wearing on thick carpets and Hari found herself envying the girl who seemed to have everything in life she could possibly want.

There had been reports in the pages of the *Cambrian* newspaper about Miss Grenfell attending the Race Ball in the Assembly Rooms. There was a description of her fine crinoline gown and of the Grenfell emeralds she had worn.

Hari remembered standing in the darkened street, watching the parade of carriages driving along Mumbles Road and into Gloucester Place. She had glimpsed Emily Grenfell who had been leaning forward in her carriage, staring out into the crowded roadway, her emeralds shining at her throat, the green richness of the stones glittering in the light from the street lamps. She thought wistfully of the shoes she had fashioned for Emily's triumph.

Hari's hands were suddenly still, the leather clinging to the last, while she tried to envisage herself wearing fine crinolines and rich jewels, it was like something out of a dream. But of course to Miss Hoity Toity Grenfell, it was nothing less than she expected.

Suddenly Hari thought of the man who had escaped from the prison, he was the same sort as Emily Grenfell, no doubt before he fell from grace they would have met and socialized.

The door swung open and a ragged boy stood framed in the early spring sunshine. 'Got a crust, misses?' he said softly. His shoulders drooped, he expected nothing, but a small flicker of hope showed in the uptilting of his chin.

'Aye, got better than that, William Davies,' Hari said,

'come on, I might be able to find you a bit of soup as well as some bread.'

She led him into the kitchen where the fire burnt cheerfully in the grate. There was a stock of food in the larder and coal in the cellar and she even had money to pay the rent for a month. Just when she had been on the brink of despair, one of her rich customers had given her a handsome order.

Mr Edward Morris wanted several pairs of boots to be soled and heeled and what's more he had paid for the work in advance.

'Here, Will, sit down and I'll warm the soup for you and then after you've eaten perhaps you'll deliver some repairs for me.'

She watched as the boy ate ravenously, he was one of a large family and though his father was in regular employment at the copper works, he drank a great deal and kept his wife and children short of even the bare necessities of life.

It made Hari so angry to see the little ones neglected but there was very little anyone could do, poverty was a fact of life in places like World's End.

She glanced at the clock, it was a wonder mother wasn't banging on the floor with her stick by now, it was way past dinner time.

Quickly, Hari ladled the soup into bowls and cut a few thick pieces of bread, suddenly realizing that she was hungry too.

'Get on with it, Will,' she said, 'I'll be down in a minute, got to see to my mam.'

'*Duw*, where you been then, Angharad?' Win Morgan had obviously just woken from sleep, her eyes were heavy and her thin grey hair ruffled. 'Been waiting all the morning for a bit of attention from my only daughter, not much for a sick mother to ask, is it?'

'Sorry, mam,' Hari replied absently. 'Here have your dinner and then after I'll bring a bowl of water for you to wash, right?'

'Soup again, is it? I'll be looking like soup, can't we have a change sometimes, Angharad?'

Hari looked at her mother in exasperation. 'I don't know, mam, you're never satisfied.' She spoke loudly because her mother was a little deaf and smiled to soften her words. 'If I give you bread and cheese you don't like it and if I give you too much soup that's not right. What would you like? Just tell me and I'll try to get it for you.'

Win Morgan smiled with a flash of humour that was rare because she was a woman grown old before her time, worn by the constant pain of her bone ache and wearied by the persistent cough that racked her.

'How about a bit of jugged hare or perhaps a nice plump breast of chicken,' she said, knowing full well that such delicacies were beyond the reach of the poor worker.

But a neck of lamb made an excellent *cawl* and a knuckle of pork was cheap and nutritious. Meat was a treat kept for good days and when the pickings were poor, Win and her daughter were lucky to have enough potatoes and bread and cheese in the pantry.

There was a loud clatter from the kitchen and Win Morgan lifted her head. 'Who is that downstairs?' she said suspiciously. Hari smiled.

'It's only young Will Davies, dropped his bowl on the floor by the sound of it.' She patted her mother's hand. 'He's going to do some errands for me so I thought it only fair to give him a bit of food.'

'Too soft you are, girl,' Win Morgan broke her bread into small pieces soaking them in the soup, 'can't be responsible for the whole neighbourhood, can you? Just like your dad, you are and didn't I tell him that teaching you reading and writing wouldn't bring any good?'

Hari moved to the door. 'If I couldn't read and write, mam, I'd have a hard job running my boot and shoe round, wouldn't I?'

She hurried back down the stairs to find Will mopping up the remains of his soup from the stone-flagged kitchen floor. 'Sorry, misses, didn't mean to spill it, lovely it was.'

Hari shook back a strand of hair that had fallen from the pins. 'Don't worry, after you've done the deliveries for me, you can take the rest of the bread and soup home with you. Now, come into the workshop and I'll give you the boots I want delivered.'

Will followed her willingly and listened while Hari explained that the boots were to be taken to Edward Morris who lived in the big white house in Chapel Street.

'You can't miss it,' Hari said reassuringly, 'it's the only one in the street with railings around it.'

When Will had disappeared from sight, Hari set to work on the slippers once more, they must be just so because Emily Grenfell was a good customer if a very exacting one.

She was easing her back with her hands, happy with the shoes near to completion, when young Will returned. He stood in the doorway, his nose bloody, his face marked with tears. Hari felt a chill fall over her.

'What's wrong, Will?' she asked apprehensively and at the sound of her voice, he burst into tears.

'I couldn't 'elp it, misses,' he sobbed, 'bigger than me he was, this boy set about me and when I was on the floor he kicked me and took the boots away from me. I tried to fight, honest I did, but he were too strong and my head was hurting and . . .' Unable to continue, Will put his hands over his eyes and the tears flowed through his small thin fingers.

Hari felt cold panic wash over her, she had done the unforgivable, she had lost a customer's boots. It was something that had never happened before and she stood for a moment trying to control the thoughts that raced through her head.

'It's all right, Will,' she said at last, 'come on, be a man now, no more crying.' She drew a shawl around her shoulders. 'You must show me where the boy went after he took the boots, we'll get them back, don't worry.'

William looked up at her, hope shining through his tears. 'Will we, misses?' he asked and his air of total belief in her banished the last of Hari's uncertainty.

She followed Will along the mean cobbled streets until he paused alongside a narrow alley. A woman was leaning against the door of one of the houses, her gaudily painted face revealing her trade.

'He ran down there,' Will said. 'There's the one, down the alley, look!'

The boy was ragged and dirty and for a moment he stood transfixed staring at Hari and Will as though he couldn't believe his eyes. Then suddenly, he vanished into the doorway where the woman had stood and Hari lifted her skirts and ran after him, her hair flying behind her.

The door was shut fast but Hari hammered on it, anger lending her strength. She tried the handle but the door had obviously been bolted from the inside. Nothing daunted, Hari moved to the side of the house and saw that a small window was open. 'Will,' she said quietly, 'if I help you to get in, can you open the door for me?'

His face was pale with fear but he nodded willingly. Hari half lifted half pushed him through the window and then she waited breathlessly for any sounds that would indicate that Will had been discovered, but when there was nothing, she moved to the door and to her relief, she saw it swing open.

'Good boy!' She kissed his cheek. 'Now get out of sight

until you see me come back. If I'm not out in ten minutes fetch a constable.'

Hari moved along the dark passageway and from the kitchen at the back of the house she heard the sound of voices. She knocked loudly on the kitchen door and waited for a moment, aware of the total silence from within the room. She was lifting her hand to knock again when the door was flung open and she was confronted by the woman she'd seen outside who stared at her defiantly, her painted face incongruous against the fall of grimy hair over her shoulders.

'*Daro!* What do you think you're doing coming in here without so much as by your leave?'

Hari looked over the woman's shoulder and the first thing she saw was the leather boots standing on the table. Of the boy who had taken them there was no sign. Hari pushed past the woman and picked up the boots hugging them to her in a rush of relief.

'These boots do not belong to you,' Hari said fiercely, and as the woman moved menacingly towards her, she held up her hand.

'The constable is on his way so don't do anything foolish, will you?'

The woman paused and stared at her suspiciously. 'If the constable is coming anyway what have I to lose by giving you a good pasting and throwing the boots in the canal?'

'A great deal,' Hari spoke with more confidence than she felt, indeed, she was trembling inside and she could only hope her nervousness didn't show. 'If I go now I'll meet the constable on the way and tell him it was all a misunderstanding.'

The woman rubbed a dirty bare foot into the sawdust on the floor. 'How do I know you're telling the truth? How would the constable know where to come?'

'I had help getting in here,' Hari said quickly, 'I didn't get in through a bolted door on my own now, did I?'

The woman thought about this and after a moment looked up at Hari with venom in her eyes.

'My name is Maria Payton, remember it well,' she said. 'See this gob,' she pointed to her painted mouth, 'it can talk a lot and these peepers can see a lot, they'll remember you, mind, and if there's anything I can do to hurt you any time then I will.'

Hari moved past the woman and as she negotiated the narrow passageway, her legs would hardly carry her.

Outside, she took a deep breath and, after a moment, Will appeared and stood silently at her side.

'Come on,' Hari said quickly, 'let's get out of here.'

She sighed with relief when the seedy, rundown houses were left behind. 'Go on home, Will,' she said, 'I'll take the boots to the customer.' She saw a look of disappointment cross the young boy's face. 'Oh, and on the way,' she added quickly, 'don't forget to pick up that bowl of *cawl*, all right?'

He sped away, his bare feet barely touching the cold stone of the roadway and, with a sigh, Hari turned towards Chapel Street.

The houses here were of the same structure as the mean buildings where Hari lived but the properties were well maintained, the outsides freshly painted, the windows gleaming with cleanliness and hung with rich drapes. Here the houses would be occupied by one family and not by a dozen or more assorted tenants.

But at the end of the road was the big white house where Edward Morris lived, a gracious house standing out from the others because it sported white railings which guarded the small, well-kept garden.

Hari knocked on the door and it was quickly opened by a young maidservant who looked her over in disdain. Hari became suddenly aware that her hair was flying loose over her shoulders and the hem of her dress was stained with mud.

'Please to go round the back,' the maid said and, without another word, closed the door in Hari's face. With a sigh, Hari moved to the back entrance and knocked again. She waited what seemed an interminably long time before the same young maid again confronted her.

'What is your business?' The maid looked at a point above Hari's head.

'I have a delivery for Mr Morris,' Hari said shortly, 'I should have thought that much was obvious even to you.'

'Step inside.' The girl didn't deign to rise to the bait. 'I'll see if Mr Morris will speak with you.'

After a time, the girl returned and, with obvious reluctance, led Hari into the sitting-room. It was a high-ceilinged, gracious room with thick carpet under-foot and rich curtains over the windows.

A visitor sat in a chair near the elegant grate where a huge fire burned, he glanced up at her and his eyes narrowed. He had dark eyes, thickly lashed and they regarded her steadily almost as if he knew her. And strangely enough she felt that she knew him but that was absurd, she had never seen him before.

The silence was broken by the entrance of Edward Morris, he smiled at her warmly and she returned his smile for this was a generous customer, a rare being who had paid her in advance for her work. And she had almost lost him by the attempted theft of his best boots.

'I want to be measured for some more boots,' Edward said, 'but you look a little shaken so I'm sure it can wait until another day.'

'I'm sorry I look such a state.' Hari decided to be truthful. 'Your boots were stolen from young Will as he was delivering them.' She smiled, 'But I made sure I got them back again, mind.'

Edward took the boots and glanced at the man sitting in the chair. 'Isn't she a remarkable girl, Craig?' he said, 'Not only does she repair shoes as good as any man, but she fights for her rights, too.' He smiled at Hari, 'I admire your spirit young lady.'

Hari felt her colour rising. 'It's nothing, I was only doing my job.'

The man in the chair spoke for the first time. 'Who taught you the trade?' His voice was cultured, he spoke with a more cosmopolitan accent than Edward Morris who though obviously educated and quite well to do had a marked Welsh accent.

'My father, Dewi Morgan taught me shoemaking from the time I was a little girl,' she said quickly, almost resentfully, 'and I'm better at the work than many men.'

'I see.' The man smiled at her and though she didn't understand why, she felt he was laughing at her.

Hari moved to the door. 'If that's all then, I'll be getting back home.' She bobbed a curtsy and put her hand on the gleaming brass door knob. 'I'll come and do some measuring in the morning if that suits,' she said. Edward Morris smiled and nodded but it was the stranger who spoke.

'*I'll* definitely keep you in mind,' he said and as his dark eyes met hers he seemed again to be laughing at her.

Hari hurried back along the street anxious to get home, it was turning colder and the night was closing in. She ran through the last few streets and saw with relief the familiar tall building rising against the night sky.

She let herself into the kitchen and sank into a chair before the fire that urgently needed mending. Hari rubbed her hand over her eyes, it had been a strange day, an eventful one in which she had quite clearly made an enemy but perhaps she had also made a friend of Edward Morris.

And yet it was not the face of her customer that she saw in her mind, but the strong lean jaw and the dark unfathomable eyes of a stranger.

3

Craig Grenfell stared moodily through the window of his friend's house in Chapel Street, his hands were thrust into his pockets, and his shoulders were slumped. He was remembering the bitterness of his arrest and the ignominy of being imprisoned behind the grim walls of Swansea Prison. He looked out into the roadway without seeing the rain beating mercilessly against the cobbled surface or the leaves of the trees dripping constantly as they shivered in the breeze, he was seeing the four walls of his cell and remembering his feeling of helplessness as the door slammed shut behind him.

Craig glanced down at the sheaf of papers lying on the small table beside him, brought to him earlier in the day by Edward Morris, papers that proved Craig's innocence. But at what cost?

Craig rubbed at his forehead in a mingling of anger and despair. To clear himself he would have to implicate his young brother in the embezzlement of a large amount of money from the family business, it would break his mother's heart.

Spencer had always been the favoured one, beloved by mother since his difficult birth made it impossible for her to have any more children. Spencer had been spoiled, treated for far too long as a baby and he had grown up knowing how to twist his mother around his little finger.

Spencer had always appeared to conform, he wore neat

35

clothes and acted the gentleman. He was the sort of son that Sophie Grenfell had always wanted, the pity of it all, from his mother's point of view, was that he was the younger son.

Edward entered the room and stood before the fire. 'Well, Craig, what conclusions do you draw from the pages I managed to "borrow" from the firm's accounting books?'

'The same conclusion as you I imagine. My brother is a very cunning young man.' Craig lifted one of the pages. 'The accounts have obviously been falsified.' Craig pointed to a duplicate sheet. 'Here, figures as they should read.' He glanced up at his friend.

'Spencer has been taking money from customers and only entering a part of the amounts in the books. He must have embezzled thousands of pounds over the years.'

Craig looked at Edward curiously. 'As accountant for the firm, did you never question the validity of the books?'

Edward shrugged. 'I doubted the figures, yes, the drop in profits was apparent but without the both sets of accounts, there was no hard evidence of any malpractice. Markets do fluctuate, you know.'

Craig moved restlessly from the window. 'The stupid young fool!' he said angrily. 'Why jeopardize what he had going for him by getting greedy? If he'd been moderate in his thieving he would never have been caught.'

'They are all caught sooner or later,' Edward said sagely and Craig stared at him.

'Perhaps you're right but there are not many who would shift the blame on to a brother's shoulders. Spencer was very clever, putting money into my account and hiding banknotes in my room. I wouldn't have thought even he could have been so calculating.'

Edward shook his head. 'Some folk will do anything for money, money makes many a man into a fool or a villain.' He poured a brandy and handed it to Craig before helping himself to a good measure. 'The question is, what are you going to do about it now?'

Craig lifted his glass admiring the slant of light through the brandy. 'I have to think about it. One thing I do know, I'm not going back to that God-awful prison whatever happens.'

He sank back into his chair. 'I've a great deal to thank you for, Edward,' he said, 'not many would have helped me the way you did or taken me in the way I looked that night.'

He smiled wryly. 'I'll never forget, playing sick to get out of my cell and then the waiting for the bread van to come and pick me up. You must have given the driver some bribe, Edward, I don't know how he managed to help me at all, he was terrified of being caught.'

Craig looked into his glass. 'The whole thing seems unreal now except perhaps the look on the face of the shoemaker's daughter when I pushed my way into her house. She must have been very frightened. I must say I admired her spirit.'

'And she yours,' Edward said drolly. 'Hari Morgan didn't give you away, did she? The old Grenfell charm must have been working even under all that hair not to mention the scruffy beard.'

'She warned me that the constables were on their way, right enough, and I'll always be grateful to her for that. But, in the end, the kindest thing to do was to get out of her way.'

'She's wonderful,' Edward said, his voice warm, 'looking as you did, she would have been justified in turning you in. I hardly recognized you myself.'

Edward smiled, 'But a bath and a shave and some clean clothes worked wonders.'

Craig stared into the fire, it had been over a week since he had escaped from the prison, lying in the back of the van, smelling the fresh mouthwatering tang of bread and listening to the clip clop of the horses' hooves.

And the terrible moment when he heard the sound of officious voices calling to the driver to stop and Craig had taken his chance and leaped from the back of the van and disappeared into the dark streets of World's End. If it hadn't been for the proximity of the tall dour houses and the unexpected kindness of a young girl, Craig would have been recaptured at once.

'It was good of you to give the shoemaker's daughter work,' Craig said taking a sip of the brandy. It stung his throat, tasting rich and hot as he swallowed. 'I don't think you could have thought of a better way of rewarding her, she seems such an independent little thing.'

Edward stared at him eyebrows raised. 'Lovely, isn't she? Such fine features and blessed with thick lustrous hair as well as a shape that would fill any man's dreams.'

'I see,' Craig said in amusement, 'so your kindness to the young lady wasn't entirely for my benefit.'

'I had noticed some time ago that the shoemaker had a beautiful daughter and the more I saw of her, the more I liked her.' He smiled. 'I always make sure I have several fittings before I'm satisfied with my boots, that way I get to talk to Hari.

'And she's a fine shoemaker, she has real talent and with a little help she could go far. Some of the ladies from the finest houses have their fancy shoes made by Hari Morgan.' He paused stroking his chin. 'You know she carried on the business alone when her father died, got guts has that girl.' He smiled wickedly, 'And she moves so gracefully, too.'

There was a sudden, loud knocking on the door. Craig set down his glass and taking up the papers moved swiftly across the room.

'It must be the police,' he said tersely. 'My dear brother

must have guessed I'd come here and tipped them off, but then he wouldn't know I had these.' He held up the papers. 'Keep them talking as long as you can, Edward, give me a chance to get out of here.'

Craig hurried up the stairs as the knocking became more insistent and paused for a moment staring back to the hallway. Edward was demanding that the callers be patient, he was coming as fast as he could.

Craig made his way to the attic and looked about him, quickly assessing the situation. There was a skylight in the attic but the sloping roof was higher than he had anticipated and he needed something to stand on.

He moved a pile of old furniture and found a broken chair with its back missing. He stood it beneath the skylight just as he heard footsteps pounding up the stairs.

He pushed at the skylight, it would not budge. Cursing, he thrust at it with his elbow and the glass shattered in fragments around him.

The footsteps were getting nearer and from the sound of it there were at least a dozen men. With strength born of desperation, Craig heaved himself up and pushed his way through the broken window just as the door burst open below him.

The roof sloped away alarmingly and, for a moment, Craig almost lost his balance. Steadying himself, he made his way over the roof and on to the parapet that ran along the side of the building. A yawning gap opened up before him and, down below, he saw a group of people staring up at him, arms waving.

He moved back a few paces and, without pausing to think, took a running leap out into the chasm between the two houses. He heard a gasp from the crowd of people gathered below, he seemed to hang forever in mid-air and then, miraculously, he was crashing down on to the opposite roof.

His foot slipped and he grasped at a piece of jutting tile and dragged himself back to safety. Carefully, he crawled the breadth of the building and, to his relief, he saw that the house beneath him was one of a row. He realized that he was following the pattern of the streets, moving into the poor area of World's End.

More easily now, he made his way along the roof-tops, hidden from sight by the forest of chimney stacks. He was breathless with the effort of clinging precariously to the limited footholds and it was time, he decided, to risk climbing down to the ground.

He let himself into one of the houses through the skylight and waited, hardly daring to breath, to see if he had been detected. There was no sound from below and, carefully, Craig opened a door and stared out into the shabby passageway.

The place in which he found himself was a tall grimy building with a long passageway and the whole place reeked of cheap perfume. He had entered, he realized with a flash of amusement, into what was obviously a whorehouse.

He brushed down his hair and straightened his clothing and made his way down the narrow stairs towards the street. A woman appeared in the lower passageway and smiled up at him, her painted face shrewd.

'Did you enjoy your visit, sir?' Her eyes appraised him and her thin fingers were spread towards him fanwise, it was clear she expected some money. She peered closer, 'Aren't you Mr Spencer Grenfell? It's me, Maria Payton.'

'That's right.' He smiled at her and touched her cheek with his fingertip. 'And I did indeed enjoy my visit but I think I have missed the best treat in the entire house, what a pity I didn't see you first.' He bowed over her outstretched hand and then left quickly before she had

40

time to gather her wits. So that was where Spencer wasted some of his ill-gotten gains, was it?

It was growing dark, the moon hung between the trees in a misty haze as though unwilling to appear at all. Craig looked around him and realized he had been here before. It was the place where the young shoemaker's daughter lived. Perhaps it would be just as well if he paid her another visit.

Hari was working late and the candle over her shoulder provided little enough light. Two candles would be wasteful but the small stitches she was making in the soft leather swam before her eyes in the poor light. She straightened her shoulders, perhaps she had done enough for today, mam would be getting restless wanting a bit of attention after her long day spent mostly alone. It was not an ideal situation, Hari found it difficult to cope with the hard exacting work of a shoemaker and the demands of her short tempered mother.

'*Chware teg*, mam's not that bad.' The sound of her own voice in the shimmering candle-light startled Hari and she rose to her feet, conscious of the silence around her.

Then she heard the noise, a creaking of wood, it was repeated and Hari looked round nervously. But she was being absurd, she was over tired and imagining things.

But she was not imagining things, the latch on the door from the street was being lifted and Hari waited, holding her breath. So far, none of the ruffians from World's End had bothered her even though she was a young woman alone. Villains they might be, but they had a certain code of practice and the rule was that you looked after your own kind.

'Who is it?' Hari said with a boldness she was far from

41

feeling. The door opened wider and a man stepped inside from the growing darkness of the street.

Hari recognized him at once, he was the friend of Edward Morris, she had seen him earlier sitting before the fire in the comfortable house on Chapel Street.

'What . . . ?' she began but he put his finger to his lips in a warning gesture. Hari tensed, there was something about the situation that was familiar. A week ago a man on the run had come into her house, he had been unkempt, his hair curling thickly about his face, he had not been as well groomed as the man standing before her now, but the breadth of shoulder was the same and something about the dark eyes staring into hers touched a chord.

'You are the escaped prisoner,' she said softly and he nodded wryly.

'That's right, I'm not begging food this time but clothing, have you anything to make me look like a man from these parts?'

Hari gestured that he follow her through the door into the small back yard and from there into the small workshop.

'Here.' Swiftly, Hari selected some of her father's working clothes and returned to the kitchen.

She found she was trembling, not with fear but with excitement, there was something about helping the most unusual villain she'd ever seen that stirred unknown feelings deep within her.

He came into the kitchen looking strange in her father's trousers and leather waistcoat. He came and stood close to her without touching her, but Hari was as tinglingly aware of him as though he'd embraced her.

'I'll see to the fire and then I'll make you some tea.' She knelt on the cold stone floor and carefully placed some coals on the dying embers in the grate. She was foolishly irritated by the lack of warmth and the slowness of the coals to light and all the time she was asking herself if she was completely mad harbouring an escaped criminal in her kitchen.

She heard the sounds behind her of her father's leather apron being tied in place and, for a moment, she could imagine her father was with her again, big and comforting, a shield between Hari and the world. Then she turned and saw the stranger.

As she watched, he took up his discarded clothing and thrust the garments into the nearest cupboard. 'There may be a search,' he said apologetically.

'Who are you?' Hari said quietly, 'There's things I need to know before I take any more risks for you.'

He stared at her steadily for a moment and then nodded. 'You're right. Sit down.' He thrust his hands into his pockets and the leather apron creaked as he moved. Hari thought again of her father and sitting there on the edge of her seat she believed that the man standing before her, handsome and young though he might be, was the same kind of man as Dewi Morgan, upright and steadfast, his eyes clear and direct as they looked down at her.

'I'm Craig Grenfell.' The words fell into the silence and Hari waited for him to continue. 'Some months ago I was convicted of embezzling a considerable amount of money from the company I share with my brother. I was innocent but the evidence was damning.' He frowned as he moved about the room.

'I could do nothing while I was behind bars so I was forced to make a run for it.' He was looking at her but now there was a far-away look in his eyes as though he'd forgotten her presence. 'Now I'm almost there, a little more time and I'll prove my innocence.'

Craig ran his hand through his hair so that it sprung into small curls giving him a rakish appearance. 'Oh, it's all been very cleverly done.' He sank down into a chair opposite Hari. 'But perhaps my brother has become over-confident.'

Craig's jaw tightened. 'I have papers that prove the books have been forged but now I need someone to help me. I can hardly walk into a lawyer's office, I'd be arrested again and I don't intend going back into prison, not even for a few days.'

'What about Mr Morris?' Hari asked. 'Couldn't he do it for you?'

Craig shook his head. 'I couldn't let Edward take that risk, he might get himself arrested for stealing pages from the account books, they are company property after all.'

'Could I see a lawyer for you?' Hari was amazed to hear herself making the offer.

Craig shook his head. 'No,' he smiled apologetically, 'I'm afraid you would not be given a hearing.' He smiled suddenly. 'Not that anyone as beautiful as you could be ignored of course.' His dark eyes stared into hers.

Hari's wash of hurt pride and anger vanished as suddenly as it had come, though she realized that Craig's words were no more than flattery. He was a man capable of great charm, but she would have to be careful that she didn't get taken in by it, Hari told herself sternly.

'Don't feel insulted, please,' he said. 'I'm refusing your generous offer as much for your sake as my own. I don't want you to get hurt.'

'Who then?' Hari said softly and Craig looked at her and sighed heavily.

'My fiancée, Emily Grenfell,' he said, 'she is forceful and strong, her background gives her standing and she won't be easily outwitted.' He rubbed his hand through his dark hair.

Hari was surprised at the rush of pure jealousy that swept over her at the mention of Emily Grenfell. But she was being absurd, she scarcely knew this man and what

44

was it to her who he was betrothed to? He'd made it abundantly clear that Hari was of no account in the community, that she could not be trusted to carry any weight with lawyers and the like.

She rose from her chair. 'I've got things to do,' she said stiffly, 'my mother is an invalid, I have to go and see to her.'

She took some bread from the pantry cupboard and placed it on the wooden table. 'If you are hungry there's some cheese,' she said, 'I can't wait on you, I'm too tired for that.'

He came and stood close to her, his hand resting on her shoulder. 'I've made you angry and I'm sorry.' His hand was warm and strong and Hari resisted the urge to turn into his arms and rest her head against his broad shoulder.

'I'm not angry,' she said flatly. 'But it's not very nice to take a convicted criminal into your home and then to have him tell you that you're of little consequence.'

He turned her to face him. 'If I gave that impression then I can only apologize once again,' he said. 'You are a very brave young woman and a very beautiful one.' He released her abruptly. 'And I'm keeping you from your duties.'

Hari quickly moved to the foot of the stairs, her head bent to hide the blush that warmed her cheeks. 'I won't be long,' she said and hurriedly left the room.

When Hari returned she saw that Craig was standing at the window looking out into the darkness. His shoulders were tense and there was an air of waiting about him that troubled her.

'The constables are coming,' he said tersely as he moved back into the room. 'I hope you are a good liar.'

Hari shook her head in fear and looked around her as though expecting a solution to present itself.

Gathering her wits, she hurried into the workshop and picked up a last and a half-tapped boot. Returning to the kitchen, she indicated with a nod of her head that Craig sit on the stool near the fire. She put the last in his lap. 'Hold it between your knees,' she hissed and then she stood behind him, leaning over his shoulder as though instructing him.

'*Duw*, what's this interruption then?' Hari said as the door was pushed open, looking over her shoulder. 'Oh, it's you, Dai the Cop-shop, poking your nose in my business, is it? Well, since you are so interested, this is my cousin come from the Neath Valley to help in the business. Want to make anything of it then?'

The constable looked at Craig's leather apron and rough flannel shirt and, at last, his eyes slid away from Hari's challenging gaze.

'Haven't you always known me to be a respectable girl then, Dai?' She leaned on Craig's shoulder as if she'd known him all her life. 'And don't go making a noise and waking mam, now, I know she's deaf but you lot sound like a herd of cattle, mind.'

Dai backed away. 'All right, Hari Morgan, only doing my duty I am.' He turned to look over his shoulder. 'Nothing suspicious here, boys,' he called, 'get on with the search.'

For a long moment after the door had closed, Craig and Hari remained motionless, so close together that she could feel his breath against her cheek. His mouth, so strong beneath the dark moustache, was tantalizingly close. And then she moved and with trembling hands smoothed down her skirt.

Craig rose to his feet, placing the last on the table. 'You are a very resourceful woman, Hari.'

'It was nothing,' she said quickly. 'Sleep by the fire, you, I'm going to bed.'

As she lay between the sheets, Hari felt a great restlessness grip her, she thought of Craig's face so close to hers

46

and she could barely breathe for the confused emotions that raced through her. But, she told herself sternly, she was nothing but a foolish girl, men the like of Craig Grenfell were not for Hari Morgan.

Suddenly and inexplicably tears were running hot and bitter down her cheeks as Hari buried her face in the pillow and wept.

4

Emily Grenfell looked up from her book as the maid entered the room bobbing a swift curtsy, her face red with indignation.

'What is it, Letty?' Emily said, impatient at being disturbed. She hadn't been reading at all but had been glancing out of the window not seeing the gracious gardens that surrounded Summer Lodge, but planning ways to help Craig when he came to her. And now that he'd escaped from that awful prison, come he would, she knew that as certainly as she knew daylight would follow darkness.

'There's a *girl* to see you, Miss Emily, insists on it she does, quite cheeky she is, mind.' There was a world of disdain in the young maid's voice.

Emily frowned. 'Insists? Who *is* she exactly?'

'The shoemaker's daughter, miss, says she got a message from Mister Grenfell.'

Emily's thoughts raced, could the girl possibly know anything about Craig?

'Bring her in to me, I'll soon sort out just what it is she wants,' Emily said, rising to her feet and shaking the creases from her crinoline gown.

Letty seemed about to demur but Emily lifted her chin challengingly and the maid bobbed and left the room.

Emily paced around the book-lined study and blamed her father for his hostile attitude to Craig. It was that sort of attitude that would prevent Craig from coming to her directly for help.

Her father was kindness itself, but he was the sort of man who gave little credit to anyone who had fallen from grace.

Letty knocked and glancing up Emily saw a slight figure with a mass of dark hair following the maid into the room. The shoemaker's daughter was pretty enough but poorly dressed with a Welsh shawl over her shoulders and not even a hat to cover her hair.

Emily waved her hand to Letty, 'I'll send for you when I want you.' She moved towards a seat and regarded the girl steadily for a long moment. If she'd hoped to unnerve her the way she did Letty then she was wrong.

'Yes?' Emily said sharply, 'What do you want?'

'I'm Angharad Morgan,' the girl began, her dark eyes challenging Emily to interrupt. 'I was asked to bring you these papers.'

She brought from under her shawl an untidy sheaf of documents and handed them to Emily without so much as bobbing a polite curtsy.

Emily took them, glancing at them quickly. 'So? These are sheets from an accounts book, what are they to me?'

The girl lowered her voice. 'They might clear the name of Craig Grenfell. Anyway,' she said challengingly, 'he thought you'd be able to help him, perhaps he was wrong.'

Emily sank down into a chair and studied the pages closely, controlling the urge to slap the insolent hussy's pretty face. On closer inspection it became clear there were two sets of figures for the same period of time for the Grenfell Leather Trading Company. The profit margin on one sheet was much lower than the other and Emily drew in her breath sharply. It was obvious that someone had robbed the company of a great deal of money and Craig was trusting her to find out who.

Emily frowned, 'Have you looked at these?' She glanced up at the girl standing before her and shook her head. 'How silly of me, I don't suppose you can even read let alone add all this up.'

'Indeed I can!' the girl answered with quiet confidence. 'The figures mean that someone has been defrauding the company and it wasn't Craig Grenfell because if you look at the dates you'll see that the fiddling went on even when Craig was in prison.' The girl fell silent as Emily approached her.

'Mr Grenfell to you. And what do you know about him?' Emily asked in a dangerously quiet voice. The girl shook her head.

'You must get all this seen to properly if you want to clear Craig's name, that's all I know.'

Emily felt anger run through her. 'How dare you try to tell *me* what to do?' she spoke icily. 'You are an ignorant, uneducated girl and now you've delivered your message, you'd better leave.'

Angharad Morgan lifted her head with an air of dignity that infuriated Emily still further. With a last disdainful look, the shoemaker's daughter turned towards the door.

'I've said my piece, it's up to you.' Her voice was controlled even as she lifted her hand to silence Emily. 'I'm going, don't worry.'

Emily caught her arm in sudden desperation. 'If you know where Craig is you must tell me, don't you understand, he and I are going to be married, I must see him.'

Angharad looked at her from under thick lashes. 'Would you put him in danger then?'

'Of course not.' Emily straightened. 'Very well, pass on the message that I *will* clear Mr Grenfell's name.' She smiled in triumph, 'Then he will be back where he belongs, with his own kind.'

Emily didn't know why she was being so defensive with

this girl from the lower order in her simple garments and with her wild hair. Was it because the girl had something indomitable about her, a presence even?

Emily rang the bell and when Letty bobbed in the doorway, she spoke coldly.

'See this woman out by the tradesman's entrance. Oh and before you go, Miss Morgan, tell your father I shall no longer be requiring shoes from him, I will purchase my goods elsewhere.'

Angharad Morgan stared at her defiantly. 'That won't be possible,' she spoke with dignity. 'My father died some months ago and, as for me, I can find work from far more rewarding customers.'

At the door she turned. 'I will bring the shoes I am making for you now, the ones with the amethysts as decoration and I will expect payment for the work I've done, mind. And there's something you should know, the amethysts are stones of tranquillity, it might do you a bit of good to wear them.'

She smiled. 'From now on you will have to find a shoemaker skilled enough to make the sort of shoes you like and you might find that difficult. You see the other shoemakers in Swansea are men and not interested in fiddly little slippers. *Bore da*, Miss Grenfell.'

As the door closed behind the girl, Emily somehow felt that she had been bested. Angharad Morgan had spirit and intelligence as well as beauty. Emily bit her lip, the girl was obviously in touch with Craig, perhaps they were even living in the same house.

Emily moved to the desk and sat down, spreading the pages of figures out before her. She must forget the girl and concentrate on helping Craig. She chewed her lip anxiously. It was clear that funds were being embezzled but who could be doing it? Could it possibly be the accountant Edward Morris?

Emily rubbed her eyes as the figures swam before her, that didn't make sense. Edward was Craig's friend, surely he wouldn't have allowed Craig to go to prison in his place?

There were several other people who had access to the accounts, Spencer Grenfell for one. The two brothers had not always got along very well but in spite of their differences, Spencer would never do anything to harm the firm or his brother.

Emily drew a sheet of writing paper towards her and picking up the pen began to write . . . *Dear Spencer, there is something I think you should see . . .*

Hari was angry as she walked back through the streets towards her home, Emily Grenfell was nothing but a snob, she thought everyone beneath her. It was infuriating to be told she was stupid. What did Emily Grenfell know about people like her?

A warmth filled her, Hari smiled as she thought of Craig Grenfell waiting for her, eager for news of what was happening to clear his name.

Hari smiled, she knew more than Emily, she knew where Craig was, and she was learning all about him, how kind he was and what a real gent he could be.

She had been surprised to find that he didn't feel it beneath him to help her in the house. He got up early that first morning and lit the fire for her. He even made a pot of tea and poured her a cup when she got up for work. He'd even tried his hand at tapping boots, they were done with more enthusiasm than skill, but so far there had been no complaints from the customers.

She entered the kitchen from the back gate closing the door on the small yard with a click of finality. She had done her best for Craig, now it was up to his own kin to sort his problems out for him.

He was kneeling before the fire, his hands and face

black with coal dust. Hari looked at him with raised eyebrows.

He smiled. 'I've been out picking coal,' he sat back on his heels and shrugged, 'it's not strictly legal of course, but I don't think that matters in the circumstances.'

'You must be more careful!' Hari said quickly, 'You could be recognized.'

He got to his feet. 'I don't think so,' he said, 'not looking like this.'

He stared at her as she shed her shawl and sank into a chair.

'Well, Hari, what has happened?' He rubbed his fingers through his hair and she could tell he was anxious.

'It'll be all right,' she said at once, 'I gave the sheets to Emily Grenfell herself, I know she'll see that your name is cleared.'

'Then what's wrong?' he said and she looked at him in surprise. He was very perceptive.

'I seem to have lost myself a customer.' Hari sank back in her chair. 'Took a dislike to me, she did.'

'Emily has a quick temper,' Craig said, 'but she's fair minded and she'll reconsider the situation, I'm sure.'

Hari said nothing, it was natural that he would take the part of Emily who was not only his cousin but was his promised bride. But Craig was wrong, to employ Hari as her shoemaker was something Emily would never reconsider.

There was a knock on the door and Craig tensed, his big hands clenching into fists.

'It's all right,' Hari said quickly, 'it's most likely the rent man, he comes today.' She smiled, 'Don't forget now, you're my cousin from Neath come to help with the business, you're big like my dad, could easily be his nephew and so long as you don't open your mouth, it should be all right.'

53

Hari took the money out of the old cracked teapot she kept on the shelf, she had just enough for the rent and she smiled in relief. It was a good thing that Edward Morris had given her another order which he had insisted on paying for in advance.

Hari knew it was mostly done to help Craig and yet Edward Morris seemed to like her work a great deal. She hoped she would keep his custom once all this drama was over.

She opened the door and handed the money over and Mr Fisher wrote something in his book.

'Got a visitor have you then, Angharad?' The man looked at her carefully as she nodded.

'News spreads fast, I suppose Dai the Cop is gossiping like an old woman again.' She asked quickly, 'Well, if it's anybody else's business I got my cousin staying here, nothing wrong in that is there, Mr Fisher?'

He closed his book with a snap and looked past Hari to where Craig was bending over the fire. His face was still covered in coal dust and he looked anything but a gent. Hari suppressed a smile.

'No course not, Angharad, glad you got a bit of help, mind. You got enough to do with the business and looking after your mam and all.'

Hari breathed more easily, for a moment she wondered if the rent man suspected the truth about her visitor.

'Duw,' she said, 'don't you worry about that, now, my mam is no trouble, it's just her legs are bad just now and that cough of hers is troublesome but she bears up well, mind.'

'Give her my regards,' Mr Fisher turned away, 'see you next week Angharad.'

'Righto, Mr Fisher, I'll be here and if I'm not in the kitchen take the money from the old teapot.'

She closed the door and turned to see Craig leaning

against the fireplace, his eyes shining through the coal dust.

'Well done, Hari,' he said, 'I think he believes that your honour is safe with your dullard cousin from Neath.'

Hari felt the colour rise to her cheeks. 'It's not funny, mind!' she said sharply. 'It's just as well that mam's here with us, isn't it, or I'd have no honour, at least not in the eyes of the people around World's End.'

'Would that matter?' Craig said. 'I didn't think you were the sort to care about other people's opinions.'

He was so innocent of the ways of the world that Hari just shook her head in amazement.

'Don't you realize I'd be a target for all the men living in World's End who are just looking for a loose woman to amuse themselves with?' She shrugged. 'My chances of making an honest marriage or even of keeping up my business would be less than dust without the good will of my neighbours. What do you think keeps the petty thieves and the people who run a bawdy house away from my door?'

'I see.' The smile had gone from Craig's eyes, 'I'm sorry, I suppose I didn't stop to think.'

Hari shrugged. 'You don't know how we people of World's End live,' she said quietly, 'so perhaps you would do well to stay indoors out of the way of any trouble.'

'My dear, Hari, don't you think I've learned anything about human nature from my stay at the prison?' he said softly.

She inclined her head. 'Maybe you learned about the ways of criminals but we at World's End are not all criminals, there are good and bad everywhere.' She glanced up at him meaningfully, 'Even in the Grenfell family, mind.'

She stared at him for a long moment wondering if in her indignation she had hurt his feelings, but his eyes were narrowed and she could not read his expression.

'I must see to mam,' she said quickly. She brought a bowl from the cupboard and filled it with water from the kettle, there were chores to be done before she could even begin to make a meal for the three of them.

She took a towel and hanging it over her arm, she made her way upstairs, her mind spinning with troubled thoughts. Perhaps it was time Craig Grenfell looked elsewhere for lodgings, there were plenty to be had. Perhaps she was being a complete fool helping Craig Grenfell, was she allowing herself to be taken in by the first handsome man to come into her life?

'Hello, mam, you're looking perky this evening.' Hari thrust her worries into the back of her mind and helped her mother to sit up against the pillows.

'Come on then, have a nice wash, it will make you feel better.'

Win Morgan sat up and stared at her daughter. 'I wish you'd stop treating me like a child, Angharad,' she said irritably. 'I may be going deaf and it's true I'm not in the most robust of health but I'm not daft.'

'I don't know what you mean, mam.' Hari damped a piece of flannel and carefully washed her mother's lined face. 'Here's the towel, I'll see to you as quickly as I can, it's a bit colder this evening.'

'You've got a man in,' her mother said suddenly. 'Don't bother to deny it now.' Her voice was stern. 'I saw him when I went down to make myself a cup of tea, just letting himself out the door he was.'

'Mam!' Hari said quickly, 'I've told you not to try to get down stairs on your own, not with your legs so bad.'

'*Duw*, girl, what do you expect me to do when you're in the shop most of the time? Anyway, you know I have my good days and when I do I like to get up and sit by the fire for a while.'

Hari sighed, it wasn't much to ask to be able to sit

before the comfort of the fire and she was well aware of the frustration her mother must suffer lying in bed all day.

'Anyway, who is this man?' Win Morgan rubbed her face briskly with the towel bringing a spurious colour to her cheeks.

Hari decided that her mother must be told the truth, as she had pointed out, there was nothing wrong with her mind.

'Well, don't go mad if I tell you all about him,' Hari said firmly, 'just hear me out before you pass any judgements.'

'I've never known a girl to make such a fuss over talking to her mother, I'm losing my temper with you, Angharad, for heaven's sake get on with it.'

'His name is Craig Grenfell,' Hari said, folding the damp towel neatly as though it was the most important thing in the world.

'One of them toffs from the other side of town?' Win Morgan said in disbelief. 'What in the name of heaven is he doing here in our house?'

'He's escaped from prison,' Hari said quickly, 'but he hadn't done anything, it was someone else who cheated and lied and Craig was the one to take the blame.'

'My dear Angharad,' her mother said sharply, 'don't you know that's what they all say? I don't suppose there's one prisoner in Swansea Jail who would admit he was guilty. The man's making a fool of you. In any case,' she warmed to her subject, 'we can't afford to feed ourselves half the time let alone a stranger, what can you be thinking about? You just can't trust these toffs, mind.'

'His cousin, Emily Grenfell,' Hari ignored her mother's outburst, 'she will prove he is innocent, you'll see.'

Win Morgan looked at her daughter shrewdly. 'You are falling in love with him!' It was an accusation and, quickly, Hari shook her head.

57

'Don't be so soft, mam, he's not one of us, I know that as well as you do.'

'Aye, your head knows it but does your heart understand, Angharad?' She sighed. 'I don't want you hurt, love, you know how much I love you even though I don't always show it. Be sensible, send this man packing.'

'Listen now, mam,' Hari said briskly, avoiding her mother's eyes, 'we won't talk any more about it just now. I've got us a nice bit of meat pie for supper and a lovely fresh bit of bread, I expect you're starving.'

'No good changing the subject,' her mother said slowly, 'don't go doing anything daft, *cariad*, this man may be as innocent as you say but his kind use people like us, remember that.'

Hari sighed, 'I'll remember, mam.' She moved to the door and glanced back, warming to her mother, it was not often she expressed affection or even concern, she was a hard woman who had lived a difficult life but now and then a little softness crept into Win Morgan's eyes that betrayed the real woman beneath the stern exterior.

'Don't worry,' Hari said, 'I can look after myself, I've been taught well by my mam and dad.'

She hurried downstairs, the water in the bowl tipping a little on the bare treads. Hari was tired, she had worked all day and then walked over to the other side of town and back and now there was supper to get. Tears came to her eyes and, as she entered the kitchen, she stumbled a little.

Craig came to her side and relieved her of the bowl. 'What's wrong?' he asked. 'Is your mother worse?'

Hari shook her head. 'No, it's nothing, I'm just so tired, that's all.'

He led her to a chair. 'You sit there and tell me what you want done, I'm not exactly helpless you know.'

'The supper,' Hari said, 'there's meat pie in the pantry and the bread has to be cut.'

Craig moved about the room lightly, he was surprisingly deft for a big man and as Hari watched him cut the bread into silly thin slices, she smiled.

'We won't save money the way you do things,' she said softly, 'thin bread takes extra butter, thick slices are more suitable.'

'I see,' Craig's dark eyes were alight with humour, 'give me time, I'll learn how things should be done.'

He cut the pie and placed a slice on one of the earthenware plates on the table. 'Here, have yours,' he said, 'perhaps with some food inside you you'll feel better. You are far too thin.'

Hari shook her head. 'I'll take mam's up first, then I can have mine in peace,' she said.

When she returned to the kitchen, she sank down at the table and tried to eat a little of the food, conscious that Craig was watching her.

'When my name is cleared,' he said thoughtfully, 'I'd like to set you up in better premises, supply you with as much leather as you need and get you an apprentice or two.'

She glanced at him sharply. 'You don't owe me anything,' she said. 'Anyway, I manage my life quite nicely on my own thanks.'

'Don't be so prickly.' Craig leaned over the table towards her, his hands almost touching hers. Hari looked away.

'You'll soon forget this part of your life,' she said to him, 'it will be like a bad dream.'

'Not all of it.' His hand rested on hers, 'You are a wonderful woman, Hari Morgan, and I won't forget you, don't you worry.'

Hari looked into his dark eyes, they seemed to hold her

mesmerized as he leaned closer, his mouth only inches from her own.

Hari pulled away from him. 'That's enough of that,' she said trying to smile, 'remember who you are, Mr Grenfell, and who I am.'

She rose from the table. 'I'm going to bed,' she said, 'I'm so tired I can hardly think straight.'

He moved to her side. 'Hari,' his voice was soft, persuasive, 'you are so lovely.' His hands rested on her shoulders and she could feel the warmth of them through the coarse material of her bodice.

'There are rules if you are to stay here,' she said, forcing a note of firmness into her voice. 'You do not make advances to me, you don't even touch me. Remember I'm no trollop to while away the hours for you.'

He did not release her, he drew her closer until her breasts were pressed against him. He stared down at her for a long moment, his mouth very close to her own.

Hari knew she should move away but she couldn't, she wanted him to kiss her, to know the feel of a man's lips against her own, it was only natural to feel that way, wasn't it?

He let her go so suddenly that she almost fell. 'You're right, Hari.' He sighed. 'And you are a good woman, more's the pity.'

He turned away and stood before the fire, his back towards her and Hari leaned against the wall for a moment trying to recover her breath.

'*Nos da*,' she said softly, 'good night Mr Grenfell.' Hari lay awake for a long time, staring into the darkness. How she had wanted him to kiss her, she didn't know what it was like to be kissed and Craig Grenfell was such a handsome man. But that was not all and Hari knew it, her mother was right, her head was filled with common sense, but her emotions were running riot.

Well, tomorrow he must go, she would tell Mr Grenfell first thing in the morning that he must make other arrangements and then he would be out of her life forever. And somehow the prospect did not make her happy.

5

Morning came bright and clear with a pale dawn streaking the skies. Hari sat up in bed and stared through the window to where the light from the street lamp paled into insignificance against the rising sun. She stepped out of bed, careful not to wake her mother and quietly washed with the cold water from the china jug.

Hari shivered a little as she drew on her underclothes, then her thick skirt and bodice, lastly pulling the welcoming warmth of the shawl around her slim shoulders. As she stood barefoot on the cold boards, she comforted herself with the thought that soon it would be spring, daffodils would raise proud trumpets to nod in the soft breezes and in the fields beyond the town lambs would be born.

But today she had come to a decision, she would tell Craig Grenfell to leave her house, his presence was beginning to disturb her, disrupt her life. She was ready now to admit that her mother was right, Hari was falling in love with Craig. It would not be easy telling him to go but it was something she needed to do for her own peace of mind.

The fire gleamed in the grate, the kettle was boiling on the hob, steam issuing from the black lips of the spout and of Craig there was no sign.

Hari made tea and sat at the table, her hands curled around the warmth of the cup. She felt unrested, her eyes heavy as she stared into the fire for the truth was that she had slept very little and, when she did drift off, dreams of being in Craig's arms tormented her.

Where was he now? Fear for his safety warred within her. Her mind worried the problem of where would he find lodgings, how could she summon the strength to put him out of the only refuge he had?

Hari rose, resolutely putting the thoughts behind her. She moved into the workshop but, for once, the prospect of work did not please her. There were the unfinished shoes for Emily Grenfell lying on the bench, the amethysts agleam against the softness of the leather. The soft pumps of pigskin were made for pampered feet that trod not on cold stone or wooden boards but on rich carpets and Hari felt resentment fill her. Emily had everything she wanted, even Craig.

Yesterday, Miss Emily Grenfell had momentarily been at a loss, wanting to know where her fiancé was and realizing to her dismay that his safety was in the hands of the shoemaker's daughter.

Emily had taken her revenge swiftly, severing the ties that had long been between the Grenfells and the Morgans. But serve her right, she had cut off her own source of fine delicate shoes, she would not find their like again, not in Swansea.

Hari prided herself that while she had the skill and the strength of any shoemaker, she also had a flair for design that most cobblers lacked, Emily would learn that lesson to her cost.

She set to work on Emily's shoes, pride insisted that she finish the job she had begun even if she was never paid for it. She stitched the soft leather uppers into place, then dampened the soles to make them more pliable. She glanced round her, there were boots to be tapped, heavy working boots belonging to Cleg the Coal with the sole hanging off like a ragged tongue. She would attend to those next for Cleg needed his boots for work, he only owned the one pair.

She heard sounds from the kitchen and she drew in a sharp breath, Craig must have returned.

The back door leading to the yard opened and Hari heard her mother's voice, sounding strangely weary, calling to her.

'What's wrong, mam?' Hari was at her mother's side in an instant. '*Duw*. There's pale you are, you shouldn't be out of bed, mind.'

She helped her mother back to the warmth of the kitchen and sat her in a chair. 'Have a cup of tea or some nice bread and milk, warm you up, you're shivering.'

'I'm afraid, Hari,' her mother looked up at her with large eyes, 'I'm that afraid.' Her lip trembled. 'I tried to call you but you didn't hear me.'

'I'm sorry, mam.' Hari felt guilt sear her, she should be more considerate of her mother and yet the work must be done or there would be no money.

'Hold my hands, *cariad*.' Her mother's voice was fainter and, for the first time, Hari felt the fear communicate itself to her. She took her mother's hands, they were cold and clammy.

'I'll fetch the doctor, mam,' Hari said, an icy coldness gripping her.

'No, girl, the doctor can do nothing, it's my lungs, they are worn out, can't draw breath no more. Don't leave me, Angharad, I don't want to die alone.'

'Don't talk soft, mam, you are not going to die!' Hari said quickly. She looked down into her mother's eyes and read the pain and fear in them.

She knelt on the floor, heedless of the cold stone beneath her knees. 'Come on, mam, let me hold you tight, you'll be all right, everything will be all right, you'll see.'

After a moment, her mother spoke and it was quite clear that each word was an effort.

'There's money for my burial,' her voice was thin and threadlike, 'hidden in the bedroom it is, under the mattress. I want to go decent with a wooden cross above my head, promise me, Angharad.'

'Don't, mam,' Hari said brokenly. As she held her mother, she noticed how thin she'd become and Hari blamed herself for not realizing sooner how sick mam was.

'You'll be all right, you'll see, when you've had a warm and a bit of breakfast, you'll feel better.'

Then her mother's head was heavy against Hari's shoulder, the hands that had clasped her fell away and the tortured breathing had died away to an ominous silence. Hari rocked her mother to and fro.

'You are going to be all right, mam, you are, you'll see. You can't die, mam, you just can't die like that so sudden without me being ready.'

She didn't know how long she knelt on the cold floor with her mother still and silent in her arms. She didn't hear the door open or feel the hands that eased her to her feet.

And then she was looking into the compassion-filled face of Craig Grenfell. 'My mother . . . ?' Her words trailed away as he nodded. She turned slowly and looked at the figure in the chair.

It was not mam, oh, it was her features and her wispy greying hair that fell about the thin face, but her mother no longer inhabited the thin frame, the light had been extinguished and all that was left was a shell.

The tears came then with the tearing sobs that racked Hari and set up a trembling within her as though she had the ague.

After a moment, Craig took her in his arms and held her close and, smoothing back her hair, whispered to her gently, the very same words she had used to her mother.

'It's going to be all right, you'll see, it will be all right.'

They were useless words, meaningless now because it was not all right, mam was dead. And yet Craig meant only to be kind, reassuring, and gradually, Hari's sobs subsided.

She moved from his arms and slowly untied her leather apron. 'There are things to be done,' she said, her voice heavy, 'and I think it best if you are out of the way for a while.'

He nodded and, after a moment, moved to the door. 'Are you sure you can manage?'

Hari drew a deep breath. 'There's no point in you being here. Please go.' She wanted to thank him for his kindness, to tell him how grateful she was that he had offered to help but the words would not come. After a moment, she turned away and she heard the door close quietly behind him.

Hari sighed and, pressing her eyes tightly shut, felt unequal to the task before her. There was old Ma Feeney to call for the laying out, the coffin maker to see, the burial to arrange.

She covered her face with her hands. 'Oh mam,' she whispered, 'why did you have to die and leave me alone?'

The cemetery had emptied of people, the cold winds swept in from the sea and the still bare branches of the trees shivered like thin fingers against the dark sky.

Hari had remained in the cemetery long after the few neighbours who had attended Win Morgan's funeral had gone. She stood staring down at the fresh earth of the new grave, at the wooden cross bearing her mother's name and she could not believe that this nightmare was real. She would surely awake from the nightmare world where she was without her mother?

She felt a hand resting lightly on her shoulder and she turned to look at Craig, almost unrecognizable now with his beard grown and his moustache thick and dark above his mouth. He looked like a buccaneer of old except that he wore not the wide-sleeved shirts and breeches of the past but the rough working clothes that had been her father's.

Craig had been wonderful to Hari during the past days, she didn't think she could have got through it all without him. He had sat with her in the long dark evenings, had made sure she ate at mealtimes.

'Come home,' he said softly, 'there's little point in catching a chill, is there?'

Wordlessly, she allowed him to lead her on to the roadway and down the hill towards home.

'You know I haven't walked so much during my entire lifetime as I've walked these last few days,' he said with an effort to divert her from her dark thoughts. 'At least I've seen more of the town where I live than I ever saw from a carriage or on horseback.'

'Hush now,' Hari warned dully as they drew nearer to World's End, 'your posh voice will give you away if you're overheard.'

Craig opened the door to the house and stood aside for her to enter. The kitchen seemed dark and cheerless and Hari wondered how she could go on living and working in a house that held so many memories.

She sank down into a chair and watched as Craig knelt before the fire, building it back into a glowing warmth.

'I'll make you some tea,' he said swinging the big black kettle effortlessly on to the coals. 'You look as if you could do with a cup.'

She stared up at him, touched to tears by his thoughtfulness, he had come into her life such a short time ago and yet he had been so good to her, so strong and kind.

She looked up at him, unable to keep the trembling from her voice. 'Thank you, Craig.' He knew she was grateful for much more than the gesture of making some tea and, instinctively, he held out his arms.

Hari moved into them, resting her head wearily against the roughness of his shirt. He held her close, smoothing back her hair, his big hands so gentle. She could hear the beating of his heart and she closed her eyes, thankful for his presence for she could not bear to be alone, not now, not yet.

He released her. 'You must get back to your work as soon as possible,' he said. 'Work will ease the pain, in time, believe me.'

He meant well but how could Hari ever get over the shock of her mother's sudden death?

He made her tea and sat holding her hand until the light faded and the lamps in the street were lit, shedding a faint light into the room.

'I must go out,' Craig said, 'but I promise I won't be long.'

Hari sat up straighter in her chair. 'You must not worry about me,' she said quickly, 'you are not responsible for me, mind, and I will not be beholden.'

He smiled down at her and, in the light from the fire, he looked so handsome, so strong and safe that she wanted to cling to him.

'I know,' he said, shrugging into his coat. 'But remember, far from you being beholden to me, it is the other way around, I should be grateful to you.'

He crouched before her, his big shoulders against the light from the window so that she could not see his expression. 'You are harbouring a criminal and that is something that takes courage. You do have courage, Hari Morgan, and never are you going to need it as much as you do now.'

He let himself quietly out of the house and the silence closed in around Hari, smothering her. She rose quickly and lit the candles, all six of them which was wasteful, but she needed to be in the light for the shadows in the corners frightened her.

Tomorrow she would work, she would finish the shoes belonging to Emily Grenfell in the morning and then in the afternoon she would sole the heavy boots that Cleg the Coal so badly needed for his round.

It was about time she stopped feeling sorry for herself, the hurt and pain of losing mam would be with her for a long time, but Hari knew she could not let her grief incapacitate her, if she did not mend and make shoes she did not eat.

A sudden rapping startled her. Hari could just see a shape outlined against the uncovered glass, she had forgotten to put dad's apron over the window.

'*Duw*. Who is that then?' she said, her mouth dry. 'What do you think you're doing frightening a girl half to death?'

She opened the door and peered out. 'What do you want?' She saw the man draw nearer.

'I want to pay my respects, Angharad,' Mr Fisher stood on the threshold, his hat in his hand. 'There's sorry I am about your mam, would have come to the funeral if I hadn't had to work, mind.'

'What are you doing here this time of night, Mr Fisher?' she asked. She looked beyond him into the darkness afraid that at any moment Craig would return.

'Your cousin at home, is he, Angharad?' he asked mildly and Hari felt herself grow tense.

'No, not right now. Thank you for coming, Mr Fisher,' Hari felt the tears of weakness brim in her eyes. 'But my mam was only buried today and I'm not fit company for anyone.'

'Right, I understand, but if there's anything you want, Angharad, any help you need, then don't hesitate to ask.' He moved away into the night and Hari watched until he had disappeared from sight, then she closed the door.

Mr Fisher's visit had underlined the position she was in, she was now a woman alone.

She rubbed a hand over her eyes, she would have to talk to Craig when he returned, he could not stay with her now and, anyway, he would not wish to compromise her.

It was late when he returned, his brow was creased and there were circles of darkness under his eyes.

'I've had bad news,' he said, 'Edward Morris has been taken into Swansea Prison, he is accused of fraud.' He sank into a chair. 'I never thought that Emily would warn my brother, how could she do it?'

The words she had been about to say died on Hari's lips. 'Your brother?' she echoed. 'You didn't say anything about your brother so I never mentioned him to Emily Grenfell. *Duw!* It's all my fault.'

'No,' Craig said softly, 'it's my fault for not warning you about Spencer. What a fool I've been.'

Hari looked down at Craig's bowed shoulders, she couldn't ask him to leave not now. 'Sit down, Craig,' she said softly, 'let me fetch you some tea.'

6

Emily lifted her head and breathed in the sweet March air, it was good to stand in the garden of Summer Lodge looking out over a tranquil sea with timid waves reaching for the shore. Soon the fine weather would come, she would be able to take rides along the coast road, get away for a while from the interminable drawing-room meetings and card calling that wearied and bored her.

She wished she had been born into a different age, an age when women had been allowed to be more than a decorative possession. All that lay before a young lady of breeding was duty to parents and hopefully a good marriage.

Emily sighed, unless Craig's name was cleared she would remain an old maid for ever, she would never accept second best whatever her father said.

'Emily.' A voice spoke close to her ear, 'It's good to see you looking so well.' Spencer Grenfell stood a little behind her, looking down at her. She turned to him, her heart beating swiftly as he leaned forward and kissed her cheek. 'I'm sorry, you seem surprised to see me.'

She shook her head not willing to admit that for a moment she had thought he was Craig. The brothers were very much alike, the same strong shoulders and the fine head of hair, but physical appearances were deceptive and there was about Spencer a weakness that showed in the line of his mouth and the almost shifty look in his eyes.

'Any news?' she asked quickly. 'I can't wait to hear what you've found out.'

'Patience, Emily, all in good time, what about inviting me in and offering me a drink, the grass here is quite damp you know, and in those silly slippers, you'll catch your death.'

She warmed to him, he was concerned about her as a cousin should be. 'Come inside we'll have some cordial.'

The drawing-room was lit with the pale promise of spring, daffodils were everywhere, on the occasional tables, in the window, yellow trumpets strong and bright against the damask wall-covering.

When drinks had been served and the door closed after the bobbing maid, Emily leaned forward in her chair.

'What of Edward Morris, is he guilty?' she asked. 'And when will Craig's name be cleared?'

'My brother will have to come forward before anything can be done,' Spencer sipped the hot cordial slowly. 'He must tell the judiciary that it was this accountant Morris who abused the trust the firm showed in him.'

Emily shook her head. 'No,' she said firmly, 'Craig can't risk it, what if he was arrested again?'

'Why should he be?' Spencer said smoothly, 'If my brother is innocent he has nothing to fear.'

Emily rose to her feet in agitation. 'That's just not true,' she protested, 'his innocence didn't prevent him from being wrongly accused in the first place, did it?'

Spencer put down his glass with a sigh. 'Has it occurred to you that this Morris fellow and my brother were in this thing together?' he said softly.

'That's absurd,' Emily said hotly. 'Why should Craig want to steal from his own company and what's more share the proceeds with an accountant?'

'But it isn't entirely Craig's money, you know, a substantial part of it will be mine once my father's estate is sorted out properly.'

Emily shook her head. 'I don't believe Craig would be involved in anything illegal, certainly nothing that would harm your prospects, Spencer.'

'There's such a thing as greed, Emily, and sad to say brothers are capable of hating each other, take Cain and Abel for example.'

He rose and put his hand on Emily's shoulder. 'Let's leave the subject, shall we, I don't want us to quarrel, there's a more serious matter I want to talk about.'

'What could be more serious than the trouble Craig is in?' Emily asked quickly.

'It's your father,' Spencer said, 'I'm sorry to be the one to tell you but you have to know, he is in financial difficulties.' He paused to let his words sink in. 'Your father is a worried man and he is looking to you to make a good marriage, that way at least your own future will be secure.'

Emily bit her lip, 'I didn't know, my father hasn't said anything to me.' It couldn't be true that her father's leather business was failing, could it, and yet hadn't he urged caution on several occasions lately? Even to refusing her new boots. She thought guiltily of the money she had been spending on new clothes and of the new slippers she had ordered with the amethyst decoration. And then the full implication of her cousin's words fell into place.

'Marriage? But I've been promised to Craig for years, I can't break my word.'

'You may have to break your word, Emily.' There was something spiteful about the way Spencer spoke the words, they held an almost gloating ring.

Emily moved away from her cousin, anger forcing a harsh note into her voice. 'No, if I can't marry Craig, I will never marry.'

'We'll see,' Spencer said softly. He put down his glass and rose to his feet. 'I've taken up quite enough of your time, my dear cousin.' He moved into the hallway and in the hazy light falling through the stained-glass window, he might have been Craig. Then he looked down at her and the similarity was gone.

The maid came through from the back of the house and bobbed a curtsy to Emily. 'That person is here again, Miss Grenfell, she says she has slippers for you, shall I show her in for the fitting?'

'Tell her to wait,' Emily said quickly, she didn't want Spencer to learn anything about where Craig was hiding.

'Hold on there,' Spencer said easily, as though sensing Emily's wish to get rid of him. 'I need some boots repaired, I'd like to see the workmanship of this shoemaker.'

'She does mostly ladies' slippers,' Emily said, 'I don't think she would be of any use to you.'

Spencer smiled and turned back into the room. 'Nonsense, I must decide that for myself.' He seated himself in a chair and Emily paused for a moment, she could hardly ask the maid to bring the girl into the drawing-room where Spencer would be listening to every word. Resolutely, she moved swiftly towards the kitchen.

The girl was standing near the back door, obviously she had not been invited inside. Over her arm was a basket covered with a snowy cloth.

'Your slippers are ready,' she said, her eyes challenging. 'If you are not pleased with them then don't pay me.'

Emily swallowed her pride. 'My cousin is here,' she said in a low voice, 'Craig's brother, be careful . . .'

'Oh, there's the little shoemaker, bring her inside, Emily, let me see her workmanship.' Spencer had followed her and was standing smiling at her.

'Come in,' Emily said shortly. She was very conscious of the girl following her towards the drawing-room and a sudden sense of jealousy bit like sharp teeth as Emily imagined them together, Craig, and this girl who, however poor she might be, had beauty as well as dignity.

Spencer was staring with obvious delight at the young girl standing before him.

'I understand you are a shoemaker.' He said thoughtfully, 'I would very much like you to make a pair of boots for me. How do you work, do you buy in the uppers or do you do the entire job yourself?'

'I'd prefer to do it all myself, sir,' the girl said. 'I can buy uppers from abroad if French calf is required but there is nothing wrong with our own leather.'

'What about design? But then it's probably beyond your powers to design boots as well as make them.'

'*Duw*, there's nothing I like better than to work on my own ideas.' The girl spoke quietly but with conviction.

Emily watched as the shoemaker's daughter uncovered the amethyst-decked slippers.

'See,' the girl said proudly, 'these flowers made of gems, I created the pattern for them and designed the slippers in such a way that the amethysts would be shown to the best advantage.'

Emily impatiently took the slippers away from the girl. 'Send me your bill and it will be paid in full.' She waved in a gesture of dismissal and turned back to her cousin.

'I'm sure you have enough boots to provide for an army,' she said jokingly. 'In any case you can shop in London any time you choose.'

'Where do you have your workshop?' Spencer ignored Emily's words and continued to gaze at the girl who had paused near the doorway.

'Oh, I think Miss Grenfell is right,' she said guardedly, 'my work is not up to the standard you require.'

She left abruptly and Emily closed the door after her with a sigh of relief.

'That was uncalled for, cousin.' Spencer said easily, 'I think you might have been a little more enthusiastic about such lovely slippers, they are a work of art, you must be very pleased to find someone with the talent to work as well as the best London shoemakers and at a fraction of the price, if I'm any judge.'

'Forget the girl,' Emily said, 'let's talk about my father, shall we?'

Spencer shrugged. 'Nothing to say, dear girl, your papa is flat broke, that's all there is to it.'

The words fell harshly into the silence and Emily looked at her cousin in disbelief.

'If this is true, don't you even care?' She spoke accusingly and Spencer shrugged again.

'I would like to help but then the business is not entirely in my hands. If Craig were to show up now, he could perhaps bale uncle out of the difficulties. After all, it's Craig who will own Summer Lodge after your father's day.'

'What do you mean?' Emily's throat was dry as she stared up at her cousin. He moved to the door. 'Don't they tell you anything? The house is entailed to Craig, no-one else can have Summer Lodge.' He carried on speaking without giving Emily a chance to catch her breath.

'What I suggested earlier might be a solution to all your problems, marriage, my dear, and I know just the man for you.'

'Oh, do you now,' Emily said sharply, 'and who may I ask have you got in mind?'

'Me, of course, I'm young and handsome, aren't I?' He smiled, 'What more could a girl want?'

'You can't be serious!' Emily said. 'You are joking, aren't you, Spencer?'

'Think about it, dear girl,' Spencer said softly, 'anything is better than disgrace to the family name, don't you think, and between us, you and I could rescue the old family firm? I'm not badly off, you know, I have some money from my mother's side.'

Emily turned her back without answering, she could scarcely talk, marriage to Spencer was unthinkable. She sighed with relief as she heard her cousin leave the room.

She stood in the window, holding back the heavy curtains, watching as Spencer climbed into his carriage and, with a wave to her, bowled off down the drive towards the roadway. When the carriage was out of sight, she sank down into a chair and put her hands over her face.

'Oh, father,' she whispered, 'why didn't you tell me you were in trouble?' No wonder her father had not been well these last few weeks, he was worried about money. His temper was uncertain and he was drinking a great deal of brandy during the evenings.

She rose suddenly and brushed back the tears, crying would get her nowhere. She crossed the hall with determined strides and pushed open the door to her father's study. She was not used to searching through his private possessions but she needed to learn the truth before he returned home.

She looked through the drawers of his desk and found nothing to indicate the financial problems her cousin had spoken of. But the middle drawer of the desk was locked and there was no sign of the key.

Emily picked up the knife from the desk and inserted it between the top of the drawer and the desk and after a struggle, the drawer burst open.

It was crammed with unpaid bills for food and clothing. Emily stared at them in horror but then a few bills didn't mean anything, most people hung on to their money for as long as they could, it was simply the way of businessmen.

She closed the drawer and stood thinking for a moment, then she moved into the drawing-room and rang for the maid.

'Letty,' she said as the young girl bobbed in the doorway, 'ask Mrs Beynon to come in please.'

The housekeeper glided into the room and stood tall and gracious with greying hair under a black cap. She maintained silence, but it was clear that the sudden summons had surprised her.

'How long has my father had outstanding bills with the tradespeople?' Emily tried to sound casual. The housekeeper's eyebrows lifted a fraction. 'For some time, Miss Grenfell, indeed only this morning the butcher refused to send around any more meat until he was paid.'

Emily felt cold. 'And the servants, have they been paid properly?'

'Not for some time but we are not worried, miss, it's not unusual for the gentry, if you will excuse me saying so, to keep folks waiting for payment.'

'Right,' Emily said with more confidence than she felt, 'please send Letty in with a tray of tea, I'm quite thirsty.'

The housekeeper inclined her head and silently left the room. Emily sighed with relief, she must be alone, she must have time to think things out.

Later when her father returned from his office, Emily greeted him with her usual kiss. 'Hungry, father?' she asked quietly. 'We've some fish for supper.'

'I'm not very hungry, truth to tell.' Her father handed his topcoat to Letty and made his way into the drawing-room.

'I could do with a drink, though.' He poured himself a large brandy and Emily watching him tip the liquor into his mouth noticed how thin he'd become. In a few short months he had changed, his hair was greyer, his face more drawn and the gold Albert hung loosely around his once corpulent stomach.

Emily had meant to wait until her father had eaten but she couldn't bear the suspense a moment longer.

'Papa, something is very wrong, please tell me, I'm not a child any more.'

He looked at her and frowned as though he would make a denial and then he saw from her face that she knew the truth.

'I'm sorry, *cariad*,' he said wearily, sinking into a chair, 'I've done my best to keep things going but someone has been poaching my customers. One by one my orders for leather have fallen away,' he paused, his voice sinking lower, 'now I'm almost ruined.'

He handed Emily his glass and, without a word, she refilled it.

'I've not even the money to see you properly married, Emily,' he said softly. 'How can you ever forgive me for I shall never forgive myself.'

Emily felt a moment of pure terror, the spectre of the workhouse on Mount Pleasant Hill rose before her eyes, the poor house where the homeless lived a life of sheer drudgery and hardship.

Suddenly an unsuspected strength flowed through her. 'We'll survive, papa,' Emily said with a certainty that brought a light of hope into her father's eyes. 'But you must show me the books, tell me everything about the business.'

Emily rose to her feet and moved restlessly around the room. 'I need to know who your customers are, what orders they have placed in the past and why they no longer wish to trade with you. I will personally see them all myself and talk them into offering us their business again.'

'It's impossible, Emily,' her father said at once. 'No lady can enter business and keep her reputation intact. Folk will think you eccentric at the very least.'

'Let them,' Emily said. 'Anything is better than starving, isn't it?'

He shook his head. 'But you don't understand, there's

no money to buy in the leather stocks we need, how can we sell a commodity we haven't got?'

'I don't know all the answers,' Emily said fiercely, 'not yet but I will not let us sink, I will not.' She smiled. 'Now come on, let's go and eat, you look as if you need to keep up your strength.'

Her father accompanied her into the dining-room and though he made a pretence of eating, he barely touched the food on his plate. Emily noticed that he was drinking excessive amounts of brandy, his cheeks became red and his eyes glazed and when the meal was over, he rose from his chair unsteadily.

'I'm going to bed, Emily,' he said, his voice slurred, 'I don't think I'll bother to go to my office tomorrow, it would only be in order to wind matters up in any case.'

Emily watched him go and then, rising, she threw her napkin down furiously on to the table.

She would not give in! She paced around the room thinking desperately, she needed free reign to look over her father's books and records and to speak to the men in his employ.

She moved into the drawing-room and stared into the fire, tears misting her eyes. According to her father they were ruined, poverty stricken. She glanced around at the house, she would lose her home; entailed as it was it would pass to the next male heir of the family. Craig would inherit Summer Lodge.

'Damn Craig!' Why did he have to be so careless that he'd ended up in prison? He could have sorted out all her problems if he'd been here.

She bit her lip, she must avoid financial ruin at all costs, what did she have that she could sell to raise money?

There was her jewellery, the Grenfell emeralds that had belonged to her mother, they were hers, hers to sell if she so chose.

Emily stood up and stared at her reflection in the ornate mirror that hung over the fireplace. The emeralds must go, they would bring in enough money to pay some of the debtors sufficient to keep them quiet for a time.

She moved to the window and stared out towards the sea, the moon lit the bay with pure light, the craggy rocks of Mumbles stood out dark against the sky. It was a lovely night, a night for calling on all her courage and all her resources to pull herself and her father out of this crisis. And she would do it, Emily clenched her hands into fists, she would fight to the last breath to keep her heritage and to preserve the good name of the Grenfells.

In the morning, she rose early and dressed in her plainest clothes, flounces and frills had no place in business. She drew on sensible boots and a warm woollen cape and called for the carriage to be brought round to the front.

Sighing, she looked around the elegant hallway, drastic cuts would have to be made but she could manage with just a cook and a maid, the others would have to be paid off.

She climbed into the carriage knowing it would perhaps be for the last time; maintaining the horses and the grooms was a luxury she would have to forgo.

As the carriage rolled down the driveway, Emily looked straight ahead, holding herself erect, determined not to give in to the tears that threatened to overflow.

The large old building, with its sign over the door bearing the Grenfell name, stood silent and empty. Emily unlocked the front door and stepped inside. She moved up the stairs past the few skins that lay on a table and made her way into the office.

A man who was vaguely familiar was seated at the desk, his hair was grey and his eyes peered short-sightedly at the books before him.

'Good morning,' Emily said quietly, 'I'm Emily Grenfell,

I've come to find out what's happening to my father's business.'

He smiled at her and his kindly eyes almost hidden beneath straggling brows were sympathetic. '*Bore da*, Miss Emily, I'm Joey and I've worked for your father since I was a boy. If there's anything to do to help, then I'm at your service.'

Emily took off her cape feeling she had found an ally. 'Good,' she said, 'I want to know anything you can tell me about the problem with the business, daddy is honest and straight, he has a good name and what's more, he knows how to choose good leather, so what can have gone wrong?'

'I wish I knew,' Joey sighed. 'What I suspect is that someone has deliberately caused delays in delivery of leather and has been undercutting your father's prices.'

'But who?' Emily asked and the old man shook his head.

'Perhaps you can find that out, go to the old customers, ask them face to face. They might well talk to a pretty lady when they would hesitate to confide in an old man like me.'

'Right,' Emily said firmly, 'let me have a list of the best customers and a list of the people my father owes money to.'

She smiled, feeling suddenly alive and full of energy. 'I am going to save the business, Joey, I don't know how I'm going to do it but somehow I will.'

She took a seat and drew a piece of paper towards her and began to write, the Grenfells weren't beaten yet, not by a long chalk.

7

The street was alive with the sound of ragged children playing noisy games. Girls with hair flying were being chased by shouting boys. It was holiday time for the Catholic children of Greenhill.

Hari knocked on the door of Cleg the Coal's house, smiling as a small girl rushed past her, eyes wide with excitement. Cleg's boots, a heavy weight in the basket over Hari's arm, were mended at last.

After a moment, the door swung open and a woman stood staring with big eyes in a pale face, her apron unable to conceal the fact that she was heavily pregnant.

'Morning, Beatie, there's Cleg's boots all mended and ready to wear.'

'Come in, Hari, sure Cleg will be that glad to see you, he's been wearing his brother's boots to work in and them pinching him like the devil.'

The house was spotlessly clean though the furniture was sparse and the floor covered with sand. On the walls were hung religious pictures of Christ with a glowing heart.

In the kitchen at the back of the house, Cleg was eating his breakfast of thick brown bread and great hunks of cheese.

'*Bore da*, Hari, there's a good girl you are finishing my boots for me and you with your mam so recently passed away. So sorry to hear about Win Morgan I was, fine woman, your mam.'

He drew out a chair. 'Sit down and have a cup of tea by here with us.'

Beatie crossed herself quickly at the mention of the dead, the young Irish woman was sometimes ashamed of her husband's bluntness.

'Don't speak of death, Cleg,' Beatie said, 'not now with me in this condition.'

'*Duw*, don't take on so, woman, got to pay my respects, haven't I? Too superstitious you are, that's what comes of going to church so much, mind.'

Beatie put her hands on her full hips. 'Don't you pick holes in my religion, Cleg Jones, being Catholic is better than being a Welsh heathen like you.'

Hari sat down and put her basket on the floor, pushing back the white cloth, she was well used to the way Cleg and his wife carried on, it didn't mean a thing.

'See, I've put toecaps on for you, Cleg, make the boots last a bit longer they will.'

'There's a good girl, work better than any man you do and me glad to give you my trade.' He looked at her steadily. 'Though I've got to tell you there's some gossip going around about the cousin you've got staying.' He leaned forward, his great forearms bulging beneath the rolled-up sleeves of his flannel shirt.

He frowned. 'None of my business, mind, but with your mam gone folk don't think it proper. I don't want you getting in bad with the ruffians who live around World's End.'

Hari took the tea Beatie handed her and set it down quickly on the scrubbed wooden table. 'There's nothing I've done that I'm ashamed of, Cleg,' she said softly, 'my father brought me up to be respectable and that's what I am.'

'I know,' Cleg's big hand covered hers, 'but, for your own sake, send your cousin packing or marry him out of the way, then no-one will have room to talk.'

Hari smiled ruefully at the thought of Craig marrying her and yet there was a sadness deep inside her, a longing that she knew would never be fulfilled.

'You're right, Cleg,' Hari sipped the hot weak tea, enjoying every mouthful, the Jones family were one of the few families in Greenhill who could afford tea at all.

'I suppose it's time I asked my cousin to leave. It's no good putting it off any longer though he's been a great comfort to me, mind.' The thought of being alone without Craig's warm presence in the house made her want to weep.

She placed her empty cup on the table and rose to her feet. Cleg stood up too and put his hand into his pocket.

'Here's the money for the boots and my brother Dai wants you to repair some shoes. Can you call round to him? He lives down near the bottom of Wind Street, got a shop he has, a well-to-do sort of man, better off than me at any rate.'

Hari nodded, she was glad of the trade, orders had dropped off lately and now she no longer had the boots of Edward Morris to repair, she was finding work hard to come by.

'I know your brother by sight, big built like you, Cleg, but with greying hair, lives at the end of one of the courts, doesn't he?'

'That's him, strike while the iron's hot, *cariad*, go see him straight away, Dai's a generous man, he'll pay you well.'

Cleg smiled. 'Got four sons he has, they'll all need shoes too, I shouldn't be surprised.'

Hari left Greenhill and made her way towards High Street. It was a pleasant walk down a gently sloping hill past the toll house. The spring sunshine was almost warm and a soft breeze was blowing in from the sea. Hari took a deep breath and tasted the tang of salt in the air, soon it would be summer but she would be facing it alone.

She had been much comforted by Craig's presence in the house these past weeks, but in her heart she had known the situation was an explosive one and couldn't last.

She stared ahead of her to where Wind Street met High Street but she didn't see the portico of the inn she was passing or the ornate façades of the tall houses; she was acknowledging to herself that she was falling more and more in love with Craig Grenfell.

It was foolishness of course, nothing could ever come of her infatuation for a man from another world, a world of comfort and security. And a world, she reminded herself sharply, that at this moment had turned against him.

At last she found the shop belonging to Dai Jones, it was spread well back from the front door, a long dimly lit store that sold everything from flour and salt to patent medicines.

Behind the counter stood a young man who smiled broadly when he saw her.

'*Bore da*, miss, what can I get you?' he asked pleasantly and his blue eyes looked into hers with obvious admiration.

'Cleg Jones advised me to come and see his brother, Dai is it?' she asked tentatively. 'Needs some boots mending, I believe.'

'That's my dad, I'm Ben Jones, youngest son and the most put upon.' His cheerful smile belied his words and Hari found herself responding to his warmth.

'Hello Ben, I'm Hari Morgan, shoemaker.' She saw the lift of his eyebrows and she smiled. 'I know, I'm only a woman but I can make and mend just as well as any man, if not better.'

'I don't doubt it,' Ben said at once. He took her hand

and made a pretence of examining it and Hari drew her fingers away quickly.

'Is your father at home?' she asked and felt a sinking disappointment when Ben shook his head.

'Not just now but tell me your address and I'll be sure to bring you any boots that need working on, right?'

Hari smiled ruefully. 'Right. I live just off Wassail Square, there's a sign over the workshop with my father's name and trade on it, Dewi Morgan, boot and shoemaker, you can't miss it.'

'I'll make sure of that,' Ben said smiling. A group of chattering women in torn dresses and faded shawls entered the shop and Hari moved quickly towards the door, she must not hamper Ben when he should be working.

Ben lifted his hand in farewell and Hari smiled politely before closing the door behind her.

All the way home, she practised the words she would speak to Craig Grenfell, she must tell him to leave, to find another place to stay but the feeling of emptiness that swept over her whenever she thought of saying goodbye to him brought tears brimming to her eyes.

When she entered the house, it was silent and empty. The fire was burning low in the grate and the kettle was cold on the hob.

Hari mended the fire and sat back on her heels, looking at her blackened fingers. Where was he, had he been taken by the constables? Was he even now locked up in some prison cell to become once again the unkempt figure he had been when she first set eyes on him?

Later, Hari forced herself to enter the workshop and get on with her repairs. She had enough work for several more days and then after that, she would need to tramp around the streets seeking new customers.

Where was Craig? Her hands fell idle in her lap and she stared around her at the bits of leather on the floor, at the row of wooden lasts along her bench, at the boots that needed new soles and heels and, with a sigh of despair, she dropped her knife and rose to her feet. It was no good, she could not concentrate on anything, not while her every nerve was alive with fear for Craig's safety.

In the early evening, Hari restlessly drew on her shawl. She must get out of the house and breathe in some air that was free of the scent of leather. She set out for the cemetery where both her parents were buried. It was situated on a hill where the winds raced over the open ground and the sea below laved the shore with small, agitated waves. It seemed that here, there was never any spring, only wind and rain and the dull ache of loss.

She knelt on the tufted rebellious grass and closed her eyes. In her mind, she saw her mother, not dead but full of life with her eyes bright and a smile on her lips. It was a dream, it had been a long time since Hari had seen her mother smile for the death of her husband had knocked all the spirit out of Win Morgan.

She felt a hand on her shoulder and she looked up into the thin face of Edward Morris. She scrambled to her feet, the wind tugging at her hair.

'Mister Morris, you've been set free then?' Hari felt him take her arm and lead her beneath the overhanging trees.

'It seems that I still have some friends in Swansea,' Edward said softly, 'no-one could convict me on such trumped-up evidence.' He smiled. 'And Craig proved my innocence all right.'

'How did he do that?' Hari asked, her mouth dry. Edward smiled down at her.

'He sent a message to the governor explaining that the thefts continued to take place at a time when the firm had transferred me to England for a period of six months. As I had no access to the Swansea accounts during that time, it was clear I couldn't have embezzled anything from the company.' His expression became sober.

'Unfortunately, in all the confusion of evidence, it seems to have come down to one brother's word against the other.'

'But the balance sheets that you gave Craig and the fact that the thefts went on while he was in prison, didn't all that prove it was his brother's fault?'

'Those papers conveniently disappeared after they were presented to Spencer Grenfell and poor Emily couldn't be blamed, she didn't fully understand the situation.'

'Where is Craig now?' Hari asked softly and Edward looked down at her with a shrewdness that disconcerted her.

'Don't let your heart rule your head, Miss Morgan,' he said, 'Craig is a fine chap, a loyal friend but he has neglected the business and paid rather too much attention to the worldly pleasures instead, so be warned.'

Hari moved away from him, her cheeks hot with embarrassment and anger. 'He has been a perfect gentleman,' she said quickly.

'I'm so pleased to hear it.' Edward smiled warmly, 'Because I have something to tell you. I came searching for you at the shop and one of your neighbours told me she'd seen you come this way.'

He paused and touched her hand. 'I have to tell you that Craig will not be bothering you any longer, he has found somewhere else to stay.'

'I see.' She paused, her head bent, 'There's strange, because I'd made up my mind to tell him to go anyway.'

'That's all right then.' Edward's grip on her hand tightened. 'You have been very brave, Miss Morgan, and I want you to know that both Craig and I are very grateful, a gratitude that will be shown in practical terms as soon as possible.'

'I don't want any charity,' Hari said at once, her chin lifted, her eyes angry. So Craig would pay her off, would he, leave her house without any word of his departure? She shrugged. What else could you expect from the gentry?

'I was thinking more in terms of work, not charity,' Edward smiled and lifted his hat. 'I feel sure I can persuade some of my friends how good you are. Now, may I walk you home?'

'No, thank you,' Hari said quickly, she wanted to be alone to sort out her muddled thoughts.

'Well then, good day, Miss Morgan, I hope to see you again quite soon.'

He walked away across the uneven ground and, as Hari watched him, she felt her anger subside leaving only the dull ache of disappointment. If only Craig had come to her, told her what he intended to do, left her a small message even. She sighed and turned away from the graveyard, drawing her shawl closer around her shoulders. It was getting cold, time she went home.

Once inside the house, Hari lit the candle and sank down at the table, her eyes heavy with tiredness and unshed tears. The silence closed in around her and her loneliness was almost tangible. Craig had been staying with her for some weeks now and she had grown used to seeing him there in her kitchen.

She had known that she was playing with fire, her own emotions had been awakened and she no longer trusted herself to be level-headed where Craig was concerned and yet wasn't that half-fearful desire a challenge, a part of the fascination she felt for Craig Grenfell?

Well, he was gone now and she would probably never see him again. Slowly, she rose and pushed the kettle on to the flames, she would make herself a cup of hot sweet tea and then she would go to bed.

She was crouching near the dying fire, hands around the cup for warmth, when she heard a scratching sound at the door. She lifted her head, listening, all her senses alert. The sound was repeated. Craig, he had returned.

She rose and hurried to the door and opening it saw not Craig but the small figure of Will Davies crouching in the street. She drew him inside and led him towards the candle-light. It was clear he had been beaten, his face was bruised and his ragged clothing was hanging from him.

'What happened, Will?' Hari asked softly and the small boy shook his head.

'Nothing different, miss, dad came home from the inn and took his belt to me.' He shook his head. 'Can't stay there, see, he'll kill me in the end.' He sank on to the floor, hugging his knees. 'Can I stay by here, miss? I'll work and I'll be no trouble.'

Hari took a deep breath. 'Of course you can stay, William, we'll sort something out.' She clasped her hands together and tried to think.

'I'd like to have you as my apprentice but would your father be willing?'

Will's pinched face brightened. 'I got a job, see, working in Jonah's bakery, hate it I do, sweeping up the floor and chasing the mice away and, worst of all, I has to get inside the ovens and clean them. For that, I gets a whole sixpence a week.'

His face fell. 'But my dad takes that.' He paused. 'If I had a bit more pay, he would let me come to you, you would have to keep me in grub if I was an apprentice wouldn't you? But I would have to give the money to him, mind.'

'How old are you, Will?' Hari asked, feeling pity for the boy wash over her.

'I think I'm nine, miss,' Will said doubtfully, 'perhaps ten, I don't rightly know.'

'Have you never been to school?' Hari asked softly and

when the boy shook his head, Hari sighed. 'Well,' she said trying to sound confident. 'I know my father's apprentices used to get quite good money but then I can't afford the proper rate. I think I could pay you two shillings a week for the first year and we'd have to see how things went. I don't know if I could ever afford to give you more.' She took a deep breath. 'But, if we can turn out plenty of work between us, we should manage nicely.'

Hari knew that the two shillings a week would be crippling unless Edward Morris lived up to his promise of bringing in extra business. And then of course there was the promise of repairs from Dai Jones and his four sons, that prospect offered some hope.

'I'll tell my dad in the morning.' Will's young face was grave, 'The ale will have worn off him by then.'

On an impulse, Hari hugged Will and then with a grimace held him away from her.

'One thing I must insist on, my boy,' she said, 'a good wash and then a hair cut. I'll get you some clothes from Ma Popits so at least you won't put the customers off.'

The boy smiled cheerfully. 'I could steal some things out of the rich folks' washhouses, mind. Done it before I have.'

'No,' Hari said sternly, 'there'll be no stealing, you must promise me that.'

'Why not?' The boy was genuinely puzzled. He looked up at Hari his eyes wide.

'Look,' Hari pushed the kettle on the fire and then sat down and faced Will, her hands clasped together. 'Our customers must trust us. We should be able to go into the big houses and let the gentry know that we are honest, that's the only way they'll give us their business. We must keep up our good name, right Will?'

'Righto, Miss Morgan.' He still sounded doubtful and Hari smiled.

'Remember when you were delivering boots for me and that boy took them from you, how did you feel then, Will?'

'*Daro!* I was mad with him, could have battered him into the ground I could if I was strong enough.'

'Why did you feel like that, do you think?' Hari said watching the young boy's face. He frowned.

'Cos he took them boots and it was my job to take them to the big house for the gentleman.' He looked at Hari, 'And I didn't want it to look bad for you.'

'That's it, Will, if we are dishonest, it looks bad for me and soon I wouldn't have any more customers.' She rose to her feet.

'Right now, I'm going to fill the big bowl with nice hot water and you are going to have a scrub and I want every bit of you to be clean, mind, including your hair.'

Hari left the boy while she went to search upstairs for one of her father's night-shirts. They were yellow with age and patched many times but at least the boy would be clean and warm. Tomorrow Hari would go to Ma Popits first thing and see what cast-off clothing she could buy for young Will.

When she entered the kitchen, she stood still, the night-shirt slipping from her fingers. Will was standing in the bowl of water and Craig Grenfell was kneeling before the boy, scrubbing him thoroughly with a piece of flannel.

'What are you doing here, Craig?' she asked. 'I thought you weren't coming back.'

'Just a quick visit,' he replied looking up at her briefly. 'I came to say goodbye and to thank you for all you've done.'

'Second thoughts, was it?' She moved towards him and he patted the boy on the shoulder as he rose to his feet.

'No, I just wanted to say goodbye in person.'

'Goodbye,' Hari said unforgivingly. He stared at her for

a moment and then shrugged and moved out of the kitchen and towards the back door. Hari followed him, suddenly flustered.

'Thank you for coming,' she said, 'but please don't wait around any longer. I don't think you should have come here at all.' She looked up at him, he was very handsome in the moonlight.

'You have somewhere else to stay now so you needn't risk coming here again.' Her words were an implied criticism and he read her well.

'Hari, I'm sorry.' He took her by the shoulders and his face was very close to hers. She longed to reach out to him, to draw his lips on to hers. She almost succumbed but then common sense came to her aid.

'I was going to ask you to leave anyway.' Her harsh words fell into the silence. 'I don't see why I should take any more risks for a man I hardly know.'

He looked down at her, his face tightening and then, so suddenly that she had no time to read his intentions, he pulled her to him.

His lips hovered for a moment above hers and then he was kissing her, his mouth hot against hers. Hari could not breathe, she felt lost in a flurry of emotions. Love flared through her, she felt desire and sadness too because she knew this was a fleeting moment.

She allowed herself to cling to Craig's broad shoulders, she pressed close to him, her lips parting under his. It was a moment of magic that she must cherish for it would never come again.

A hammering on the door startled Hari and, abruptly, she moved from Craig's arms. 'Get away from here!' she said sharply, 'go out through the back yard, God knows who could be hammering my door this time of night.'

As Craig disappeared into the darkness, Hari hurried into the kitchen. William was crouched before the fire,

94

dressed in the too-long night-shirt. His face was pale as he stared wide-eyed towards the door.

'What if it's my dad?' he asked fearfully. Hari straightened her shawl with trembling fingers and moved towards the door.

'Who is there?' she called and waited with a feeling of dread.

'It's Dai the Cop, open up, Hari girl, or I'll have to break the door in.'

Hari flung the door wide. '*Duw*. No need for violence, mind, but no woman alone opens the door to anybody, not at this time of night and in a place like World's End.'

'Enough of playing the innocent.' A big constable elbowed his way past a sheepish-looking Dai and stared suspiciously round the room. 'Where is this supposed cousin of yours?' He spoke aggressively.

'He hasn't been here for some time,' Hari answered. 'Why, what has he done?'

'I don't think this man was a cousin at all, indeed, I think you've been harbouring a criminal from jail.' The constable towered over her. 'Tell me Miss Morgan, where are you hiding him? He was seen coming here tonight so don't deny it.'

'No,' Hari shook her head. 'You are mistaken, there's only me and young William here, look around if you don't believe me.'

'I will, be sure I will.' The man nodded and behind him Dai gave a shrug of resignation and began to search the small house.

'You,' the constable pointed to Will, 'what have you seen, was there a man here a few minutes ago or not?'

Will licked his lips and looked uncertainly towards Hari. She thought of the lecture she had just read him on honesty and trembled.

'No-one has been here only me and Miss Morgan, just

been bathing me, she has, see?' He pointed to the cooling water.

The constable closed his lips in a firm line and made his way through to the yard. Hari heard him beating at the bushes with his truncheon and then he opened the door to the workshop. After a few moments he returned.

'You have been sailing very close to the wind, miss,' he said as Dai returned to the room. He pointed his truncheon at her. 'This house will be watched, make no mistake about it, we shall be out for blood.'

Hari sighed in relief as the door closed behind the men. She sank into the chair, her hands over her eyes.

'I did right, didn't I, miss?' Will said anxiously. 'It is right to tell lies sometimes, isn't it?'

Hari held out her arms and drew him close. 'Aye, it's right to tell a lie to protect a friend, Will, it is necessary to lie sometimes.'

She took a deep breath. 'Right, let's make you a bed on the couch, is it? I'll fetch you some blankets from upstairs and I'll put a bit more coal on the fire to keep you warm, just for tonight. Tomorrow I'll clean out mam's bedroom for you.'

She smiled at him softly, he looked so young and vulnerable in the too-big night-shirt, a child who until now had borne the responsibilities of a man.

'Well done, Will,' she said, as she hurried from the room. There was a constriction in her throat and her eyes were brimming with tears. Though if they were for young William or for herself, she could not be sure.

8

Summer Lodge was in mourning, dark drapes were closed against the pale, spring sunshine and the gloom within the rooms was accentuated by the soft sound of women weeping.

Emily, entering the drawing-room, stood for a moment, watching her aunts in their black mourning silk and jet beads and, for a moment, they appeared like birds of prey, dark and menacing in the dim light.

The family had gathered to mourn the death of Thomas Grenfell, weighed down by the shame of losing all his money, overcome by a sickness that he had no will to resist.

Pride gave a lift to Emily's chin as she braced herself to move further into the room and greet her kinswomen.

'Emily, my poor child, what will you do with no-one to protect you against the world?' Aunt Sophie embraced her warmly and the soft scent of lavender rose from the pleated bodice of her gown.

'Don't worry about me, aunt,' Emily forced a note of firmness into her voice. 'I am quite capable of taking care of myself.'

'Nonsense, you are little more than a slip of a girl, you would be prey to all sorts of men, fortune hunters and the like. You need someone to look after you.'

'You forget, aunt, I have no fortune,' Emily said, secretly appalled at the prospect of being 'looked after' by her well-intentioned aunt. 'I shall be all right.'

'But the business,' Aunt Sophie said in dismay, 'what are you to do about that?' She patted Emily's shoulder, 'We all know that our dear Thomas's affairs were not . . . settled. Let Spencer help you, my dear, my youngest son always did have a good head for figures.'

Sophie regarded Emily steadily for a moment. 'I know you were promised to Craig, but no-one would blame you for trying to forget him.' She lifted a gloved hand to fan her hot cheeks. 'Craig is my first-born son and I love him dearly,' she paused, 'but, after what he's done, Craig must consider himself disowned by the entire Grenfell family.'

Emily felt angry words rise to her lips but quickly suppressed them, this was neither the time nor the place to argue Craig's innocence.

Emily glanced through the curtains; outside in the driveway stood a group of her kinsmen, come to pay their last respects to Thomas Grenfell.

She could see Spencer quite clearly, he appeared to be holding court among the elderly distant relatives who had travelled from all parts of the country to be at the funeral. Spencer lifted his arms in a flamboyant gesture and Emily felt physically sick at the mere thought of marrying him. She turned away and rubbed her eyes wearily.

After the first shock of her father's death, Emily had felt a searing anger against him, furious with him for leaving her to face her misfortune alone. Then came the terrible sense of disbelief and at last the dawning realization that she would never be held in his embrace, breathe in the scent of his cigars or hear his kindly voice ever again.

And yet she had not cried, not even now, when the coffin was to be taken from Summer Lodge and carried to the graveyard on the hill overlooking the sea, could she give way to tears.

If only Craig was at her side it would be so different, she

needed his strength to see her through the ordeal, not only of the funeral but of the days and weeks that were to come.

Emily felt a momentary sense of panic, she had no means of supporting herself, her father's business was in ruins, he had left great debts that she could not meet.

Then, an iron resolve began to grow within her, she would fight to make a future for herself, she wasn't stupid or helpless, the problems would be tackled and every effort made to save the business.

'Come along, Emily, dear,' Aunt Sophie was at her side, catching her arm, leading her back into the centre of the room where the vicar stood over the coffin, ready to pay his last respects to Thomas Grenfell.

Emily did not listen to the emotion-filled words, she would not allow her grief to show, it would be a sign of weakness. She must conduct herself as though she was in complete control. And so she would be she vowed, as she stared stony-faced at the gleaming brass and the glowing wood of the coffin.

She lifted her head and though her eyes burned and her throat ached with unshed tears, outwardly, she was a picture of perfect composure.

Craig Grenfell stood on the hilltop looking down at the scene in the graveyard below. He had been fond of his uncle, Thomas had been a bluff hearty man but unfortunately he did not have a head for business.

The leather trade was one which did not take a great deal of effort to run successfully but then Craig believed that his brother had a hand in the unprofitable deals Uncle Thomas had made and had profited from them.

Craig's hands tightened into fists as he saw his brother, flanked by his mother and Emily, step forward and throw a little earth into the grave.

'Blasted hypocrite!' he said savagely. Well, let brother

Spencer enjoy his ill-gotten gains while he may, the day was coming shortly when his fraud would be exposed for all to see.

Craig watched as Emily, stiff backed, moved away from the grave. Her face was a white blur under the dark cloak and hood she wore as protection against the fierce wind coming in off the sea. He felt his heart contract in pity, Emily was a fine woman, he admired her composure and he knew how much the façade must cost her, she had loved her father dearly.

He made his way from the hilltop and down into the valley, this was an ideal opportunity to search his mother's house.

He walked quickly. Glancing at his fob watch, he had at least an hour before Spencer returned with their mother to the family home. Funerals in Wales meant a large feast after the burial and knowing Emily, she would present a good face to the world in spite of her misfortunes. There would be a table groaning with smoked ham, with thick succulent slices of cold beef and crusty fresh bread. Hunger gnawed at him, he had not eaten properly for days.

He had spent his time in a lodging house on the Strand, eking out the small amount of money Edward Morris had been able to lend him.

He entered the house by the front door and was confronted by a flustered maidservant. She bobbed a curtsy to him as he handed her his topcoat and if there were any questions at the appearance of a man who should be in prison, they were not voiced aloud.

Craig made his way at once to the study, the desk was locked as he had expected. He took up the brass paper knife and with a turn of his wrist had the drawer open, his stay in prison had served some useful purpose.

As he expected, he found nothing incriminating,

Spencer would be far too careful for that. Quickly, Craig made his way upstairs to his brother's room. He stood for a moment, looking around him. Spencer would hardly keep important documents in the mahogany chest of drawers or the huge wardrobe.

Craig drew back the carpets and examined the floorboards inch by inch. He saw a fresh cut mark on a board near the fireplace and, quickly, he lifted it.

The books and papers were wrapped in a silk cloth and, smiling, Craig knew he had found what he had been looking for. He heard the front door being opened even as he unfolded the cloth and began to read.

After a moment, there was the noise of voices in the hallway and then footsteps pounding up the stairs. Craig tucked the books inside his coat and as the door was flung open, he strode past his open-mouthed brother and down towards the drawing-room.

Spencer hurried after him and as Craig flung wide the doors, he felt himself being grasped from behind.

Craig shook his brother off easily and moved towards the fireplace.

'Hello, mother,' he said, 'and Mr Cummings, our respected solicitor, too. Isn't it fortunate that you should be here.'

'Get the constable,' Spencer said hastily. 'There's no knowing what this lunatic will do or say.'

'Yes, bring the constable by all means.' Craig brought the books from his coat and looked down at them thoughtfully. 'I've just found these under a board in your room, Spencer, I think they will prove that I am not the one who's been defrauding the company.'

'What rubbish!' Spencer said quickly. 'It was not I who interfered with customers' accounts, taking out large sums of money.'

Craig smiled. 'Then how did you know which way the

fraud worked?' He flicked through the pages of the book. 'The Honourable Charles Griffiths, for example, has lost, over a period of time, quite a lot of capital.'

'I know nothing about it, nothing at all,' Spencer protested. But his mother was staring at him strangely.

'Continue, Craig, if you please,' she said sternly.

'My dear Sophie,' Cummings stepped forward, 'I don't think you should listen to all this, your eldest son has been tried and convicted of the fraud, that should be enough proof for you that he is guilty.'

'You are in this too, then, Cummings,' Craig said with deceptive gentleness. He looked down at the book again.

'I see that the method used was to divert large amounts of money into a fund under the name of another firm, a non-existent firm I imagine.' He paused as his mother stared at him in bewilderment.

'I don't understand, Craig, can't you explain more clearly?'

'Look, mother,' Craig held the book towards her, 'Mr Faraday's account is short by several hundreds of pounds, this loss has partly been made good by taking money paid in to the company by General Webber. That way no-one misses too much money at one time.'

Sophie Grenfell looked at her youngest son in horror. 'Spencer, explain yourself, what does all this mean?'

'It means, mother, that Craig is trying to put the blame on me for the thieving he's done.' Spencer turned to Craig and said challengingly, 'How do we know you found those books in my room? You could have just planted them there.'

Craig smiled. 'Oh, I think an investigation into the bogus account will be very revealing, I don't see how I could have managed to go on robbing the customers from inside Swansea Jail, you should have stopped when you were ahead, Spencer.'

'You fool, Cummings!' Spencer was breathing heavily, 'I told you we should hang fire for things to cool off.'

'Be quiet!' Cummings said angrily. 'You don't have to say anything.'

Sophie looked at both her sons and then sank into a chair. 'I can't see Spencer go to prison for this,' she said brokenly. 'Craig, can't you do something?'

Craig shook his head. 'Mother, you amaze me,' he said. He thrust his hands into his pockets and moved to the window, staring out into the sun-dappled drive flanked by swaying trees.

'But Craig, you know Spencer has never been strong like you, he could not survive in prison, his health . . .' Her words fell away into silence.

After a long moment, Craig turned to face his mother. 'Send one of the servants for Edward Morris,' he said, 'and for a solicitor, an honest one.'

Craig stared directly at his brother. 'The best I can offer you is a head start, get out of here and don't ever come back.'

Spencer stared at Craig with venom in his narrowed eyes. 'Don't think you've heard the last of this matter,' he said through his teeth, 'you won't get away with it, taking from me my home and my birthright, I should have been the eldest son, I am more worthy of the position. I'll never forgive you for what you've done to me.'

He stood before his mother. 'I'm innocent, believe me, Craig has fooled you but he can't fool me, he wanted it all, the property and land, the business and every penny of the money. Well, he won't get away with it, one day I'll have my revenge.'

He swung out of the room and after a scared glance in Craig's direction, Cummings followed him.

Craig looked into his mother's white face and saw lines of pain etched around her mouth. 'What have I done?' she said, her voice trembling, 'my baby, I've lost him for good and it's all your fault, Craig.'

Craig took a deep breath, controlling his anger. He moved forward and pulled at the bell rope, it was about time he put the wheels into motion, the wheels that would prove his innocence. And Spencer would be caught, there was no doubting that, and then he would learn what it was like to be imprisoned behind grey walls and iron bars.

Emily sat in her father's study, staring at the mass of figures that danced before her eyes. The first thing she would have to do was to raise some capital so that she could rescue something from the dregs of her father's business.

It was clear that Thomas Grenfell had made more than his share of mistakes, it seemed that The Fine Leather Trading Company had been overspending on labour and without the expected turnover in goods moved and sold.

Poor prices had been asked, ridiculously low prices for expensive imported French calf so that losses on the leather had been sustained. It was clear that her father had been wrongly advised and Emily thought she knew exactly who was responsible.

A great deal of Thomas's trade had passed through the hands of Spencer Grenfell who seemed to have trouble bringing in payment to her father on time. In short, Thomas Grenfell had been gulled.

'Spencer Grenfell, you have a great deal to answer for,' Emily said bitterly. She picked up the stock records, she had studied them for so long that her head ached. In the warehouses there were still some bales of fine leather and if sold to an honest dealer, they would bring in enough at least to pay off some of her father's debts.

She pushed away the papers and rubbed at her eyes, she would have to visit the creditors, pay them a little of their money and then beg them for time to pay the rest. If most of them accepted her terms, then she might just survive.

Then there were the contents of Summer Lodge, fine antique furniture, exquisite china, carved marble figures, all would have to be sold.

Emily covered her eyes, it would be so humiliating, selling everything she held dear, but there was nothing else for it, it would have to be done. When it was all over, she would rent rooms in some small lodging house with perhaps one maid. And from the sale of the contents of the house, she could buy in more leather to keep the suppliers happy.

She felt tears blur her vision, she was weary and the grief of her father's death hung over her like a dark cloud. A great silence filled the house, the servants were asleep, not knowing that tomorrow they must find themselves other positions. It would be hard saying goodbye to the servants, some of whom had been around since she was born, but it was something she would have to do, she simply had no choice.

Slowly, Emily rose from the chair where she had seen her father seated many times, not knowing the problems he faced or understanding how troubled he was. She was at fault for not taking a hand in the business before now, she could have helped him, been her father's right hand. At least with her young, keen eyes she would have seen that he was being duped by his own nephew.

Emily felt a sudden anger against the Grenfells, they had allowed this to happen to her father, even Craig had not been innocent, he should have seen what was going on in his own business. Instead of spending most of his time shooting game and striding about in the parks of his estate, he should have stopped Spencer from ruining Thomas Grenfell's life and casting a shadow on Craig's own business.

She moved to the stairs and stood for a moment in the silence of the hallway, the candle flickering in her hand. She felt so alone, so very frightened of the future and all the challenges it held. Slowly, she mounted the stairs and went into her room and, sinking down on the bed, she began to weep.

In the morning, she rose early and already the fires were lit and breakfast cooking on the range. She had taken it all for granted for so long, her creature comforts had been assured and she had not given a moment's thought to how they were provided.

After breakfast, she called the housekeeper and asked her to summon the rest of the staff. 'Bring them into the kitchen, please,' she said, her hands clasped tightly together, 'I must tell them all the bad news personally.'

The housekeeper looked at her with concern. 'What is it, Miss Emily?' she asked anxiously.

'I'm sorry,' Emily said, 'I have to let you all go, Summer Lodge is no longer mine and, in any case, there is simply not the means to keep going as we have been.'

The housekeeper bit her lip. 'Let me come with you wherever you go, please, Miss Emily, you are the only family I've ever known, I won't need paying, just my keep, I can still work hard, mind.'

'We'll see,' Emily said softly knowing in her heart that the old woman could hardly bend, let alone light fires and carry coal.

The servants were subdued by the occasion, sensing at last that something was badly wrong, it was a rare occasion when all of them were summoned before the mistress at the same time.

Emily paced around the room, her skirts swishing against the carpet. At last, she paused and looked at the assembled staff.

'There is no easy way to say this,' she began haltingly,

'my father died a ruined man, I have to let you all go, there's nothing else for it.'

The butler stepped forward. 'May I speak, Miss Emily?' he said gruffly and, when she nodded, he gestured towards the rest of the staff. 'I think I am talking for us all when I say that we will gladly work for nothing, just until matters improve, we have all been so happy here at Summer Lodge and each and every one of us would like to stay with you wherever you go.'

Emily felt tears constrict her throat. 'Your loyalty is very touching,' she forced herself to speak, 'thank you all for this fine gesture, but I can no longer afford to maintain a staff of servants. As to Summer Lodge, it will as is the custom pass to the next male heir of the Grenfell family.'

She turned away and hid her tears. 'But I will tell you this, I shall not be beaten, I will rebuild my father's business and when I do, I want you all to return to work for me.'

She swallowed hard and turned to face them again. 'There will be enough wages to keep you all for a few weeks at least, until you have a chance to find another situation. Of course, there will be fine references for you all. Thank you.'

The servants filed silently from the room until only the housekeeper remained.

'What is it?' Emily asked, forcing back the tears. The older woman rubbed her hands together.

'I may be speaking out of turn, Miss Emily, but you are young and innocent and I am concerned about you.'

'Go on,' Emily said encouragingly, 'I won't bite your head off.'

'It is not ladylike to run a business, Miss Emily, that's a job for a man. Why you would have to travel abroad and choose leather and see that those in your employ did not cheat you, you are too sweet and beautiful to survive in such a harsh world.'

'Thank you for your concern, but I shall be all right,' Emily said firmly. She turned away and heard the door softly closing and knew she was alone. Alone, she sank into a chair and covered her eyes with her fingers, moved to tears by the way her staff had reacted to the bad news. They had not worried for themselves, only about what would happen to Emily.

She realized she had never seen the servants before except as part of the backdrop of Summer Lodge, now she saw that they were part of her life, real people with loves and loyalties especially to her and it made her feel suddenly humble.

She rose and stared through the window to the hills outside, to the sea running gently into the embracing arms of the bay. She would fight for a new future and she would succeed. And yet, even as determination rose within her to right the wrongs that had been done her father and to make the name of Thomas Grenfell respected again in Swansea, she was trembling with fear.

9

Hari stood in Goat Street staring up at the façade of the old theatre and swallowed hard, trying to pluck up enough courage to walk into the ornate portico. The theatre was not something of which her parents would have approved, such frivolous pleasures were not for the likes of hard-working shoemakers.

The basket on her arm contained assorted shoes, soft satin slippers, pumps of French calf as well as stout leather shoes for walking. She was taking a gamble, already Hari had spent precious time and materials making footwear that might never be bought and paid for.

And yet she must seek new outlets for her work; she greatly wanted to expand her range of shoemaking outside the humdrum jobs of soling and heeling heavy working boots.

It was true that she had gained a few customers lately, Dai Jones, Cleg the Coal's brother being one of them. Dai and his sons were always needing boots tapped for they were big men all of them and heavy on their feet.

Once Edward Morris had been set free, he had recommended her to some of his friends and so trade was looking up. But Hari had ambition, she wanted to raise her business to great heights; to one day own an emporium where there would be shoes of all descriptions, serving the best customers in the country.

Well, she would do none of that standing here in the

street, she told herself firmly. She pushed open the door and moved into the strange world of sparkling glass and soft carpets. The scent of rose water hung in the air, covering the stale smell of pipe tobacco and strong drink.

Hari stared around the silent building, there was no-one about, the silence hung heavily over the rows of seats, the stage was hidden by a thick curtain and yet Hari had the eerie sensation that she was being watched.

She moved down one of the long aisles; the body of the hall was in darkness and she stumbled a little as the floor sloped downwards. She felt panic rise within her, what was she doing here in this strangely unreal world? Her place was in her workshop, sitting before her bench moulding shoes upon a last, cutting and stitching, working the leather into a recognizable shape. That was the part of shoemaking that she loved. This plying of her trade was foreign to her and she felt unsure of her ability to carry it off.

'And what might I ask are you doing here, young lady?' A voice boomed at her from a small door at the side of the stage. Hari stopped abruptly and peered into the darkness, trying to see the face of the man addressing her.

'I'm a shoemaker, sir,' she said, forcing a confidence into her voice that she did not feel. 'I wondered if I could be of service to anyone in the theatre.'

'Come with me.' She followed the sound of the disembodied voice out of the darkness of the theatre and into the lighted area of a long passageway.

The man looking down at her wore an imposing set of whiskers, a grey beard hung down over his brightly coloured waistcoat and thick, waving grey hair sprouted back from his forehead, giving him the look of an ageing lion.

'I am Charles Briant,' he spoke with a flourish as though addressing an audience. 'I am the owner of this theatre and you should have sought my permission before you ventured inside, young lady.'

Hari tried to conceal her surprise, she had believed the man to be a famous actor, he seemed so colourful and too theatrical to simply be a businessman.

He saw the lift of her eyebrows and smiled. 'Oh, I used to tread the boards, I am an actor all right but there aren't many roles for a man who sustained an injury that left one leg shorter than the other. None of your boots would remedy that, young lady.'

Hari frowned. 'I don't know about that,' she said, 'but it's certainly something I would like to think about.'

He laughed with forced heartiness, as limping badly he began to walk along the corridor, leading the way, and Hari realized that he had used the laugh many times to conceal his true feelings.

'I won't promise anything,' she said following him, 'I've never tackled a job like it before but I might just be able to make a built-up boot for you.'

'In that case, young lady, you would have my un-dying gratitude.' Charles Briant glanced back over his shoulder.

'I am taking you to the dressing-room where the ladies are gathered, they would be your best customers, I don't doubt.'

He took her to a surprisingly small room furnished with dark leather sofas and lit by harsh gas light.

Curious faces turned in her direction, faces some plain some pretty but all innocent of paint and powder. Hari felt a sense of disappointment, she had expected something more from players at the theatre, exactly what she didn't know.

'What's this then, Charlie?' One of the women rose to her feet, she wore a tight corset and bloomers, and pink ribbons trailed from the silk robe that hung loosely over

111

her shoulders. 'Heaven forbid that you've brought us another budding actress.'

'My dear Meg, this lady,' Charles Briant said with dignity, 'is a boot and shoemaker, she simply wants to be of service to us, to make, like us all, an honest living.' He stepped aside with a flourish and, after a moment's hesitation, Hari removed the cloth from her basket and took out the satin slippers.

With cries of delight, the ladies of the theatre gathered round Hari, exclaiming loudly that they had never seen anything so pretty.

'Can you make these to fit any foot?' the actress in the pink robe asked, touching the satin almost caressingly.

Hari nodded. 'I can make anything you like, here are some fashionable French calf slippers decorated with glass beads that glitter as you walk.'

'I want some,' Meg took the shoes lovingly in her hands, 'they are so beautiful, a work of art, you are very clever, Miss Shoemaker.'

'My name's Angharad Morgan, Hari. My workshop is in World's End.' Hari smiled. 'You'd be welcome to look around any time you like.'

'I'm Clarisse,' the actress said, 'well, that's my stage name of course, my real name is Meg.' She shook back her curled hair. 'But you wouldn't catch me venturing into World's End for love nor money. Why don't you get respectable premises somewhere more suitable.'

'Because I can't afford to move,' Hari said with a flash of anger. 'In any case I was born in World's End, everyone there has been very good to me.'

'I'm sure,' Meg said quickly. 'I'll order a pair of these French calf shoes for a start but I won't have green beads, do you hear? Green is unlucky, don't you know that?'

'No, I'm sorry, I didn't.' Hari put her basket down and

took out her paper patterns. 'Right then, let's have some measurements,' she said firmly.

Within the hour, Hari had measured several pairs of feet and had enough orders to keep her busy for several weeks. She felt jubilant but apprehensive too, how was she going to cope with all the work?

She would just have to give young William the task of cutting out the leather soles, he had learned very quickly and his hands, though small, were strong and deft.

Meg was trying on the satin slippers. 'These are so comfortable,' she said happily, 'and they fit beautifully, I'll have them.' She held out her hand to Charles Briant, 'Give me some money, Charlie, take it out of my wages.'

'Wait just a minute,' Meg said as Hari moved towards the door, 'next week, my friend Benny the Clown is appearing here in Swansea, he wears these enormous shoes for his act, he could be a very good customer for you.'

'Next week?' Hari said in dismay. 'Do you mean you won't be here then?'

Meg laughed, 'Bless you, no, chick, we'll be off to Somerset in a few days. Some fine shoes down there in Street, you know, made by Mr Clark, you must have heard of him.'

Hari remained silent not wanting to admit her ignorance. Meg smiled. 'You will have the shoes ready in time, won't you?'

'*Duw*, course I will,' Hari said firmly though she had no idea how she was going to live up to her word. 'I'll be back in a few days with your orders.'

Her head was buzzing as she followed Charles Briant out of the theatre and into the sunlight. Blinking a little, she looked up at him.

'Will you be going to Somerset too?' she asked and it was with a sense of relief that she saw him shake his head.

'Dear me, no, I'm a permanent fixture here in Swansea,

113

this is my home and this,' he waved his hand towards the ornate façade of the theatre, 'this is my domain.'

Hari sighed. 'When I've done the orders for the ladies, I'll try out some ideas for a boot for you, all right?'

'That will be wonderful, my dear. In any event, come again, we always have a great deal of variety here at the theatre and if you are a speedy worker, you should do very well.'

When Hari returned home, she found William in the workshop hammering leather soles on to a pair of small boots. He looked up happily as Hari put down her basket and took off her shawl.

'There's nice to see you back, it's quiet as the grave in by here on my own.'

Hari sank down on the bench beside him. 'I see you're getting on with the boots for Edward Morris's nephew, doing a good job too by the look of it.' She leaned forward and examined the leather which had been well cut, fitting the boot with just a little to spare. Hari sighed heavily.

'What's the matter, no job for you down at the theatre then?' William looked up at her and Hari smiled, pleased with the way his cheeks had filled out and that the set of his shoulders was straight now, his fear of violence having given way to a new confidence in himself.

'Don't talk, Will, there's too much work, six pairs of shoes to be made by the weekend! I don't know how we're going to do it, even if we work flat out every day.'

William bit his lip. 'We could get somebody else in to help us, just for now, like. Got to be a cobbler round who is having a lean time of it.'

'Will, you're a genius,' Hari said, eagerly. 'I could go to see Lewis Watts, he was my dad's apprentice for five years when I was a little sprout like you just learning the trade. I think he'd help us out if he's not too busy.'

She stood up and straightened her back. 'Let's have

something to eat, William, then afterwards I'll go and see Lewis, I expect he still lives down near the docks.'

William took a tack from between his teeth and hammered it into the leather and then picked up a file.

'I'll just tidy up these boots and then they're ready to be delivered.' He said smiling, 'That's one job off our hands.'

Hari felt the impulse to ruffle William's hair but she knew he would resent being treated like the child he was, boys grew up quickly in the harsh realities of World's End.

William insisted on accompanying Hari as she left the house and made her way towards the docks. It was not yet dark but soon it would be and then the town would come alive. Sailors from off the boats would be looking for a good time and public bars would resound to the sound of many voices.

William kept close to Hari's side, though for his own protection or hers Hari wasn't sure. She smiled down at him and realized that in the few weeks he'd been with her he had not only put on weight but had grown a few inches in height too. For the first time in his life, William was having enough food to eat and was not being beaten into submission by his bully of a father.

The boy was still obliged to give his earnings every week to his family, otherwise he would have been dragged unceremoniously home and that was something Hari would not allow.

'There's the Watts's house down by there near the public bar.' Hari pointed to the building tall and narrow sandwiched between two other houses. It looked neat and clean from the outside and the curtains were freshly washed.

Hari knocked on the door and after a time it was opened by an elderly lady who stared down at her with a frown.

'If you're begging, there's nothing here for you,' she

said sharply and was just about to close the door in Hari's face when Lewis appeared behind her.

'Mam, for heaven's sake don't be so hasty.' He smiled with dawning recognition. 'It's Angharad Morgan,' he said smiling warmly, 'my master's daughter, come inside.' He stepped back from the door.

'Mam, this is the daughter of Dewi Morgan who taught me my trade. *Duw*, there's sorry I was to hear of his death, a fine man was Dewi Morgan. Your mam's gone too, Angharad, there's sad for you.' He led the way into a warm pleasant kitchen. '*And* you've grown up since last I saw you.'

Hari, aware of the admiration in Lewis's eyes, felt her colour rising.

'Sit down,' Lewis said, 'and who is this lad, then?'

'William is my apprentice,' Hari said, 'and though he may look very young he's a good cobbler and a great help to me.'

'Glad to hear it,' Lewis said smiling. 'You stick with Angharad, my boy, she's almost as good a cobbler as her father before her.'

'She's very clever,' William said at once, 'making lovely shoes she is for them actresses in the theatre.'

Mrs Watts sniffed disapprovingly, 'Actresses, is it? Hussies the lot of them.'

'Now mam, go and put the kettle on the fire and get our visitors a nice cup of tea.' Lewis sat opposite Hari and she was suddenly aware of how handsome he was. Thick, dark hair curled around his face and his rolled-up sleeves revealed strong, well-muscled arms. He saw her regarding him and smiled.

'You've changed a great deal, Angharad,' he said, 'you were just a little girl when I finished my apprenticeship and now look at you.'

Hari returned his smile, liking his friendliness and

116

enjoying his open admiration. 'Yes, look at me,' she said ruefully pushing back her tangled hair and straightening her skirts.

'Anyway,' she said in what she hoped was a businesslike manner, 'I've come to see if you can help me out on a special job.'

'Oh?' He looked at her questioningly and Hari leaned forward eagerly in her chair.

'I've got rather a big order,' she said, 'mostly for slippers but one or two pairs of shoes I have to make in French calf.'

'Expensive,' Lewis said thoughtfully. 'I hope your customer is prepared to pay you well.'

'I think what I'm asking for a pair of shoes is fair enough though I am keeping the prices low as an incentive for my customers to come back for more.'

'These are the theatre people?' Lewis said. 'Not best known for their reliability, mind, travelling about the country, never being in one place for more than a few weeks, got to be careful there.'

'That's my problem,' Hari said firmly, 'what I want from you is help in making the shoes, perhaps you could work a few evenings for me?'

Lewis leaned back in his chair as his mother came forward with the teapot, setting it on the china stand.

'Why should I help you, Angharad, I've got my own job, mind, working for Maunders boot and shoe emporium. It's long hours and when I get in I've seen enough shoes to last me a life-time.'

Hari thought quickly. 'If I build up my business the way I hope I can, I may well need a partner. Just think, you'd be your own boss, up to a point, master of your own destiny, not slaving away for a pittance while someone else makes all the profit.' She paused as Mrs Watts handed her a cup of tea.

117

'Thank you for the tea,' Hari said, trying to thaw the iciness of Mrs Watts's expression. 'It's very kind of you to bother.'

'No bother, just good manners.' Mrs Watts sat in a deep chair in a dark corner of the room but Hari had the impression that the woman was like a cat sleeping with one eye open, watching everything that went on.

'What have you to lose, Lewis?' Hari returned to the attack, 'A few hours of your time, that's all.'

Lewis's smile was full of charm. 'I'll think about it,' he said. 'Now, have one of mam's Welsh cakes, beautiful they are, mind.'

Hari felt a rush of disappointment, she had expected Lewis to jump at the chance of earning some money but it seemed he was reluctant to take her venture seriously. Well, she would do it without him, if need be, she would not let this chance slip away from her.

When she left the Watts's household, Hari rested her hand on William's shoulder. 'It seems I've failed to get myself a helper,' she said. 'I thought Lewis would agree straight away.'

'He'll agree,' William said with conviction, 'but in his own good time.'

'What do you mean, Will?' Hari asked in surprise. 'In his own good time?'

'It's pride, see, not many men would like working for a lady, mind.'

Hari walked along in silence for a moment, breathing in the salt tang of sea air. 'You know something, William?' she said at last. 'You are a very wise person.'

It was the next day that Lewis turned up at the door of the workshop his tools in a bag and his leather apron over his arm.

'Right, then,' he said smoothly, 'where's the French

calf? It's a long time since I've had some first-class leather to work with.'

Hari led him to the bench and watched as Lewis tied on his apron. He looked down at her, his expression sober. 'If you are to go into this business in a big way, you want to think of buying in ready-made uppers for men's boots, that would cut down the work a lot, mind.'

'There's something in that,' Hari agreed, 'but, for the moment, I have to concentrate on the ladies' shoes so that they are ready for the people from the theatre to take with them when they move on to Somerset.'

'They're going to Somerset?' Lewis said in surprise. 'There's a lot of good leather down that way, why aren't they buying shoes from Mr Clark's factory?'

'It might just be,' Hari said sharply, 'that I am making something a little bit different, giving personal attention to what the ladies require in a way that a big factory could not do.' She had read about Mr Clark since her visit to the theatre, he was doing very well and turning out shoes and boots of good quality.

'Good point,' Lewis said with a rueful smile. 'I'll consider myself put in my place.'

He sat down at the bench and picked up one of the patterns Hari had made on paper.

'This the right size, you've checked with the customer?'

'Lewis,' Hari said in exasperation, 'please give me credit for some sense, how do you think I've survived on my own since my father died? Certainly not by making the wrong size shoes.'

She settled herself beside him at the bench and took up the satin slippers she was decorating for Meg. 'I must remember, no green beads,' she said under her breath. 'Green beads are unlucky.'

'What?' Lewis said and Hari smiled at him cheekily.

119

'Just talking to myself, it's the only way I can get any sensible conversation round here.'

Lewis pretended to be angry. 'That's nice, isn't it?' He appealed to William who was cutting leather at the other end of the bench. 'I never thought I'd end up working for a bossy woman.'

Hari could almost feel the silence as the three of them worked industriously, cutting, stitching and shaping the leather into something beautiful. She sighed with satisfaction, the job was going to get done on time after all and that, she promised herself, was only the beginning.

IO

The elegant drawing-room at Summer Lodge was filled with people; intruders who lifted priceless objects and studied them trying to assess their worth. One man, corpulent and a little seedy looking, took an occasional table and upended it, examining the workmanship with cool appraising eyes.

Emily felt a sudden anger at the way her home was being violated, how could she bear to have the things she'd held dear being haggled over like so much rubbish?

Already the auctioneer was positioned outside on the lawn, a table before him and a wooden gavel in his hand. Soon, her possessions would belong to strangers, the familiar well-loved objects that had surrounded her since childhood would be gone.

The summer sun spilled over the gardens, the trees swayed gently, the leaves rustling like soft, applauding hands. Emily sighed heavily, no more would she sit beneath those trees reading or idling away her days so carelessly as she had done, was it only a few short weeks ago?

The voice of the auctioneer rang out, hushing the expectant crowd. The bidding began and Emily turned away from the window, unable to watch.

People were drifting away from the house, moving into the garden. Wide crinolines brushed against the grass and men in fine suits made bids with a raised finger or a simple nod of the head. Emily found her gaze drawn irresistibly to the scene outside, she longed to rush to the auctioneer and put a stop to the proceedings.

She turned abruptly and moved quickly through the hallway, hearing from outside the open front door the sound of muted voices. A woman laughed, a carefree tinkling laugh and Emily paused in wonder, it seemed so long since she had felt like laughing. Suddenly she envied the unknown woman.

In the kitchen, Letty was standing near the black hob staring listlessly as the kettle hissed a rushing jet of steam towards her. The mistiness seemed to well from the maid's eyes, but perhaps, Emily thought, she was being fanciful.

'Let's have some tea.' Emily sat at the scrubbed table and the startled look on Letty's face made her smile ruefully.

'We are both going to get used to the old order being disrupted,' she said softly. 'I'm glad you are coming with me to Chapel Street, Letty, I know it's only lodgings but it's clean and respectable and it won't be for long, I promise you.'

'What's going to happen to Summer Lodge, Miss Emily?' Letty sniffed a little as she made the tea. 'Will it have to be sold like all the other stuff?'

Emily shook her head. 'No, it passes to the next male heir, that's my cousin, Craig Grenfell.' Emily sighed heavily, 'It just isn't fair!'

She had not been surprised to learn that the accountant Morris had been proved innocent of any crime and had pointed the finger at Spencer Grenfell. His accusations backed up with the evidence found by Craig would be enough to convict Spencer and send him to prison for some time, once his whereabouts were discovered, for Spencer seemed to have vanished from the face of the earth.

Emily had not called on Aunt Sophie recently, she wasn't in the mood for visiting nor for the lecture her aunt would surely give her on humiliating the family by openly selling her possessions.

And if Emily had expected Craig to ride in on a white charger and save the day, she had been doomed to disappointment. He had left Swansea without even sending a message and, as empty day ran into empty day, Emily's anger and resentment towards her cousin continued to grow.

No doubt Craig was ashamed to face her, he had allowed her father to be duped into losing everything and now Craig would benefit from Emily's misfortune. He would inherit Summer Lodge. No wonder he wasn't anxious to see her.

Emily drank the tea, suddenly aware of the incongruity of the situation: here she was, sitting in the kitchen like one of the servants, something that would have been unthinkable just a few weeks ago.

She rose restlessly and moved to the door. 'I'm going up to London tomorrow, Letty,' she said quickly, it was best she got things moving as soon as possible. 'I have some business up in town. Perhaps while I'm away, you'll see to moving our bags to Chapel Street, I'll make sure you have some money for the cab.'

'Yes, miss.' Letty bobbed a curtsy and Emily smiled with a sudden feeling of gratitude towards the maid.

'I think you can dispense with the formalities, Letty, curtsying would look out of place in a few rooms in a lodging house, don't you think?'

'If you say so, miss, but it's going to be hard getting out of the habit, mind.'

Emily stood in the hallway for a moment staring into the garden, the sun still shone brightly and the inexorable voice of the auctioneer rose and fell in the summer air.

Emily turned and walked up the wide staircase, looking painfully at the bare walls where paintings of her ancestors had hung for generations. It would be hard to leave Summer Lodge but there was no other choice, it was no longer her home, it belonged to Craig Grenfell.

In her room, she sat on the bed and opening her travelling bag carefully took out the satin-lined box. Opening the lid, she stared down at the emeralds glinting up at her like cat's eyes, her mother's emeralds and her grandmother's and many generations of Grenfell women before her.

She closed the lid with a snap of finality. Tomorrow, she would go to the finest jeweller in London and sell the gems for the best price she could get. She was determined not to look on it as the ending of a chapter but the making of a new beginning. Why then were tears burning against her closed lids?

Emily sat in her small room in the lodging house in Chapel Street working over the books and she rubbed her eyes tiredly. A slight chill the day after the sale had delayed her journey to London and so she had been forced to leave Summer Lodge with her few possessions in a bag and watch as the cab carried her from the large estate on the hill to the cramped rooms of the house in Chapel Street.

Almost immediately, she had written to her father's supplier in London and made an offer to pay off some of the debt he owed. Now, she held the letter of reply before her and sighed; it seemed that Croydon and Cooper, Leather Importers, wanted more than she was able to offer.

There was nothing for it but that she visit the company directors in person and see if she could persuade them of her determination to rebuild the business.

Emily hated travelling by train, the noise and the steam and the cinders made her head ache and the feeling of not being able to control the iron monster frightened her. But go to England she would for she was determined to make the directors of Croydon and Cooper see sense. And at the same time she could sell the emeralds, a task she had been dreading.

She glanced at the clock, it was barely eight thirty and the train would be leaving within the hour. She might as well get ready for the journey.

'Letty!' she called, 'check my overnight bag, see that I've got all I need, there's a good girl.'

Letty appeared from the kitchen and looked at Emily with concern. 'Going off to London today, are you, miss, and on your own too, won't you let me come with you?' Letty said coaxingly.

Emily sighed. 'You've no reason to worry, I'm not a child and anyway the fare is dear enough for one of us, let alone two. But I will have a cup of tea, Letty, please.'

Emily had become accustomed to taking her meals with Letty; there was no dining-room in her lodgings, only one small sitting-room apart from the two bedrooms and it was convenient to eat in the kitchen, keeping the sitting-room as an office.

'There's some cold beef and a nice fresh loaf I brought from the bakers early this morning,' Letty said. 'Shall I make you up some nice sandwiches?'

'That will do nicely.' Emily thought ruefully of the sumptuous meals she used to eat at Summer Lodge, the tempting courses of meat and fish and then a carefully concocted pudding that melted in the mouth. It was a wonder she had not grown fat.

Letty disappeared and Emily turned her attention to the letter on the table before her.

'Well, Croydon and Cooper, you shall see me face to face soon enough and then you will know that Emily Grenfell is not a woman to be trifled with,' she said grimly.

The station was practically empty of people and Emily felt so alone as she stepped on to the train. She watched as the town moved past the grimy train windows and Emily felt that she was tugging up her very roots.

She must have dozed a little and the train grew stuffy as the sun hit the windows. When she woke it was to the incessant chattering of the wheels against the rails and Emily thought she would never arrive at her destination.

It was hot in London, the pavements seemed hard beneath her feet. People passed by without a glance in her direction and it was as though she had suddenly become invisible.

Not so long ago she had been loved and cherished with the world at her feet, now she was a woman alone. Emily shook back a stray curl of hair and held herself upright, she must stop feeling sorry for herself. Before papa died she had been a child, spoiled and cosseted and it was a pity she had not grown up a bit more quickly.

As she made her way to the modest Grenfell town house, Emily felt the beginning of a headache coming on. The house was no longer papa's property, although she still held the key; it rightly belonged to Craig, just as Summer Lodge did.

Nevertheless, she meant to make use of it. Emily unlocked the door and moved into the cool of the hallway, putting down her bag gratefully. She went into the drawing-room and sank down into a chair. The silence hung round her like a shroud and, looking around, her feeling of resentment against her cousin burned into a fierce anger. Where was he when she needed him most? Her fiancé, the man who was supposed to love her, had not come near her since her father's death.

But that was wholly unreasonable for when papa had died Craig was still under suspicion of fraud, how could he come to her? She rose and moved to the window and stared out into the silent square. The hot sun fell between the buildings throwing great shadows, the trees dotted along the road waved greenly reminding Emily of home.

But home was Summer Lodge with its lawns and flower-beds, not the cramped lodgings in Chapel Street.

Suddenly Emily was weeping, she put her hands over her eyes fighting the feelings of pain and frustration. She had lost everything, first her father and then her home, to a man who cared nothing for her.

A sudden sound in the doorway startled her and she looked up in fear.

'Emily!' The voice was gentle. 'Emily, I'm here, everything is going to be all right.' Craig was suddenly in the room, moving towards her, holding out his arms to her as though he had never been absent.

'What are you doing here?' Emily realized that she sounded hysterical. Quickly, she wiped away the tears.

'Come to claim the town house have you? Having a wonderful time in London I don't doubt and at my poor father's expense.'

Craig's expression hardened. 'I'm in London trying to sort out my own affairs,' he said gently, 'I'm making an effort to repay customers who have been cheated.' He paused staring at her with half-closed eyes so that Emily could not read his expression.

'And what about me!' Emily demanded. 'I suppose now that I'm penniless I'm no longer suitable for the wonderful Craig Grenfell. Your firm might have problems but you are still solvent, that's more than I am.'

'I'm sorry, Emily, I know I should have been there to help Uncle Thomas with his business long ago.' He shrugged. 'I suppose I was careless but in any case your father never welcomed interference in his affairs, he was his own man.'

127

'That's an easy thing to say now, isn't it? It was your precious brother who stole customers away from papa, took the profits to put in his own pocket. You are a fine pair, you and Spencer.'

Craig's jaw tensed. 'And why should you care about *my* customers, is that it? Why should you worry if they are losing much of their investment?' He paced around the room. 'You always were a selfish little madam, wrapped up in yourself to the exclusion of everyone else. Just see how you've walked into this house without a thought for if I wished to use it.'

He looked down at her. 'However bitter you may feel about it, the properties were entailed and I am the heir to them, like it or not.'

He sighed. 'And I have a great many debts to repay before my affairs are sorted out. I am sorry for your problems, Emily, and I'll try to help, of course I will, but I have worries of my own too.'

'What worries?' Emily said, her voice hard, 'Paying back a few paltry debts. I have watched my most treasured possessions being sold to strangers, I have moved out of my home to accommodate you, my precious cousin.'

She rose and faced him angrily. 'I am here to plead my case with my father's creditors and to sell the family jewels, I suppose it *is* selfish of me to be concerned with such trifles when you have such pressing concerns like where you shall live, in the London home or at Summer Lodge.'

'Emily,' Craig said suddenly, 'why are we quarrelling? We should be helping not blaming each other.' Craig made to put his arm around her shoulders but she held up her hand.

'I don't want your pity!' She picked up her bag, 'And I don't want your charity either, keep your house, long may you enjoy the fruits of my father's labour.'

She was out in the street before she knew it, walking along the hard pavements beneath the swaying trees. She longed to cry, to dissolve the hard knot of tears that was inside her but pride would not allow her to make a show of herself in the street.

She waved her hand to call a cab and when, at last, one stopped, she leaned towards the driver.

'Where can I find decent lodgings for the night?' She heard her voice tremble but could not control it.

'Don't worry, misses,' the driver said staring at her in open curiosity, 'I'll take you to a very respectable lodging house run by a real lady. Mrs Simons will look after you.'

With a sigh, Emily sank back in her seat and closed her eyes, listening to the clip clop of horseshoes ringing against the roadway with a feeling of unreality closing in on her. This was all a nightmare from which she must one day awake. But for now, she would not allow herself to think, she would rest for a few hours and then make arrangements to deal with business matters.

It was early the next day that she was ushered into the offices of Croydon and Cooper. Mr Cooper was not present but Mr Croydon sat behind a huge desk, a bland smile on his face.

'My dear Miss Grenfell, this is a surprise,' he said jovially. He was a big man with a fine moustache about the same age as her father had been, Emily guessed, but it was quite apparent that he considered himself quite a dandy. He wore a richly coloured waistcoat beneath a fine linen jacket and in his cuffs were large gold links.

Emily smiled, she knew instinctively that here was a man who thought of women as merely creatures of decoration and, if it would serve her purpose, it was a view she would exploit to the full.

'Please help me out of my problems, Mr Croydon,' she

said softly, despising herself for the wheedling tone in her voice. 'If you will only accept the offer of payment I made to you earlier, then the rest of the debt will be paid very shortly.'

'And who, my dear lady, is handling your business interests and why are you here in person on such an unladylike errand?'

Emily looked up at him from beneath her lashes. 'My cousin is indisposed, he will, of course, handle everything once he is well again.'

'I see,' Mr Croydon stared at her shrewdly. 'Isn't there talk of some sort of scandal involving your father's nephews, some . . . dubious business dealings?'

Emily looked down at her hands, she knew it was useless to deny it, the man was no fool. 'Alas,' she sighed, 'there's one black sheep in every family, I suspect.' She smiled again and Mr Croydon leaned towards her over the desk. 'But fortunately,' she continued quickly, 'the rest of the Grenfells are honest, upright citizens.'

'Quite so.' He shuffled some papers before him and regarded the figures in silence for a moment. Then he looked up and met Emily's eyes.

'Your father does owe us rather a lot of money, you know, will your cousin meet the obligations?'

Fat chance! Emily thought, Craig was too wrapped up in his own schemes to care about her father's debts. 'Once he is quite well, he will take up the reins and the business will be booming again,' she said out loud.

Mr Croydon leaned back in his chair and smiled ruefully. 'Right now,' he said abruptly. 'Let's be done with the play acting, what is really going on, Miss Grenfell?'

Emily sat up straighter in her chair feeling the colour rise to her face. 'I'm sorry,' she smiled ruefully, 'I shouldn't have tried to fool you.' She twisted a scrap of lace handkerchief between her fingers. 'I'm going to run the business myself, I have plans for paying off the bills of each creditor in instalments and then trying to build up the business again.

'First thing I must do is to sell the emeralds I inherited from my mother, they will bring me in enough to buy in leather and begin to trade again.' She stared hard at Mr Croydon. 'But I must have your good will.'

He remained silent for a long time, staring at Emily as though summing her up. At last he spoke. 'Very well, you have it,' he said. 'Now that you are being honest with me, I think I can help you.'

He leaned forward. 'Let me see your jewels, I might be able to find you a buyer who will give you a good price. Then, we will talk again.'

He rose to his feet and extended his hand. 'I can't say I approve of it, young lady, you going into business, but I admire your courage and any help and advice I give willingly.'

He led her to the door and opened it for her. 'One hint, don't be so coy with the men you deal with, they might misconstrue your intentions and try to take advantage of you.'

He smiled as she walked past him her cheeks burning. 'And get yourself a good shoe designer and a good cutter, make your own shoes, begin an emporium instead of just importing and selling the leather, at least then you would not find yourself out on a limb in a man's world.'

Emily took a cab back to Mrs Simons's house and went directly to her room. She sank on to the bed and closed her eyes, ideas racing through her mind.

Mr Croydon was right, she must open her own shop, have shoes made to order at first and then perhaps import goods from the English shoemakers such as Mr Clark of Somerset.

She would need the services of a talented shoemaker and the best one she knew of in Swansea was Hari Morgan. Emily swallowed hard, how could she lower her pride so far as to approach the girl she had been so scornful of?

And yet she knew that swallowing her pride was something that must be done, she would offer Hari Morgan the inducement of her own premises, a free hand in design and the services of experienced boot and shoemakers to work under her direction. But would Angharad Morgan be willing to give up her own independence?

Determination surged afresh through Emily's consciousness, she *would* rebuild her father's reputation and his business, she would show the world that Emily Grenfell was no weak-kneed lady of leisure, but as strong as any man when it came to business. She would *make* Hari Morgan interested in her scheme for an emporium however much it cost her in lost pride for in Hari lay the key to success.

Emily was astute enough to recognize that Hari had a singular talent, a fine touch for design that eluded most men. She also had the gift for innovation, something the more practical-minded Emily lacked, a fact she readily admitted to herself.

The ringing of a bell from downstairs announced that it was time for supper and Emily realized quite suddenly that she was hungry. She rose from the bed and stared at her reflection in the speckled mirror on the wall. She was unremarkable to look at and far too tall for a woman.

But Emily did herself an injustice, her hair was lit with copper tones enhancing her creamy skin. Her figure though slender was well formed and her height gave her an almost regal appearance.

She moved away from the mirror and walked slowly to the door, she would eat her supper, make pleasant conversation with her landlady and then return to her room.

Tonight, she would rest and not think about her future until the morning. Tomorrow would come all too soon and then her problems would really begin.

11

The foyer of the theatre was ablaze with lights, music drifting from behind closed doors carried to where Hari stood in the street with William at her side.

Her eyes felt heavy, she had worked much of the previous night and most of the day to have the shoes for the theatre people ready in time.

'*Noswaith da*, Miss Morgan, going to the theatre like the rich folks now, is it?'

Hari turned to see Ben Jones smiling down at her, his cap in his hand. 'Good evening to you, Ben.' Hari smiled ruefully. 'No such luck, I'm just working as usual.' She moved the basket from one arm to the other.

'You haven't brought me any boots for repair, lately, Ben, anything wrong with my cobbling then?' Hari smiled. 'No offence intended, mind, if you want to go to someone else that's up to you.'

'*Duw*, it's not that,' Ben protested. 'I didn't like to tell you before but I've learned to be a dab hand at tapping the boots myself. Had to do it see, dad's been complaining about me being lazy.' He shrugged.

'I like the cobbling, that and driving the van is about the only work I'm fit for, having very little brains for the counting and stock taking.'

Hari liked Ben's open friendly manner and his honesty. 'Well then, I can't complain about a man who does his own boots, can I? But when I'm rich and have my own emporium

I'll hire you as part-time cobbler and van driver, right?'

'Right,' Ben said solemnly, 'but for now can I wait by here for you and walk you back home, it's no time for a young lady to be out alone.'

'I'm here, mind!' William said indignantly. 'I wouldn't let Miss Hari go out by herself.'

'My apologies,' Ben said at once, 'I didn't notice you by there.' He winked at Hari. 'May I still have the pleasure of walking to World's End with the both of you?'

'Well, I'm willing,' Will said reluctantly, 'if that's what Hari wants but there's no need, mind.'

Hari moved purposefully towards the foyer. 'See you in a few minutes, Ben,' she said smiling. 'You're welcome to walk back home with Will and me and have a cup of tea for your trouble.'

The theatre was alive with the sound of voices and Hari realized with relief that the show must be over. She led the way along the back passages towards the small dressing-rooms and she could hear William's well-soled boots clattering against the stone floor.

The corridors were ill-lit and cheerless and Hari shivered, the backstage life of the theatre folk was far from the glamour portrayed in front of the public.

'Ah, our little shoemaker.' Charles Briant welcomed Hari into the bright lights of his office. 'You've come just in time because tomorrow the cast moves on to Somerset.'

He sat on a huge leather chair with a sigh of relief and it was clear to Hari that his leg had been giving him trouble.

'Let me see what you have been doing for us,' Charles said smiling widely beneath his white moustache. 'I'm sure Meg and all the ladies are very anxious to take possession of their fine new footwear, but I shall have the privilege of seeing it first.'

'There's something for you to try.' Hari took a pair of boots from her basket. On one of them, the leather sole had been built up fairly high and yet by the sheer elegance of the design the modification scarcely showed.

'You know I took all those measurements?' Hari said smiling. 'Well, I'm hoping I've made good use of them.'

Charles frowned and cleared his throat, tentatively he took the boots from Hari and kicking off his leather slippers, bent forward and gingerly drew the boots on to his feet, lacing them up with trembling fingers.

Slowly, he rose to his feet. He took a step forward and then another free from the characteristic rolling movement caused by the shortness of one of his legs.

He turned to Hari, his eyes moist. 'For the first time in years, I can stand proud like any other man.' He took her hand and kissed it. 'I can't find enough words to thank you.'

Hari swallowed hard. 'No thanks needed,' she said briskly.

'I shall pay you well for the boots, of course,' Charles said in a matter-of-fact tone that did little to conceal his emotions. Then, with a return to his flamboyant self, he flung his arms wide. 'But more, I shall spread your name far and wide to all parts of the country, you will be as famous as any of the actors who have trod the boards at this theatre, that I promise you, Hari Morgan.'

A sudden wash of laughter and raised voices shattered the silence as the doors opened and from the area of the stage, the performers returned to the small dingy dressing-rooms.

'Hari!' Meg's voice was joyful, 'you've brought our shoes, thank the Lord for that, I thought you'd forgotten.'

She fell silent, staring in wonder as Charles walked towards her, hands outstretched. 'Look what the wonderful girl has done for me, my darlings,' Charles waved his hand to encompass the entire cast, 'I can walk straight as a tree, no more will I have to endure the taunts and jeers of the ignorant, I am a new man.'

'Hari, you are so clever,' Meg said warmly, 'you can see what happiness you've brought dear Charlie, you are a genius. Come now, let us all see what you've done for us, then you must celebrate with a glass of champagne, mustn't she Charles?'

'Indeed, she must,' Charles said emphatically. 'The first toast shall be to Hari Morgan, shoemaker extraordinaire.'

It was much later when Hari, with William at her side and her empty basket swinging on her arm, left the theatre. Of Ben Jones there was no sign and Hari sighed, she could hardly blame him for not waiting, she had been in the theatre for over an hour.

'Looks like your follower didn't want to hang around,' William said with obvious satisfaction.

'Looks like,' Hari agreed hiding her amusement. 'Never mind, you and me will manage on our own, right?'

'Right.' William walked swiftly to keep stride with Hari.

Although he was growing fast, Hari was still taller than he was, a matter which quite clearly irked him. Hari rested her hand on his shoulder.

'But I have you at my side, Will, and I know we'll be all right.'

Nonetheless, she was happy to reach the tall narrow house in World's End, she didn't like the darkness of the streets and the distant sounds of drunken voices. She closed the door behind her with a sigh of relief.

'Bed now, Will,' she said softly, 'you look worn out.' She threw off her shawl. 'As for me, I must write what I am owed in my book and then I too will go to bed. I'm sleeping on my nose.'

She sat at the table and painstakingly wrote down the sums of money that should have come in for the work already done. She had expected to return home with full payment for the shoes she'd made, but it seemed the theatre people were not too quick in settling bills, a practice they shared with the gentry. The only payment she had received was from Charles Briant who had given her a generous bonus for her extra work on his boots.

Hari closed her book with a snap of finality, the outstanding balance she owed for the French calf hung like a weight around her neck. She stood for a moment staring round at the flickering shadows thrown by the lone candle, the fire had died long since and the room was cold and suddenly lonely.

'Time for some sleep, Hari, girl,' she said softly, knowing that in the morning her worries would subside and her natural optimism take over once again. She would face the future with renewed determination but, for now, all she wanted to do was to crawl into her bed and sleep.

Emily climbed down from the cab and stood looking uncertainly around her, World's End was a far worse place than she could ever have imagined. Tall narrow houses stood back to back and grimed curtainless windows stared blankly at her as though reflecting the hostility of those within. Her lodgings at Chapel Street were a palace in comparison with this place and Summer Lodge a far-off dream of perfection.

And yet, amidst the dirt and grime, grew the occasional camomile, white flowers pressing strongly towards the sun. Perhaps it was fanciful to think of Hari Morgan as a defiant camomile flower and yet that was the picture which came to Emily's mind.

She saw to the side of one of the houses the faded sign for Morgan and family, boot and shoemakers, fastened over what appeared to be little better than a shed. Surely

Hari Morgan would be only too grateful for the opportunity to get away from such an unprepossessing background?

She pushed open the door and saw a small counter before her arrayed with pieces of leather and a variety of lasts. The smell of leather permeated the air and at once Emily was back in her father's storehouse where he had kept mountains of skins ready to be cut and fashioned into boots and shoes.

She straightened her shoulders, harking back to the past would do her no good at all, it was all gone, like a once-cherished dream. She was alone now, she had lost not only her father but her possessions, her beloved emeralds and her home and all because of the neglect of Craig Grenfell.

Prison had been too good for him and although he declared himself innocent of any crime, he was most certainly guilty of fecklessness, leaving important matters of finance in the hands of his greedy younger brother. It was ultimately Craig's responsibility and yet he had stood back and allowed himself to be duped and Emily's father to be ruined. How could she ever forgive him?

A small boy appeared from the table behind the counter, he smiled at her politely and waited for her to speak.

'I'm looking for Miss Hari Morgan,' she said stiffly, not taking kindly to having to explain her business to a mere boy, however clean and polite he might appear.

'Are you a customer, misses?' the boy said eagerly, touching his cap, and Emily nodded.

'That's right, is Hari Morgan here or not?'

'I'll fetch her now, misses, won't be a minute.' He ducked out of a back door and Emily heard the sound of his boots ringing on the cobbles.

She looked around at the bare, cheerless workshop, at the roughly made counter and the cold bare flags of the floor and shivered, what a place to have to work, even in her own reduced circumstances she was so much better placed than Hari Morgan. Why was it then that she almost envied the girl?

Suddenly, Hari Morgan appeared in the opening of the back door, her hair fanning out darkly on her shoulders, an incongruously large leather apron swamping her small frame. She looked very vulnerable and Emily wished that they had started off on a more pleasant footing.

'May I talk to you?' Emily asked awkwardly, not quite knowing what to say. 'It's about business.'

'Aye, come through into the kitchen,' Hari spoke guardedly and Emily couldn't blame her for being suspicious. Emily followed her across the yard into the surprisingly sunny warmth of the kitchen. The room was poorly furnished but it was spotlessly clean and a cheerful fire blazed in the blackened hearth.

'Yes?' Hari said and there was a note of hostility in her voice that was unmistakable.

'I want to make you a proposition,' Emily said, almost wishing she hadn't come. 'I intend to start up a business.' She paused for a moment looking for the right words.

'I want to make shoes and sell them in large quantities and yet I would like them to be different, individual, and to achieve that, I require a designer.'

The words were rushing out and Emily realized with surprise that she was actually nervous of this composed young woman standing before her. 'You could be my designer if you so wished.'

'Me?' Hari said with disbelief. 'You want me to work for you after the way you've treated me? You must be daft then.'

Hari raked the coals beneath the kettle on the fire, more, Emily imagined, to give herself time to think than for any other reason. Hari looked up suddenly, catching Emily off her guard.

'You've got plenty of money, why should you want me when you could pay the best in Swansea?'

'You are the best in Swansea as far as I'm concerned,' Emily said. Ambition burned within her, she wanted Hari to work for her so much, to make the business an outstanding success and Hari's reticence only made Emily more eager to have her services.

'I can take any debts you might have on to my books and raise the money I need to start the business off, but I must tell you one thing,' Emily said, 'I am not rich, don't make that mistake, I need the business to succeed or I'm finished.' Silence hung heavily in the room as Hari seemed to be assessing her words.

'With your talent and my management,' Emily went on, 'we could make the names of Grenfell and Morgan known throughout the country. It's a wonderful opportunity, please don't discard it out of hand because of pride or pique, just think it over for a few days and let me know your decision when you are ready.'

'I can let you know my decision now,' Hari Morgan's face was tight with controlled anger. 'I don't want to work for you, I'm employed very nicely working for myself and the name of Morgan is respected already in town, which is more than can be said for that of the Grenfells.'

'I see.' Emily felt as though she had been slapped in the face. Well, this little upstart would see that the Grenfells had dignity. She moved towards the door. 'In that case, I'm sorry I troubled you.'

'Wait!' Hari said quickly. 'That was rude of me, I'm sorry.'

Emily smiled bleakly. 'Yes, I'm sorry too, we could have made a good team, in business at least, though I realize we could never be friends or anything of that sort, but I'm convinced it could have worked. If you change your mind, please call to see me.' She opened the door.

'I am in lodgings in Chapel Street, you must know that all my possessions from Summer Lodge had to be sold?'

'Yes, I know,' Hari said ruefully, 'I don't suppose you realize how lucky you were to have things to sell, that's more than I ever had, mind.'

Anger surged through Emily and she bit her lip hard to stop the rush of bitter words. After a moment, she took a deep breath.

'Yes, well, if you feel it's lucky to see all the things you held dear being handled and bought by strangers just to pay off your father's debts, then I suppose you could say I'm lucky.'

'I'm sorry.' Hari smiled suddenly. 'It seems I'm making a habit of saying sorry to you. Look, sit down, have a cup of tea, let's be civilized to each other at least.'

Emily hesitated then moved to the scrubbed table and sat down abruptly, her legs shaking so badly it seemed they wouldn't support her. Hari made the tea silently and deftly pushed the cup towards Emily.

'It's very weak, mind, got to make the tea last, it's so expensive these days.' She leaned forward and looked earnestly at Emily. 'I don't mean to be nasty or anything but I don't really think we could work together, do you?'

Emily sipped the tea gratefully. 'Perhaps you are right,' she said flatly. 'In any case, we would both have to be committed to the idea, half-heartedness won't do, it's all or nothing.'

'I agree,' Hari seemed ill at ease, 'I would like to help but I'm all right here, I've got people working for me, see I owe it to them to make a success of my own business. I have never worked for anybody but my father, I like being my own boss.'

Emily finished her tea and rose to her feet. 'Well, if you'd rather be a big fish in a very small pool, that's up to you, I suppose. Personally I would have thought you had more ambition than that.'

'I have got ambition,' Hari said quickly, her cheeks suddenly flushed and Emily could see that her words had stung.

'I'm making shoes for the theatre folk just now and I intend to build my business up bit by bit.'

Emily smiled. 'I suppose it's my turn to say I'm sorry,' she said. 'Of course you must do things your own way, I was silly expecting you to take a big risk with me when you can get along quite nicely alone.'

Emily left the house, her mind in a turmoil, she couldn't allow Hari to stand in her way, the girl was refusing her offer out of sheer pride, Emily was certain of it. But perhaps there would be some way of persuading her; at any rate, Emily would not give up her ideas.

When she arrived home, Emily shrugged off her coat and kicked her shoes across the room; they were not comfortable shoes, the leather was hard and ill-shaped, nothing like the wonderful shoes Hari Morgan used to make for her.

Letty appeared with a tray of tea and Emily smiled her appreciation. 'You must have read my mind,' she said, 'a good strong cup of tea is just what I need.'

A little later, Emily was looking through her accounts and came across a bill for French calf; thoughtfully, she turned it over in her hands, Hari would need to buy the calf too and the usual practice was to pay for it at the end of the month.

There was no doubt that Hari would buy from the same supplier as the Grenfells and what if Hari had an outstanding bill? Emily might be able to persuade the supplier to call the debt in, just as a favour of course, then Hari would need money at once, she would have no choice but to throw in her lot with Emily. Emily reached for some paper and began to write.

It was almost a week later when Hari Morgan was shown into the small sitting-room of the house in Chapel Street. Emily rose to her feet and smiled.

'Good morning, I'm very pleased to see you, does this mean you've changed your mind about my business proposition?'

Hari nodded. 'I'll be honest with you, I didn't want to come but I've got no choice.'

'Sit down, please.' Emily avoided Hari's eyes, unable to suppress the sudden dart of guilt that brought the colour rushing to her cheeks.

'I owe a large bill for leather,' Hari said, 'and I haven't yet been paid by the theatre folk.'

Hari's face was pale and Emily told herself sternly that it was all for the best, together she and Hari would prosper.

'As I told you when we first spoke,' Emily said quietly, 'I can take your debts on my own books and I can raise enough money to start us off in quite good style. For your part, you will bring your undoubted talent as well as your customers to the business. Eventually, we shall build our clientele from the richer people of Swansea.'

Hari nodded. 'Agreed, but one or two things I must make clear, William comes with me and I choose the cobblers who work for us, I'm not putting the name of Morgan to any inferior work.'

Emily smiled. 'I understand. Together we will make it work, Hari, believe me, we shall have the finest business in the country.'

Hari moved towards the door. 'I will go on working in my shop until you get the premises, then.'

'I've got the premises already,' Emily said and then she saw the surprised look on Hari's face. 'Nothing definitely decided, of course.'

'Where is it?' Hari asked. 'I hope it's nothing too grand.'

'It's an old building at the bottom of Wind Street,'

Emily said. 'I can rent it cheaply because the owner was a friend of my father's.'

'It's handy to have friends like that,' Hari said drily. 'Do you plan on us living in?'

'Yes, I think it will be cheaper that way and more convenient,' Emily said. 'Don't forget, we will be equal partners.' She moved forward and held out her hand and, after a moment's hesitation, Hari took it.

When she was alone, Emily allowed herself a smile of satisfaction, nothing could stop her now, she was on her way up and all thanks to her own ingenuity.

Into her mind quite suddenly came an image of Craig. Emily covered her face with her hands, she should be making plans for her marriage right now, but he had failed her miserably, she no longer wanted anything to do with him, did she?

Emily stood in the centre of the shop staring round happily at the crowd of curious customers. The sound of voices and the clink of glasses was like music to her ears, the shop, *her* shop was actually open for business.

One of the singers from the theatre had stood in the doorway declaring to the crowd who had gathered to watch that the Grenfell and Morgan boot and shoe emporium was providing the best leather goods in town.

Charles Briant had spoken in his fine voice that carried to the very edge of the crowd, telling the people of Swansea how talented and gifted was Angharad Morgan.

'She made me walk straight and tall again, made me feel a complete man with her excellently designed footwear,' he had boomed.

And then the crowds of crinolined ladies with their escorts had moved into the interior of the store, eager to drink the champagne that Emily had insisted upon and to look at and touch the merchandise.

Hari was at Emily's elbow. 'How do you think it's going?' she asked anxiously and Emily smiled.

'Very well attended, as an opening occasion should be, but I think half of these people have come to stare at Emily Grenfell who has done the unthinkable and gone into trade.'

'Don't be so downhearted,' Hari said quickly, 'I'm sure that toffs aren't all like that – are they?'

Emily smiled. 'I don't suppose so, I *am* feeling a little self-conscious, I'm not used to being on display in this sort of way.'

'You must be more used to it than I am. You've always been one of the gentry, used to grand balls and such.'

Emily shrugged. 'Look, Sir Charles is coming over, I must thank him.' Emily smiled at the surprised look on Hari's face.

'Sir Charles, do you mean Charlie from the theatre?' Hari said.

'Of course, why do you think I asked him to attend the opening of the store?' Emily said easily.

Hari shook her head. 'I thought you'd asked him because he was a kind considerate man and a customer. You are a snob.'

Emily was not a bit offended. 'Well, one of us has to be,' she said coolly as she moved forward, holding out her hand.

'Well done, ladies,' Charles winked at Hari, 'I see the rich have come to stare, let us hope that they are as free with their orders as they are with drinking your champagne.'

'Thank you, Charlie,' Hari said, 'there's good of you to spare the time to come to help us out.'

'Wild horses wouldn't have kept me away, my dear Angharad.' Charles smiled at her before moving to the centre of the room.

146

'Ladies and gentlemen,' he said, his voice easily overriding the hum of conversation. 'I shall be the first one to give in my order to these dear ladies, I shall have three pairs of the best leather boots the house of Grenfell and Morgan can supply.'

He turned to Emily and kissed her hand and then took Hari in his arms in a bear hug of an embrace.

Emily found herself inundated with people wanting to make orders and cursed herself for not being prepared. She held up her hand for silence.

'Please have another glass of champagne and in the meantime I will bring my order book from the office.'

She smiled at Hari as she moved towards the stairs, there was no order book but from now on there would be one and, if today was anything to go by, it would always be full.

As she moved up the stairs, Emily felt a sense of triumph, she was on her way to a big success and no-one was going to stop her.

12

Craig Grenfell stood in the sitting-room of Summer Lodge staring out into the garden, it was good to be back home in Swansea. The trees waved luscious leaves in the wind and the soft scent of roses drifted in through the open window.

He glanced around him ruefully, the house bore very little resemblance to the Summer Lodge he knew, the floors were bare of carpets and little of the old furniture remained, the best of it sold off to reduce his uncle's debts.

And all because Craig had allowed his brother a free hand both to pilfer money from his own customers and to interfere in Uncle Thomas's business. Could he wonder that Emily believed him to be feckless and irresponsible and wanted nothing to do with him?

Careless he had certainly been, allowing his complete trust in his brother to blind him to the way the business was being mishandled. Just the same, Emily was forgetting that her father, who was taking an active part in his own affairs, had been taken in by Spencer's cleverness.

Nonetheless, Craig should not have quarrelled with Emily, she was his fiancée as well as his cousin and she had been bitterly hurt by her father's death. The humiliation of seeing her possessions sold must have been a great blow to her pride. And Emily was proud, too proud for her own good, perhaps it was time she learned some lessons about the real world.

The fact that he had inherited Summer Lodge was inevitable, the property was entailed and, in any event, the eldest male heir always took precedence over the female relatives. Unfortunately, Emily was still responsible for her father's debts and she had no choice but to accept the situation.

Summer Lodge would be Emily's home again once they were married and then Craig would take Emily's debts and deal with them as best he could.

He smiled, in view of Emily's bad temper last time he'd seen her, it seemed almost certain that she had other ideas rather than marriage, at least for the time being.

As for himself, Craig knew he had enough on his plate sorting out his own complex problems. He believed that, with Edward Morris's expert help, it would not be too long before the books were in order.

The business, fortunately, was still viable, the profits continued to come in and now that he had taken the trouble to placate and reimburse the more injured of the customers, putting right what he had referred to as 'accounting errors', there was a good chance that the worst of the crisis was over.

He looked around him, once he got his business life in order, he would begin to replace the furniture, hang some drapes, make the place look more like home. But it all cost money and that was something he could not spare, not just yet.

In any case, the choice of furnishings he had hoped to leave in Emily's capable hands, when the time was right. But he didn't think she was in any frame of mind to offer advice gladly on the refurbishing of Summer Lodge, not just now.

He heard the sound of the front door being pushed open and foosteps ringing across the uncarpeted hallway.

'Craig, it's Morris, are you there?' Edward was peering

around the tall doors of the sitting-room, his dark hair falling straight across his forehead, giving him the appearance of a small boy and yet he was a most capable accountant, brilliant even. It was good to have Edward working for him.

'Guess what? Your brother has been arrested up in Newport.' Edward smiled, 'I've just heard the news from an accountant friend of mine who lives there.'

'My mother won't be pleased about that,' Craig said, 'but then I don't suppose Spencer will serve a very long sentence, he'll plead ill health or something.'

'Feel like a drink?' Edward asked. 'I've got another little bit of gossip you might like to hear about.'

'Why not?' Craig moved towards the door. 'I could down a mug of ale and not notice it passing my tonsils. Come on, let's get out of here, the place is like a mausoleum.'

'Then why not rent the place out?' Edward suggested. 'You're doing all right renting the town house out and the proceeds from that are providing a timely and regular infusion of money into the firm.'

'Renting out the place is probably a good idea,' Craig said, 'but I don't want to take such a drastic step unless I have to.' He smiled. 'Emily would never forgive me if I allowed strangers to occupy her precious family home.'

Edward strode out swiftly towards the town. 'It's about Emily I have some gossip.' He glanced at Craig and smiled ruefully. 'Why can't you live somewhere civilized like Chapel Street? I only have to fall over and I'm in some tavern or other.'

'What about Emily?' Craig asked. He felt sure Edward had very little to gossip about where Emily was concerned, she was a lady to the tip of her fingers and very conscious of being 'proper'.

Where was all the spirit and fire of the Grenfell blood? It seemed to be entirely missing from Emily's character.

'All in good time, my friend,' Edward said, 'let's settle ourselves in the comfort of the Mackworth Hotel with a cooling mug of ale in our hand and I'll tell you all that I know.'

And that wouldn't be very much, Craig mused, Emily was nothing if not predictable. Not like the young girl from World's End. Hari now was another sort of woman entirely, beautiful and somehow very wise, but with a proud and defiant streak in her nature that was compelling. Why had he not taken her to bed while he was under her roof? He must be slipping.

He should not allow the seriousness of his business problems to cloud his judgement too much, his rakishness was what had endeared him to the ladies in his life. Did his failure to seduce Hari Morgan mean he was in danger of becoming completely reformed?

And yet he knew, had always known, that Hari Morgan was too good for a mere casual dalliance. He smiled thoughtfully, perhaps he should get his halo out and dust it up a little.

'What's so amusing?' Edward asked. He had turned into the High Street and was walking slightly uphill in the direction of the hotel, ahead of him was Greenhill and to his right and just out of sight was the curving line of the River Tawe.

'Mind your own business,' Craig said pleasantly and Edward returned his smile.

'A woman, no doubt, when have you ever had anything else on your mind, you hot-blooded ram!'

'Right, of course,' Craig said, but he did not enlarge on his statement as he pushed open the doors of the hotel and narrowed his eyes against the sudden gloom after the bright sunlight in the street.

The Mackworth was a well-established hotel with plush carpeting and a plethora of potted palms brought no doubt from the moderate climate of the English South Coast.

He lifted his hand and a waiter was at his side at once. Craig ordered the ale, settling himself on one of the big comfortable chairs in the coolness of the hotel with a sigh of relief.

Edward leaned forward, arms resting on his knees. 'You won't believe this,' he said eagerly, unable to keep his news to himself any longer, 'but Emily and the little darling girl from World's End have set up a shoe shop together at the bottom of Wind Street.'

Craig looked at him in disbelief. 'Emily and the shoemaker's daughter, you must be mistaken.' He smiled ruefully, 'My cousin is far too much of a snob to actually work with a girl like Hari Morgan.' He raised his eyebrows. 'Emily would not see Hari as we see her, an attractive beddable young woman, remember.'

'I knew you would be surprised,' Edward said laughing out loud, leaning back in his chair, enjoying Craig's reaction. 'But every word of it is true. Hari has given up the premises in World's End and Emily has left her lodgings in Chapel Street.' He paused. 'I saw your dear cousin move out myself, she was lodging only a few doors away from my own house, if you recall.'

'What are they doing setting up a shop like that?' Craig felt slightly irritated. 'I can't quite see Emily as a captain of industry somehow.'

'That seems to be a fault of yours, if you don't mind me saying so,' Edward spoke solemnly. 'You sometimes fail to see what is right under your nose.' He stared morosely at the mug of ale the waiter put down on the table before him. 'You didn't even notice that Hari Morgan was madly in love with you, lucky sod.'

He leaned forward again. 'The shop looks well appointed, I must say, and it's only been opened for a short time and already it's gaining a reputation for the finest footwear in Swansea.

'It seems the crowd from the theatre in Goat Street was at the opening,' he continued, 'some lady singer doing the honours and Charles Briant, *Sir* Charles Briant giving the place his special commendation.'

'Who on earth is Sir Charles Briant?' Craig asked. 'I don't think I know him, do I?'

'Apparently not.' Edward smiled. 'He's somewhat eccentric, come over from Bristol way I believe, working at the theatre, though from all the talk, he is extremely rich and needn't work at all.'

'Rich, is he? Well, that will please Emily, I dare say,' Craig said drily.

'Ah, but it isn't Emily he is interested in, it's Hari. The clever girl made some boots that corrected a foot defect or other, earned Sir Charles's undying gratitude. I should think the ladies' shop would do well with the benefit of such an illustrious patron.'

Craig admitted to himself that he was more than a little surprised. It didn't seem at all credible that Emily would have the courage to launch out into the business world and even more doubtful that she would employ the services of the girl she had so openly despised.

'I didn't think Hari would agree to work for Emily,' he said aloud, 'not after the way the two behaved to each other.'

Edward took a deep drink of ale before replying. 'They are partners,' he said. 'Equal partners.'

'And how do you know so much?' Craig asked, amused by Edward's proprietary manner.

'Because, my friend, at Hari's request, I am the accountant acting for the ladies. Who else would they come to? They both have had dealings with me, know me to be honest and hard working, what more can I say?'

'How about adding how modest you are?' Craig said smiling. 'Well, I wish them every success, I am pleasantly surprised at Emily's courage in not sinking under the strain of her father's debts.'

He sipped some of his ale. 'I meant to have helped her with her problems when my own affairs were in good order but now, it seems, my help won't be needed.'

Edward had a far-away look in his eye. 'It's Hari I admire,' he said warmly. 'Such a beautiful young girl and such skill and talent. You know that even the French are asking for her designs?'

Craig stared at Edward thoughtfully. 'She will go far, will that young lady.'

Edward pressed his fingertips together. 'I would very much like to call on Miss Hari Morgan,' he said. 'Oh, I know she is what some might call beneath my station, but I don't give a fig for that. Look how both you and I have been wrongfully accused of theft, how easily we could have spent the rest of our lives in prison. That experience has given me a finer sense of values, believe me.'

Craig knew what Edward meant, being unkempt and considered less than human as he had languished in a prison cell had certainly given Craig an insight into the way the less affluent lived, an experience he was not likely to forget in a hurry.

'Wouldn't it be fine if when you married Emily, we could make it a double wedding with Hari marrying me?' Edward said slowly. Craig stared at him, wondering why he didn't find the prospect at all fine.

'Drink your ale,' he rose to his feet, 'I've just remembered something important I have to do.' He put some money on the table and without a backward look left the surprised Edward sitting at the table alone.

Outside in the warmth of the sunshine, Craig found himself striding along High Street in the direction of Wind

Street. He had no clear idea of what he intended to do or say but he knew he must see for himself what Emily was up to. Or was it Hari Morgan who aroused in him the most concern? He wasn't really sure.

The sun was still high overhead, the sky cloudless, it was a bright summer day but Craig didn't notice, he was deep in thought.

He saw the sign above the elegant shop front while he was still a short distance away. It read, Grenfell and Morgan Footwear Specialists.

Craig noticed the group of ladies in large crinolines gathered outside, bonnets bending and dipping as they talked excitedly. He moved closer and saw that the window was dressed with dark blue velvet upon which rested surprisingly few pairs of boots and shoes.

Satin slippers decorated with buckles and beads stood alongside elegant leather boots as if worn by a couple about to step into a dance. A string of black jet hung over a pair of black stark shoes intended to be worn by a lady in mourning. It was an imaginative display and Hari's hand could be seen written all over it.

He moved past the ladies into the interior of the shop. The room was long and cool and a few ornate chairs were strategically placed next to stands holding a further variety of boots and shoes. At one end was a sun-lit conservatory where some customers sat at leisure sipping what appeared to be cool drinks.

Craig became aware of the small figure walking towards him and, with a shock of surprise, he recognized Hari Morgan. Her thick hair had been tied up and back with a ribbon and she wore a plain but fashionable dress that emphasized her slim waist and firm breasts.

'Can I help you, sir?' she asked and there was a smile in her eyes that made him slightly uneasy. He had the distinct impression that she was laughing at him.

'I'm just curious,' he said bluntly. 'I didn't think that you would ever work with my cousin, what happened?'

Hari gestured around the room. 'This happened, Emily and I made it happen.'

'Very impressive,' Craig said. 'I hope you enjoy a great success with it all.'

'There's no worries about that,' Hari said emphatically, 'we are going to *make* it succeed.' She paused.

'Do you want to talk to Emily? If so, I don't think it's a good idea, not just now.'

'I see.' Craig moved past Hari, his eyes on the stairs that led upwards apparently to the offices. He took them two at a time aware that Hari was quickly following him, her face flushed with indignation.

'Where do you think you are going?' she demanded as, hampered by her skirts, she struggled to catch up with him. 'You've no right to push your way into our private quarters.'

Craig moved into a modestly furnished sitting-room and there as he expected was Emily. She rose to her feet and stared at him with angry eyes.

'How dare you intrude in this way!' she said with quiet fury. 'You have no rights here, do you understand?'

'No rights?' Craig replied with some amusement. 'I'm not only your cousin but I am supposed to be your fiancé.'

'You can forget all that!' Emily said sarcastically. 'You are nothing to me except the man who took away my home and my pride and dignity. I am fighting hard to win all that back and I shall do it without any interference from you. Understood?'

Craig looked from Emily's set face to where Hari stood in the doorway, staring at him with hostility in every line of her taut body.

He shrugged. 'Very well, if that's the way you want it to be, fine, I'll get out of your life and stay out.' He moved to the door and stared down at Hari. Her eyes were large, her expression suddenly uncertain.

On an impulse, Craig took her in his arms, his mouth crushing hers. She stood unmoving and, after a moment, he released her.

He hurried down the stairs and out into the bright sunshine and walked quickly away without looking back.

Hari sank into a chair, her hand to her lips, hating herself for the desire that had blazed into a fire when Craig had held her in his arms. She knew he didn't mean the kiss as any sort of caress, it was more a gesture of dismissal, an insult.

Emily paced about the room, her hands clenched into fists. 'I hate that man!' she said with feeling. 'I could cheerfully take a gun and shoot him.' But her face was suddenly pale, her eyes brimming with tears.

Hari bit her lip. 'I don't think you should talk like that about him,' she said defensively, 'I felt just a bit sorry for Craig, I'm sure he came here to make amends.'

'Oh and you know all about him, do you?' Emily rounded on her. 'Perhaps you know more than you are willing to admit. That was a pretty intimate kiss just now.'

Hari rose to her feet. 'It was not! It was just Craig getting his own back, it didn't mean anything.'

'Well, in that case why did you not slap his face?' Emily said hotly. 'That's what any lady would have done.'

'So you are reminding me that I'm not a lady, are you?' Hari said in a low voice. 'Well, I've never pretended to be anything I'm not, it was your idea that I put on these posh clothes and tie back my hair and go and talk nicely to the customers.' She moved to the door.

'Well, I won't do it any more, it's not what we agreed, I want to make designs, supervise the workshop, I don't want to prance about acting saleslady to a lot of snobbish

157

women who only look down their noses at me. You can do all that in future.'

'I can't serve in a shop!' Emily was outraged. 'I've never done anything like that in my life before.'

'Well, it's time you started then, isn't it?' Hari said quickly. 'I am not your paid help, mind, I'm your partner and so far you haven't pulled your weight, Emily Grenfell.'

'What do you mean?' Emily said. 'I do the books, don't I? I contact suppliers, I . . . I . . .' She lapsed into silence.

'Aye and what do I do, make the designs, direct the boys in the cutting and sewing, spend hours decorating the slippers with beads and such *and* I'm expected to serve in the shop, well, it's too much and I've had enough of it!'

Hari watched as Emily sank down into a chair. 'You know what we're doing, don't you?' Emily said, wearily. 'Just what Craig wanted, we are snapping at each other like two fishwives. I tell you my cousin doesn't want us to succeed.'

Hari sighed heavily. 'Perhaps you're right. In any case one good thing about all this is I've had my say. I can't do it all, Emily, with the best will in the world, I just can't. You must help a bit more, can't you see that?'

'Go on,' Emily said, 'we'll talk this out reasonably like two sensible women and then we'll think about what's to be done.'

'I want to go out more,' Hari smoothed the creases out of her dress, 'I want to go to Goat Street and mingle with the theatre people. I want to make specialized boots like those I made for Charles, I don't want to spend my days kowtowing to a lot of bored rich ladies.'

'I see your point,' Emily said and Hari sighed with relief.

'I'm not grumbling, mind,' she added quickly, 'but now

that it's all out in the open, I'm glad.' She smiled. 'Seems like Craig did us a favour after all.'

'Maybe,' Emily said slowly, 'but I really don't think that's what he intended.'

'Don't be too hard on him,' Hari said gently, 'I know you feel he let you down but he's had a bad time of it too, mind, it couldn't have been much fun in prison.'

'But if he hadn't been so feckless, Craig would have kept an eye on business matters. It was he who allowed his brother the freedom to dip into the till.' Emily smiled suddenly.

Emily moved to the door, 'Don't let's talk about Craig any more. You'll be pleased to know that I'm going to have my first experience of being a saleslady.' She paused. 'You are quite right, Hari, this is a partnership and I shouldn't expect you to do anything I won't do.' She took a deep breath and Hari watched as Emily made her way downstairs to the shop floor.

Hari followed her and stood just outside the door watching, she saw Emily approach one of the ladies who was tapping her foot impatiently, waiting to be served. There was in fact quite a queue of ladies, all of them fretting impatiently, at this rate, Hari mused, they would be losing customers. Perhaps it was time that the company of Grenfell and Morgan branched out and took on some extra sales staff. But in the meantime Emily needed help. Hari took a deep breath, fixed a polite smile to her lips and walked out on to the shop floor.

Craig was immersed in the task in hand, he stood in the warehouse near the docks and ticked off the shipment of leather just come in from abroad. There had been an increase in the demand for French calf and Craig had enough foresight to buy all the existing stocks.

It had taken a great deal of cunning to persuade the

French company to make him the sole agent in Wales, but he had done it on the grounds that it was cheaper to sell to him in bulk.

It made sense to send the leather on one trip to Swansea rather than transporting small amounts to various parts of the country, a point the French after some argument had appreciated.

He closed his book with a smile of satisfaction, now the small boot and shoemakers would all have to deal with him if they wanted the good calf from abroad. And that included dear Cousin Emily, now she would have to overcome her pig-headed pride.

He knew that he could sell the calf at a good profit; it seemed his business was recovering, at last, from his brother's mishandling.

Edward Morris had employed another accountant to work with him and to Craig's great pleasure had delegated the accounts of Grenfell and Morgan to the new young man.

Craig nodded to the warehouse man and moved towards the door.

'Time for a drink, Ianto, I'm sure you could use one, we've worked hard this afternoon.'

'Aye, could that, Mr Grenfell, sir.' Ianto locked the warehouse door. 'The smell of the leather there don't half make a man have a thirst.'

The two men walked towards the Castle Inn in silence, leaving the sounds of the docklands behind them. As he strode along Wind Street towards Castle Square, Craig could not help glancing towards Emily's shop with its usual gaggle of women outside on the pavement.

'Fine boot and shoe place there, mind,' Ianto said conversationally. 'And not just for the rich folks, mind.' He paused and rubbed at his eyes a little self-consciously.

'The little lady shoemaker, Angharad Morgan, made

160

the finest pair of boots for my youngest boy, you never seen anything like them and him with a gamey leg since he was born. Fit him like a glove they do and built up like, so the boy don't have to limp any more. Didn't charge over much either. Grateful I am to that little lady, would help her in any way I could if she should ever need it.'

Craig was thoughtful, he could see a ready market for special shoes for people like Ianto's son. It seemed that Hari and Emily along with her was going to be a very successful businesswoman.

But then he'd always known she had spirit from the first moment he'd set eyes on her in the small kitchen of the house in World's End. In spite of her fear, she had hidden him from the constables, given him shelter when he needed it and, all things considered, he owed her a great debt. Perhaps, he mused, it was time he repaid that debt, the only problem was working out the best way of doing it.

13

It was hot in the workshop and Hari pushed back a curl of hair that had fallen over her eyes. 'No, William, not like that, let me show you.'

Hari took the thick needle from William and caught the leather upper neatly to the sole with a deft stitch. 'Try it again and don't worry, it took me years of training with my father to handle the waxed thread.'

She moved along the bench watching Ben Jones who, though not a cobbler by trade, was skilful and strong and coped well with the ordinary repairs which against Emily's wishes Hari had insisted they continue to do.

'That's a neat job of soling and heeling if I ever saw one. *Duw*, Ben, I'm that glad you came to work for me, I don't know what I would have done without you.'

He winked at her. 'Nor me, either! Between sitting in the boiling heat smelling leather in my nostrils all day and driving that van, I'm having a high old time of it. I must be mad, risking my life I am with that scatterbrained horse every time I make a delivery.'

He smiled. 'Not complaining, mind, glad to be doing a proper job instead of standing behind the counter in my dad's shop. Felt like an old woman there I did.' He looked round. 'Where's Lewis today?'

Hari sighed. 'When I employed him, I knew his mam was very poorly and he'd sometimes need time off to look after her, though I really can't really spare him, these days.'

'Too soft you are, Hari.' Will spoke up with the knowledge that he was privileged to air his opinion.

'Oh?' Hari crossed her arms over her leather apron and stared down at William with raised eyebrows. 'And pray why am I too soft?'

'Well, I'm not saying it's Lewis's fault but his mam puts it on, mind. Strong as a horse she is, I see her often enough when I'm out on errands. She's in Swansea Market more times than the women who sell cockles, Lewis's mam is.'

'Poor Lewis,' Hari said softly, 'I think his mother is more demanding than a wife.'

Ben smiled over his shoulder at her. 'I wouldn't know about that, nor would young Will there.' He nudged William's arm. 'We are both in love with our boss, aren't we Will, can't settle for any other lady.'

'Well,' Hari smiled, 'don't wait for me or you'll wait for ever my lads.' She took off her apron. 'I'm a career woman now and I've got a long way to go before I settle down for marriage and children.'

'Wait till you fall in love with someone.' It was William who spoke, 'I've seen it happen with my sisters, all five of 'em. Go all goggle-eyed they do when they fall in love, daft women.'

'Don't worry,' amused, Hari put her hand on Will's shoulder, 'I won't go all goggle-eyed I promise you.'

Hari moved to the door of the workshop situated to the rear of the shop premises in Wind Street and paused for a moment in the doorway, comparing the spacious well-equipped room to the small shed she rented in World's End. The difference was marked and Hari felt a sense of achievement as she stared round her.

She sighed with pleasure as she moved into her office, sunlight spilled into the room slanting across her drawing board on which was pinned one of her latest designs.

It was a good feeling to be successful.

She stood before the board, examining the design, it was for a soft kid shoe with a pattern punched in holes on the instep and a removable bow that slid into two of the holes. The bow would come in a choice of colours to match any occasion and Hari felt it was an innovation that would be very pleasing to her customers.

She worked silently for some time, modifying and clarifying the drawing and then sank into her chair, brushing her face with her hand. It was very hot in the office and she looked longingly out into the street.

The traffic was quite heavy with delivery vans and pony and traps jostling for prominence. Not far away was the bustle of the docks with the hooting of ships and the scents of spices mingled with rope and tar and the salt of the sea.

The sea, how wonderful it would be to plunge into the cool of the gentle waves that lapped Swansea Bay. But dreaming didn't get the work done and, reluctantly, Hari returned to her drawing board.

While Hari worked alone at the back of the large premises, Emily was busy taking orders from one of her customers.

'I want only the most exclusive of your designs, nothing is too good for my daughter's drawing-room with the queen.'

'Of course, Lady Caroline.' Emily smiled politely. 'Coming out is a really special day and I think Lisa will have a wonderful time.'

'My dear, I do think in the circumstances you should refer to my daughter as Miss Elizabeth, I mean you are not quite on the same footing with her now, are you?' She didn't wait for an answer.

'Of course my daughter will be seen by the queen herself.' Lady Caroline stared at Emily shrewdly. 'I understand some people have to make do with one of the princesses. Of course, you never came out, did you? Not properly, I mean.'

'You are quite right,' Emily said forcing herself to speak evenly. 'My first ball was at the Assembly Rooms but it was still a fine occasion with the ladies dripping in diamonds and precious stones.' She stared dreamily into the distance, 'I remember daddy wearing his gold Albert and I had on my mother's emeralds.'

'Yes, well, it's a great pity that coming from such a once-rich family you had to go into trade, isn't it?'

Emily looked at her sharply. 'Trade is not prostitution, Lady Caroline, it is quite honest and respectable.'

Lady Caroline sniffed into a lace handkerchief. 'All right for a man but not quite the thing for a lady, but I suppose it's needs must when the devil drives. And your marriage to Craig Grenfell came to nought, such a handsome man and doing so well for himself now I believe.'

'Shall I take your order, Lady Caroline?' Emily's patience was fading fast. 'I really do have other customers to see to you know.'

'Oh, very well,' Lady Caroline fanned herself with her scrap of lace. 'Make it six pairs of shoes, in French calf and let's say about five pairs of satin slippers.'

She paused. 'That's just for my dear Elizabeth, I shall need at least a dozen pairs of shoes for myself, some riding boots and say half a dozen pairs of slippers. Only the best calf, remember.'

'Of course, excuse me a moment.' Emily spoke quietly to the new assistant she had recently employed.

'Sarah, will you pop along to the office and ask Miss Morgan if she can spare me a moment.' More loudly she said, 'I have a very important customer who requires to be measured for new shoes.'

Sarah bobbed a curtsy and hurried to the rear of the

shop, disappearing into the nether regions where the office and workshop were now situated.

'Shan't be a moment, Lady Caroline,' Emily said quietly. 'In the meantime would you like some iced tea in the restaurant? We have moved it upstairs so that our customers have a fine view over the town and the hills beyond.' The view was just a glimpse of the rooftops but Emily doubted if someone as insensitive as Lady Caroline would notice anyway.

Sarah returned shortly, following Hari at a respectful distance. It was clear that Sarah did not quite know what to make of Hari Morgan who though seeming equal in status to Miss Grenfell spoke very much the same way as did Sarah herself.

Emily drew Hari to one side. 'We have boring Lady Caroline here, full of airs and graces as usual but with a very good order for us. She wants several dozen pairs of shoes and slippers for herself and her daughter and some best riding boots as well.'

Emily saw Hari frown. 'I'm sure we can manage that,' she said. 'Could we just have a word before I see to the fitting?'

'What is it?' Emily was slightly impatient. 'Surely it can wait, Lady Caroline is about to spend a great deal of money with us.'

'I'm running short of calf,' Hari said, 'and I've just learned that the French company I buy from have made Craig Grenfell the sole supplier for Wales.' She paused, 'I'm so angry that I don't know what to do about it.'

'Damn my cousin!' Emily said, her colour rising. 'So he's sinking to underhand dealings now, is he? Just wait until I see him, he'll have a fine piece of my mind.'

'Wait a bit,' Hari said quickly, 'let me speak to him, if we upset him he might not let us have the calf and then we'd be in a pretty pickle.'

Emily clenched her hands into fists, she knew what she'd like to do to Craig and that did not include toadying to him like some poor supplicant.

'Damn him!' she repeated. 'I'll go down to Bristol and buy calf from there.'

'That's all right as a last resort,' Hari said gently, 'but think of the extra cost involved, we'd have to pay for the leather to be transported across the Bristol Channel for a start and then brought over here from the docks. Apart from being expensive, it would take a lot of time.'

Emily bit her lip, she knew Hari was talking sense. She wanted to stamp her foot and rail at her cousin but there were customers in the shop and, in any case, such conduct was not becoming to a lady of business.

'Let me talk to him first,' Hari coaxed, 'and if he's going to be difficult, we'll go to Bristol.'

Emily sighed. 'All right, Hari, but don't demean yourself to that man. I won't have you lowering your pride.'

Hari smiled. 'I can lower my pride like the best of them if it will get me what I want. There's more than one way of beating a man, mind.'

Emily felt her anger dissolve. 'All right but I don't envy you going cap in hand to Craig Grenfell.'

Hari arched her eyebrows. 'Perhaps I won't have to. But now, I must go and see our customer.'

Emily watched as Hari walked away, her head high. She really was a beautiful girl, so small and delicate looking and yet with such strength of character. It was difficult now to believe she once looked down on her, just like Lady Caroline looked down on them both. Emily turned smiling to greet her next customer.

'I hope you don't mind me calling unexpected, like.' Hari stood in the doorway of the sitting-room in Edward

Morris's house, blinking against the glare of the sun slanting through the windows.

'I'm delighted to see you.' Edward dismissed the maid with a nod of his head and stepped aside to allow her inside. 'Is it business or pleasure, may I ask?'

Hari glanced up at him from beneath her lashes, 'A bit of both really, Mr Morris.'

'Come in.' Edward pushed aside some papers he'd been working on and plumped up a cushion. 'Can I get you something cool to drink?'

'That would be lovely.' Hari sat down and arranged the folds of her pale linen skirt neatly around her legs. She refused point blank to wear crinolines, compromising instead by having made for her some full skirts with matching bodices and replacing her woollen shawl with a shawl of fine lace.

Her shoes as always were hand made and dashing and, to her amusement, it seemed she was setting a bit of a trend in attire around the more elegant circles in town.

Edward was not away for more than a few minutes and returned with a tray loaded with a jug of iced cordial and some tall glasses. Setting down the tray, he poured out the cordial and handed her one of the glasses.

He smiled and Hari returned his smile, thinking that he really was very nice to her; he had been since the first time he'd set eyes on her.

'What can I do for you, Hari, is it the accounts?' He seated himself opposite her and leaned forward eagerly in his chair.

'No, the accounts are fine, we leave all that sort of thing to your firm of course.' It wasn't quite true, Emily made a point of going over all the figures industriously. Probably worried because of the way her father had let the business slide.

'I have finished your boots and if you will try them on, I

will check that they are what you want.' She handed him the boots and watched as he pulled a footstool close and tried on the boots, looking down at them in satisfaction.

'Wonderful!' he said. 'But then I didn't doubt they would be. Now what else was there?'

'I need an order of French calf, at once,' Hari said. 'It seems that Craig has been given sole rights to sell the leather in this area and I feel a bit hesitant to approach him myself.'

'Why?' Edward said in genuine surprise. 'I can't see any difficulty in making such a request.'

'Can't you?' Hari asked. 'Well, it seems Emily can, she feels Craig might not be willing to sell to us in the circumstances. You must know they are not friends any longer.'

'But that should not extend to you or to the business,' Edward said quickly, 'I really can't see Craig being biased in such a way, he wants to sell calf, you want to buy like any other customer, it's as simple as that.'

'In other words you do not want to help me?' Hari said putting down her glass.

'My dear, don't think that,' Edward replied, 'if you wish me to approach Craig on your behalf then I shall certainly do so.'

'Good, that's settled then.' She leaned back in her chair and smiled at him and Edward, encouraged, leaned closer.

'Will you honour me by coming to the theatre with me one evening, we shall take a chaperone of course?' He sounded so much like a little boy requesting a treat that Hari could not bring herself to refuse.

'Yes, that would be lovely, then you could come backstage with me and meet my friends.' She was relieved that she'd thought so quickly, if she introduced Edward to some of the players, it might just take his mind off her.

'Meg is in town this week, perhaps we could all have

supper together later?' Hari said brightly, she didn't want Edward Morris thinking she wanted anything but friendship.

'Oh, yes, that would be fine,' Edward said reluctantly.

'You'll let me know when you've spoken to Craig about the leather then?' As Hari rose to her feet the front door was pushed open and footsteps could be heard crossing the hallway.

Edward smiled, a little relieved. 'I believe this must be Craig now, no-one else walks into the house as though he owns it.' There was a world of affection in Edward's voice.

Hari would have liked to make a run for it but there was nowhere to go, then the door to the sitting-room swung open and she and Craig were standing face to face, his eyes alight as they rested on her.

'This is a pleasure,' he said moving closer, 'Edward, you are a dark horse having secret meetings with a lovely lady.'

In the uncomfortable silence that followed his words, Hari took a deep breath. 'I was just on my way out, sorry I can't stay.'

Craig barred her way. 'Don't go on my account, it's a great pleasure to see you again, it's been far too long.'

'Hari is here with a simple business request,' Edward said. 'But I think you can talk directly to each other now that you are here, Craig. Go and make yourselves comfortable while I fetch some more iced cordial.'

Hari felt she had no choice but to bow gracefully to Edward's request. She moved back into the room and sat down. She was tinglingly aware of Craig's presence and she felt suddenly clumsy and ill at ease.

'You look very well,' Craig said softly leaning over her, too close for comfort. 'But I think I liked you best in your simple gown covered with a leather apron.'

She eyed him steadily. 'In other words you think I should keep to my place, is that it?'

'Don't be so touchy,' Craig said, 'I was paying you a compliment.'

Hari wished he would move away, and yet she found herself breathing in the scent of freshness about him, the smell almost of sunshine in his crisp shirt. She remembered the feel of his mouth on hers, the strength of his arms around her. But never in tenderness, she reminded herself, to Craig Grenfell she could never be anything but a shoemaker's daughter.

'I need some French calf.' She spoke more abruptly than she'd intended. 'I tried to buy some from my usual supplier but I found that you had the sole rights to sell the leather in this area.'

'Quite right,' Craig said. 'I suppose Emily sent you to persuade Edward to do the buying for you.' He smiled, 'My cousin would be too proud to make the request to me personally.'

'*I* am the buyer for the business.' Hari felt angered by his criticism, 'It was me who thought of asking Edward, he has more chance of seeing you than I have.'

'That simply is not true,' Craig said at once, 'I have an office in Gloucester Place where anyone can find me.' He leaned over her once more. 'And I would very much like you to find me far more often than you do.'

Hari turned her shoulder so that her back was almost towards him, she didn't want him to see the sudden colour in her cheeks.

'What's the truth of it, Hari? A deliberate ploy to ignore me, Emily's idea no doubt.'

Exasperated, Hari rose to her feet and moved away from him. Strange how she could hate Craig even while she loved him. Loved him? Nonsense, how could she love a man who treated her like a fool?

'I am not playing at being in business, mind,' she said, 'I am deadly earnest about making a success of my life. I am using my own skills and innovations.

'As for Emily, she is very efficient, she has great business acumen and, with all her contacts, we have a good thing going between us, so long as someone doesn't come along and try to ruin us.'

'And you think I am trying to ruin you?' Craig said soberly.

Hari shrugged. 'I don't know, why else would you want to control the importing of calf, you must realize that I need it for my shoemaking.'

'So do a lot of other shoemakers and cobblers in the town, you are not the only ones who now have to buy from me.' Craig paced about the room, his hands thrust into his pockets, his hair falling in curls over his forehead.

'I, too, want to make good in business though that might come as a surprise to you. I have dragged myself and the firm back from the brink of ruin and disgrace and I haven't time for indulging in games, pandering to a few women.'

He faced her suddenly. 'You can buy calf from me at the same price as any other buyer in Swansea, call round to the office any time you choose and you shall have a list of the new prices.'

'New prices?' Hari's throat was dry. 'They have gone up then?'

'Naturally, if I am paying for importing calf in quantity I must make a profit, the first rule of business, I thought you would have known that.'

'Well, thank you very much for your time, Mr Grenfell,' Hari said forcing an even note into her voice though anger flared through her and fear too. With the calf at a higher price, they would need to make increases themselves, a change the customers would not like, especially the ones like Lady Caroline who had already put in her order and been given a price. Without the calf they could not supply the goods, or could they? Perhaps she could improvise somehow.

Edward came into the room with a fresh jug of cordial and Hari smiled at him. 'I must go now, Edward, but I won't forget our plan to go to the theatre some time this week, come over the shop and see me, we can talk in private then.'

At the door she turned. 'Good-day to you both.' Her eyes lingered for a moment on Craig before she moved into the hallway and opened the front door.

She walked quickly along Chapel Street, breathing deeply of the balmy summer air. Her heart was still racing and anger ran in her veins as she thought of Craig's attitude of indifference. He intended to treat the firm of Grenfell and Morgan exactly as he would any other, but then why shouldn't he?

Emily had retired to her rooms above the store and, as Hari went upstairs, she could hear her talking to Letty. In her own rooms, Hari slipped off the shawl which even though it was light as gossamer seemed to encase her in heat.

She took off her shoes and walked barefoot towards the small communal kitchen and saw that Letty was just brewing a cup of tea. The maid's face was streaked with perspiration as she bent over the fire and Hari felt an immediate sympathy with her, remembering the many times she had worked over a fire in the summer heat cooking food for herself and mam.

'I'll get the cups,' she said and opened the cupboard door. She set the crockery on the neat table-cloth and sank into a chair, looking round her appreciatively.

The quarters above the shop were small so as to accommodate the new tea rooms, but they were just about adequate according to Emily's standards.

To Hari, the rooms were far more luxurious than anything she had known before. Good carpets covered the floor and, though the kitchen was shared, she and Emily had their own sitting and bedrooms.

Emily's part of the building was more spacious being at the front but then Letty had to be catered for because under no circumstances was Emily prepared to do without the girl.

It was something Hari readily understood because she had insisted on William moving in with her. Emily had agreed on the understanding that the boy slept down in the shop. It would not be proper, she maintained, to have a male however young sharing the same accommodation as three women. In any case, William's presence in the shop would deter thieves.

Hari had agreed, knowing that even the makeshift bed downstairs was better than Will's own home had been. And certainly warmer and drier than the place she'd shared with him in World's End. But she sometimes wondered at Emily's unseeing selfishness, a result she supposed of being cosseted all her life.

She watched as Letty set out the tray with a dainty cloth and a small vase containing a rose and smiled a little. Emily liked things nice and it was to her credit that she clung to her standards even though now she was no longer living in a big house with a huge staff to take care of her.

'Tell Emily I'd like to speak to her, please, Letty,' she said and the maid glanced at her.

'I shall *ask* Miss Grenfell if it is convenient, miss,' she said and Hari concealed a smile, Letty was far more of a snob than ever her mistress had been.

Letty returned in a few minutes. 'Miss Grenfell will be pleased to receive you in her sitting-room,' she said. 'And if you like you can take your tea in with you.'

'Thank you, Letty, that's very kind.' Hari refused to be

irritated by the girl's manner which was much the same as that of Sarah who helped in the shop, a grudging deference that stopped short of being sincere.

'Well, what happened?' Emily came straight to the point. 'I can see from your face that my cousin intends to be his usual obstructive self. Do sit down, Hari.'

Most of the time, Hari felt at ease with Emily except when she was in the inner sanctum, the name Emily gave to her rooms. There she felt Emily was inclined to get on her high horse and act the lady.

'He was difficult, yes,' Hari admitted. 'Unfortunately he arrived at Edward's house as I was about to leave.'

'How was he looking?' Emily leaned forward, lines of strain appearing around her mouth, it was clear she still cared a great deal about her cousin whatever she claimed.

'As handsome as ever,' Hari said ruefully. 'He says he bought in the leather as a good business move and that we shall have to pay the same for it as any other firm would.'

'In other words he's doing this to spite me.' Emily rose to her feet and moved about the cramped room with small, agitated steps.

'No, I don't think so,' Hari said slowly, 'I think he really needs to build up his own business again and he made a very shrewd move in buying in the calf. I wish we could have done it instead of him.'

'You always defend him,' Emily said, 'but then you don't know Craig as I do.'

'Then again perhaps you are too close to him,' Hari said. 'I don't think he would stoop to being spiteful to what he regards as a couple of women playing at business.'

'And doesn't that anger you?' Emily demanded. 'To know that he does not treat our business with the seriousness he would give to a venture undertaken by a man?'

'It makes me very angry,' Hari agreed, 'it also makes me more determined to succeed.' She took a sip of her tea. 'I've been thinking things out and I've an idea that I can make very good boots just as well with calf from our own country.'

'But people like the French calf,' Emily said, 'it has a sort of prestige about it.'

'I know,' Hari smiled, 'and I can make Welsh calf just as sought after, I shall play on the fact that it is not foreign but best of Welsh.' She spoke excitedly. 'I shall appeal to the patriotism in the townsfolk and, more, I shall make such excellent designs that customers won't care where the leather came from so long as it bears the stamp of Grenfell and Morgan.'

Emily smiled widely and she looked very beautiful when she smiled, Hari thought enviously.

'I think you've got something there, Hari.' She sank into her chair. 'I shall advertise our goods in the *Cambrian* newspaper, claiming that we are the first company to produce all Welsh leather boots and shoes.'

She was flushed with enthusiasm. 'I shall emphasize the fact that our goods are exclusive and while anybody can buy French calf, only our valued customers can buy hand-crafted goods in fine Welsh leather.'

On an impulse she moved over to Hari and hugged her. 'Hari, you are a genius! Together we shall make our boot and shoe business the finest in the country.'

Unable to relax, Hari decided to go to her office, she would begin to work on her designs straight away. But as she made her way downstairs, Hari heard the sound of weeping.

'Will, what is it?' The boy was sitting on his makeshift bed, tears running down his cheeks, grubby now where he had tried to dash the tears away.

'It's my mam,' he said in a broken voice, 'she's been

taken bad, real bad. My sister just came for me, told me to come home, says mam might have the fever and won't last till morning.'

'I'll come with you, Will,' Hari said at once. She stood at the bottom of the stairs.

'Emily,' she called, 'I've got to go out, I don't know how long I'll be.'

She locked the door of the shop behind her and stared at William's tear-streaked face, he was only ten years old and already he had known violence and poverty. Now it seemed he would have to cope with death as well.

She sighed heavily, how easy it had been in her few months of pleasant living to forget the mean streets from where she'd come. But the old ways would not be forgotten so easily, she was not, she realized, inured from the pain and anguish of the poor of World's End.

Will went home regularly with his wages and, for all she knew, he might have already contracted the disease that was taking his mother's life.

She squared her shoulders, disaster had risen up to confront her and all she could do was face it head on.

14

As soon as Hari entered the hovel where Will had once lived with his family, she smelled the scent of death. She moved to the bundle of rags in the corner upon which lay Bella Davies, her skin an unwholesome yellow, her frame emaciated; skeletal fingers were clawing at the tattered shawl that covered her.

'Sorry to learn of your trouble, Mr Davies,' Hari spoke softly to Will's father who stood moodily near the window, smelling, as usual, of ale. 'I wondered if there was anything I could do.'

He shrugged. 'I don't know, girl, I sent the kids to their auntie further down the block.' He rubbed at his head. 'Give the misses a bit of peace, like, not that all the peace in the world could cure what my Bella got.'

Hari could see that he was right, Bella Davies was past medical aid. Still, her suffering could be eased by a little laudanum perhaps.

'Go for the doctor, Will,' she said softly and Bill Davies's head swivelled round.

'Can't afford no doctors, don't you think I'd have fetched one long since if there was money?' His eyes were moist and Hari saw that he was grieved by his wife's sickness. She bit her lip, the man wasn't all bad.

'I'll pay for the doctor,' she said and seeing his face flush she added quickly, 'I can always take it back a bit at a time out of Will's pay.'

This seemed to appease Bill Davies and he nodded abruptly to his son. Will hurried out and, in the silence, Hari could hear the sound of his good boots ringing against the cobbles.

She rolled up her sleeves. 'I'll boil up some water and give Mrs Davies a nice wash, is it?' Hari knew the task would be easier for the doctor if some of the grime was cleaned from the woman's wasted body. 'It might make her more comfortable, like.'

He nodded his assent and then looked out of the window as though distancing himself from the proceedings. Only by the tightening of his knuckles could Hari tell that he was hurting inside.

Gently she washed Mrs Davies and small groans came from the pallid lips.

'You hurting her, girl?' Bill Davies demanded and Hari shook her head.

'No, just disturbing her from her sleep, that's all. Don't worry, I'm being very careful.'

But both she and the man looking at her beseechingly knew that it wasn't disturbed sleep that was causing Bella Davies's moans but the sickness that racked her body, the fever draining away the last of her resistance.

The doctor, when he came, nodded abruptly to Bill Davies and glanced curiously at Hari who appeared too clean and well dressed to be part of the family living in such a hovel.

'Hari Morgan,' she said by way of explanation, 'Will here is my apprentice.'

'James Webber,' the doctor said briefly and bent over the still form of Bella Davies, frowning in concentration.

His examination was brief and then he administered a small potion which he forced between Bella Davies's lips.

He looked up and shook his head. 'She will rest easy until the end,' he said gently.

Hari followed him to the door. 'Send your bill to me, doctor,' she said. 'Hari Morgan at the boot and shoe emporium in Wind Street.'

'You shouldn't be here, young lady,' he said, 'the sickness is called yellow fever and it's very contagious, you must know that.' He sighed, 'It seems it was brought in to the port by a ship called the *Hekla*; no-one took the illness on board seriously at first but now the townspeople are being infected. Go home and don't come here again, that's my advice.'

Hari looked at him gravely. 'Like you, doctor, I just had to come and do what I could.'

He nodded. 'Well, you can do nothing more. Discard the clothes you are wearing, burn them if you can and then wash yourself thoroughly.' He smiled bleakly.

'Most doctors would laugh at me and in truth nothing can keep away the sickness if it is your lot to get it but, in my experience, cleanliness helps.'

He walked away then, his shoulders slumped in an attitude of dejection and Hari had the awful feeling that he feared there would be many more outbreaks of the sickness.

She turned back into the room, she must persuade Will to come home with her, she would see that he washed too and got rid of his clothes, she must do all she could to protect him.

He was kneeling at the side of his mother and Bella's eyes were open. She tried to smile at her son and then held up her hand shakily to her husband. She could not speak but her lips framed the words, 'God bless.'

Suddenly Will was weeping, loud gulping sobs that shook his thin frame. Hari swallowed hard as she saw Bella's frail hand had fallen back on to the shawl and her eyes were suddenly unseeing.

Bill Davies didn't utter a sound but his head had sunk

on to his calloused hands and tears slipped between the grimy fingers.

Hari turned and left the room, this was no place for her, she was an intruder on the family's grief. And Will would come home to her when he was ready.

Hari walked for a long time without thinking where she was going. It was only when the salt breeze drifted into her face that she realized she was on the pier, staring out at the restless sea. If only she could have done more to help Bella Davies but then it would take riches more than she would ever have to alter the lives of the people of World's End.

Hari rose and returned home entering the premises from the rear, avoiding any contact with customers or staff. Emily came to the door of her rooms and stared curiously as Hari waved her away.

'Don't come near me,' Hari said hoarsely, 'at least not before I've washed and changed.'

She hurried into the washhouse at the back of the building and stripped off her clothing, pushing the garments deliberately into the flames of the fire.

She took up the bar of carbolic soap and, with the jug of water that was always kept on the floor near the door, she began to scrub herself thoroughly. Her skin felt raw by the time she'd finished but, at last, she was satisfied that she was as clean as she could be.

With just a towel to cover her, she moved towards her rooms and, shivering, opened the drawer of the chest. Listlessly, she took out some fresh clothing and got dressed. Then she moved towards Emily's rooms.

'I must warn you,' she said softly, 'the sickness that has come to Swansea is yellow fever, it's very contagious.'

Emily was suddenly pale. 'How do you know?' she asked quietly.

'William's mam has just died, she may be the first victim but she won't be the last or so the doctor seemed to think.'

'Saints preserve us,' Emily said and Hari waited for the tirade of abuse and accusations that must surely come. By going home with Will, by coming in contact with the sickness directly, Hari was risking not only her own life but Emily's too.

The anger did not come. 'You were very brave, Hari,' Emily said, her chin lifting, 'I don't think I could have done what you did, I do admire you. Please, come in and sit down, we shall have some tea, Letty has just made a fresh pot.'

Hari felt tears constrict her throat. 'You know something, Emily?' she said hoarsely, 'you're not so bad.'

Emily smiled. 'I take that as a great compliment – coming from you.'

Emily poured the tea and Hari took the delicate china cup, with hands that shook. 'It's Will I'm sorry for,' she said, 'he's young to have so much grief.'

'We'll help him all we can,' Emily said softly, 'and the boy has character, he'll be all right. I've been thinking of giving him lessons, perhaps English and arithmetic to start with. I don't suppose he's had the benefit of very much schooling.'

Hari sighed, 'I don't suppose he has.' She finished her tea and put down her cup. 'But the first thing I have to do for Will is to see that he is washed and that he has some fresh trews.'

'Always practical.' Emily smiled, 'And yet so artistic, a strange combination.'

Hari rose to her feet. 'I'm going before we start to get really soppy, I'm more used to us quarrelling than being nice to each other.'

As Hari moved to the door, she was aware of Emily rising to her feet.

'Hari, have you thought what this sickness could do to our business?'

'No.' Hari turned to face Emily. 'What could it do?'

'If it spreads, people will be afraid to go out, afraid to be in contact with too many people and boots and shoes will be the last thing on their minds.'

'You're right,' Hari said thoughtfully, 'but let's hope it won't come to that, is it?'

Back in her room, Hari sank into a chair and closed her eyes but she could still see the scene at Will's hovel of a home, the picture of Bella's gaunt face and the thin hand outstretched in a final blessing on the family she was leaving and, suddenly, Hari was weeping.

The sickness did not become as widespread as Hari had feared but the streets were almost empty and only those who had to venture out did so.

The shop was far from busy but the occasional maidservant brought an order, delivered it quickly and then disappeared. Most of these hurried exchanges were dealt with by Emily, while Hari worked on her designs and supervised the actual making of the shoes.

Will's family, it seemed, were doomed, one by one the children had succumbed to the sickness, half-starved and weak as they were, they had no resistance to the sickness.

Even Bill Davies who had been a bull of a man was taken and Hari, witnessing the man's grief, believed that he no longer wished to live.

Hari was forced to break the news to Will. He sat staring up at her, his young face white and strained but he shed no tears.

'I'm on my own then,' he said flatly. Hari took him in her arms and held on to him tightly.

'You're not on your own, Will, I'm your family now and you are mine, neither of us has anyone else alive in the whole world, we shall comfort each other.'

Will nodded, dry eyed, revealing his grief only by the trembling of his lips.

'Please Will,' Hari urged, 'say you'll stay with me always and be like the brother I never had. You must look after me as I shall look after you, all right?'

Will could not speak, he just nodded and then stood passively in the circle of her arms, his face set and the control he showed was that of a man not a boy of ten years of age.

It was Hari who cried, hot tears that scalded her eyes, and William patted her awkwardly not knowing what to say. At last, Hari had dried her eyes and smiled ruefully at Will.

'The tears are over now, *cariad*, we must try to make the best of our lives from now on.'

It was the next morning when Hari awoke to the sound of wailing that she had thought was in her dreams. She rubbed her eyes and, as the sound became a reality, she sat up in bed aware that the noises were coming from Emily's rooms.

She hurried through the hall between the two sets of rooms and saw Letty standing near the door to Emily's inner sanctum, uselessly wringing her hands.

'What is it?' Hari heard the fear in her own voice and tried to get a grip on herself.

'In there.' Letty gestured towards the sitting-room, her voice barely audible. Hari moved past her and saw that Emily was sitting in her chair shivering violently in spite of being fully clothed.

It was clear she had been there all night, her dress was crumpled and her hair hung untidily over her face.

Hari moved closer. 'Emily?' She leaned forward and touched Emily's cheek with the back of her hand. Seeing the yellowness of Emily's skin, Hari drew a deep breath. 'Yellow Jack!' she said softly.

Emily was burning with fever. Her eyes were staring, seeing nothing and her lips moved soundlessly.

'She been right bad for days now, wouldn't let me say nothing to you. Did you say it's the yellow fever?' Letty spoke fearfully, backing away from the door. 'Oh my God, we'll all be dead in a few days!' Her voice rose hysterically, 'I can't stay here, I can't.'

'Stop it!' Hari turned on her angrily. 'Control yourself!' She clenched her hands into fists, fighting her own fear.

'Look, if you were going to get the sickness, you'd be as bad as Emily is now. Calm yourself, we'll be all right, you'll see, now run for the doctor, as quickly as you can.'

Letty took a shuddering breath. 'I'm afraid to go out, Miss Hari. I can't help it, please don't send me into the streets.'

A quiet voice spoke from the doorway. 'I'm not afraid, I'll go.'

'Oh, Will, there's brave of you, I could kiss you!' Hari said in relief and then smiled as William made a wry face. 'But I won't, don't worry.'

She followed him to the door. 'Tell Doctor Webber to come as soon as possible, explain that Emily Grenfell is sick and needs urgent attention.'

Will nodded. 'I'll run as fast as I can.'

Hari followed him down to the stairs and stood on the door watching as he sped along the silent street. The shops were closed and somewhere a church bell was ringing out yet another death.

Hari longed to walk down to the beach to feel the sea breezes against her face, to stare out towards the far horizon and distance herself from what was happening but Emily needed her and, with a sigh, Hari turned sharply and went into the gloom of the empty shop.

Determinedly, Hari began to roll up her sleeves, there was work to be done and only she was able to do it.

Craig was in Bristol when he read the news that Swansea

185

had fallen prey to the sickness called yellow fever. The newspaper was careful not to raise panic among the people and the report was guarded mentioning only a few deaths. He sat at the table in the tap-room of the Bristol Arms and frowned as he wondered how far the epidemic had really spread.

Emily would be all right, he was sure of that, she may even have left Swansea and taken refuge in the country somewhere far from the crowds. But Hari, Craig could not believe she would run away from her responsibilities, she was made of sterner stuff, she would stay and fight to the bitter end to keep what she had worked so hard to achieve.

He rose to his feet so abruptly that he overturned his chair and the landlord who had been dozing in the afternoon sun opened his eyes lazily and having decided that nothing was amiss closed them again.

Craig moved to the bar. 'Make up my bill.' He spoke forcefully and the landlord was on his feet instantly, his air of indolence vanishing.

'I'll be leaving at once.' Craig mounted the rickety stairs to his room and began to throw his belongings into a bag, he must get home, his business in Bristol had been concluded yesterday and the order he had taken for French calf was most satisfying.

A frown creased his brow, he had the orders all right, plenty of them but if the fever was to spread, he wondered how long it would be before the ships from abroad would refuse to enter British ports.

He picked up his bag and stared around the small, sparsely furnished room savouring for a moment the silence and the peacefulness of the countryside surrounding the inn on the outskirts of Bristol, then, with an unconscious squaring of his shoulders, Craig picked up his bag and made for the door.

Emily tossed and turned feverishly in her bed, her hands plucking at the covers and Hari, watching her, knew that the ministrations of the doctor however well meant were doing no good at all.

Hari moved away from the bed and put her hands over her eyes trying to recall what her mother had told her about the epidemic of fever that had occurred some seventeen years earlier when Hari was a child.

Mam had made up some herbal remedy, a concoction she had sworn by but, however hard she tried, Hari could not remember how to make the potion.

But she must do something, Emily was getting worse, she had grown thinner and there was an unnatural pallor to her skin. Hari bit her lip in anger at her own lack of knowledge.

'Letty!' she called and, as the girl came hesitantly into the room, Hari indicated that she take a chair.

'You are going to sit with Emily,' Hari said firmly, holding her hand up for silence as the maid would have protested. 'Don't argue, I've got to go out and I'm sure you'd rather be left here than go on an errand for me, wouldn't you?'

Letty nodded sullenly, not at all pleased with the responsibility that had been laid squarely upon her shoulders.

Hari ignored the maid's angry expression and hurried from the shop in Wind Street walking swiftly towards her old home at Wassail Square.

The house still bore the faded sign that her father had erected and the windows were still curtainless. The house looked even more neglected than when Hari had lived in it and she had to summon all her courage to knock on the door.

After a time, a woman came along the passageway and stared suspiciously at Hari.

'What do you want?' she demanded. 'You don't look like a beggar. Are you one of them do-gooders from the posh part of town? If so, clear off, we don't want your sort around here.'

'No,' Hari spoke quickly as the woman moved to close the door in her face. 'I'm Dewi Morgan's daughter, the shoemaker, I used to live here.'

'Oh aye, well what do you want?' The woman didn't sound quite so hostile and Hari smiled.

'My mam had an old book, I wondered if it was still here in a cupboard or something.'

'Doubt it, I chucked out a load of rubbish only last week.' The woman shook her head. 'Sorry, misses, can't help you.'

'Where?' Hari asked. 'Where did you put the rubbish?'

'Out by the back, have a look if it's that important, mind. Go round the back way, it may be in the yard, though I'm not promising anything.'

The door was closed and Hari stood biting her lip for a moment and then moved without hope towards the back yard. In the corner was a pile of rags, some bottles jutted from the heap and Hari could see bits of broken china strewn about the place.

She took up a stick and probed the pile of rubbish doubting that she would ever find the book of herbal remedies. After a moment, the stick probed something hard and, pushing aside the rags, Hari unearthed the green-covered book.

She shook the dust from it and flicked through the pages and saw with relief that it was still intact. She hurried back through the streets, trying to read as she walked.

Angelica, that's what she needed, but would she be able to get any?

She turned towards the market knowing that some of

the stall holders had herbs for sale, they would not be fresh herbs but ones that had been dried in the warmth of country kitchens.

'They will have to do,' Hari said under her breath. 'One way or another, I am determined that Emily will get better.'

But as she hurried into the almost empty market, her hands holding the herbal book were trembling and she knew that she was afraid.

15

Hari ground the angelica root into a fine powder trying not to hear the soft moans that came from Emily's dry lips. Swiftly, she mixed a few spoonfuls of treacle in the carduus water taken from the boiled leaves of the angelica and added a little wine, stirring vigorously.

She paused, looking at the potion anxiously, praying she had mixed it correctly for Emily's life might depend on it.

'Letty!' she called, 'have you mixed the mustard for the footbath?'

Letty came in from the kitchen with the bowl of hot water and stared vacantly at Hari who was lifting Emily's head, encouraging her to drink the liquid in the cup.

'Move the bedclothes, there's a good girl,' Hari instructed, 'I'll sit Emily up and you put the hot mustard cloths on her feet. Come on, don't stand there looking stupid!'

With set mouth, Letty obeyed, touching with distaste the thin yellowed ankles of her mistress.

'I'm not employed as a nurse, mind,' Letty said truculently.

'You won't be employed as anything if you don't pull yourself together,' Hari retorted angrily.

Letty was silent but Hari knew by the hot colour in the maid's face how annoyed she was at being ordered around by a mere shoemaker's daughter.

Emily seemed to rest a little easier during the afternoon

and Hari took the opportunity to catch up on a little sleep, the work could wait. She felt overwhelmingly tired and, as soon as she settled down in her bed, she was asleep.

It was dark when she woke to find William standing over her, a cup of steaming tea in his hand. Hari sat up at once, sleep banished.

'What is it, Will, is Emily worse?' Her tone was hoarse and fear washed over her in waves.

'It's not Emily, it's Letty, she's just sitting by the fire shivering.'

'Oh God in heaven, what next!' Hari took the tea, giving herself a moment to find the strength to face this new crisis. 'Right then, Will,' she pushed the bedclothes aside and slid out of bed, 'let's see what's wrong.'

Letty was slumped forward in her chair crouching as near to the dying embers of the fire as she could get. Hari put her hand gently on the maid's shoulder dismayed at the yellow tinge to her skin.

'Letty,' Hari said gently, 'how do you feel?'

Letty looked up at her very slowly as though it was an effort to focus her mind on what was being said.

'My eyes, they hurt so much,' her voice was thin, 'and my head aches and the pains are everywhere, in my chest, even in my legs. I got the sickness, haven't I, Hari, I'm going to die?'

Hari touched Letty's forehead, it was burning hot, the skin dry. 'I'm going to give you some medicine,' Hari said calmly, 'you'll feel much better when you're tucked up in bed and don't worry, I'll look after you.'

Hari bit her lip as she poured some of the elixir made from angelica into a cup. 'Drink this, Letty and then I'll help you into your room, rest is all you need and you'll be fine, you'll see.'

'I want the doctor,' Letty said, 'I want proper medicine, please Hari.'

'All right,' Hari said placatingly, 'but drink this first and then when I've got you comfortable we'll get Doctor Webber.'

Hari drew William towards the door. 'Fetch the doctor for me, Will,' she said in a low voice, 'and then I want you to go to Edward Morris. Ask him can you stay with him till the sickness is past.'

'I don't want to leave you alone, mind,' Will said. 'I've faced the sickness before, remember.'

'I know,' Hari said, 'but it would give me peace of mind, Will, please do as I ask.'

Will's mouth trembled slightly and then, without another word, he turned and left the room. Hari stood for a moment, eyes closed, listening to the sounds of his footsteps ringing down the stairs and she felt suddenly as if she was now alone in the world.

Hari settled Letty into her bed, talking soothingly to her all the time but Letty's eyes were closed now and Hari doubted if she could hear anything she was saying.

Hari sighed and then moved towards Emily's room, almost dreading to go in. Emily was still asleep, her breathing seemed a little easier but then perhaps that was just wishful thinking. Hari covered Emily with the quilt, brushed a curl of hair from her face and then retreated to the kitchen to mend the fire.

It was almost an hour later when the doctor came, he was falsely cheerful but Hari could tell that he held out little hope for the recovery of Emily or her maid.

'You are doing a splendid job with your home-made potions,' he said, 'you could do some good and you certainly won't do any harm. But be prepared for a short period of improvement in the condition of your patients which is usually followed by a relapse and death. I'm sorry.'

Hari went with him to the door, the doctor appeared tired and upset. 'The source of the infection has been confirmed,' he said, 'it was brought in by a ship to the North Dock. The *Hekla* stayed only a few days but it was long enough to bring the fever ashore.'

'Does that mean shipping will not be admitted to the docks?' Hari asked but the doctor shook his head.

'No, it would take more than a few people falling sick to stop trade in our ports,' he said ruefully, 'there have been comparatively few deaths so far, hardly enough to cause concern.' He smiled. 'Except to the unfortunate ones who have to deal with the fever.'

When the doctor had left, Hari sank into a chair in the kitchen and stared down at her hands, not so long ago all she'd had to worry about was making designs for shoes, promoting Welsh calf and making a success of the business. Now here she was in charge of the lives of two women and the responsibility suddenly weighed very heavily on her.

She must have dozed because she was roused by the sound of vomiting from Letty's room. Sighing, Hari forced her tired limbs into movement, there was work to be done.

She picked up the jug of elixir, it was almost empty, she glanced through the window, it was dark outside, the market would long since have closed, she would not be able to get any more herbs till morning.

Hari bit her lip, she had two patients and only enough elixir for one, what could she do? Uncertainly, she made her way to Emily's room and stood staring down at her. In the flickering light of the candle, it seemed that some of the yellow had gone from Emily's skin and, by now, her breathing was definitely easier.

And yet hadn't the doctor warned her that a period of recovery might be followed by a relapse? Hari had to choose who should have the last of the elixir and suddenly the burden seemed too great.

Suddenly, Emily's eyelids fluttered and then she was looking up at Hari. 'Thank you,' her lips framed the words and Hari felt relief flow through her, Emily had regained consciousness.

Hari felt tears burn her eyes, she lifted Emily's head and held the cup to her lips. 'Drink this, Emily, it will make you feel better,' she said.

Obediently, Emily drank and then sank back against the pillows exhausted. Hari sat beside her and took her hand.

'You are going to be all right, now,' she said infusing confidence into her voice. 'I want you to rest and in the morning I'll feed you some gruel.'

As she returned to the kitchen, Hari wiped away the tears and yet she knew, somehow she knew, that Emily was going to get well.

She heard footsteps on the stairs and sighed, William had come back in spite of all she'd said.

'Craig!' He came into the room and immediately held his arms out to her and, with a small moan, she went into them. The tears came then, hot and fast, tears of weariness and of hope.

Craig held her silently, his cheek resting against her hair and Hari knew that whatever happened in the future, she would be grateful to Craig for his kindness to her when she most needed him.

'Sit down,' he said at last, 'let me make you some tea, you look exhausted. Why didn't you ask for help, Hari, you must know I would have come.'

Hari watched him in silence as he brewed the tea and it reminded her of the days in World's End when Craig had been a fugitive from the law. In spite of everything, they had been good days.

'How did you know?' she asked as he handed her the cup and sat close to her, his face full of concern.

'I read about the sickness in the papers and I came home right away.' Craig reached out and touched her cheek. 'I always knew you had courage, Hari, but to manage alone was foolish of you.'

He stood up abruptly. 'You must go to bed now, I'll look after Emily, the maid too, you catch up on some much-needed sleep.'

Hari rose to her feet, for a moment being in Craig's arms, seeing the concern in his face, she had imagined he cared but it was Emily he had come to see. She left the room and sank on to her bed, how silly she'd been to believe even for a moment that a man like Craig Grenfell could fall in love with a shoemaker's daughter.

She slept the sleep of the exhausted and a pale light was streaking the room when she woke to find Craig beside her. He sank down on to the bed and smiled warmly.

'You look like a little girl there with your hair all tangled over your eyes.' Gently he brushed away the curls and, leaning forward, kissed her gently.

At first the kiss was a salute but then his lips became hot, searching. Hari found that she was responding to him, her arms were around his broad shoulders, she was pressing him close to her as though she would never let him go.

'Hari, my beautiful, lovely girl.' His mouth moved to her neck and Hari closed her eyes, wanting to hold him and possess him, to be one with him.

When his hand touched her breast, she felt a momentary sense of panic, how could she give herself to Craig without a word of marriage spoken between them and with no ring on her finger?

But that was absurd, tomorrow she might well die of yellow fever and, for now, all she wanted was to be in Craig's arms and to learn what it was like to be a real woman.

The force of her feelings almost frightened her, she wanted Craig as she'd never wanted anything in her life. She clung to him, not protesting when he loosened her clothing, losing herself in the heat of the passion that flared between them.

She heard herself moan his name as unknown sensations drowned her, she felt the silk of his skin against hers as she moved with him like the waves of the sea reach for the shore. And then rational thought deserted her and she gave herself up to the sheer joy of the moment.

They spent the next few hours in each other's arms and, afterwards, Hari slept once more, a smile curving her mouth, her naked arms were outside the covers and she slept softly in contentment.

When she awoke, she could hear Craig in the kitchen raking the coals. She rose quickly and washed in the water from the jug on the stand and quickly dressed in fresh clothes.

Timidly, she moved into the kitchen not knowing what to expect from Craig. He was placing coals on the fire and he looked up and smiled.

Hari hoped he would take her in his arms but he didn't. 'Sit down, have something to eat,' he said, 'you're far too thin.'

She felt her spirits droop, this was not the response of a lover. She glanced down at her small frame, had Craig been disappointed in her, had she somehow failed him?

He put a plate of bread and cheese before her. 'Now, take your time and eat it,' he said, leaning across the table, his strong arms bare, his shirt sleeves rolled above his elbows.

'I've seen to the invalids so you just think about yourself for a moment.'

Hari forced the food between her lips, the last thing she felt like doing was eating. She wanted to throw herself into

196

Craig's arms, to beg him to say he loved her, reassure her that she hadn't just been a moment's pleasure for him.

He did no such thing. He drank his tea and then rose to clear the table, putting everything neatly away before taking the cloth and folding it carefully.

Suddenly, he smiled at her. 'You see, I've learned to be somewhat domesticated, a result of spending so much time with you, I suppose.'

Hari rose abruptly, she was sensing criticism in his every word, it was time she made herself busy. 'I'll go and see Letty, I suppose you've already checked on Emily,' she said and quickly left the room.

Letty was lying completely still, her skin was even more yellow than Hari remembered and her eyes were wide open staring unseeingly upwards. Letty was dead.

Hari put her hand to her mouth, she had never been close to her and yet she felt devastated by her death. Hari had tried so hard to save Letty's life but at the last she had failed her by not having enough of the elixir.

She felt Craig's hand on her arm. 'Come away, there's nothing you can do now.'

Hari shook off his hand and, rushing into her bedroom, flung herself down on the cover and the tears came hot and painful.

Craig stood in the doorway. 'Don't blame yourself, Hari,' he said softly, 'and remember, you did save Emily's life.'

Hari looked up at him, 'How do you know, what's to say she won't die too?'

'Go and see for yourself,' Craig said and disappeared from the doorway.

After a time, Hari washed her face and, straightening her clothes, made her way to Emily's room.

'Hari,' Emily held up a trembling hand, 'I'm so grateful to you.' The traces of jaundice had almost vanished and there was a light in Emily's eyes that had not been there for some time.

Hari sat on the bed and, on an impulse, hugged Emily. 'No need for gratitude, love, I only did what anyone would do,' she said thickly.

Emily patted Hari's shoulder. 'No, not anybody,' her voice was muffled. 'It takes a woman of courage like you, Hari, to face death to help a friend.'

Hari became aware of Craig standing in the doorway and moved away from the bed. Emily looked up and then turned her face away.

'Send him away, Hari,' she said. 'I don't want to see him.'

Craig moved forward. 'Emily,' he said her name chidingly, 'after being so sick, don't you think our quarrels are trivial?'

Emily turned over in the bed and faced the wall and her hunched shoulder was a rejection of him.

'Come on,' Hari caught his arm. 'Don't worry her now, Craig, let her rest.'

In the kitchen, she picked up her shawl. 'I'd be obliged if you would stay here until I've been to report Letty's death and then I'll call at the market for some herbs.' She said not looking at him, 'You'd better go back home, no point in you risking catching the fever.'

'I've been out this morning,' Craig said, 'I've seen to all the arrangements regarding Letty, she'll be taken out of here today, don't worry.'

Hari moved to the door. 'There's good of you to think of it,' she said, her hand on the latch, 'but I still have shopping to do.'

Craig came up to her and took her shoulders. 'Hari, why the coldness? You were happy enough in my arms earlier.'

She waited for him to go on, to tell her he wanted her for

his wife, that their lovemaking was born out of his wish to have her with him always, but he said nothing.

She looked him in the face. 'Perhaps that is something we'd better both forget,' she said stiffly.

She left the house and her thoughts were in a turmoil, she didn't know what to make of Craig Grenfell, one minute he was caressing her, loving her as though he would never let her go and the next he was like a stranger.

But then hadn't mam warned her long ago that men like Craig only wanted their fun with a girl like Hari, she wasn't the sort he would ever consider marrying. The thought hurt.

She made her purchases in a daze, walking around the market hoping against hope that she could sort out her confused feelings. But she was still going over and over the events of the last few hours in her mind when she heard a warm voice speaking close to her ear.

'Hari, I'm so pleased to see you.' Edward Morris took her arm and smiled down at her in concern. 'I've been so worried since William came to the house, I was about to come over to see you.'

'Better for you to stay away but I'm grateful to you for taking William in, how is he?' she asked anxiously.

'Fit as a flea,' Edward said, 'but you, young lady, are looking decidedly peaky.' He moved a little closer to her. 'I know this is a bit sudden, we haven't even been able to go out together but in the circumstances that doesn't seem to matter. Hari, won't you let me take care of you as well as William?'

Hari looked up at him uncomprehendingly and Edward smiled.

'I'm asking you to become Mrs Edward Morris,' he said, 'is that so difficult to understand?'

Hari put her hand on Edward's arm, she was warmed by his words, at least he didn't consider her beneath him.

'Thank you for the compliment, Edward, but I can't seem to think straight just now . . .' Her words stumbled to a halt as he held up his hand.

'Of course not, how inconsiderate of me, just take your time and think it over, Hari, that's all I'm asking. Now, how is Emily? I hear there's an improvement in her condition.'

Hari nodded, 'Yes, she's over the worst,' she said softly, 'but poor Letty, I couldn't save her.'

'I'm going to call a cab to take you home,' Edward said firmly, 'you look far too weary to be tramping the streets. Go home and rest, Hari, and I'll see you when you are not feeling so tired.'

'You are such a kind man, Edward,' Hari said, 'there's glad I feel to have you as a friend.'

'I could be far more than that, Hari,' Edward said, 'but I won't press you now.'

As Edward hailed a cab and helped her into it, Hari knew that she could never think of any other man as a husband now, she was committed to Craig even if he never asked her to marry him.

Edward kissed her hand and then stepped back as the cab jerked into motion. Hari leaned back against the cold seat and closed her eyes, how simple life would be if she had only fallen in love with Edward not Craig.

When she returned home, there was a pot of stew on the hob and a note pinned to the mantelpiece. It seemed that Craig's brother had been released from prison. Spencer was sick with the fever and Craig had gone to bring him home.

Note in hand, Hari wandered round the rooms feeling lost and alone. Letty's bed was empty, stripped of clothes, the undertaker had been very prompt.

Hari peered into Emily's room, she was asleep, her shoulders hunched as if to ward off anyone who tried to wake her. The silence of the rooms closed in on Hari as she returned to the kitchen.

Downstairs, the showrooms were empty and silent, the doors locked against the public to protect them from the fever.

Hari sank into a chair and put her arms on the table, resting her head wearily. She had to face the facts full in the face, she had given herself to Craig and he had taken her lightly, to him she was nothing more than a tumble in the hay. The thought was bitter and yet Hari could not cry, it seemed that now, after all that had happened, she was beyond tears.

16

Craig stood in his new warehouse on the docks and stared at his alarmingly large stock of French calf, the venture, the buying in of all existing stock from abroad, though a good idea, had not worked out in practice and Craig had just discovered the reason why.

'Damn all women!' He moved into his office and seating himself at the desk took out his order book. He had precious few pages filled. Previously, the calf had been in great demand, the requests had poured in from all over the country, everyone had been anxious not to be caught without the leather that had been so popular. It was popular no longer, at least not in Wales.

He stared out of the window and a wry smile curved his lips, Hari Morgan was shrewd, no doubt about that and she had courage. Her bravery in the face of the yellow fever had more than testified to that.

She had nursed Emily back to full health and it seemed that the two women had their business back in full operation.

Craig had his hands full looking after Spencer. He had been sick for some weeks but had at last shaken off the fever. However it had left him weakened and irritable.

Mrs Grenfell had made up her mind that when he left hospital, Spencer would stay at Summer Lodge with Craig until he made a complete recovery; it seemed she wanted little to do with her youngest son.

By the time Craig was able to deal with business matters once more, he found that Hari had more than paid him back for taking the monopoly on the French calf. She was doing nicely with Welsh leather, thank you very much.

Hari had advertised the home-made products as more patriotic as well as more desirable than foreign goods. Now, a great many people were taking her at her word and Craig could see the day when in Swansea at least the Welsh leather would be more popular than ever the French had been.

As her trademark, Hari tooled into her products a tiny exquisitely formed daffodil making it her own symbol of Welsh products. He closed his book with a snap of finality, it was time he was going home.

He locked up the warehouse, breathing in the tang of the sea and the ever-present smells of tar and hemp and dreaded the thought of returning to Summer Lodge, with its sparse, barely furnished rooms and the brother who never ceased to whine.

He must pick up some food for Spencer, something to tempt his brother to eat for the yellow fever had left its mark. Spencer was thin and drawn and his skin still retained a faint yellowish tinge and worst of all his temper, at the best of times uncertain, was like a fire ready to flare at the least provocation.

A dark-haired young woman was walking briskly along the other side of the street, her skirts swinging and, for a moment, she looked so much like Hari that he actually paused before realizing she was a stranger.

Hari, she had been so soft in his arms, so responsive one moment and the next cool as ice. Women, they were unpredictable creatures at the best of times.

But Hari had an inner strength that Craig admired, he admired too the way she had nursed Emily back to health with her own unorthodox remedies so successfully that it was hard to believe Emily had been sick at all.

Perhaps he should talk to Hari about his brother, it would do no harm to give Spencer something that might at least put some spirit into him. And it would give him an excuse to see Hari again.

And yet many would consider him a fool, it was Emily he should be pursuing. He should have married Emily by now. As soon as her father had died, he should have made her his wife. But then he'd had nothing to offer her, his own business in debt, his fortunes at the lowest ebb, how could he have afforded a wife?

And now it was too late, he had lost Emily for good, she would not even offer him her friendship. He had lost her to the business and that Emily was proving a business-woman to the tips of her fingers was in no doubt.

The emporium was booming. Not even the outbreak of yellow fever had prevented the townsfolk from patronizing the shop except for a few of the worse weeks.

Craig heard quick footsteps behind him and, looking over his shoulder, he smiled.

'Edward, just the man I wanted to see. Come for a pint of ale in the Burrows? I've got a thirst that could drink the sea dry.'

Edward inclined his head in agreement. 'Not working today?'

'Nothing to do, I've laid off most of my men,' Craig replied. 'If there's no leather to load, why have the labourers in?'

'Give in,' Edward said. 'Go back to buying Welsh or English calf, anything's better than sitting around selling nothing.'

'You could be right,' Craig stopped outside the door of the Burrows public house and the aroma of ale rose tantalizingly from the barrels behind the bar, 'but I built up my stock and advertised it as French calf and I'm stuck with it.'

'Well, take it up to England then, sell it in Bristol or Manchester, get off your backside and think, man, it's not like you to sit around and mope.'

'Thank you for your plain talking,' Craig said with a glint of humour in his eyes, 'and it doesn't come any plainer than that.'

Suddenly Craig felt charged with energy, Edward was right, he was sitting down under what he saw as his defeat when he should be up and fighting. Was he going to let a little Welsh girl beat him?

'Come on, Eddie,' he said, 'let's forget that drink, I've got work to do.'

Emily sat in the window staring out into the Strand below. She was still very weak but, to her relief, the yellow staining on her skin was diminishing, even the whites of her eyes were returning to their natural clarity.

She thought of Hari, working hard at the business and guilt racked her. If it wasn't for Hari's careful nursing she would not be here now and hanging over her like a great weight was the knowledge that she had tricked Hari into working with her by arranging the calling in of her debt.

She wondered for the hundredth time if she should come clean with Hari, tell her everything and yet, they had become so close, would the relationship be shattered for ever if Hari knew the truth?

Emily heard footsteps on the stairs and she pulled herself up and made her way shakily into the kitchen. Throughout the afternoon, she had been slowly preparing a meal of stewed lamb and vegetables, sitting frequently in a chair to regain her strength, every small effort a mountainous achievement. But now the aroma of the stew rose tantalizingly, emanating from the black iron pot, making Emily's mouth water.

'*Duw*, there's a lovely smell, what have you been up to, Emily?'

Hari looked tired, her dark hair was escaping from the satin ribbon and there were shadows beneath her eyes.

'I thought I'd surprise you.' Emily smiled wanly. 'I won't serve the stew though if you don't mind, I don't think I could stand for long enough to fill the bowls.'

'Sit down you, doing too much you are, we really must get somebody in to cook for us, you are not fit and I'm too busy to waste my time in the kitchen.'

'You're right,' Emily sank gratefully into a chair, 'why don't you put a notice in the window? Someone is sure to see it.'

'Good idea.' Hari busied herself with the meal, cutting inelegant slices of bread and putting out three bowls.

'Will!' she called, 'come on up here and have your supper.'

She returned to the fire; her face flushed with the heat she looked so pretty and so very dear that Emily felt weak tears rise to her eyes. Hari was like the sister Emily had always longed for and never had. What a far cry from the days when she had looked upon the shoemaker's daughter as a mere underling, what a snob she had been.

'Thank you, Hari,' she said softly and Hari glanced at her with surprise.

'For what?' she asked, her eyebrows raised.

'Just for – everything.' Emily stopped speaking as the sound of Will's footsteps echoed on the stairs.

'You are daft sometimes!' Hari said but her tone was warm. 'Who would have thought that you and me would become such good friends? You were such a toff in the old days, Emily, looking down your nose at the cobbler's daughter.'

'I know,' Emily said humbly, 'I was just thinking that myself and I'm sorry for all the things I did, so very sorry.'

If only Hari knew how sorry, Emily thought guiltily.

'Here, Will,' Hari said briskly as the boy entered the kitchen, 'Emily has made us some lovely nourishing stew and we could both do with it, worked ourselves to death today we have but not complaining, mind.' Hari smiled.

'It seems our Welsh leather is putting Craig's nose out of joint, more and more people are asking for the shoes with the little daffodil on them, a mark of excellence one customer called it.'

'Your work is excellent,' Emily said, 'I only wish I was well enough to pull my weight.'

'You will be,' Hari said sitting at the table, 'be patient, you were at death's door, mind.'

Emily fell quiet, she realized how close she had come to dying, especially when she heard the news about Letty, poor Letty had been the unfortunate one.

Sixteen people in the town had died and many more fallen sick with the fever. 'If it wasn't for you . . .' Emily's words trailed away and Hari smiled.

'Come on now, it's not like you to be sentimental. Eat up your supper, I want to discuss some patterns with you later on.'

'Right, miss,' Emily said smiling. But she was happy that Hari was including her in the business even in such a small way.

Emily was impatient now to be well, to be back in harness, organizing and running the business although it seemed that Hari had done very well without her.

She glanced at William, he was growing up, there was an air of solemnity about the boy that belied his years. He was still beardless, his smooth young chin innocent even of a baby growth of hair, but his eyes were sad and the frown of concentration would have sat better on the face of a mature man rather than a young boy.

As though sensing her scrutiny, Will looked up and his

eyes met Emily's. She was suddenly aware of the hostility in William's face. She drew back a little as though she had been slapped and then he turned away and she wondered if she had imagined it.

'This stew is lovely,' Hari said warmly, 'don't you think so, Will?'

'Lovely,' he repeated but there was no warmth in his voice. She hadn't imagined it, Emily thought, for some reason Will was wary of her, she would go so far as to say he disliked her. Why?

Later when Hari went to the workshop to fetch her pattern book, Emily faced the boy squarely.

'What's wrong, William?' she asked evenly. He glanced at her sullenly.

'Nothin',' he said defensively. He moved toward the door.

'Wait, are you afraid to face me with whatever is on your mind?'

Goaded, he turned on her. 'I know what you did to Hari,' he said. 'When she sent me to the bank the other day, the manager was talking about the business, I heard him telling another man about how you asked him to call in Hari's loan putting her in a corner.

'A shrewd move, the bank man called it, I call it sneaky and underhand and cheating on Hari.'

Emily felt her face flush as she faced Will's accusing eyes. She sank down into a chair.

'I agree with you, William,' she said softly, 'I didn't know Hari then, I didn't realize how fond I would become of her.'

William's mouth fell open in surprise at her lack of denial.

'I've wondered many times if I should tell her the truth,' Emily continued. 'But I don't know if it would only hurt her more than it's worth to ease my own conscience. What would you do, Will?'

208

He shook his head. 'I don' know. You shouldn't have done it in the first place then you wouldn't be in a pickle, would you?'

Life was so clear cut to a child, Emily mused, no grey areas, only black and white.

'You are right, of course.' She glanced towards the door, and, hearing Hari's footsteps on the stairs, she took a deep breath. 'I'll leave it up to you, Will,' Emily said, 'if you feel you must speak then so be it.'

'Oh, no!' Will said emphatically. 'You don't get me to do your dirty work, you must be the one to make up your own mind, right?'

Hari returned to the room and placed the pattern book on the table. 'Look, how about a pair of riding boots with buckles for decoration, do you think that would be a good idea?'

'I don't know.' Emily found it difficult to concentrate, 'Perhaps the buckles would hurt the animal, what do you think?'

'Well, no, I'd put them on the outside of the boot, they wouldn't touch the horse.'

Emily shook her head. 'No, it's not a good idea, if the rider were to fall the buckles might cause some damage.'

Hari sighed. 'Yes, good point. What if I just tool some patterns across the instep then, make our boots a bit different to everyone else's?'

'That sounds just right,' Emily said, 'why don't you inscribe the words "Welsh leather" on the boots.'

'Hmm.' Hari considered the matter. 'A bit too abrupt, what about the initials of our three names, E, W, H?'

William smiled, 'My name on a pair of boots, *duw*, that would be real good, I'd be famous, mind.'

'Well, it would only be your initial, Will, but I'll do it.'

She looked down at her pattern. 'And what if I emboss the initials of the owner of the boots on the other side in larger script, do you think they'd like that?'

'Well,' Emily said, 'if Will's reaction is anything to go by, I'd say they'd be delighted.'

Hari worked on the drawings for a moment in silence. Emily glanced at William but he avoided her gaze.

'I'm making a pair of boots for Charlie from the theatre at the moment,' Hari said abstractedly, 'should I put his title do you think or is that going a bit far?'

'Hari,' Emily said suddenly, 'I must speak to you, privately, it's very important.'

Hari looked up in surprise and immediately Will rose to his feet.

'I got something I want to do downstairs anyway,' he said quickly and vanished from the room.

'What is it? Are you sick?' Hari sounded anxious and Emily moistened her lips nervously.

'No, I've got a confession to make, no, don't stop me, I've got to tell you the truth.'

Hari gave Emily her full attention. 'The truth about what?' she asked in a small voice.

'I tricked you into coming into the business with me,' Emily spoke in a rush, 'I asked a friend of mine in London to pressure the bank about the debt you owed for leather, I forced you into doing what I wanted.'

Hari rose to her feet and moved to the window, staring out into the darkness, though Emily was sure she couldn't see anything except perhaps the lights from the other buildings around.

'But it was for the best, wasn't it? You have enjoyed being in the business with me, we've made a marvellous success of things.'

'Why are you telling me this now?' Hari turned to face her, she was white and trembling and her voice was edged with anger. 'It's something to do with Will, isn't it, he knew the truth?'

She shook back her hair. 'Oh, my God!' she covered her face with her hands. 'I've been such a blind fool all this time. I've actually trusted you, Emily Grenfell, you and Will were all I had left in the world, don't you know that?

'I noticed Will's hostility to you lately, how he looks at you so strangely but I never guessed at anything so underhand, so despicable! Oh, Emily, can you ever understand how used I feel?' Her voice ended on a high note of anguish.

'I wanted to tell you,' Emily said desperately, 'I've become so fond of you, Hari, I owe you so much, my very life.'

Hari turned on her bitterly. 'How can I believe a word you say now? You've cheated and lied to me from the start and you've only told me the truth when your scheme was discovered. You Grenfells are all the same, take what you want at whatever cost, I hate you for what you've done, Emily.'

Hari moved to the door and flung it open. She didn't pause to look back but ran swiftly down the stairs. Emily heard the sound of the outer door slamming and she put her head down on her hands and wept.

After a moment, she felt a soft touch on her shoulder. 'Shall I make you a cup of tea, Emily?'

William was looking down at her, compassion in his young face. 'You did what was right, Hari will get over it and then you can start afresh, a good honest start.'

'I hope you are right, Will,' Emily said softly, 'I do hope you are right and I haven't ruined things for ever.'

Hari moved through the darkened streets, her head in a whirl, how could Emily have been so deceitful? But then she had been foolish, expecting a woman of Emily's kind to change, once a snob always a snob. She had cultivated Hari coldly and calculatedly, using her talent, using her trusting friendship. 'Oh, Emily!' There was a wealth of despair in Hari's voice.

'Hey! Where are you rushing to in the darkness?' The voice was familiar, the hand on her arm gentle and Hari looked up gratefully into the smiling face of Edward Morris.

'Edward, I need a friend, can I talk to you?' Hari leaned against his shoulder and at once Edward was full of concern.

'I'll call a cab, I'll take you back to Chapel Street, you can stay with me for as long as you like. And Hari, there will be no demands on you and that's a promise.'

Thankfully, she let Edward take charge, he was kind and good, he would never use her and discard her once he'd had his way. Edward loved her, really loved her and now, at this moment, the thought was like a healing balm to her wounded spirits.

He hailed a cab and settled her on to the leather seat, his arm around her shoulders. The rhythmic clip clopping of the animal's hooves was soothing and Hari leaned back sighing with weariness.

'You've had a hard time, poor love,' Edward said softly, 'you have looked after two sick women as well as keeping the business going and you forget you are only human, you can't do everything, Hari, however strong you think you are.'

Hari's head sank on to his shoulder, she was so grateful to him for taking care of her, making decisions for her, cosseting her. She closed her eyes, she was so tired, so very tired.

She was barely conscious of the cab reaching Chapel Street. Edward guided her into the house and up the stairs and called his housekeeper to bring some hot lemon tea.

Blushing, he gave her a cotton night-shirt. 'Wear this in bed,' he said, 'I don't have any use for the things myself.'

She drank the lemon tea with her eyes refusing to stay open and when Edward would have crept from the room, she held out her hand to him.

'Stay, Edward, wait with me until I'm asleep,' she begged.

Her hand curled in his and she felt warm and loved. She turned on her side and fell into a sleep with tears on her cheeks.

She stayed with Edward for two weeks before she decided she would marry him. She was sitting in the room he'd given her, staring out into the fields at the back of the house, when Edward came to her with a bouquet of flowers held towards her, a sign of his devotion.

As she took them, Hari made her decision. 'Edward,' she said, 'the answer is yes.'

'What do you mean, Hari?' A light of hope flared in Edward's eyes and Hari smiled.

'I mean I'm being a shameless woman, I want to marry you, Edward Morris.'

He knelt at her feet, his face alight as he took her hands. 'Hari, I know you don't love me as I love you but I'll make you a fine husband, I will be faithful and loving and . . .' He stopped speaking as Hari put her finger over his lips.

'Eddie, my dear trustworthy Eddie, don't you think I know all that?' She paused. 'And I will be honest with you, I have not been a perfect lady, always, I . . .' It was Edward's turn to stop her speaking.

'I don't want to know anything about your past, it's the here and now I'm concerned with.'

Hari lifted her face to his and as Edward tentatively kissed her lips, she knew that there was little passion in her response, but there was loving and caring and there was trust, something that had been singularly missing from all her relationships in the past.

The next day, Edward presented Hari with a fine antique ring of rubies and diamonds. 'It was my mother's,' he said softly, 'I would be honoured if you would wear it as a token of our betrothal.'

'A token of our love,' Hari corrected and Edward took her in his arms.

'I can't believe it, Hari,' he said, 'I can't believe that you are really mine.'

'Believe it, Edward,' she said simply, 'when we make our marriage vows they are for ever and ever, amen.'

Three days later, Hari came face to face with Craig Grenfell. He entered Edward's house as though he owned the place and crossing the room took Hari's hand in his.

'I hear congratulations are in order,' he said, his eyes probing hers. Hari drew her hand away quickly.

'You are quite right,' she said, 'I'm going to marry Edward as soon as he can make the arrangements.'

'So you are finished with the emporium?' Craig asked and Hari looked up at him uncomprehendingly, she had not thought that far.

'That is my business,' she said briskly, 'it's up to me and to my future husband.'

'Well, I hope you stay out of the leather trade from now on,' Craig said equitably, 'you and my dear Emily have practically ruined me between you.'

Hari turned away as Edward entered the room. 'Craig is so relieved to see me get married to you,' she said, her voice brittle, 'he is losing a business rival, something that seems to make him very happy.'

Edward tucked her arm in his. 'Not half as happy as it makes me,' he said smiling. 'Now old friend, would you like a nice slug of brandy?'

The two men moved to the sideboard and the muted

sound of their voices seemed to wash over Hari. Bitterness rose within her at Craig's reaction to her marriage; they had after all been lovers, however briefly.

But then, Craig was a Grenfell, none of them could be trusted, she was better off without either Emily Grenfell or Craig.

She moved quickly to Edward's side and took his hand. 'Come along, my lovely,' she said brightly, 'we can't waste time here, we have lots of arrangements to make.' She smiled up at Craig, 'I'm sure you'll forgive us,' she said, 'but Edward is needed and though I do not wish to spoil your friendship, I do for the moment want to monopolize the man I love, I'm sure you understand.'

Craig inclined his head. 'I understand perfectly,' he said and Hari knew that he did. She was telling him in effect that he was no longer free to roam in and out of the house in Chapel Street as he pleased.

'Finish your drink, lovely,' Hari said, smiling at Edward, 'and then come and look at the patterns I've made for the shoes I hope you'll wear at our wedding.' She moved to the door.

'Goodbye, Craig, I expect we'll be seeing you some time.'

She saw the look of displeasure cross Craig's face at her abrupt dismissal of him and yet there was no sensation of satisfaction; instead, Hari suddenly had the overwhelming desire to fling herself on to her bed and cry as she had never cried before.

17

Hari's marriage to Edward Morris was a quiet affair with only a few of Edward's distant relatives as witness to the ceremony. At Hari's side was the faithful William; Lewis and Ben her helpers and Cleg Jones and his wife with another baby on her arm.

Craig Grenfell was naturally enough Edward's grooms-man and when Hari looked at him, standing staring straight ahead, she felt a moment of panic, what was she doing, marrying one man when she loved another? But then, Craig was indifferent to her, he'd used her as a night's pleasure, something Edward would never do.

The ceremony was very simple and as Hari stood at Edward's side in the slant of spring sunshine she felt strangely removed from the occasion. It was almost as though she was an onlooker instead of a participant in the solemn marriage service.

She had bought a plain dress of cream satin with just a trace of blush pink to emphasize the folds of the crinoline skirt. The neckline was scooped and her dark hair, braided with blossom, swept up from her slender neck.

Edward smiled down at her, love shining in his eyes, and Hari felt humbly that she must do all in her power to make him happy.

But as he slipped the ring on to her finger, she suddenly felt trapped. She stared into the sunshine seeing not Edward but Craig standing beside her.

She had always known that she meant nothing to Craig and yet his indifference now hurt her beyond measure, but that was the rich folks for you, Craig and his Cousin Emily were two of a kind, they were the takers in life without the ability to give.

Edward was different. True he was quite wealthy by Hari's standards, he owned his own fine house in Chapel Street and he had flourishing offices in the Strand and yet Edward was ordinary, he spoke with the Welsh intonations in his voice as she did and there were no airs and graces about him.

She was fond of him, there was no great passion on her part but Hari trusted Edward, he was good and kind and he would care for her and never deceive her.

They left the church to the rousing sound of organ music that brought tears to Hari's eyes. The sun splashed over the couple as they stepped out of the arching doorway and blossoms fell from the trees scattering their path with petals.

'A good omen, Hari,' Edward whispered in her ear, 'we shall be very happy, you'll see.'

On an impulse Hari stood on tiptoe and kissed him and Edward's face lit up with pleasure. Behind them, Hari glimpsed Craig, his face seemed set and grim and his eyes meeting hers were hostile. Hari looked away quickly.

Suddenly, Hari felt a presence beside her and she glanced around, feeling nervous.

'Emily!' she said stiffly. 'What are you doing here?'

'I had to come.' Emily was still pale and thin and her hand holding a wrapped parcel trembled.

'Whatever you might think of me I couldn't allow your wedding day to pass without seeing you. Please, Hari, if we can't work together again let us at least be civil to each other.'

'Thank you.' Hari did not have the heart to refuse the gift. 'It's kind of you to think about me.'

'I think about you constantly, Hari,' Emily said quickly, 'I am so grateful to you and I feel so guilty at the way I tricked you, please try to forgive me.'

Hari knew what it cost Emily to apologize, to humble herself before others.

'It's past now,' she said, 'we must all look to the future.'

Edward's hand was on her arm, guiding her towards the carriage. He would take her home to change into travelling clothes and then they were going to the coast of Cornwall for a few weeks before Edward resumed work once more.

'Bye, Will,' Hari said quickly, 'look after things at Chapel Street while we're away, won't you?'

William nodded and then, after hesitating for a moment, he leaned forward and kissed her. Hari squeezed his arm, Will was another anchor in her life, he, like Edward, would never let her down.

After she had left the premises in the Strand, Hari had sent Edward to fetch William, he was her brother, not by blood but by choice and, until he was old enough to make his own decisions, she would take care of him.

In any case, he was still apprenticed to her and it was her bounden duty to give him employment. That was something she must think about later, when she returned from Cornwall. She needed to have work to do herself, but now that she was no longer in partnership with Emily, there were problems to be sorted out.

It was silent in the house on Chapel Street, the afternoon sun slanted into the hallway, dappling the carpet and highlighting the stairway. After a moment's hesitation, Hari moved upward towards the master bedroom and blushed as she heard Edward's quick footsteps behind her.

'Help me with the buttons of my dress,' she said softly and his fingers were warm on her bare neck. The gown slid into a pool of shimmering satin on the floor and Hari stood in her shift looking up shyly at her new husband.

With a soft groan, he took her in his arms and tenderly, almost reverently, he kissed her. She fell back against the pillows, her arms around Edward's slim shoulders, holding him close. This was right and proper, it was no sordid affair, they were husband and wife and were bound by the words of the ceremony to become one flesh.

Edward was a tender lover, he teased her with surprising expertise, rousing her as she had never expected to be roused by him. She was a young healthy woman and she needed to be loved. In any case, Edward and she were now legally bound and in time she would grow to love him, she was sure of it.

When it was over, she sighed softly, at least now she had proved herself to be a proper wife and if there was an ache inside her for another man, then her husband would never know it.

It was beautiful in Cornwall, the rugged clifftops stretched away as far as the eye could see and the rolling waves crashed ashore, white with foam that raced and chattered over the rocks.

But after a week of enforced idleness, Hari's mind was racing with ideas for a new business, her own business that she would run without help from anyone. Emily might have had the contacts to start with but now Hari had her own following of customers. It was her own skill that was in demand, her flair for design and the ability to make up the boots and shoes to the customers' exact requirements.

She would invite Lewis and Ben to come to work for her, after all what could Emily do with them now? Unless she found another talented shoemaker who could match Hari's designs, the business was finished anyway.

Hari recognized that she would need to find some modest premises, indeed, she might not bother with a shop at all but just rent a workplace. Customers could be fitted in their homes and perhaps they would even prefer the convenience of not having to stir from their own firesides.

Hari could take patterns with her, show samples enough to gain the customers' interest. As for designing, she could do that in one of the many rooms in Edward's house, her house, she felt sure he would be only too delighted to make her happy.

'You are far away, my love.' Edward was sitting easily in a rattan chair placed strategically on the lawn of the elegant house he had rented, where the full benefit of the splendid view could be observed.

'I know, I am impatient to be back at work.' Hari leaned towards him her arm resting easily around his shoulders. 'You will let me work, won't you Eddie, you won't stop me from designing and making shoes?'

'When could I ever deny you anything?' He laughed, 'Anyway, I'd be a brave man if I tried to stand in your way, you are a little virago when you get started.'

He leaned over and kissed her and, as his lips warmed against hers, Hari suppressed a sigh. Edward was a demanding husband, he seemed to want her at any hour of the day or night. But they were married, it was her duty to please him, no, more than her duty, it must be her pleasure.

She allowed him to lead her into the coolness of the big house and up the elegant curving staircase to the bedroom. To her shame, her initial response to him had not been often repeated and now she clung to him more in despair than passion as he made love to her.

Had she made a dreadful mistake? Should she have stopped to think about the step she was taking before rushing into marriage?

Edward fell asleep almost the moment their lovemaking ceased and, as Hari stared down at him, she knew deep in her heart that good and kind though he was and fond though she might be of him, she would never love him, not in the way a woman should love a man.

She cursed Craig Grenfell, it was him she loved and the fact that he cared nothing for her didn't alter her feelings one jot. She had lain in his arms, given herself in love as well as in passion and he was the only man with whom she could ever be truly happy.

But she must put him out of her mind, she was married to Edward, that's all there was to it. She would make Edward a good and faithful wife, she would do anything she must do to please him and after all once they returned home, they would both have their work to occupy their minds. Perhaps then, Edward's ardour would cool a little.

She slipped from the bed and made her way into the dressing-room where the jug of water stood ready for use on the marble table, the rose-covered bowl standing beside it.

When she had washed and dressed, she slipped from the room and made her way downstairs to the writing-room.

Her only materials were some writing paper and ink and a worn-out pen but she was soon lost in her work, her mind rested, the ideas flowed and soon the paper was covered in drawings with small notes beside them and Hari felt alive for the first time in weeks.

Emily sat in the shop and looked around her fearfully, the stock of shoes that she and Hari had built was almost gone, the shelves depleted, the displays dusty and bare. She must do something before she was ruined, she owed rent on the premises as it was and the landlord would soon be getting impatient.

What did other shop owners do? They did not all have a Hari ready at hand to provide endless ideas and designs.

221

Suddenly it came to her, she would buy in stocks from other areas.

There was Mr Clark's factory in Street in Somerset and in addition the famous Lotus shoes had become fashionable; these would surely appeal to the ladies of the town. She would call her new store Emily's Emporium.

Emily felt a pang of guilt, what about Hari? But then Hari was married, she need never work again and she had left of her own free will, Emily must think only of herself now.

She would have to travel to Somerset, she decided, see the Clark factory for herself, then she would have to raise capital to buy in stock and transport the shoes to Wales. Emily sighed, Craig could have been a great help to her right now but she would sooner starve than go to him for anything.

As though he'd been drawn to her by the thread of her thoughts, Craig entered the doorway of the shop and paused for a moment as though adjusting his eyes to the gloom. He took off his hat and stared at her, his eyebrows raised.

'Am I to be welcomed or thrown out?' he asked. Emily did not answer him but, as he drew nearer, she couldn't help the thrill of excitement that his presence aroused in her.

But he would never have known it, her expression was stony as she looked up at him. 'Are you enjoying living in *my* house?' she asked icily.

'It would have been our house if you hadn't been so headstrong,' Craig said easily. 'In any case Emily, the male heir inherits, it's just a fact of life, you know that.'

'Don't patronize me,' Emily said hotly. 'I know you had to have the house but it doesn't make it any easier for me to be shut out of my own home.'

'Why didn't you marry me as we'd planned then?' Craig

said reasonably. 'And the house would have been yours again.'

'Don't go making *me* out to be the culprit.' Emily stubbornly shook her head. 'You were to blame for my father's disgrace, if you hadn't been so idle and useless, papa would not have lost a fortune to that brother of yours.'

'I was remiss,' Craig said in a hard voice, 'but don't you think I paid for it? You think it's hard to lose your home, I lost my liberty and my good name, not so easily regained, my dear Emily.'

'It's no use talking to you,' Emily said, 'I wouldn't marry you if I remained a spinster all my life. I have to make my own way in the world, I want to be my own woman, to be a success.'

'In other words you want to make up for your father's failings. And he did fail, Emily, if I was wrong then so was he, we both trusted Spencer and that's where we made our biggest mistake.'

Emily inclined her head. 'You may have a point but, in any case, I don't want marriage, at least not yet.'

'Well, who is to say you'll be offered marriage, Emily?' Craig asked, his eyebrows raised and she had the feeling he was making fun of her.

'I don't want *you* to offer me anything!' Emily said angrily. 'Who do you think you are?'

'You are a cold, carping woman, Emily,' he replied, 'perhaps you are right, you are not cut out for passion, you certainly don't have the blood of the Grenfells running in your veins.'

Emily had difficulty controlling her breathing, far from being cold, his words had aroused a bitter anger in her. But she was not a woman to let her emotions run away with her, that was something Craig would learn.

'Cold am I? Well, just because you fooled poor Hari into

thinking you were wonderful, you needn't think all women are that easily duped.'

Craig's face darkened, he imagined they had been talking about him, about his night with Hari, he could not know that Emily was merely using Hari's infatuation as a weapon against him.

'Jealous because I slept with Hari, are you?' he said angrily, 'well, at least she's a normal, hot-blooded woman not a cold fish like you, cousin.'

Emily gasped. She felt anger and an unexpected sense of jealousy pour through her like hot strong wine, she had not expected to hear such words from Craig, she had only been taunting him, not trying to extract a confession.

She clenched her hands into fists. 'I presume Hari's new husband doesn't know about all this? How could you betray your friend that way?'

'Don't be foolish, "all this", as you so elegantly put it, was long before Edward proposed to Hari.'

'And you think that makes it all right? I despise you, Craig, and I despise Hari too, to think I was apologizing for deceiving her and all this time she has been your paramour! You'd better go, I have work to do even if you have not.'

'Why blame Hari?' he demanded. 'You had made it quite clear that you wanted nothing to do with me.'

Emily wanted to lash out and hurt Craig. 'I see you are defending her!' she said hotly. 'And that you are continuing your life of indolence, doing nothing to make a secure future for yourself. Don't you want to see Summer Lodge restored to its former elegance?'

'Summer Lodge, possessions, is that all you can think about, Emily?' Craig said in exasperation.

She didn't deign to answer him, as she swept up the stairs, Emily's legs were trembling but she held her head high even though tears blurred her vision. She hated

Craig, he was a ne'er-do-well and a deceiver, it seemed he could not be faithful to one woman even if he tried.

She began to pack a bag at once, the sooner she got her ideas put into practice the better, it was clear she had no one to depend on but herself.

Emily took lodgings in the Street Inn and settled down to rest, wanting to be at her best before she approached Mr Clark with her proposition. And yet the last thing she thought of before she fell asleep was Hari in Craig's arms and bitterness filled her at the duplicity of the two people who once had been dear to her.

Mr William Clark's factory was a gracious-looking building more like a large private house than the hive of industry it was. Its many windows looked down the High Street towards Glastonbury Tor.

It was with some surprise that the foreman showed Emily into the office and asked her politely to sit while he ascertained if Mr Clark was available.

The man introduced as Mr Clark was younger than Emily had supposed, perhaps twenty-five years of age. He sported a beard and his eyes were bright and intelligent as he looked questioningly at Emily.

'I own a boot and shoe emporium in Swansea,' she said without preamble, 'and now I wish to expand my stock by bringing into the area some of your leather footwear. I have heard many good things about your boots and shoes, Mr Clark.'

William Clark's quick glance betrayed his astonishment at the thought of a young lady of breeding being in business but, after a pause, he inclined his head and waited for her to continue.

'This is a new departure for me so I propose that I take several hundred pairs of boots and shoes, show them in my emporium and in the event that they do not sell, return them to you without delay.'

He smiled. 'In other words, I take all the risks, Miss, what was it, Grenfell?'

'I'm sure that you and your forefathers have not built up your business by avoiding certain risks,' Emily said softly. 'I should expect you to send some representative to my emporium before you agree to assure yourself that I am running a legitimate business and then perhaps we can talk again.'

When William Clark didn't reply, Emily searched in her bag for the references she had brought with her from various suppliers and from her solicitor in London.

'These may prove that I am a legitimate businesswoman with a blameless character. I would like you to look at them, Mr Clark.'

He read the documents in silence for a few moments and then nodded.

'I will take a chance on you, Miss Grenfell,' he smiled, 'I can not approve of a lady working in the trade but for all that I will send one of my men with a small load of boots and shoes to your emporium in Swansea and we shall see how you get on.' He rose from his chair.

'Perhaps you would like to see the factory before you begin your long journey home?'

Emily rose to her feet, she wasn't particularly interested in the mechanics of the factory although Hari would have been agog to see the newest equipment and the famed machines that the Clark family had imported from America.

'That's very kind of you, Mr Clark,' she said politely and followed him from the office.

The clatter of the treadles was the first thing Emily heard as William Clark opened the door to the long room. Men and women worked side by side, some of the women hand stitching and finishing on a small side table. Some younger girls rhythmically pressed the footplate that turned the wheel operating the needle.

In spite of herself, Emily was interested in the sole-cutting machine, with its various wheels and handles. It was an ungainly monstrosity but what a lot of time and effort it saved, doing the work of several cobblers in only a few minutes. How Hari's mouth would have watered at the sight.

But she must forget Hari, she no longer felt guilty about deceiving her for Hari's deception had been greater.

When she took her leave of Mr Clark, the sun was sending long shadows over the High Street. Emily made her way to the inn and ordered a meal of cold meat and fresh crusty bread.

She felt enthusiasm rise within her at the prospect of selling the boots and shoes and the soft Clark's slippers with lamb's-wool linings to the inhabitants of Swansea. She'd show them a thing or two, Emily Grenfell was not easily beaten.

The next day, Emily had barely arrived home, travel weary and longing for a cup of tea, when a van clattered to a halt outside the shop.

Written in bold letters on the side was the name C&J Clark, Street, Somerset.

Emily had no-one to unload the goods so she paid the driver handsomely to bring the footwear into the shop. The man touched his cap thanking her in his soft Somerset drawl as he handed her a bill.

'Mr Clark said you'd see him personally about that.' He indicated the sheet of paper and Emily nodded.

'That's right and thank you once again for your help.'

Emily watched as the man took his leave and then turned back to the room that seemed filled with the Clark merchandise. She would have to get the salesgirls to return to work and have them fill out the stands. None would have Hari's flair for display, but did that really matter? All that was needed was for the buying public of Swansea to be apprised of her new stock and that would simply involve advertising in the pages of the *Cambrian* newspaper.

She locked up the shop and wearily made her way upstairs, she was tired after the long journey and her nerves were tense as she anticipated the difficulties she might have persuading the people of the town to buy Clark's shoes.

She rubbed at her forehead, distractedly, she had to admit that she missed Hari's inventive mind, an eye-catching slogan would have come easily to her, she would know instinctively how to present the goods to the best advantage.

Well, Hari was not here, she was safely ensconced in the respectability of marriage. Respectability, that was a laugh, Hari, who had been sleeping with one man, had now married another.

The large advertisement in the *Cambrian* attracted a crowd of curious people to the emporium. It seemed like the old days when there had been a constant ebb and flow of customers.

Emily made a point of telling people that Mr Clark was world renowned, a boot and shoemaker exporting his goods as far afield as Australia.

The response was better than Emily could have anticipated, the gap left in the market by Hari's abdication from the job of shoemaking had left the townspeople at a loss what to buy next. And it seemed, Emily thought gratefully, that she had stopped that gap with her new ideas.

At the end of the first week, she was able to mail to Somerset the good news that she needed more stock. She informed Mr Clark that she would be employing her own van and driver who could transport the goods and at the same time pay her outstanding bill.

As she surveyed her satisfyingly empty shelves, Emily congratulated herself that once again, she was back in business. She should feel on top of the world so why was it she felt so alone?

18

Craig Grenfell stared down at his books and read the satisfying balance at the foot of the page. At last he had disposed of his stock of French calf and what's more he had orders coming in from Northampton, Kendal and Stafford, enough to keep him busy for several months.

With a sigh he closed the books, his business prospects had improved but his personal life seemed empty and dull.

Most days, he spent some time with Edward and his friend's happiness, though gratifying, was also a thorn in Craig's side. He concealed his feelings of envy well enough for there were times when he lusted after Edward's wife, remembering the one time they had been together with some regret for what might have been.

And now he had dallied too long, by his stupidity he had lost both Hari and Emily, neither of them had any time for him and could he blame them? He had trifled with both of them, treating Hari with unforgivable casualness and Emily with complete lack of sensitivity.

What did he really want? he asked himself, Emily as a wife and Hari as some sort of mistress, waiting for him in a scented room ready to offer him pleasure. He was dreaming.

Perhaps he didn't know the meaning of the word love. He rose from his chair, scraping it back angrily so that it almost fell. Damn it! He would go down to the Burrows, have a cooling mug of ale, forget about women or the lack of them in his life.

He was crossing the road with rapid steps when he bumped into a woman hurrying in the opposite direction. He raised his hat and looked down about to apologize when he saw that Hari was staring up at him, her eyes unreadable.

'Mrs Morris,' he said with forced lightness in his voice, 'I do apologize for my clumsy behaviour.' He fell into step beside her as Hari moved quickly along the street. 'May I accompany you to wherever you are going?'

'Do you have to be so sarcastic all the time?' Hari said bluntly.

'I'm sorry,' Craig said softly, 'it's just my way.' How could he tell Hari that he hated seeing her married to his best friend, that he wanted to take her to bed this minute, to untie her thick dark hair and watch it tumble over her white shoulders? He was no monk, he was a man of flesh and blood and he wanted Hari like hell.

'Will you come to the Mackworth for some tea with me, Hari?' he asked. 'I have a favour to ask you.'

She looked up at him in surprise. 'A favour, what do you mean?'

He improvised swiftly. 'I was wondering if I should branch out into the shoe business. Instead of simply selling the leather to the big towns, perhaps I should take samples of the specialized shoes you used to make. We could go into business together.'

He could see that Hari was intrigued in spite of herself. He took her arm and steered her towards the doors of the hotel.

'Come along, not even Edward would object to us being together in the tea rooms, would he?'

'Of course not,' Hari said quickly, 'Edward knows that when I made my vows I meant them.'

He held the chair for her to sit down and speculated how different Hari looked from the first time he'd seen her in

231

the slum area of World's End. Then she had been simply dressed with a cotton blouse covering her rounded breasts and a long drab skirt that did nothing to conceal the curve of her hips. Her hair had been a tangle of curls and she had looked at him with frightened but defiant eyes.

Now she was a lady of fashion, she wore a crinoline nipped in at the waist, high at the neck, and she looked equally as lovely as the first time he'd set eyes on her.

'How are you enjoying being the wife of a respectable accountant?' he asked with a return to his bantering tone. Hari gave him a level look.

'Please don't be so patronizing, Craig, there's no need of it.'

'You're right,' he said quickly. 'Well, how about you making shoes again, do you like the idea?'

'Of course I do but why should I work with you when I can work for myself?' Hari pointed out. 'I had a partner before and it didn't turn out very well.'

Craig leaned back in his chair. 'Your partner is doing very nicely for herself now,' he said.

'Yes, I'd heard that Emily was running a large emporium, buying in shoes from Mr Clark in Somerset. Good luck to her.'

'But aren't you just a little envious?' Craig asked.

Hari shook her head. 'No, that's not what I want to do, I want to design and make individual shoes just as I did before and I really think I'd be better off working alone.'

'With Edward's money?' Craig asked challengingly. Hari looked up at him startled. Craig smiled.

'You hadn't considered that aspect, had you? You'll need capital to get started and I can offer it to you as a business proposition, I can also take your designs and make them known all over the country. Why don't you think about it?'

'I already have a good reputation,' Hari replied quickly, 'Charlie has seen to that in his own small way. I think that now any bank would be ready to advance me money, don't you?'

'Probably,' Craig said. He leaned towards her persuasively. 'But no bank could offer you the outlets that I could. I travel all over the country these days, from Bristol to Northampton, just think, your designs could become famous.'

Hari took the teapot that the waiter placed before her and, as she poured for both of them, Craig knew she was giving herself time to think.

'I'll have to talk to Eddie,' she said at last, 'I couldn't do anything that my husband didn't approve of.'

'I wouldn't expect it.' Craig smiled inwardly, he had won. Edward was not about to deny his wife any reasonable request she might make and he had spoken often enough of Hari's desire to return to work. What better than that she should work with Edward's oldest friend?

Did Edward know what had happened between Hari and his best friend? Probably not, in any case all that was long before Edward's marriage to Hari, best forgotten. But could he forget ever? Craig doubted it.

He leaned forward. 'Have you any designs ready?' He smiled, 'I would lay odds that you have not been idle, I expect there are sheets and sheets of paper covered with your ideas.'

'You seem to know me well,' Hari said and Craig resisted the urge to tell her that he would very much like to know her much better. Hari would not approve of flirting.

'I'm right then?' Craig found himself warming to the idea of promoting Hari's work; specialized shoes were always in demand especially by the rich young ladies who were anxious to come out in style.

'Yes,' Hari smiled, 'but don't sound so smug about it.'

'Then I may take some of your ideas when I go away in a few weeks' time?' he asked and he felt triumphant as Hari nodded.

'I don't suppose it would do any harm.' She put down her cup and rose to her feet. 'Now I must talk to Eddie, if he agrees, then we have a bargain.'

He rose, 'Fair enough, Hari.' After a moment, he held out his hand and then his fingers were curling around Hari's. She drew her hand away and Craig knew then, without doubt, that he had lost Hari for good, she had never been the sort of woman who went easily into an illicit relationship and now that she was married anything other than business between them was out of the question.

Strangely enough, Craig found himself wanting her even more, she was a beautiful woman and one of principle. 'Edward is a lucky man,' he said softly.

He sank back into his seat, watching as Hari's small figure disappeared through the doors of the hotel. At least, he thought ruefully, he had Hari as a partner if nothing else and it seemed he would have to be grateful for that.

Edward returned home from the office, his face flushed, perspiration beading his forehead. Hari moved towards him quickly and took his coat.

'Eddie, what's wrong, you look awful!' She led him into the sitting-room, calling to the maid to bring some iced coffee.

'I think you have a temperature, my lovely.' She rested the back of her hand against his forehead. 'I'd better get the doctor.'

Edward shook his head. 'No, it's all right, I get these bouts of fever, something to do with being abroad when I was a child, it always passes after a few days in bed.'

'I'll find you one of my herbal remedies for curing a

fever then,' Hari said quickly, 'but after you've had your coffee, I'd like you to go up to bed.'

'Yes, mam.' Edward hugged her around the waist, resting his head against the softness of her breasts.

'I love you, Hari, don't ever leave me, will you?'

'There's soft you talk sometimes, Eddie, you are my husband for ever and ever, of course I'll never leave you.'

When Edward was settled in bed, Hari brought a bowl of cool water and bathed his face.

'That feels wonderful,' he said, 'I'm so grateful to you, Hari.'

'Nonsense! No need for gratitude between husband and wife, you'd do the same for me, wouldn't you?'

'Like a shot,' he said softly, 'I'd wrap you up in velvet and keep you all to myself if I could.'

This did not seem the time to tell Edward about her encounter with Craig. Instead Hari searched for her book of herbal remedies and flicked through the pages.

'Yes, this is it, I'll get some borage and mix it with a little bugloss, that will calm down the fever and strengthen your heart.'

'My heart is yours, my lady,' Edward said with mock severity and Hari smiled.

'Well then, it will do as I say.' She sat beside him. 'The heart begins to beat more swiftly when you have a fever and it must be calmed, trust me, I will take care of you, I'll have you well in no time.'

Edward took her hand. 'I have complete faith in you.'

'Right then, let me get on with it, talking about a remedy is no good, I have to make it and you have to drink it.'

'Bully,' Edward said trying to smile though it was clear by the flush on his cheeks that he was in some discomfort.

In the kitchen, Hari ground the roots and leaves of the herbs together and then poured hot water over them. The mixture would need to stand for an hour and then it would be ready to strain. She wished she could hurry the process for Edward's sake but she would just have to be patient.

She sighed staring down at the jug of liquid, thinking of when she had nursed Emily, how different her life had been then.

Her thoughts switched to her meeting with Craig. Why did he still have the power to stir her blood? She was a married woman, she loved Edward, he was a dear sweet man and yet Craig's touch on her hand was enough to send her into a turmoil of emotion.

But it would go no further, she had done wrong once, she had allowed her desires to overcome her common sense. Now she was a respectably married woman and she would remain faithful to Edward whatever it cost her.

Later, as she gave Edward the soothing remedy and settled him back against the sheets, she felt affection for him overwhelm her. 'You should rest more easy now, my lovely.' She covered him with the sheets. 'Try to sleep a little, sleep is very healing, mind.'

Downstairs, she drew out her sketchbook and began to make rapid drawings. It was as if the meeting with Craig had inspired her, her pen flew across the pages and she was unaware of time until she realized quite suddenly that the light had faded.

She put down her book guiltily, it was time she saw to Edward.

He was awake and some of the fever had abated. The hectic flush had left his cheeks and he smiled when he saw her.

'I'm starving,' he said, 'how about something to eat?'

Hari smiled. 'That's very good news, what do you fancy? I can send Will out to the baker's for some fresh crusty bread and there's some soup in the pot. I made it myself so I know it's full of goodness.'

'That will do very nicely, *cariad*,' he said, 'but first come and give your husband a kiss.'

She hugged him to her, her cheek resting against his. His hand strayed to her breast and she drew away from him with mock anger.

'That will be enough of that! An invalid needs rest not strenuous exercise, you wait until you are fit again, my lad.'

'Tyrant,' he said but he was smiling. Hari sat on the edge of his bed with a bowl on her knee and it pleased Hari to see Edward enjoy a little of the soup she'd made him.

'Eat up,' she said, 'that's the way to recover your strength.' She moved away from him knowing that she had been glad of an excuse to avoid intimacy with her husband.

Matters had failed to improve in that sphere of her life, much as she was fond of Edward, she could not give herself completely, it was as though a small part of her was holding back, waiting for something but she knew not what. Edward was her husband till death did them part so what possible reason could there be for withholding anything from him?

Within a few days, Edward was almost back to normal, he was up and about, doing his work at home instead of in the office and yet Hari sensed that he was not feeling as well as he should be.

She hesitated to tell him about her meeting with Craig, waiting until he was quite well again and then it was too late, Craig called to see how Edward was progressing.

The two men were in the sitting-room and Hari was in the kitchen, supervising the supper. She entered the room to see Edward looking up at her with a strange expression in his eyes.

'Edward feels that we should make a go of our venture,'

Craig said. 'He is more than willing to act as accountant for our little business enterprise.'

Hari felt herself grow cold, she had not yet discussed the idea with her husband; the news coming from Craig must have been quite a shock. But if it was, Edward hid his feelings well.

'That's very kind of you, Edward,' Hari said knowing instinctively that Edward wanted Craig to believe he had known about the matter all along. 'It would be a great help to have someone like you keeping an eye on things.'

'My pleasure.' Edward sounded distant, his eyes refused to meet hers and Hari bit her lip. Edward was an easy-going man but it was quite clear that he was hurt by what he must see as her deceitful behaviour.

'Would you like some supper?' Hari asked Craig. 'We're having poached fish and then some saddle of lamb with a lovely sponge cake to follow, you'd be welcome to join us.'

Craig rose to his feet, sensing perhaps that all was not well. 'No, I have to get on, there are things I must do but thank you all the same.'

He moved to the door. 'I shall be seeing you soon, Edward, I have my other books ready for you and I'm sure you will be impressed with the improvements I've made in my leather business.'

Edward murmured something and sank back into his chair as Hari saw Craig to the door.

'Is something wrong?' Craig asked. 'Edward does approve of the business idea, doesn't he?'

'Yes, of course.' Hari could not let her husband down, if Edward's pride demanded that she pretend he knew all about the venture then so be it.

'We must get together soon, then,' Craig took his hat and coat from the maid, 'we have a great deal to talk about, if this affair is to flourish.'

Hari was well aware that the maid was listening avidly to the conversation. She knew that conclusions could be drawn from Craig's statement.

'I'm sure our business venture will succeed, don't worry about that, and Edward will see that the books are sorted out properly.'

When Craig had left, Hari took a deep breath and returned to the sitting-room. 'Supper smells wonderful,' she said brightly. 'I hope you are hungry, Edward.'

He looked at her searchingly. 'I seem to have lost my appetite, Hari, and enough prevaricating, I think you owe me an explanation.'

Hari shrugged. 'I have nothing to hide, Edward, I didn't talk all this over with you because while you were ill it didn't seem important.'

'That's all too easy,' Edward said, 'but what I want to know is when was this business venture discussed, when did you meet Craig, were you alone with him and how many times have you had discussions about this business you are so keen to set up with him?'

'I saw him once in town,' Hari said quickly, her temper rising. 'We had tea in the public tea rooms and the idea just came to Craig quite suddenly. He thought I might be interested in starting work again and to be truthful, Edward, I am very interested.'

He looked at her, his mouth set into a line, he was so much like a whipped child that Hari went to him and took him in her arms.

'You've always known that marriage and a home wasn't enough for me, Eddie, I love working, designing shoes is in my blood, I thrive on it. I'll become like a cabbage if I just sit at home like some doll doing nothing all day.'

'But isn't being my wife rewarding enough?' Edward said. 'I want you to be here waiting for me when I come in at night from the office. I don't want a wife who is so involved in her own ideas that she doesn't know what time of day it is.'

Hari moved away from him. 'Then I'm sorry, Edward, you have married the wrong woman. I was a working girl when you met and fell in love with me, why try to change me now?'

He didn't reply, he stared down at his hands, his face drawn and pale. 'Edward,' Hari said calmly, 'we took each other for better or worse, we made our vows and I shall stick by mine. But let me tell you this, you are going the right way to lose my respect.'

He drew her close then and kissed her eyelids. 'I'm sorry, my darling, I'm a jealous lout, I know you are not a woman to flout your vows, what am I thinking about?'

He took her hand and led her from the room, through the hallway and up the stairs. He pushed open the doors of their bedroom and led her inside, bolting the door after them.

'Edward,' she protested weakly, 'what about your supper?'

'To hell with supper!' he said eagerly. 'What I want now is you and it won't wait.'

He drew her on to the bed and began to open the buttons on her dress, his hands then were freeing her breasts, caressing them, teasing the nipples with his tongue. Hari tried to respond, she wound her arms around her husband's shoulders closing her eyes against the thinness of his chest.

He took his time undressing her, caressing every part of her until she could have screamed at him to get on with it, get it over and done with, for Edward's lovemaking was the last thing she wanted.

But it seemed to go on interminably, he smoothed the flat planes of her stomach with his hand, looking down at her with a strange look in his eyes.

'I want to fill you with my child,' he said softly, 'give you babies, Hari, then you will be satisfied to be at home with me instead of playing the fool with Craig and this shoemaking business.'

When he came to her at last, she knew she was cold and unresponsive, much as she tried to summon passion, her body refused to comply. But Edward did not realize that he was unwelcome and how could Hari explain that she felt as though he was smothering, suffocating her.

At last, it was over and she rose from the bed and spent a great deal of time in the dressing-room adjoining the master bedroom. She heard Edward leave the bedroom and then she dressed herself with trembling fingers.

She did not go down to supper but summoned the maid to light a fire in the bedroom, she knew the girl's curiosity was aroused but she didn't care.

When eventually Edward came upstairs, he was smiling and a little the worse for drink, Hari could smell the port on his breath quite strongly. He went into his dressing-room and she heard him make preparations for bed and she closed her eyes wearily.

How could she go on like this, dreading Edward's touch, hating it when he caressed her? She would have to tell him the truth, perhaps move into the spare bedroom and yet hadn't she agreed on her wedding day to be obedient to him in all things?

At last, she crawled into bed beside him and tried to sleep but the morning light was streaking the skies before she at last closed her eyes.

When she arose, feeling as though she'd had no rest at all, there was a note from Edward telling her he had gone to Bristol on business and he would return within the week. Hari sighed heavily with relief.

It was William who told her of the gossip that was circulating Swansea society via the servants' quarters.

'They're saying that you are carrying on with Mr Craig Grenfell behind your husband's back, Hari,' Will said softly, 'seen out to tea together and then him coming to the house a lot. Sorry to be the one to tell you.'

'*I'm* glad you've come to me, Will,' Hari said, 'and I needn't tell you that none of it is true, need I?'

'No, you needn't!' William said fiercely. 'You are a real lady, Hari, not like these rich fancy pieces who say one thing and do another.'

'Will,' Hari said softly, 'are you grown too old for a hug?'

Will put his arms around her and hugged her and Hari became aware that he was growing up, he was almost a man now, the lines of his face were losing the childish softness and hardening into an expression of determination and strength.

'My brother,' Hari said in a choked voice, 'I might have known you would believe in me.'

'Of course I believe in you. Now what are you going to do, let the gossips spoil your life or will you go ahead with the business you were planning?'

Hari smiled suddenly, 'What do you think?'

Will returned her smile. 'In that case, you will want to keep the appointment Mr Grenfell asked me to make with you?'

'When for?' Hari asked in surprise.

'In about five minutes' time in the tea-rooms where everyone can see you.' William smiled. 'There's a cab waiting outside.'

'Will,' Hari said, 'has anyone ever told you, you're a bossy boots? But I love you just the same.' She took up her shawl. 'I want you to come with me, Will, from now on you are going to take a more active part in the management of the business and this is as good a time as any for you to start learning.'

Together, they left the house and, as Hari climbed into the cab, she glanced back and, seeing the face of the maid framed in the window, stared back at her coldly. 'She will have to go,' she said to Will.

Craig was sitting waiting for her, he rose when she entered the tea-rooms and Hari felt that every eye was upon her. She held her head high, aware of Will's reassuring presence at her side.

'*Bore da*, Craig,' she said taking a seat. He smiled at her warmly.

'And good-day to you, Hari, I'm happy to see you.'

'You are aware of the gossip I'm sure,' Hari said and Craig nodded.

'Of course, but then gossip never worried me unduly; after being in prison, having my name trailed through the mud, I am impervious to gossip.'

He leaned forward. 'Let's forget the rest of Swansea, let us talk of our future plans for the business, I'm sure we shall make an unqualified success of it.'

Hari suddenly felt warm, his tone inspired her and, for the first time in days, the future seemed to hold the promise of hope.

19

Emily surveyed the crowded shop with satisfaction. At first the customers had come to Emily's Emporium out of curiosity, eager to see the boots and shoes brought up from Mr Clark's factory in Somerset. Then they had come to buy, admiring the fine leatherwork and neat machine stitching that was a feature of the Clark's footwear.

'Good-day Emily, I see you are no longer making bespoke boots and shoes but these, these *manufactured* articles.'

'Good-day Lady Caroline, and of course we are only selling the best these days, no longer do you have to wait several weeks for a special pair of shoes, your demands can be met immediately.'

Lady Caroline sniffed. 'My daughter has such delicate feet you know, she can only wear *hand*-made leatherwork. I don't see how any machine could gauge the exact measurements of my Lisa's little feet.'

'You must bring her in and let her try some shoes for herself,' Emily said a trifle acidly. Her patience with the snobbish attitude of people like Lady Caroline was fast wearing thin.

The woman drew herself up to her full height. 'I have always known what's best for my daughter, thank you very much. I shall patronize that talented shoemaker Hari Morris in future.'

Emily looked at her sharply. 'But I didn't know Hari

was making shoes these days.' She could have bitten out her tongue as soon as she had spoken because a gloating smile came over Lady Caroline's face.

'Oh yes, she has set up a business backed by the Grenfell Leather Company, they have taken over some lovely new premises in the High Street.'

She looked round. 'Not cluttered like this place, mind, oh no. In Hari Morris's shop there are sensible chairs to sit on and footstools where you can be measured in comfort. There you are given personal attention, not expected to buy boots and shoes made on silly machines and from outside Wales at that.'

Lady Caroline, having gained the attention of many of the other shoppers, moved out of the door like a ship in full sail, her skirts billowing behind her.

Damn Hari, Emily thought, seeing with dismay that customers were leaving her shop, influenced by the arrogant attitude of Lady Caroline.

'Anything wrong, Miss Emily?' Sarah Miller had returned to Emily's employ as soon as possible once the business got under way again. She was happier working for Emily than she had been for Hari, she knew a lady when she saw one.

'No, but I'd like a cup of coffee if you don't mind,' Emily said rubbing at her eyes wearily. 'Bring it up to my rooms, please Sarah, and have some refreshment yourself, you look worn out.'

In her room, Emily stared out on to Wind Street, the long winding roadway that flanked the front of the emporium. It was busy with traffic, several vans were drawn up outside shops, horses, used to the routine, were standing patiently, heads down in submissive acceptance.

Cabs and carts clattered along the roadway that was teeming with people, Swansea was a town full of shoppers and suddenly none of them seemed to wish to spend their money at Emily's Emporium.

So, Hari and Craig were working together, were they? Very convenient especially for her cousin who had always known when he was on to a good thing. He would use Hari shamelessly, play on her affections for, married though she might be, Hari was still in love with Craig.

Emily felt a pang of regret, how she wished she had not quarrelled with Hari, she realized now that Hari was as much a victim of Craig Grenfell's machinations as she herself was. It was obvious he had merely been dallying with Hari and had dropped her once he'd had his way with her, otherwise Hari would not have married another man.

Emily missed Hari's company desperately and she had no wish to see her exploited yet again by Craig, there was gossip about them as it was. Not that Emily believed it, however emotional Hari might be, she would never break her marriage vows, she was too upright and honest for that.

Perhaps she should go and see Hari, try to talk her into coming back to the emporium? And yet there was still an unreasoning pang of jealousy within her whenever Emily thought of Hari and Craig together. 'Forget Craig!' she said out loud. 'He's not worthy of any consideration from Hari or me.'

Emily sipped her coffee thoughtfully, her first step would be to walk up Wind Street and into High Street, see the new premises for herself. It could all be done quite casually, she would just be out shopping, strolling aimlessly along. If she could somehow have a good look at the shop Craig and Hari were managing between them, she'd have some idea of what she was up against.

It was a fine day so Emily simply drew on some gloves and a hat and leaving Sarah in charge of the younger, newer employees, made her way out of the shop.

The mellow walls of the old castle reflected the sunlight

as she walked up through Castle Street and Emily narrowed her eyes against the glare. The sky was a blue bowl overhead with just a few fluffy clouds drifting lazily above her. It was a beautiful spring day and suddenly Emily felt nostalgia for the way things used to be.

She was so alone now, friendless, relying on paid help for company and as the warm blood surged in her veins she knew that she would give anything if she could put back the clock, her future as Craig's fiancée secure.

But that was simply wishful thinking; her mind told her that Craig was not worthy of her slightest regard and her mind would rule over her emotions every time.

It was a simple matter to locate Hari's new shop, the crowd gathered outside the premises, peering at the artistic display in the window, was enough to draw anyone's attention.

The window was large, the display spartan. The backdrop was a scene depicting the red dragon of Wales against a field of daffodils. At the centre of the stage stood a pair of ladies' boots buttoned high and beautifully tooled. Different coloured leather had been used to form a pattern over the instep and the rest was polished to a mirror-like finish.

On the other side of the doorway was a smaller window; this was obviously a showcase for the theatre folk. Shoes of all description from the exaggerated hugeness of the clown's red leather pumps to the dainty dancing slippers in soft satins were spread out in apparent disarray over the stands. But the leatherwork was so cleverly displayed that each and every pair of boots and shoes caught the eye.

Emily moved back across the open doorway; within was a board with clear lettering proclaiming that specialized shoes, personally made to suit the individual taste and pocket, were available at short notice from Hari's own boot and shoe shop.

It was all very cleverly done to play on the loyalty of the

townsfolk. Hari might as well have gone into the street and cried to people to buy Welsh but then she was far more subtle than that. Renewed anger against Hari flared up within her.

'Admiring our display?' Craig had come to stand next to Emily and the tone of his voice was impersonal, as if he was addressing a stranger.

'Yes, it's very clever indeed. Make your store look good at the expense of mine that was the idea, wasn't it?' she said angrily.

'Not at all,' Craig said, 'but if that happens to be the result who am I to quibble, all's fair in love and business, don't you think?'

'No, I don't.' Emily was not amused. 'You are setting out to take my business away from me, coldly and deliberately, you and Hari want to ruin me.'

'Rubbish!' Craig said. 'You didn't hesitate to use up Hari's stock when she left you and then when that was gone to buy in stock from Somerset. Did *you* stop to consider what that might do to Hari's trade should she wish to start up in business again?'

He didn't wait for a reply. 'No, of course you didn't, you went your own usual selfish way without a thought for anyone else.'

'That's just not fair!' Emily protested. 'Hari was safely married and, in any case, I didn't think she would want to work with me again, what else could I do but go on and make my own plans?'

Craig looked at her without speaking for a long moment. 'You know, Emily,' he said at last, 'you never did deserve a friend like Hari, she saved your life remember. You never knew her at all, otherwise you wouldn't have believed for one minute that she would be content with home and hearth for evermore.'

He shrugged. 'But then, you were never receptive to the

248

feelings of others. Excuse me, I have work to do.'

He disappeared into the shop and Emily stood there blinking in the sunshine, trying to stem the tears that threatened to spill over on to her cheeks.

Was Craig right, was she selfish and unreceptive to the feelings of those around her? She drew herself up to her full height and made her way back down the road to her own emporium.

Suddenly she was filled with a sense of determination, she would not let anyone rob her of her courage and she was confident of her ability to run a business profitably, what more was there to think about? Craig and Hari, both of them could stew in their own juice.

A few days later a large advertisement appeared in the pages of the *Cambrian* extolling the virtues of Clark's famous footwear. It also announced a cut back in prices of styles that were going out of production in favour of new lines. If Emily's Emporium could not take the trade of the rich and pompous of the town, then it would take its business where it may.

Emily was rewarded by a flood of people from doctors to coal merchants and to her great satisfaction she was able to suit most of the requirements asked of her.

Where her service was lacking was in the repair of boots and shoes once they were bought and Emily made up her mind that she would have to employ skilled cobblers who could remedy that situation.

'Sarah,' she spoke softly to the sales assistant, 'would you do me a favour and accompany me on a scouting mission?'

'A what, miss?' Sarah's eyebrows lifted, her shapely figure emphasized by the tight black dress she wore in the shop seemed to quiver with curiosity. Emily smiled.

'I want to employ some men, cobblers who will sole and heel boots and shoes preferably in the comfort of their own homes, that way I will save on overheads.'

Sarah smiled. 'That's easy, my dad is a cobbler, got a little shop up in Morriston he has, busy he is, mind, but for a secure wage I'm sure he'd work for you.'

'That's an excellent start,' Emily said, her enthusiasm showing in the light of her eyes. 'And can you think of anyone else who would work for me?'

'My dad is sure to know someone, Miss Emily, got lots of friends in the trade, mind.'

'All right, when the shop is closed will you take me to meet your father, Sarah?'

Sarah looked doubtful, 'Our house isn't what you're used to, mind.'

Emily smoothed back a strand of hair that had escaped from the dark ribbons. 'I have become "used to" a great deal of things I wasn't familiar with before, Sarah. Whatever you might think of me, I'm not a snob.'

With a sudden sense of surprise, Emily realized that she spoke the truth. Once she had been a snob of the worst kind, looking down her nose at people like Hari as though they were less than the dust beneath her feet. But that had been before disaster had struck at her, since then she had been grateful for the help anyone chose to give her.

'All right,' Sarah said at last, 'but we haven't got much, mind, my mam's been gone these years now and we've got just a little house in a street of houses all the same as ours and only dad to keep it tidy now that I'm living in.'

'Don't worry so much!' Emily touched Sarah's arm. 'I need men like your father, just remember that.'

'You are nice, miss,' Sarah said warmly and Emily smiled ruefully, what a pity her cousin didn't see her that way.

John Miller was, surprisingly, a handsome active man in his forties. Emily for some reason had expected him to be old and white haired. He took her hand warmly and his smile was much like that of his daughter.

'So you'd like me to do work for you, Miss Emily.' He said, 'Well, you've chosen the right sort of skilled bootmaker for the job.' He spoke with a certain pride in his craft and Emily liked that.

'I'm sure I have.' Emily smiled, 'I've only got to look round me and I can see the evidence of your fine workmanship everywhere.' She indicated the boots and shoes in various states of repair around the small workroom.

'Would you like a cup of tea, miss?' His eyes crinkled at the corners, they were very blue eyes. Emily realized quite suddenly that she more than liked this man, she felt attracted to him. Which was absurd, she might not be a snob any more but an alliance with a bootmaker was not the sort of thing a woman like Emily allowed herself to think about.

'Yes, thank you, I'd like that,' she found herself saying as she followed him from his small workroom to the parlour where she settled herself into a chair.

'I'll do the tea, dad,' Sarah said quickly, 'you and Miss Emily got business to discuss.'

Emily found it embarrassing to talk to this man about money so she brushed over the subject quickly. 'I'll give you five shillings a week above what you are earning now,' she said and then smiled. 'That is if you want to work for me, of course.'

'I shall work for you, never fear, and a more loyal willing worker you'll never find.'

Emily found it difficult to make small talk to this ruggedly handsome man. She saw his hands were idly shaping a piece of leather and she knew instinctively that she had found as good a substitute for Hari as she would ever find. This man, John Miller, actually loved the leather he worked. Given scope, he might rise to great things.

When Sarah brought the tea, Emily took the cup and her hands were trembling. A little of the liquid spilled into the saucer and Emily blushed as she felt John's eyes upon her, smiling blue eyes that seemed to look deep inside her.

What arrant nonsense! What on earth had come over her? Emily finished her tea as soon as she decently could and, shaking out the folds of her skirt, glanced toward Sarah.

'We'd better be getting back to the shop,' she said and she was embarrassed but not surprised when John Miller insisted on accompanying them.

'It is not right for two young ladies to be out alone at night-time.' He led the way out into the narrow street of terraced houses and ignored Emily's protests that they would get a cab.

'Won't get one around here, miss,' he said reasonably. 'Folks in this sort of area walk everywhere.'

There was something magical about the spring evening as Emily walked on John Miller's right hand with his young daughter Sarah on his left. He was a big man and he gave Emily a feeling of great confidence, he could cope with anything that came along, she felt sure of it.

She risked a glance at him and in the light from the gas lamp their eyes met for a brief instant. Emily's stomach seemed to turn over, her mouth was dry and, even as emotions raced through her body, she recognized them as the response of a woman starved of affection.

Perhaps, she thought, almost angrily, it was time she made her peace with her cousin and settled down into a safe and suitable marriage.

Hari was bending over the last, working a piece of sole into place when suddenly she felt faint and ill. She glanced up and saw that Will was regarding her with concern in his young face.

'Hari, what's wrong, are you bad?' he asked anxiously. Hari made an effort to keep the waves of darkness at bay.

'Fetch Edward, please,' she said and her voice was distant and far away.

It was perhaps moments later that she regained consciousness, finding herself resting against the softness of her bed. Edward was bending over her and in the background stood Will, his face white with fear.

From far away Hari heard him speaking in a whisper. 'Hari hasn't got yellow jack, has she?'

'I doubt it,' Edward said with false heartiness, 'but the doctor will be here soon.'

Hari tried to rise, 'I don't need a doctor, I'm all right, really I am, Eddie.'

'No arguments,' Edward said hoarsely and, by the look in his eyes, Hari knew how worried he was.

The doctor came and Hari recognized him at once. 'Doctor Webber,' she said weakly, 'sorry to call you out.' She saw Will shrink against the door and was thankful when the doctor indicated that Edward should take the boy from the room.

The examination was gentle and thorough and Hari had never been so embarrassed in her life. When the doctor drew the sheets over her she moistened her lips.

'What is it, doctor, what's wrong with me?' she asked fearfully.

'Not very much, my dear, this is simply nature taking her course, you are expecting a child, congratulations.'

Hari was speechless, a child, that was not a possibility she had even considered.

'I can't be!' she said in disbelief. The doctor smiled.

'No such thing as can't, my dear, not when you are a young healthy married lady.'

'When?' Hari asked, her voice trembling with a mingling of excitement and fear.

'I'd say in about six or seven months' time, Mrs Morris, but I really can't be accurate to the hour, you know.'

Hari was incredulous, 'How could I not know?'

The doctor was closing his bag. 'I suppose it didn't occur to you to check your dates,' he said smiling. 'The lack of courses is something many women overlook for quite some time.'

He moved to the door. 'I shall leave you now to break the good news to your husband, tell him from me to look after you, not let you work too hard.'

After a few moments, Edward returned to the room, his face long with anxiety. He sat at the side of the bed and took her hand.

'The doctor said you had news for me, what sort of news, Hari? Tell me quickly before I die of fright.'

'We're going to have a baby, Edward.' Hari still could not bring herself to believe it. 'You and me, we are going to be parents.'

Edward looked as incredulous as Hari felt and then with a whoop of joy, he took her in his arms and hugged her close.

'My clever little girl,' he said, his voice hoarse, 'my dear clever little girl.'

Hari held him away laughing. 'All right, don't smother me, you had something to do with it too, remember.'

Edward sighed. 'It will be a boy, I just know it will, our son, what shall we call him?' He cradled her gently, his cheek against her hair. 'Joseph perhaps after my father.'

'Or Dewi after mine!' Hari retorted. 'Mind, it could easily be a girl, a sweet pretty little thing who will grow up to be a lady like her mam.'

'Don't talk such rubbish,' Edward said, 'being a lady means having kindness and good manners not material possessions, remember that.'

'Call Will,' Hari said on impulse, 'after you, he must be the first to know.'

'Aye, all right. While he's with you, I'll slip round to the office, bring some work home, I can't bear to leave you for a whole day, not today at least.'

Will was so pale and worried that Hari held out her arms to him.

'Will,' she said softly, 'I'm not sick, I'm just going to have a baby, it will be like a brother or sister for you. Will, what do you think?'

Will nodded thoughtfully. 'Well, we'll have to take good care of you because my mam was very bad with the last baby, mind.'

'I know, Will.' Hari held him close for a moment. 'But I am more fortunate than your mam, remember, I've got a husband who can look after me and Will, you are older now, you can look after me, too.'

'I suppose so.' He sounded doubtful, 'But what about your work with Mr Grenfell, you'll have to give that up, won't you?'

Hari felt a cold chill run over her, that was something she had not thought about. What would Craig make of her news, would he be upset that she was spoiling his plans?

But she could still do some of the work, she could at least make designs and have Lewis and Ben execute them, they were both skilled enough.

But could they add the little touches, the tooled patterns, the dainty hand stitching, for ladies' slippers?

Hari sighed, some of her exuberance vanishing. 'I shall work for a few months anyway, Will,' she said, 'a little bit of stitching and sewing won't harm me.'

'Did you know that Miss Emily has employed shoe-makers to work for her?' Will asked. 'I know she's got Mr Miller who is a good man and some other boot repairers are working from home soling and heeling, taking our work, they are, mind.'

So Emily wasn't content to buy in stock from outside, she wanted the repairs as well. 'No, Will, I didn't know,' Hari said softly. 'Where did you hear about it?'

Will shrugged, 'The news is everywhere, all the boot and shoemakers want to go to work for Emily, offering over the odds in pay, she is, five shillings on top of the normal earnings for a week, no-one can afford to turn that down.'

'I suppose not,' Hari said softly, wondering if her own hitherto loyal workers would want to leave and work for Emily too.

'Be a pal, Will,' Hari said, 'go and make me a cuppa, there's a good man, I'm gasping with thirst.'

Will walked to the door and stared back at her gravely. 'Have to have a new maid now, I know the other one was so nosy that she had to go, but you'll need more than a housekeeper now mind, can't have you doing house cleaning and washing sheets, that's what got my mam down, see.'

'I think you are right, Will.' Hari felt tears constrict her throat at the concern in the boy's voice. 'I'll speak to Edward about it when he comes home.'

When she was alone, Hari sat up and stared out of the window into Chapel Street, a baby, she Hari Morgan, no Hari Morris now, she was going to have a baby, it was scarcely believable. And in the midst of her joy and excitement, Hari knew that there would be choices to be made and the choosing would not be easy.

20

The hot summer day had brought out the crowds; Wind Street was thronged with people, mostly women looking for bargains in Emily's Emporium.

Emily stood in the doorway and welcomed her customers, smiling and nodding, addressing the regulars by name.

Suddenly business was booming, Emily no longer need worry about money for stock, her shop was excellently equipped and there was money in reserve in case the cold winds of trouble began to blow.

A large figure loomed in the doorway, dark against the sunlight. Emily blinked and then frowned. 'Craig, is there anything I can do for you?'

'Yes,' Craig said easily, 'I think it's time we forgot our differences and acted like civilized beings again.' He seemed unusually subdued.

'Is there anything wrong, your mother?'

'My mother is well enough,' Craig said, 'indeed she wants to see you again, quite soon, she insists it's been too long since we all had dinner together.

'But I am worried,' he continued, 'it's Spencer I want to talk to you about.'

Emily sighed, she and Craig were kin after all and she owed him some loyalty.

'If I can help in any way then of course I will,' she said quietly.

257

Craig smiled, 'I'm glad about that, Emily, I would very much like to ask your advice.'

'Yes, of course.' Emily felt flattered and she realized, in that instant, that the ice had begun to thaw in her relationship with her cousin. He had come to her not in his usual, arrogant, patronizing way but to ask her help and she would give it gladly.

She slipped her arm through his in an uncharacteristic gesture. 'Come upstairs and have some iced tea and tell me what's wrong. I can spare a little time from the emporium, it almost runs itself now.'

'Things are going well then?' Craig said smiling down at her and Emily saw afresh how handsome her cousin was. Handsome and charming but not the man for her, or was he?

Emily had a quick word with Sarah who nodded willingly and hurried from the shop. Upstairs, with the windows of her rooms wide open, a cool breeze lifted the curtains and drifted refreshingly to where Emily stood.

'It's very pleasant here,' Craig said, waiting for her to be seated before taking a chair himself.

'Not as pleasant as Summer Lodge,' Emily said ruefully, 'but it comes a close second.'

Craig leaned forward. 'Come over there this evening, have supper with me and my mother, it's about time we began to act like cousins not enemies.'

'Why not?' Emily said avoiding his gaze, 'I'd like to see Aunt Sophie again, I'll have a cab bring me over about eight o'clock.'

Sarah bustled in with the tea tray and Craig sat back in his chair. 'Good, we'll talk then, I think it's better.'

He was looking tired, Emily thought, Craig was clearly troubled but he would talk to her, all in good time, and suddenly Emily felt glad about it, happy that she could once more be part of a family. He did not stay long and once he was gone Emily wondered if his supposed worry about his brother was simply a ploy to gain her attention, but then why should Craig bother? No, he must really have a problem he needed to talk about.

Emily looked forward to the evening with mixed feelings. She dressed with care and brushed out her dark chestnut hair until it shone. She wanted to look her best, prove to Craig that she was now in total control of her own destiny. And yet, there was a tinge of apprehension about her feelings, something must be very wrong for Craig to approach her for help.

Summer Lodge looked the same and yet different, the building was as mellow as ever outside but colourful drapes hung at the windows instead of the faded ones she had been used to.

'Come in, you are looking very beautiful,' Craig welcomed her, leading her to a chair near the fire. Aunt Sophie smiled a little frostily at her.

'It's a little chilly tonight, dear Emily, it was good of you to come out on such a night,' she said with forced brightness.

Craig moved to the sideboard. 'Would you like a glass of port, Emily?'

'Yes please.' Emily smiled. 'I feel quite strange being here in my old house again.' She took a seat and sipped the drink Craig had handed her. 'But I do realize that I was wrong to blame you for inheriting Summer Lodge, it was inevitable, really, I suppose.'

Emily glanced round her. 'It seems very quiet here, I can't hear any servants around. There used to be such a lot of activity in the kitchens when I lived here.'

'I haven't got the staff you had, Emily,' Craig said, 'I can't afford them. I only have an old couple who do a bit around the place for me. Supper is on a tray, I'm afraid, but I don't think we'll starve.'

Aunt Sophie sniffed disapprovingly, 'Keep up standards, I say, Craig, keep up standards.'

Emily held out her glass as Craig offered more wine. 'I took the servants for granted, I'm afraid,' she said, 'why didn't I wake up sooner to what was going on under my nose?'

'You were not told anything about the business, your father treated you like a child, it wasn't all your fault, Emily, so don't blame yourself,' Aunt Sophie said quickly. 'I still don't approve of you meddling in business affairs, child, that sort of thing should be left to the men of the family.'

Emily sat back in her chair, resisting the urge to remind her aunt that it was one of the men of the family who caused all the trouble.

'Tell me,' she leaned forward, 'what's the problem with Spencer, is he sick?'

Craig shook his head. 'If only it was that easy. No, he's what you might call unbalanced.'

'Don't say that!' Aunt Sophie said indignantly. 'Spencer has trouble with his nerves, that's all.'

Emily sat up straight, 'When did this . . . this nervous thing come on him?'

'It was after the fever,' Aunt Sophie interrupted, 'he never really recovered his strength, you see. I sent him to one of the aunts in the country and now she has written to say she can't cope with Spencer's moods any longer.'

'What about you, Aunt Sophie, can't you look after him?' Emily said.

'My mother is not happy about it, but she will have to take him at least for a time.' Craig spoke ruefully as his mother's mouth twisted into a grimace of distaste. 'If that doesn't work out, I have the choice of putting him in a hospital or hiring a nurse to look after him here. What would you suggest, Emily?'

Emily sighed. 'It's difficult, Craig, but if he's really sick perhaps a hospital would be the best thing all round.' She looked down at her hands. 'I'll do anything I can to help you, Craig.'

He leaned forward and touched her hand. 'I may take you up on that offer one day, Emily.'

They both picked at the supper of cold meat pie and pickles and though the freshly cut bread was crusty and fresh, Emily scarcely tasted it. Aunt Sophie on the other hand ate with relish, her worries about her youngest son seemingly forgotten.

Craig refilled her glass and Emily felt closer to him than she'd done for some time.

'Why haven't you married, Emily?' Craig spoke gently. 'You are a very beautiful and desirable young woman and haven't you got the Grenfell blood running in your veins? You'd be a wonderful catch for any man.'

Emily thought briefly of Miller who worked close to her and who was alarmingly attractive and smiled ruefully.

'If you'd asked me that before my father died I would have said I only wanted to be married to you, now . . .' she shrugged, her words trailing away.

'Don't talk about such things now,' Aunt Sophie said, 'we have more important considerations at the moment.' She rose to her feet.

'I wish to go to bed, I trust my room is ready and that the fire is well stocked with coal, I don't want to catch a chill.'

Emily rose, it was time for her to leave. 'I'll see you home,' Craig said with an impatient glance at his mother.

In the darkness of the carriage, Emily felt Craig's hand resting upon her own.

'Why not get married?' he said. 'Why don't we go ahead with the wedding as we always planned?'

'Craig, you don't mean it?' Emily said, 'I don't know what to say.'

'Why not?' Craig repeated. 'Are you in love with anyone else?'

'No,' Emily said but it wasn't strictly true, she could so easily fall in love with John Miller. But such a thing was out of the question, she couldn't even think of marrying a cobbler.

'I'm not sure,' she said, 'I suppose we could try to make a go of it. As you said, Craig, it would bring our families together again.'

The scent of Craig's soap-clean skin drifted towards her, Emily felt cocooned from reality in the close darkness of the carriage.

'This problem with Spencer,' Craig said softly, 'has made me realize we are all mortal. I want a son and heir, Emily, a child to inherit what I have built up with my own hands. You must want that, too?'

'Perhaps,' Emily said, 'and have you thought that if we amalgamated our assets we could become the biggest in the business this side of the Bristol Channel?'

Craig's fingers gripped hers. 'I think I would benefit more than you would from such a merger but yes, it would be a good move.'

Emily shrugged. 'You are doing very well now and though you have a little sideline going with Hari Morris's shop, I still feel that the two of us getting together is a commitment well worth making.' Emily paused, feeling a sense of excitement rising within her.

'What about Hari, would she agree to come in with us?' Emily wanted Hari's beautiful designs, wanted her skill.

'I'll ask her.' Craig paused. 'But at the moment she is very happy as she is, safe in a marriage with motherhood on the way. I never thought I'd see the day she'd forget about shoemaking.'

It took a few moments for his words to sink in. 'You mean Hari is expecting a child?' Emily said in surprise. Somehow the picture of Hari doing anything but working on her designs didn't seem to come readily to mind.

'Yes, Edward is over the moon about it, I think. Didn't you know?'

'How should I know?' Emily said, too absorbed in her own mixed emotions to hear the edge in Craig's voice.

'No-one has thought to mention it to me,' Emily continued.

'Well,' Craig said, 'Hari will want to go along with whatever I say and, in her broody frame of mind, I don't think she'll care much either way.'

Emily looked out of the window into the darkness lit only by the street lamps. So much had happened to her in the last hour, there was so much to take in that she suddenly wanted to be alone to think things out.

Emily alighted from the carriage with a sense of relief and, without looking back at Craig, moved into the shop. She felt as though she had been in another world, sitting there with Craig, in the darkness, his proposal of marriage had seemed to be only common sense. Now she wasn't so sure.

She hurried up the stairs and into her dressing-room and spent a long time, staring at herself in the mirror. Did she want to be married and did she want children? She wasn't sure what the answer was to any of those questions.

When Sarah entered the room, a little while later with a tray of hot drinks in her hands, Emily questioned her. 'Sarah, had you heard that Hari Morris is expecting?'

'Aye, I've heard and it seems she's not too well, mind, looking pretty peaky she was when I saw her in the market the other day.'

Emily longed suddenly to go to see Hari, she should be with her now, looking after her as Hari had nursed her when Emily was so ill. They had been such good friends then, perhaps Hari was the only real friend Emily had ever had and she missed that friendship.

Craig came to see her a few days later and, taking her in his arms, kissed Emily on the cheek and she had the oddest feeling that the gesture was forced.

'Want a drink?' she asked. 'There's some iced coffee in the jug or you could have a port.' She looked up at him, trying to imagine herself in his bed and blushed at the thought.

'Port please.' Craig took his drink and sat down, stretching his long legs out towards the fire.

'Have you spoken to Hari about our plans yet?' Emily asked seating herself opposite him.

'Forget about Hari, let's just talk about us.' Craig was frowning a little.

'All right,' Emily said. 'Then talk about us, we can discuss business later.'

'We would be good for each other, Emily,' Craig said leaning forward, shoulders hunched, 'we are alike, both from the same background, it will be a very suitable marriage.'

Emily noticed that Craig spoke as though he needed to persuade her or was it himself he was trying to convince?

But he was right, it would be a good union and then there was the business aspect of their relationship. Emily was ambitious, she wanted more than success and financial stability, she wanted to vindicate the Grenfell name once and for all and together she and Craig could do that.

'We will make a success of it all, won't we, Craig?'

'Of course,' he said cheerfully, 'we'll have the finest alliance in all of Wales.'

Hari let the sewing slip on to her lap, the tiny garment was finely stitched and was almost finished, it was a frothy white Christening gown. Her slim figure barely showed the signs of her pregnancy; except for the slight thickening of her waist, she hardly appeared any different.

Edward entered the room, the *Cambrian* in his hand. 'I've got news for you,' he said slowly, 'Craig and Emily are to be married in the autumn.'

Hari felt a sense of shock sweep through her, her hands trembled and she clasped them together quickly.

'Well, I can't say I'm surprised,' she said, 'the gossips have been at it for weeks, talking about them being together so much, speculating on a romance at last between the beautiful and rich Grenfells.'

'I would have thought Craig might have told me himself instead of allowing me to read the news in the paper.' Edward seated himself in a chair and shook out the folds of the *Cambrian*.

'I expect he'll get round to it,' Hari said, her mouth dry, 'you are sure to be his groomsman just as he was yours.'

'Do you think so?' Edward smiled. 'I suppose you're right, Craig will be round any day now to have a chat with me.'

Hari looked down at her sewing, she knew it had to come, she'd known that one day Craig would settle down and wasn't it natural he should choose Emily? They had been betrothed since childhood and, in spite of the difficulties between them, they must still love each other.

And yet it hurt to know that, once and for all, Craig would be lost to her. But that was absurd, he had been lost to her the minute Edward had slipped a ring on to her finger. What did she think was going to happen, that Craig would remain alone for the rest of his days?

Edward began to cough and Hari rose to her feet quickly. 'I'll bring you some elixir,' she said, 'it will sooth your throat, lovely.'

'I'm all right, you fuss too much over my health, my girl, when you should be looking after your own.'

'I'm as strong as a horse,' Hari protested, 'having a baby isn't like being sick, mind.'

'No, but the doctor told you not to take any risks, didn't he? So don't go rushing about like that, it's not good for you.'

Hari was resting in the garden when Craig finally did come to talk to Edward. She heard his voice and kept her eyes closed, drinking in the sound of him, anticipating the moment when she would open her eyes and see him.

What thoughts for a married woman to be harbouring, she should be ashamed of herself. And yet when she opened her eyes, she felt her nerves were suddenly on edge at the look of him, tall and strong in the sunlight, his eyes unreadable as they rested on her. He nodded.

'Keeping well, Hari?' His tone was casual. 'I've come to tell you my news, I'm getting married.'

He sat beside her and leaned forward. 'Emily is asking humbly if she may come to see you, she would like you to be at the wedding, it would make her very happy.'

'Come on, love,' Edward said, 'don't bear a grudge, not now when we all should be very happy.'

'Yes, of course I'll be at the wedding, I'll be there at Edward's side where I belong.' Hari was aware that she must sound unbearably stuffy but she didn't know what to say to the unexpected gesture of peace from Emily.

'I'll tell her,' Craig said softly. 'Thank you, Hari, you always were the fairest-minded person I know.'

What an impersonal remark when Hari longed to hear him say that he would always love her, whatever happened in their lives, he would never forget the one night they had spent together.

He seemed about to say more, then he rose abruptly to

266

his feet. He stared down at her for a long moment in silence.

'Are you happy?' The words were softly spoken so that Edward having moved to the doorway of the house couldn't hear.

Her eyes met his for a brief instant and she knew she failed to hide her emotions from him.

'I'm . . . as content as I could be.' Without you, she added silently.

'I see.' He moved away from her then and she had no idea what he was thinking, he was an enigma, a man of whom she would never know the depths.

Restlessly, she rose and moved into the house, she would go to the workshop, see how the men were getting on with the production of the shoes. Strange, Craig had not mentioned the business at all.

Edward was very much against her leaving the house. 'I don't think you should be thinking of work, not just now,' he said catching her hand in concern. 'Leave everything to Craig, just until the baby is born and then you can go back to your precious work if you so wish.'

Hari smiled. 'You would wrap me in cotton wool if you could, my lovely, well, I won't have it, I'm not sick I tell you, I'm having a baby.'

He rested his hand on her stomach. 'I know, and I'm so proud and happy, sometimes I'm afraid of being so happy.'

Hari shivered. 'Don't talk like that, Eddie!' she said, putting her arms around him. 'Don't tempt fate, it's not right. You're feeling all right, are you? Your chest isn't playing you up again?'

'Oh, go on to your workshop and stop fussing,' Edward said gently, 'forget I spoke.'

Hari tried to shake off the uneasy feeling Edward's words had aroused in her, but even though the sun shone and the trees were full of leaf and trembling in the warm breeze, she felt chilled.

William greeted her with a lighting of his eyes that made Hari want to hug him. 'How's the work coming along?' Hari asked moving into the workroom, breathing in the familiar scent of leather hungrily.

Lewis was working at his last, tapping a pair of working boots but of Ben there was no sign. Hari turned to Will questioningly.

'Ben's just gone to take some boots to his Uncle Cleg the Coal, urgent order it was and, as Cleg's a good customer, Ben took them over himself.'

'That's good, you did right, Will, we must look after the old customers, we may need them again some time.'

'Not according to Mr Grenfell,' Will said glumly, 'he keeps telling me it's a waste of time, small fry will never bring in a big catch, so he says.'

'Well, there's such a thing as the good will of the customer and Craig Grenfell would do well to remember that,' Hari said sharply.

She would have to talk to Craig, he really was taking on too much responsibility, he seemed to think that because she was expecting a child she had suddenly lost all her intelligence.

She suddenly felt nostalgic for the old days when she worked in her father's shop at the side of the house in World's End, when life was uncomplicated by mixed emotions and when her job was simply to make and mend boots and shoes.

Ben entered the shop at a run, his hair flying back from his face, his eyes ablaze. 'Know what I just heard from Cleg the Coal of all people?' he demanded. 'That bastard Grenfell is throwing in his lot with Emily Grenfell, selling us out to feather his own nest!'

He stopped short when he saw Hari and clasped his

hand to his mouth. 'Sorry for the language,' he said, his face ruddy with embarrassment, 'didn't know you were here.'

'Sit down Ben and tell us calmly what you've heard.' Hari tried desperately to remain calm herself, her blood was racing, her mind spinning with questions.

'Where did Cleg get this idea from?' she asked trying to compose her thoughts.

'Delivering coal to Miss Grenfell, he was, and the two of them was in the garden talking, the Grenfells thick as thieves discussing our shop and said they were going to go in together, Cleg heard them with his own ears. Didn't think he was telling no tales, thought I'd know all about it.' Ben paused. 'Did *you* know anything, Hari?'

Hari sank into a chair and sighed heavily. 'No, Ben, I had no idea this was going on.' She was suddenly coldly angry. How dare Craig come to her house, asking her to be friends with Emily when all the time the both of them were plotting to take her business away from her?

'Call me a cab, Will,' she said at last, 'I'll sort this out for myself.'

Will hurried out into the street, his young face pale, his mouth set in a line of anger and Hari knew with a sense of warmth that she had more than one ally in what would be a fight between her and Craig and Emily Grenfell.

The shop in Wind Street was filled with people and Hari stood for a moment and stared around her. As her eyes became accustomed to the gloom, she saw that there were lots of shelves, all of them groaning with boots and shoes imported from Somerset. Good stock, no doubt about that, but where was the flair, the individuality of her own stock?

Sarah came and stood before her. 'Can I help you?' she asked and there was something arrogant about the tilt of the girl's head.

'Excuse me.' Hari walked past her and began to mount the stairs, Sarah hurried after her and caught her arm.

'You can't go up there, you haven't got the right, not any more, this is Miss Emily's shop now, nothing to do with you.'

Hari stared at her coldly. 'Take your hands off me.' Her tone was low and dangerous and Sarah, taken aback, released her.

Emily was sitting at the table and standing near her was Craig. Both looked at her in surprise and Emily smiled tentatively imagining she had come in friendship. Hari soon dispelled that idea.

'You Grenfells will stop at nothing, will you?' she said. 'You cheat and lie and even thieve to get what you want.'

Emily half lifted her hand. 'Hari, what's wrong?' She looked at her appealingly, 'Sit down, won't you, let's talk calmly, have some tea.'

Hari turned to Craig. 'Is it true that you are planning to merge our business with Emily's?' she said staring at him, her eyes hard with anger.

Craig took a deep breath. 'It didn't seem the right time to talk to you about it just now, but it makes sense, Hari, you must see that?'

'In what way?' Hari said. 'We'd be swallowed up, we'd become little more than a cobbling service, do you think that's what I want?'

'I thought you wanted marriage and motherhood.' Craig sounded angry now. 'I asked you earlier and you said you were content.'

'How dare you decide from that what I felt about the business?' Hari's voice trembled. 'I was referring to my marriage then, not to work.'

She turned away. 'Well, now I know where I stand, I will fight you both to the last, I'm not going to let my skill and flair be sold out under my nose this way.'

'Hari,' Emily said pleadingly, 'I thought you'd agreed to all this, I was so happy thinking we'd be working together again. I don't want you to lose your skill, I want you to use it to make us a bigger and better company.'

Hari looked at her directly then. 'Do you expect me to believe that?' She shook her head, 'You Grenfells don't know when you are telling the truth any more. You may believe your own lies, Emily, but don't expect me to be so gullible again. I trusted you once and that was once too often.'

She left the shop and she was trembling with anger, she didn't see the green leaves above her or feel the sun on her skin, she just felt blind hatred for the two people in her life whom she had loved and who had once again betrayed her.

After Hari had gone, Emily stared at Craig in silence waiting for his explanation. He sank down into a chair, his long legs spread out before him.

'Well?' Emily said, 'Aren't you going to say anything?' She paced the room unable to forget the look in Hari's face. 'I thought you had won her complete support for this venture of ours, I didn't dream you hadn't even told Hari about any of it before you made your plans.'

'I thought she no longer cared about anything but domesticity,' Craig replied impatiently. 'She's scarcely bothered with the business since she's known she's going to have a child.'

'Having a child is bound to be a slight distraction.' Emily's sarcasm was plain to hear in her voice. 'Don't you give anyone the benefit of having feelings?'

'Feelings?' Craig echoed. 'I don't think you know the meaning of the word and you have the gall to throw accusations at me!'

Emily sank down into a chair and stared at him. 'We've

made a terrible mistake and I can't marry you and I can't throw back your ring because you haven't bought me one.'

Craig stared at her. 'You mean the marriage is off because of one small disagreement. Was it only the business you wanted then?'

'Perhaps,' Emily said, 'I knew that I could make a financial success on my own but I wanted more, I wanted the Grenfell name to be synonymous with original products, with the finest designs, I wanted our name to be famous and Hari could have helped me realize that.'

Craig frowned, 'You would have married me for all the wrong reasons then?'

'I suppose so,' Emily said slowly. 'And why were you marrying me, was it love or an overriding passion?' She smiled bleakly. 'I hardly think so. You are obviously in love with Hari.'

Craig rose from his chair in a swift movement. 'The business venture was a good idea even if the marriage was not.' He smiled bleakly, 'Our romance didn't last long, did it?'

He looked her directly in the eye. 'I think you are right, I am in love with Hari, but a fat lot of good that knowledge will do me now.' He thrust his hands into his pockets.

'I still think the business venture could work, I can persuade Hari that it's in her best interest to throw in her lot with us, together we will achieve such a great deal that apart would not be possible.'

Emily shook her head. 'You don't know Hari at all, do you? And you don't know me, either. I'll make it alone, Craig, from now on I'll live my own life as I want to live it not as I think other people would have me live it.' She rose to face him.

'Now if you'll forgive me, I have work to do.'

She watched as Craig strode down the street and, for a moment, she longed to call him back. What was she doing destroying her chances of respectability in this way?

Emily felt suddenly weary and alone, would she always be doomed to be alone, a woman with no man in her life? Emily was suddenly angry, angry with Hari, with Craig, but most of all with herself.

Damn respectability and damn common sense! She would put her words into actions and live her life just as *she* wished to live it and to hell with convention.

21

Hari sat in the tiny dressing-room of the theatre in Goat Street exchanging gossip with her old friend Meg. Charles, with his usual robust way of talking, intervened spasmodically to add a comment of his own. Now and then, he and Meg exchanged glances and they seemed so happy to be together again that Hari suspected there was a good deal more than friendship between them.

'So you are going to be a mummy then.' Meg sat back in her chair, her make-up completed, and stared at Hari in fascination. 'You don't look fat and ugly, you are not at all as I imagined an expectant lady to look.'

Hari laughed, 'I suppose that's to come! I'm feeling absolutely wonderful but Edward insists I'm an invalid which of course I'm not and wants me to do nothing but rest.'

'Take it easy while you can, my love,' Meg said smiling. 'I wish I had the chance.'

'Would you really like to give up work, Meg?' Charles asked and Meg smiled at him.

'I'm quickly coming to the stage when I want to put down roots, stay in one place instead of traipsing all over the country.'

Hari sighed. 'I'm one of those people who love working,' she said smiling, 'there's daft, aren't I?'

'Work, that reminds me,' Meg said quickly, 'I've got some orders for you.' She delved into a large bag and rummaged for a moment before drawing out a crumpled sheet of paper. 'Special shoes for the business, golden slippers and fancy leather boots, can you do it?'

'I'll be only too glad to oblige.' Hari didn't wish to enter into discussions about her business, the pain of knowing that Craig and Emily were double dealing was still raw. 'Have you got the patterns for the size?'

Meg laughed. 'I've got some more papers somewhere, there!' Triumphantly she produced the patterns and then carelessly dropping them into Hari's lap, peered into the mirror, tapped her fluffy hair and tucked a stray curl into place.

'Well, my love, I won't offer to make any tiny garments, that's not my sort of thing but when the infant comes along, I bags being godmother.'

'There's a good idea,' Hari said, 'and you, Charlie, will you be godfather?'

'My dear Angharad, I would be delighted to attend the child's christening and will do the honours to the best of my ability.' Charles smiled broadly, 'But are you sure I am a suitable candidate for such a responsible task? I am not exactly known for my religious fervour, you know.'

'I want you to be godfather and so will Edward, you will be reliable and caring, that's what counts.'

Hari rose to her feet and tucking the patterns securely into her bag, she felt a sudden surge of excitement, she longed to get started on the slippers and a design for the boots was already tugging at her mind. In spite of the way her life had been taken over by her pregnancy, Hari still burned with ambition to make the finest shoes in the land.

She took a cab to her premises in the High Street, clutching her hands together in a fever of impatience. She had spoken to the landlord and had taken over the rental of the building on her own behalf, Craig could do as he pleased but from now on the name of Grenfell would be erased from the business records.

Her workers were loyal to her and they remained busy in the shop expecting her to keep them supplied with work. And she couldn't, wouldn't, let them down.

Hari took the patterns into the workshop and as the men looked up at her she smiled.

'Some orders from the theatre folk, the first orders I've had for some time and I'm hoping for many more.'

'There's plenty of work still coming in from England,' Will said. 'What shall we do about it?'

Hari considered for a moment. 'Send the orders on to Mr Grenfell, I'm sure that's what he would want.'

'But that will leave us without much work, mind.' Will sounded anxious. 'And the English customers expect shoes designed by Hari Morris.'

'You are a sensible young man,' Hari said sighing, 'and perhaps you're right.' She sank on to a stool and stared absently at the pieces of leather on the long table. 'I suppose I'd better sort all this out with Mr Grenfell one way or another.'

She smiled. 'Perhaps, Will, you'll go over to the emporium in Wind Street, I expect you will find Mr Grenfell there, ask him what he wants to do about the work coming in from England.' She put her hand on Will's arm, 'You know as much about the business as I do, you may be able to get the answers we need.'

'I'll do my best.' Will took off his leather apron and shrugged himself into a jacket. He looked so grown up, so earnest and worried that Hari resisted the urge to kiss him, knowing he would be mortified at such a gesture in front of the other men.

She watched from the door as he strode along the pavement, Will was growing up, soon he would be a man. With a sigh, Hari closed the door and returned to the workshop.

Will paused outside the emporium and watched the constant flow of people who entered through the double doors. It was clear that trade was brisk and, now that Mr Grenfell had thrown in his lot with Emily, how could the venture fail?

He moved to the back of the premises and saw Sarah Miller, her sleeves rolled up above dimpled elbows, carrying a dustpan and a brush.

'*Bore da*,' he said cheekily and Sarah turning smiled warmly.

'Will, why haven't you been over our house lately, me and dad look forward to seeing you on a Sunday dinner time.'

'Didn't know what sort of greeting I'd get after the last time when you slapped my face,' Will said ruefully.

Sarah came and stood closer to him. 'Well, I've thought things over now, mind, and although you're a bit younger than me, I don't think that really matters. I've missed you, Will.'

He made a move towards her but she stepped back. 'Careful, boyo, my dad is around here most of the time, now, don't forget.'

Will smiled. 'Aye, I know, good cobbler is your dad, but he'll never match Hari.'

Sarah pouted. 'You and your Hari, I sometimes think you're in love with her!'

'Don't be daft.' Will's voice was soft, 'Hari's like my sister, I'd die for her but it's you I want as my girl, Sarah.'

'Well, you haven't shown it lately.' Sarah glanced round quickly and wound her arms around Will's neck. 'You've grown so handsome and to think when I first saw you I thought you was only a boy.'

Will kissed her holding her close but after a moment,

she drew away. 'I'll see you afterwards, I'll say I'm going out for a walk, be down at Victoria Park, right love?'

'Wait,' Will called as she would have returned to the shop, 'is Mr Grenfell here, I've got to speak to him.'

Sarah pouted again. 'Oh, so you didn't come special to see me then?'

'Course I did,' Will smiled. 'Why do you think I offered to do the errand, it was because I wanted an excuse to speak to you, that's why I came around the back instead of going through the shop.'

Sarah was mollified. 'All right then, I'll believe you.' She stared at him. 'But you won't find Mr Grenfell here, no chance of that! The Grenfells have quarrelled, not speaking again, they're like kids mind, all lovey dovey one minute, then enemies the next.'

'What have they quarrelled about?' Will asked curiously and Sarah leaned towards him.

'From what I could hear, Miss Emily thought Mr Grenfell had spoken to Hari Morris about going into business with them.' She shrugged. 'Of course he hadn't done any such thing, Hari knew nothing about it, right?'

Will frowned non-committally. 'Could be, what else was said?'

'Emily was not best pleased, felt cheated I 'spect 'cos she needed Hari's skill more than she ever needed Mr Grenfell's influence.' Sarah sniffed. 'Miss Emily got no time for Mr Grenfell for all that he's rich, she's in love with my dad, any fool can see that. But there you are, she thinks he's beneath her so she tried to get out of harm's way and marry Mr Grenfell.' Sarah smiled in satisfaction, 'It didn't work, did it? Daft I call it.'

Will was sceptical, from what he knew of the rich and powerful they didn't fall in love with their workers. But then Sarah was an impressionable girl, fond though he was of her and younger than her by a year he may be, he was still much more mature than her.

'Well, this needs thinking about,' Will said, slowly. He was sure that Hari would have nothing more to do with Mr Craig Grenfell but there was still the matter of the latest orders to be sorted out.

'There's nothing for it, I'll have to go up to Summer Lodge and look for Mr Grenfell.' He smiled suddenly, 'But don't forget our meeting in the park, will you?'

'Go away with you!' Sarah said coyly. 'As if I'd forget and why are you suddenly talking all nice like a toff?'

'Well, I intend to be a toff one day,' Will said in all seriousness.

He made his way rapidly uphill towards Summer Lodge knowing that if he couldn't find Mr Grenfell there, he was in trouble. Craig Grenfell was away a great deal on business, which was one reason for the tremendous variety of orders he had brought Hari over the past months and, if he was away, there would be no decision on the orders waiting attention in Hari's workshop.

The maid opened the door of the big house and stared down at Will with open curiosity. He was smartly dressed in a fresh white shirt and a good suit and yet a quick look at his leather-stained hands shouted aloud the fact that he was a working man.

'Is Mr Grenfell at home?' Will asked politely and the maid had him pegged at once by his voice.

'Yes, but tradesmen go to the back door,' she said snootily.

'It's all right.' Craig stood in the hallway, a drink in his hand, his collar casually open at the broadness of his throat and Will could see why all the women fell in love with this man. Still, toff he might be and handsome with it, but Craig Grenfell would never be good enough to lick Hari's shoes.

'It's about the last batch of orders.' Will stepped into

the hallway. 'Mrs Morris is not sure what you want to do with them.'

Craig led the way into the huge drawing-room that shone with sunlight and smelled of beeswax.

'Do?' Craig's eyebrows rose. 'I assume she will honour the contract made with these customers.'

Will felt his hackles rise. 'Mrs Morris is so honourable that she thinks you might want to take the orders for yourself,' he said acidly.

Craig inclined his head. 'I see and I apologize.' He moved to the table and poured himself a drink. He glanced at Will and smiled.

'Like one?' he asked and Will realized the gesture was one of conciliation but he knew his place and shook his head.

Craig sank into a chair. 'You may tell Mrs Morris that I shall be pleased if she will make the boots and shoes as arranged and in the future I will ensure that any customers who wish to do so will get in touch with her direct.'

Will felt elated, that meant they would still have business coming in from all parts of the country, Hari's business was safe.

'Thank you, Mr Grenfell,' he said feeling more kindly disposed towards the man. 'I'll go back and tell Hari, Mrs Morris, at once.'

'You are a bright young man, Will,' Craig said thoughtfully, 'you really should be educated properly, then you would be a real asset to Hari.'

'I can read and write well enough,' Will said huffily, 'and I can count and do sums.'

Craig smiled. 'I realize that but, if you wish, come up here to see me on the weekends and I will teach you how to do bookkeeping and make proper accounts.'

The thought of this fount of extra knowledge was irresistible to Will, but he would do nothing behind Hari's back.

'Do you mind if I let you know?' he asked, aware that his voice was stiff.

Craig inclined his head and moved once more to the side table and, from the dismissive set of the man's shoulders, Will knew that the interview was at an end.

He felt almost triumphant as he made his way back to town. The familiar sights of the streets, the open-fronted fish stalls and the crowded windows of the grocery stores were lost on him as he envisaged a future which included reading informative books, adding up columns of figures as he'd often seen Hari do and learning something new excited him.

Hari was alone and just finishing off a pair of slippers when he returned to the workshop in the High Street. She sewed on the last bead and then sat back and stared at him, her eyes shrewd.

'Well, what have you got to tell me, Will? Are we to make up the orders or does Craig want them for himself and Emily?'

'It's all off there, Hari, they've had a fight, no marriage, no business. We can fill the orders and Mr Grenfell is telling the customers to get in touch with you instead of him.'

'Is that right?' If Hari was surprised by the revelation, she didn't show it. 'And?'

Will smiled. 'I can't hide anything from you, can I?' He sat down on the bench beside her.

'Mr Grenfell is willing to teach me, bookkeeping, all sorts of things.'

'What do you feel about it?' Hari asked and Will sighed heavily.

'I could wish for nothing better but I wouldn't agree until I'd spoken to you, if you don't want me to have anything to do with him, then I'll say no.'

'That's my boy!' Hari squeezed his arm. 'But I want you

to say yes.' She rose and placed her hands on her back and straightened slowly.

'Why?' Will asked, excitement flaring through him.

'Because I know Craig has a lot to offer you and you would be foolish to turn it down. Knowledge is very precious, Will, and you are young enough to make full use of any you can get.'

'I'm glad you think that because I didn't want to be disloyal to you.'

'You couldn't be disloyal if you tried. Now, Will, we'll pack up for today, I think I've worked long enough, the men went off home an hour ago.'

Will was concerned by Hari's pallor. 'Sit by there, Hari,' he said quickly, 'you're not walking back to Chapel Street, I'm calling a cab.'

As he sat beside Hari in the cab, staring unseeingly into the now-darkening streets, Will felt exhilarated, full of hope and ambition for the future. With Mr Craig Grenfell's help, he would turn into a knowledgeable gentleman and then there would be no stopping him.

Hari was glad to get indoors and to make her way to the small sitting-room of the house in Chapel Street and just sink into a chair.

Edward entered the room and smiled down at her. 'You are looking pale, my girl, working too hard will do you no good, not now that you are going to be a mother.'

'I know.' She took his hand and held it against her cheek. 'But at least I've had some good news today, the orders Craig got for us, he's letting us keep them.' She drew him down beside her.

'It seems Craig and Emily won't be getting married after all,' she continued, 'it's off and so is the business merger.'

Edward regarded her silently for a moment. 'Does that mean he'll want to be involved in your business now?'

Hari shook her head emphatically. 'No! There is not a chance of that, I wouldn't have it.'

Edward sighed. 'I'm very glad of that, it always made me vaguely uneasy to have Craig around here too much.'

'He did make a very kind suggestion,' Hari said quickly, not wanting to consider the implications of Edward's remark too closely. 'He says he will teach Will some lessons and I've advised Will to take up the offer.'

'I could have done that,' Edward said at once. 'True I didn't attend such an illustrious college as Craig but I'm reasonably well educated.'

'Of course,' Hari said quickly, 'but you'll have enough to do with our own child.'

Edward's face softened. 'Of course I will, how stupid of me.' He leaned over and kissed Hari's cheek. 'I still can't believe it, not even with the visible signs that you are at last putting on weight.'

Hari was grateful for one thing, that Edward had moved into the spare room, he took her condition very seriously and feared his passions would run away with his sense of responsibility, he had no desire to endanger their child.

'Coming up to bed?' Edward said gently. 'I'm feeling a little tired and you must be too.'

'In a minute,' Hari said softly, 'I just want a bit of supper and then a few moments to relax, otherwise I won't be able to sleep.'

'Oh, my dear, you haven't eaten!' Edward was all concern. 'I will go to the kitchen myself and bring you something.'

'No need,' Hari said firmly, 'the maid will see to it, you go off to bed, I won't have you falling sick again.'

A small supper on a tray was all she required and then Hari, unable to resist it, took out her sketch-pad and began to draw. Her fingers were quick, her tiredness vanished and she covered the pages with intricately detailed designs.

It was late when, at last, she put down her pen. She yawned and moved quietly up the stairs, careful not to wake Edward.

She looked into his room that was washed by moonlight and she could hear his soft, regular breathing. She moved forward and stood looking down at her husband, loving him and yet not in the way a woman loved a man. But she knew her duty and she would do her utmost to be a good wife.

In the morning, Hari woke to the feeling of pain in her lower abdomen. Panic stricken, she called out for Edward.

He was there in an instant, the collar hanging from his shirt, a stud in his hand.

'What is it, Hari?' he asked anxiously, his face pale. She tried not to tremble as she pushed herself up from the pillows.

'Send for Doctor Webber, I think there's something wrong.'

The minutes seemed like hours as Hari waited for the doctor to arrive, she knew instinctively that she was in danger of miscarrying her child and that was something that must not be allowed to happen.

At last, she heard the sound of measured footsteps on the stairs and then the doctor was in the room, his reassuring smile having the effect of calming her at once.

'Let's see what we have here then, shall we?' He examined her carefully and taking his time over the diagnosis, he at last stepped back from the bed and moved over to the wash-stand.

'I think you are all right,' he said, 'this time, but I must insist that you give up your work at least for the time being.' He returned to the bed and sat down. 'One good thing, I believe your pregnancy is more advanced than I first thought so the danger is somewhat lessened. I'll leave it to you to discuss that with your husband.'

'Why is it better that my pregnancy is more advanced?' Hari asked anxiously and the doctor smiled.

'It is in the first three months that most miscarriages occur.'

Hari felt dizzy with relief. 'I'll keep the baby?' she asked, her voice tremulous.

'Yes, if you do as you are told,' he said sternly. 'And that means leaving shoemaking to your men, keep out of the workshop, that's my advice, benches of the sort cobblers use are not conducive to the comfort of expectant mothers.'

'I promise I shan't do any work at all,' Hari said, 'except perhaps for a little drawing, that won't harm surely?'

'No, so long as you don't try to put these drawings into practice,' Doctor Webber said firmly. 'Just drawing would be beneficial, a nice ladylike occupation, just so long as you sit comfortably in your chair and don't spend too much time at your board.'

He rose. 'Rest now for a few days at least, don't move from your bed unless you have to and then, perhaps a little walking in the park, a gentle stroll in the fresh air with your husband, but no business worries and that's an order.'

When the doctor had gone, Hari sank back against the pillows sighing with relief. She would miss her work of course and she would need to deputize the finer tasks to one of the men.

Hari bit her lip, Ben was not practised enough for delicate tooling and Lewis, though a fine solid craftsman, had the large strong fingers of a bootmaker. It would have to be Will, he must be the one to do all the finer skilled sewing, it would be a challenge for him and one she felt he would accept gladly.

As if sensing her thoughts, Will appeared in the doorway, his face anxious.

'Come in, Will,' Hari said, 'I'm all right, I promise you.'

He stood awkwardly at the bedside, a handsome young man with his future before him. His jaw had strengthened and his eyes were steady and honest.

'I'm going to have to rely very heavily on you for the next few months, Will,' Hari said holding out her hand.

'I'm willing to do anything I can,' he said quickly, 'I should have made you pack in work sooner, I blame myself for this.'

'Nonsense!' Hari said quickly. 'There's no-one to blame. In any case I'm going to be all right so there's nothing to worry about.'

'Well, you know I'll work hard, Hari,' Will said earnestly, 'I'll work night and day if it will keep the orders going out.'

'What I want you to do, Will,' Hari said, 'is to take over my job. You will do the fine tooling, the stitching on the ladies' slippers and the making up of the flower motifs when required.'

Will nodded. 'I won't be as good as you but I'll do my very best, you can depend on it.'

'I do,' Hari said. She heard footsteps running up the stairs and nodded for Will to leave. He smiled and left the room just as Edward came puffing in through the door.

'I've just shown the doctor out, it's good news then, Hari, the baby is going to be all right.'

'Yes, of course,' Hari said, 'the baby will be just fine. Sit down, Edward, you're out of breath, you'll do yourself harm if you run upstairs like that.'

'I was so worried about you, Hari,' Edward said softly. 'If I lost you and the baby I wouldn't want to live.'

Hari took both his hands and held them tight. 'Well, you won't lose us, so stop worrying. Now, how about a nice cup of tea? I could certainly use one.'

Hari sank back against the pillows, listening contentedly to the soft sounds of the house around her. From the kitchen she could hear the clink of cups against saucers and then the sound of the coals being moved in the grate.

A band of sunlight spread warm fingers into the room and the light fell across the bed, illuminating the flowers in the satin sheet. Soon it would be high summer, the fruits would ripen on the branches of the trees and blackberries would grow in hedgerows.

With the coming of the harvest, her child would almost certainly be born, a fine son or daughter to bring Edward and she close together.

Suddenly, Hari sat bolt upright in bed, her mouth dry. The doctor had said the pregnancy was more advanced than he had first thought, he had made the cryptic remark that he would leave it to her to tell her husband. Which all meant that the baby had been conceived before the marriage had taken place.

Hari covered her face with her hands as the full import of the situation swamped her. It was not as the doctor believed a case of an over-zealous bride and groom anticipating the marriage night, it was far worse than that.

Hari felt tears hot and bitter burn against her lids, she pressed fingers against her eyes in an agony of guilt, how would she explain that, if the doctor was right, the baby she was carrying was not her husband's but Craig's? She rubbed at her eyes, and how could she explain tears at a time like this when she should be so happy?

'Forgive me, Edward,' she whispered into her hands. But how could he ever forgive her if she were to tell him the child he so longed for was the result of her one night of love with Craig Grenfell? Hari sank back against the pillows and closed her eyes and suddenly the world seemed a very dark place.

22

The beach curved crescent-like for five miles ending in the promontory of rocks called Mumbles Head. The sea washed gently inward, splashed red and gold with the dying of the sun.

Emily sat on the sand, skirts drawn decorously over her ankles as she stared out to where long ships lay against the horizon. She had never felt more lonely in her life.

Her business was flourishing, there was no doubt about that, the boots and shoes brought from Somerset were much in demand and if the small sideline in cobbling was slow, that didn't really matter. She was an established businesswoman now whether the men of the town liked it or not. She had paid off her father's debts and could hold her head high, and yet there was no-one with whom she could share her triumph and so it seemed an empty thing.

For a brief interlude, she had believed that she and Craig might make a good marriage, but that had been an illusion, a silly dream. Her face was suddenly suffused with angry colour as she remembered their quarrel, Craig was a fine one to lecture her on her lack of feeling when he seemed to charge ahead without consulting anyone.

She and Craig were incompatible, they simply rubbed each other up the wrong way, his lack of concern for Hari's stake in the business had emphasized that.

'Good evening, Miss Grenfell.' The voice was deep and

melodious and entirely respectful. Emily looked up swiftly, her emotions mixed as she saw John Miller standing above her.

'Good evening, John.' Her voice was steady but she was struggling for control because suddenly her heart was pounding. 'I'm admiring the scenery, why not join me?'

He sat beside her, his long legs stretched out before him and Emily could see that he felt uneasy at what he saw as his over-familiarity.

She did her best to put him at ease. 'You are doing a good job, John,' she said, 'trade in the workshop is improving.'

'Aye, I'm all right on good stout riding boots,' John said slowly, 'but when it comes to ladies' slippers then I'm out of my depth.'

There was a long silence and Emily waited for John to continue, he had something on his mind and knowing him, he would not rest until he had spoken his piece.

'I was thinking,' he began, 'much as I like working for you, I'd be better off at my own shop up in Morriston.' When Emily didn't reply, he continued.

'I don't like being beholden, not to you especially, not now.' She turned and met his eyes and read not for the first time the love in them. It was like a balm, she drank in his regard greedily, not willing to let him go.

'Please, John, don't leave me,' she said softly. 'I need you.'

'You don't need me, Miss Emily, you are a very successful woman.'

'But I do! I need a man I can trust to advise me, to look out for me. I'm only a woman after all and sometimes I feel very vulnerable, especially at times like this when it's Sarah's night off, I feel so alone in that great building.'

John appeared nonplussed. 'I don't know what you want of me, Miss Emily,' he said almost angrily. 'I'm not your sort, I'm an ordinary working man but at least when I'm running my own shop, small though it might be, I'm my own boss.'

Emily sighed. 'I don't really know what I am asking of you, John, but please stay on in the job just a little longer, your son is running your shop well enough, isn't he? Just give me a few more weeks, that isn't asking too much, is it, John?'

He was silent for a long moment, staring out to sea, his face stern and unreadable. Then he turned and smiled and Emily knew she had won.

'Just a few more weeks, then,' he said indulgently, 'I suppose I can manage that.'

On an impulse, she put her hand on his and, for a moment, he clasped her hand warmly. He remained looking at her for some minutes and it was as if he would have said more, but then he rose to his feet and touched his hat to her and was striding away, kicking up a fine dust of sand behind him.

Emily sighed, what a pity there was a barrier between John and herself, he would have made her a fine husband. She hugged her knees and thought of the eligible men she could so easily come in contact with, if she so chose.

Of course, she was suspect being a businesswoman and therefore not quite a lady in the eyes of the town's élite circles and it was a long time since she had been invited to any of the ladies' at homes. But then she had been so busy that she had never replied to the calling cards that at first had been left at her home.

And lately there had been no calling cards, no invitations to fashionable balls, nothing but grinding loneliness.

When her very existence had been threatened, Emily had not cared about polite society, she went out and did business the way that any man would and now that she was wealthy and successful she wondered if it had all been worth it.

She rose and shook the sand from her skirts, not the crinoline worn by her peers but a smart, no-nonsense plain skirt with a formal matching jacket. She was even beginning to dress differently from all the other society ladies she realized ruefully. And she *was* different, there was no getting away from it. Spending time at afternoon teas would probably bore her to tears.

She made her way back along the shoreline towards Wind Street and saw that lights were being lit in the windows of houses along the bay. A lone horse and cart rumbled past and the streets seemed empty and deserted. She looked round nervously, with the sudden feeling that she was being followed.

Emily was glad when at last she reached the shop. She let herself inside the long dark room and stood for a moment drinking in the silence. It was Sarah's day off and she would spend the night with her father and brother in Morriston, so Emily would be alone.

Suddenly there was a scratching at the door. Emily moved back into the shadows and saw outlined against the glass the figures of two burly men, it seemed they were trying to gain entry.

For a moment, she was rooted to the spot, she didn't know whether she should turn and run upstairs to her own quarters and lock the doors or if she should stand and challenge whoever it was outside.

Then the door swung open and the men were inside the shop. Both of them stopped short on seeing her, obviously surprised.

'What are you doing here?' she demanded and the men paused but only for a fraction. One of them moved quickly and she was caught in an iron grip.

'Where is the money?' A hoarse voice said in her ear, 'No need for rough stuff if you are sensible, woman.'

Suddenly incensed, Emily lashed out with her foot

catching one of the men a blow to his shin. He let out a cry and then his hand whipped across her face and she fell to the floor in a heap.

He was upon her then, pinning her down and his laugh was cruel and full of meaning. 'This one wants a lesson, I think.' His breath was hot against her cheek and Emily pushed against him with all her might but it was useless to struggle, he was too strong for her.

'You get the money!' the man commanded his accomplice harshly. 'I'll see to her.'

His mouth was against her neck and his hand cruelly twisted her wrists together in a hold she had no hope of breaking.

'Let me go,' she said desperately. 'Take anything from the shop but let me go.'

'Too late for that, my lady,' he said, 'much too late, you can't get away from me now so you might as well stop struggling for I mean to have my way.'

'Do you indeed!' The voice came out of the darkness, harsh and angry and then the man was lifted bodily away from Emily. She heard the grating of bone against bone and the man slumped like a sack to the ground.

'John!' Emily said thankfully. John Miller stood over the fallen man, his fists clenched, his jaw a hard line of anger.

'There's another of them!' she said in panic as a shape loomed up out of the darkness. She saw John side-step the rush and calmly he stuck out his boot and the man, carried forward by his own momentum, went sprawling.

In moments, it was over, both men bolting into the street, running as if their lives depended upon it. Emily covered her face with her hands and found that she was sobbing hysterically.

John helped her to her feet and half-carried her upstairs to her rooms. She clung to him, her head against his broad shoulder, drinking in the tobacco scent of him and the freshness of his skin.

'I saw someone follow you from the beach,' he said softly, 'so I thought I'd best keep an eye on you.' He gently led her to a chair and lit the lamps and set about mending the fire, building it up carefully with the coals placed to give maximum heat.

'You sit quietly,' he said, his voice authoritative, 'I'll make you a nice cup of tea.' They were no longer employer and employee but man and woman.

She was still trembling when John handed her the cup, she put both her hands round the warmth of the china and drew comfort from it.

'You see how much I need you, John,' she said in a whisper, 'please don't leave me tonight, I don't want to be alone.'

'I'll stay by here on the sofa,' he said reassuringly. 'I'll look after you, don't worry, those ruffians won't be back.'

He rose to his feet. 'I'll see to the door, we don't want any Tom, Dick or Harry coming in here helping themselves to your boots and shoes, do we?'

The way she felt at the moment, Emily didn't care, she had been in danger and John, dear John, had come along just in time and saved her.

When he returned, she was still sitting in the chair unable to move, shock waves were running through her. Tea splashed over the rim of the cup on to the table.

He took the cup and helped her to her feet. 'Let's take off these torn things.' He unbuttoned the jacket that hung in threads over her blouse.

The hem of her skirt had been ripped upwards and, carefully, John helped her off with it.

'Where's your bedroom?' He asked the question as though speaking to a child and she pointed shakily towards the door.

He tucked her in the bed and brushed the hair back from her face. 'You are going to have a beauty of a black eye tomorrow,' he said, 'I think it best if you have the doctor to look at it, mind.'

She nodded, willing to agree to anything he said so long as he stayed with her. He held her hand, smoothing her wrists and Emily at last felt her eyes begin to close. She turned on her side, his hand beneath her cheek and slept.

In the morning, she awoke to the sounds of activity from the kitchen. She could hear Sarah's voice speaking softly and the resonant tones of John Miller as he replied.

Emily wondered what Sarah must make of the whole strange business of her father spending the night under Emily's roof. Perhaps she should get up and explain.

In the kitchen, Sarah was putting out a breakfast of bacon and eggs and John was sitting in his shirt sleeves looking handsome and at ease as though he always ate breakfast at the shop in Wind Street.

'*Duw*, Miss Emily, there's a black eye you got!' Sarah spoke almost with awe. 'Them men must have had the shock of their lives when my dad set about them. Used to be the best bare-fisted boxer in Swansea did John Miller, mind.'

Emily sank into a chair as Sarah poured her a cup of tea. The girl seemed not one bit bothered by the fact that her father, unchaperoned, had stayed the night with Emily.

'I'm so grateful to your father.' Emily spoke with difficulty, the pain in her face was quite severe. 'I dread to think what might have happened if he hadn't been here.'

'Murdered you would have been, no doubt about it.' Sarah spoke with relish. 'These footpads got no mercy on women, mind, I dread to think what they would have done with you before they killed you.'

'Sarah, that's enough,' John said soberly. 'I'm sure Miss Grenfell just wants to forget it all happened. I'd like you to go along to the doctor and ask him could he kindly call some time today.'

'It's not really necessary,' Emily said quickly, 'I'm just bruised, I'll be all right.'

'You've suffered a shock,' John said forcefully, 'I think you need to see the doctor.'

It was clear that Sarah was used to obeying her father for she picked up her shawl and left the house promptly.

'Thank you, John,' Emily said, looking up at him with searching eyes, 'I know I've said all this before but I don't know what I would have done without you here last night.'

John came and knelt before her, taking her hand in his, his air of deference had vanished. It was almost as though he saw her now as a vulnerable woman rather than a lady who was far above him in station.

'Wild horses wouldn't have dragged me away from you last night – Emily.' He said her name shyly. 'I don't know what we are going to do about our future but I can't see you living here alone, not even with my Sarah for company, you are both too much at risk from any stray villain who wants to chance his arm.'

He rose and put the distance of the kitchen between them. 'When Sarah returns with the doctor, I'll get her to open up the shop, organize the other girls, so that for a few days they can manage without you.'

Emily nodded, happy to let John take charge. 'I don't want you going into the shop until your face is completely healed, no need to give the gossips fuel for the flames, do we?'

Sarah arrived, leading the doctor into the private rooms upstairs with an air of due deference for, to the townspeople, the doctor was held in high esteem, the saver of lives, the healer of pain and suffering.

'Well, Emily my dear, what on earth have you been doing?' Doctor Webber peered at her eye, touching the bruised skin with practised fingers. 'That's a beauty, isn't it?'

He picked up his bag. 'Come into your room, I want to examine you properly, to see if there are any other injuries.'

Lying on her bed, Emily was apprehensive, her ribs ached and her limbs were covered in bruises. The doctor probed gently.

At last, he pulled a sheet over her and sat down. 'No serious harm has come to you, my dear, but you do seem to have some sort of inflammation of the abdomen.'

Emily looked up at him puzzled. 'What does that mean?' she said quietly.

'Do you often have stomach pains, Emily?' he asked. 'Trouble with your courses?'

'Sometimes,' Emily said, 'but what's wrong with that? Every woman has to go through it.'

'Quite so but occasionally, rarely in fact, such problems can affect your ability to have children.' He smiled, 'Though I doubt if that would apply in your case, at any rate don't worry about it. I'll give you something that will clear the trouble up in no time.'

When the doctor had gone, there was a knock on the door and John entered the room, a cup of hot tea in his hand. He looked concerned.

'What's wrong, Miss Emily?' he asked, standing beside the bed staring down at her, his face white. 'Bad news, is it?'

Suddenly Emily knew she had to talk to John, he was a wise, loving man who might be the only person in the world who cared a damn about her.

'Sit down, John,' she said. She took his hand as he perched on the foolish little rattan chair beside her bed.

'I'll be honest with you, John, I've fallen in love with you in spite of myself.'

When he would have interrupted, she held up her hand. 'No, don't say anything yet, just hear me out.'

'I want to marry you, John, I want to be your wife and take your name.' She sighed heavily. 'It wouldn't be all roses, we'd be the talk of Swansea and people will point a finger at you and say you are a fortune hunter. If none of that bothers you, I think we could be very happy together.'

The colour rose to John's face, he was clearly startled by her suggestion and yet there was a warmth in his eyes that encouraged Emily to go on.

'There is one more drawback, I may not be able to bear you a child.' When he remained silent, she sighed heavily.

'But it is a great deal to ask, that a man take on such a lot of problems, forget I spoke, you have your own life to lead.'

John raised her hand to his lips and kissed her finger-tips. 'I am a plain man,' he said, 'I was married to the same girl for twenty years, had two children by her. I am forty-two years of age, old enough to be *your* father and so I hope I have gained some little wisdom of the world. If you want me, I'd be honoured to have you as my wife.'

It was a long speech for a man like John Miller and tears came to Emily's eyes. She stretched up and touched his cheek with her free hand. 'You are a handsome, well-set-up man,' she said, 'you are honest and you care about me which is most important. I love you and I will be honoured to have you as a husband.'

'I'll be good to you, Emily,' John said hoarsely, 'have no fear on that score.'

'I haven't,' Emily said softly and she leaned forward and kissed him. His lips warmed to hers and, as John held her close, Emily knew for the first time what it was like to feel real happiness.

Sarah was more than a little surprised when she heard

the news. 'You and my dad, going to be married?' she said incredulously. 'Why?'

'Because we love each other.' Emily was a little annoyed by the girl's attitude but it was only to be expected, she told herself, everyone in Swansea would be showing the same surprise that the high and mighty Miss Grenfell was marrying a man from the lower orders. Well, let them talk, she was practically an outcast from society anyway. Emily had made up her mind to the marriage and that was all there was to it.

The wedding, with only Sarah and her brother Ray as witnesses, took place at St Paul's Church in Sketty. It was a fine day with the sun shining brightly.

As the ring was placed upon her finger, Emily smiled up at John, loving him so much that she wanted to cry. She felt a sense of unreality as she walked from the church into the sunshine and then John turned to her and smiled.

'Well, Mrs Miller, what is it like to be a married woman?'

'I'll tell you when I'm more used to the idea,' Emily said leaning lightly against his shoulder. There was no party, no fuss and, together, Emily and John returned to the emporium.

The arrangement of the rooms had been quickly altered, what once had been Hari's apartment was now turned into an extra drawing-room and a study where Emily could work on her books. Her own bedroom larger than the other was to be the room she shared with her new husband. Sarah was to have the night off so that the newly-wed couple could have the house to themselves.

They ate supper with Emily only picking at hers. She was nervous, strung up, not knowing what to expect of John. She had vowed to be a proper wife and yet he had been married before, comparisons were bound to be made and Emily feared she would be found wanting.

After they had eaten, Emily carried the remains of the supper into the kitchen, she would leave it, Sarah would see to the dishes in the morning.

Sarah had acted as a part-time help upstairs, the work was easy with just Emily to think about, but now Emily would need to employ a full-time maid, she could not expect her shop assistant to wait on her when she had a husband to consider.

John poured her a glass of port and sat opposite her, a little uneasy in his waistcoat and his good solid boots. He seemed to feel out of place and Emily knew it would be up to her to make the first move.

'I think I'll go into bed, now,' she said smiling as she rose to her feet. 'Give me a few minutes to get ready and then will you join me please, John?'

His face lit up with happiness. In one movement he was on his feet and gently he took her hands in his.

'Do you really love me, Emily?' he asked softly. Emily looked up at him.

'We are man and wife and those vows I made, they were made in happiness and love.' She was trembling as she undressed and when she looked down almost shyly at her nakedness, she wondered if John would be pleased or disappointed in her.

Drawing her night-gown over her head, Emily shivered and then slipped between the sheets, a little fearful of what was to come. John was a man who respected women but he was a full-blooded man nonetheless and she prayed he would see her as just a woman and not as Emily Grenfell, daughter of the landed gentry.

When he came to bed, John smelled fresh and clean and there was a hint of the fragrance of pipe tobacco about him.

He settled down beside her and she turned to him, putting her arms around him, burying her face in his warm shoulder. With a soft moan he twisted his hands in her loosened hair and then his lips were warm against her throat.

John was gentle and expert in the art of making love. He caressed her with teasing hands and lips and all the time he murmured soft endearments. Emily felt wanted and loved and, as she warmed to his embrace, she felt passion overwhelm her fear. Suddenly she knew, she could give herself to John without restraint, he was her lover, her teacher and, most of all, he was her husband.

23

Craig stood in the drawing-room of Summer Lodge and watched as the handsome youth strode up the driveway of the house. William was a well-set-up young man and extremely intelligent, his swiftness to learn was a source of delight and Craig had come to look forward to their meetings at the weekends.

Craig was sometimes able to hear a crumb of news about Hari and these he digested with eagerness. He had never ceased to regret his stupidity in letting Hari get away from him, he should have married her when she was free.

Craig had become friends with the eldest daughter of Lady Caroline Grey but Elizabeth, though pleasant, lacked the richness of spirit that characterized Hari Morgan.

'Will, good to see you.' Craig opened the front door himself, the maid whom he had been reluctantly forced to engage was busy in the kitchen helping the old couple prepare Sunday luncheon. As Craig stood in the hallway, he became aware that the smell of roasting beef was permeating the house.

'You'd be welcome to stay and share my dinner,' Craig said smiling, 'there's always far too much food cooked in this house.'

'I've got to get back,' Will said reluctantly, 'Hari isn't feeling too good, got to stay in bed so the doctor says and I'm trying to catch up with the fine work on the shoes, you see.'

Craig closed the door of the drawing-room and moved to the table where he had spread a variety of maps for the day's lesson.

'What's wrong with Hari?' He could not conceal the concern he felt and Will smiled.

'It's all right so long as she rests in bed a few days, seems the baby is due much sooner than expected, though I don't understand too much about it myself.'

'Look at these maps,' Craig forced himself to concentrate on the lesson, 'I want you to learn the names of the continents today and fix in your mind where they are in relation to each other.'

There was silence in the room as Will pored over the maps, a frown of concentration furrowing his brow. Craig sat in the window, staring out into the garden and pondered on William's news about Hari. Slowly, a suspicion began to form in his mind.

The suspicion grew into a deep-rooted certainty, Hari must be carrying *his* child, not Edward's, the baby was the result of the night he and Hari had spent together. Those wonderful hours that had gone flying past like minutes.

He rose restlessly and rubbed his hand through his hair, Hari would have a son, an heir to the Grenfell estate, he was certain of it.

Craig felt exultant, he wanted to rush out to see Hari, confront her with his suspicions, make her agree that the child she carried was his.

Then common sense asserted itself, the child would bear Edward's name, would be born in wedlock, to all intents and purposes would be Edward's child. Craig closed his eyes against the knowledge that he must keep his suspicions secret for Edward's sake and for Hari's peace of mind.

Will's voice penetrated his thoughts. 'Africa then is the biggest of the continents, is that right?'

Craig rose from his chair and moved to the table, pointing a finger at the map.

'Just study the map, William.' He tried to force himself to concentrate but the mixed emotions he was feeling drove out rational thought.

'Will, would you mind if we skipped the lesson today?' he said. 'How about a mug of ale down at the Lamb and Flag instead?'

'All right.' Will rose from his chair and stared shrewdly at Craig. 'You are worried about Hari, aren't you? You care about her, anyone could see that.'

'You're right.' Craig sighed and moved into the hallway, picking up his jacket.

The maid came from the kitchen and bobbed a curtsy, her dark eyes on William.

'Anything you need, sir?' she said deferentially to Craig.

'Thank you, Maria,' he said, 'I'm just going out for a while but I shall be back in good time to enjoy that roast dinner, don't you worry.'

It was a fine crisp September day, the late sun was warming the streets and the leaves on the trees were just beginning to turn brown. Soon, Craig thought, his son would be born and he would have no rights in the matter. He would be an outsider looking in on the happiness that could so easily have been his. And the knowledge was like a bitter taste in his mouth.

Hari was seated in the window, the patterns she'd been working on lying idle in her lap. Edward was away on business and the silence of the house suited Hari's mood of lethargy. All she had become was a child-bearing vessel, without conscious thoughts other than the welfare of her baby.

She had worried for a time about who was the father of her child and the more she brooded, the more convinced she became that the baby could not be Edward's.

Should she tell Edward the truth, she wondered, or would it be kinder to keep her doubts to herself. But at last, she had come to the conclusion that it would only hurt her husband to know the truth.

To tell Edward about the time she had given herself to Craig would serve no purpose except to relieve herself of the burden of guilt. Instead, she decided to live with that guilt, in that way only one of them would be unhappy.

The new young maid entered the room a look of avid curiosity on her face. 'You've a visitor,' she said, 'a Mrs Miller, Miss Emily Grenfell as was.'

Hari concealed her surprise and looked up slowly, struggling for composure.

'Thank you, Jenny, show her in, there's a good girl.' The maid scarcely bobbed a curtsy, after all Mrs Morris was only a working girl like herself who had come up in the world, she wasn't a real toff.

Emily entered the room with an anxious look on her face but in spite of that, she appeared to be well. Her fine-boned face had rounded out a little and there was a sparkle of happiness in her eyes that was difficult to ignore.

'Hari, I had to see you, to talk to you,' she began breathlessly. 'Please don't send me away, just listen to what I've got to say, please.'

'Thank you, Jenny.' Hari nodded meaningfully to the maid who was loitering in the doorway. When the door closed Hari indicated a chair and carefully placed the designs she'd been working on on the table, aware that her hands were trembling.

'I know we've had misunderstandings,' Emily said, 'and most of it has been my fault but now that's in the past and I really feel it's time we put it behind us.' She smiled diffidently, 'After all, we've so much in common now that we're both married women, haven't we?'

'Please sit down,' Hari said, her mouth was dry with nervousness.

Emily leaned forward. 'I wanted to talk to you as a friend, I've no-one else, Hari, and I'm so very happy that I want to share it.'

'Yes.' Hari didn't know how to react to this new, gentler Emily.

'I love my husband,' Emily continued, 'oh, I know the gossips are having a field day, the high and mighty Miss Grenfell has married beneath her but I haven't.' She rushed on without pausing. 'John is a fine man and I'm a very lucky woman.'

Hari didn't speak, the pain was deep inside her, Emily's happiness was self-evident, how she wished that she was half as happy. But she couldn't be happy, not without Craig.

But at least she could try to patch things up with Emily, it would be good to forget the past and start again.

'I'm glad you came,' Hari said softly, 'we both let Craig deceive us and there were wrongs done by the three of us, but perhaps we can put all that behind us now.'

'Craig's not so bad.' Emily sighed. 'I almost married him but realized very quickly that I was second best; I represented what Craig saw as a suitable union and, for a time, that's what I thought too. We would merge the Grenfell fortunes once and for all.'

Emily smiled, 'But it was never meant to be. I think he always loved you even though he wouldn't admit it.'

'Craig never loved anyone but himself.' Hari said, 'I was always beneath him, not good enough for the high and mighty Grenfells.' Hari couldn't conceal the note of bitterness that crept into her voice.

'That might have been true once, but now I, at least, want to make amends,' Emily said humbly, 'you are the only real friend I've ever had. You cared for me when I

305

was sick, if it weren't for you I wouldn't be alive today.'

'I'm so confused, I can't even think straight.' Hari was unsettled by Emily's belief that Craig was in love with her, could it be true, could Craig forget his background enough to love a working woman?

'Look,' Emily said softly, 'it makes sense for us to support and help each other at a time like this.'

Hari rose to her feet. 'You have the support of your husband, you love him and why should you need me?'

'I have always wanted your friendship, Hari, and admired your talent, and, if you have problems, I can be someone to talk to when things get too much to bear on your own,' Emily said reasonably.

Hari rubbed her eyes. 'Let's just take things slowly Emily, please,' she said.

Emily rose to her feet and stood staring appealingly at Hari. 'I'll go now but if you want me please, Hari, just send a message and I'll be here.'

She walked to the door in silence and when she put her hand on the shining brass knob, she turned.

'Take care of yourself, Hari,' she said softly, 'I wish you everything you wish yourself.'

'Wait,' Hari said. 'Thank you for coming, Emily, I'm not ungrateful, I just want time to think, that's all.'

She stood in the window of the house in Chapel Street and watched as Emily made her way along the road. There was something different about her, even the way she walked was less arrogant somehow. It was clear that marriage suited her, clear that she loved her husband and Hari envied her. At least Emily had chosen a reliable, honest man to love instead of the charming deceiver that Craig had become.

And yet was that fair to Craig? When had he ever lied? He had promised nothing, offered nothing but a night of love and Hari had accepted it eagerly enough and she could blame no-one but herself for the consequences.

Will was suddenly framed in the doorway, his eyebrows raised questioningly. 'Everything all right, Hari?' he asked and she forced a smile.

'Yes, of course,' she said. 'Come in, Will, tell me what's happening down the workshop.'

'I'm just finishing off those shoes for that snooty Lady Caroline, *duw*, she goes through more slippers than anyone I know and so fussy with it. Pearls she wanted this time, pearls to match the treble string she wears around her fat neck, there's a woman for pomp!'

'So long as there are Lady Carolines in this world we are kept in business,' Hari said smiling more easily now, brought back to normality by Will's down-to-earth bluntness.

'That daughter of hers has set her cap at Mr Grenfell,' Will said thoughtfully and Hari knew that this was no casual remark, Will was passing on information he believed she would want to know.

'Walking out they are, though Mr Grenfell don't look too happy about it if you ask me.'

'Why do it then?' Hari said sharply and Will leaned forward, his big hands hanging between his knees.

'He's a man, Hari,' he said quietly. 'He's not a monk, mind.' His words held a reproof and Hari acknowledged that reproof.

'You're right, of course, why shouldn't he have a normal life.' She sat straighter in her chair. 'How are the lessons going?'

Will's face lit up. '*Duw*, there's a brainy man! Mr Grenfell knows all about the world and the seas and the skies. If I end up with half his knowledge I'll be more than satisfied.'

This was a side of Craig Hari had never seen. She had known his passion, the stirring of the blood with his touch but she had never learned of the real man beneath the surface and she regretted it.

She noticed that Will was speaking with less of a Welsh accent since he'd been taking lessons with Craig, it was as though the boy unconsciously imitated the older man and it was no bad thing, if Will was to succeed in the world he needed all the advantages he could acquire.

'Well, if you don't need me for anything, I'll be off out,' Will said.

'Go on out and enjoy yourself, Will.' Hari spoke teasingly, 'A little bird told me you were walking out with Sarah Miller, is that right?'

'You can't keep anything private in this house, I suppose Jenny couldn't keep her tongue still, could she?'

'Well, is it true?' Hari asked resisting the urge to laugh at Will's indignant expression.

'Aye, I suppose so but it's not serious, mind, just walking out, that's all, not planning to get married.'

Hari wondered briefly if she should warn Will about the dangers of getting Sarah with child but on reflection, coming from a household of babies as he did, Will probably knew more about it than she did.

When she was alone, Hari pondered over Emily's visit, it was a generous gesture, to come here to Chapel Street and try to heal the breech that had yawned between them. And it would be good to have a friend, a confidante who might one day share the burden of Hari's terrible secret.

Perhaps in a day or two, she would take a cab to Emily's Emporium, sit down quietly with Emily, try to rekindle a little of the warmth that had once been between them.

Hari allowed her mind to dwell on what Will had said about Craig walking out with Lady Caroline's daughter. It was hurtful to know about his affairs and yet Will was right, Craig was no monk to sit at home and twiddle his thumbs.

The day would come when he would marry, it was inevitable and, when it came, Hari must be prepared for it.

Will strolled along Wind Street whistling softly to himself. He looked forward to his meeting with Sarah with great anticipation, she was a fun-loving girl, warm and responsive, and Will felt it was high time he gave in to the manly urges that had plagued him of late.

He knew that he had grown from a scrawny boy into a well-built youth, his shoulders had broadened and his muscles were firm and strong. His one regret was that he had not achieved the six foot in height that his father had boasted.

Sarah was waiting for him at the gate of the park, their usual meeting place, her dark eyes laughed up at him as her firm young breasts rested against the wrought-iron work, tantalizingly thrown into relief by the tightness of her bodice.

Will took her hand. 'Come on, let's go over on to the sands,' he said and for a moment, Sarah hung back.

'I know what you're after, you want to get me in the dunes, hidden from prying eyes and then the Good Lord only knows what you'll want to do.'

Protesting feebly, she allowed herself to be drawn across the width of the Mumbles Road and there, the golden sands sparkled in the September sunlight like diamonds flung from the sky.

Will watched as Sarah sank into the sand and removed her shoes and stockings curling her toes into the golden softness with the abandon of a young kitten.

Will sank down beside her and fell back, his hands beneath his head. The sky was blue as a summer sky with the mellow sun turning the sea to azure. He sighed, on a day like this it was good to be alive.

Sarah buried her head in his shoulder. 'Tell me you love me, Will, and I'll be the happiest girl this side of Cardiff.'

He turned and took her in his arms, 'Of course I love you, Sarah, you are the first girl I've ever walked out with but,' he teased, 'am I the first man in your life? I doubt it.'

'Don't be naughty, Will.' She pushed away his straying hand, though he could see that she was pleased. Sarah, like him, was teasing the edges of life, she wanted to taste its pleasures just as much as he did.

He rested his head against the cotton of her bodice and smelled the soft woman scent of her with rising excitement. 'Sarah,' he said thickly, 'don't you trust me? You know I wouldn't hurt you, just let me caress your beautiful breasts, that can't do any harm now, can it?'

She was quiescent as his fingers traced the outline of her body through her gown, her breathing quickened and a pretty flush came to her cheeks.

'I want to love you so much, Sarah,' he said in a whisper, 'I want to know all about you.' He pressed close to her and, for a moment, his senses swam as she clung to him. Then she pushed him away and sat up laughing, teasingly.

'You are shameless, would you take me here in the sunlight where anyone passing could see us?' she said.

'Yes, I would,' he said, 'what better way for us to learn the truth about life than under the sky and the sun and with the sea washing at our feet.'

He drew her down once more and this time she did not push him away. Her rounded arms clung to him and with a dart of joy he felt the bareness of her thigh against his hand.

He was heady with desire and the feeling of power that ran through him like wine. Sarah was his for the taking and the knowledge was like a starburst of happiness within him.

Later, he took Sarah back to the emporium and at the

310

back door he held her gently and kissed her warm lips.

'I love you, Sarah,' he said and then he meant it, for gratitude to a woman is a powerful thing.

'And I love you, Will, when shall we be married?' she asked softly.

Icy fingers traced a line along his spine. With sharp wits he smiled down at her.

'I won't ask you to be my wife until I can provide for you properly,' he said. 'For now our love will be enough.'

'But, Will, what if I get with child, the shame of it!' she said fearfully.

'Don't worry,' he said, 'you won't get with child, I've seen to it.' And he had, at the last moments of his passion, he had taken himself away from Sarah and did as the Good Book said and cast his seed upon the ground.

Will could not endure the sort of life he had known as a child full of poverty and babies. No, he wanted more for himself and for the woman who would eventually be his wife.

Craig closed the account book and smiled at Will. 'I don't know what's wrong with you but you are just not concentrating today. If I didn't know better I'd say it was spring fever.'

'Well, to be truthful,' Will smiled, 'it's something like that.'

'I see.' Craig smiled, 'Well, the first experience of anything is always to be savoured.'

'I know,' Will said, 'but my girl thinks it just naturally leads to marriage.'

'And you are not ready for that just yet?' Craig wondered why he felt suddenly so old. He found himself almost envying William for though the young man had nothing of worldly goods, he was on the very threshold of

311

life, ripe for new experiences and, if Craig was not mistaken, about to make something of himself.

'Women are very special creatures,' he said thoughtfully, 'you must never make use of them and then cast them aside.'

Yet wasn't that just what he had done with Hari? He had enjoyed one night of passion with her and had never declared that he loved her. He became aware that Will was speaking again.

'I wouldn't do that to Sarah but then neither do I want to commit myself to marrying her.' He shrugged, 'I suppose the proper thing to do is not to take advantage of a woman in the first place.'

'Quite right, Will,' Craig said, 'if it were only that simple!'

He sighed. He felt exactly the same as Will did now, he wanted the warmth of a woman in his arms without the commitment it invariably entailed. 'I don't have all the answers, Will, indeed I continually surprise myself with my lack of understanding of womankind. You think you know what they want and then they confound you utterly. A man who says he understands women is a fool or a liar.'

William smiled. 'I suppose you don't feel like a nice cold mug of ale, that public bar we went to last time served a good strong brew.'

Craig nodded, 'Good idea, you are learning, Will, when a man can't answer the important questions in life, the way out is to spend some time drinking ale with a friend.'

He saw the look of pleasure cross William's face and hid a smile, the boy probably thought him very old and sophisticated and quite wise. How wrong he was.

Later, as he sat in the cool of the bar with William maintaining a companionable silence alongside him, Craig thought about the mistakes he'd made in his life. He wished he could advise William how to avoid making the same errors but no-one could live Will's life for him, his mistakes must be his own, how else would he learn?

'How's Hari?' Craig couldn't resist the question, he saw Will glance at him and hesitate a moment before answering.

'Not too good,' he said, 'she has been feeling bad lately, got to rest in bed, the baby, you know.'

'Oh?' Craig felt a dart of alarm, 'Is there something wrong then?'

William shook back his brown hair. 'No, not really wrong, I think Hari is just tired, her spirits are a bit low, too.'

Craig felt so impotent, if only he could go to Hari, talk to her, tell her of his love. But it was all too late for that, much too late, he had made his mistakes and now Craig knew he would just have to live with them.

He picked up his mug of ale but suddenly the drink tasted like ashes in his mouth.

24

The pain woke her, it was like a vice clamping about her body and Hari sat up in bed, instantly awake. She stared at the pale dawn for a long minute, holding her breath, wondering when the pressure would subside.

She turned to see Edward beside her, he was sound asleep, his hair tousled over his too-pale face and with a pang of unease, Hari realized just how thin he'd become over the past months.

The pain eased, ebbing away from her like a tide, leaving her gasping and frightened. She sank back gingerly against the pillows, perhaps it had been a false alarm, the birth was early even by the doctor's reckoning.

In the early morning light, Hari examined her life calmly and with senses alert and she knew that whatever happened, she must protect Edward from the truth. It meant she must live a lie, letting him believe the baby was his, to shock him with her doubts would be too cruel. In any case how could she be sure, really sure that the baby was not Edward's?

Once the child was born and she had regained her strength, she would see things more clearly, she would put the past behind her and start afresh, determined to make Edward happy.

The pain came again fiercer this time and Hari put her hand over her mouth, determined not to frighten Edward with her cries. She closed her eyes tightly, trying to remember to go with the pain, that was the advice handed out by the old midwives, not to fight against the forces of nature but to go with the flow. But it was more difficult than Hari had ever imagined.

At last, the pain subsided and tentatively Hari reached out a hand and touched Edward's shoulder. He was awake in an instant.

'The baby,' she said, 'it's coming.' She saw the sleep vanish from his eyes to be replaced with apprehension. 'It's all right,' she reassured him, 'just fetch the midwife, everything is going to be just fine.'

'But it's too soon.' Edward was already struggling into his clothes. 'The baby isn't due yet, something must be wrong. I'd best have the doctor, I'd feel happier with him looking after you.'

When Edward had gone, Jenny came into the room with a tray of tea and an expression of avid curiosity on her face.

'Mr Morris gone for the doctor, then, baby coming early, is it?' She put the tray down at the bedside. 'No need to worry, mind, my mam got six children, they come when they're ready, she says.' She paused hands on hips, 'Mrs Crocker the midwife delivered all of us, mind.'

There was a reproof in Jenny's voice, an implication that what was good enough for the women of the area was not good enough for Mrs Edward Morris.

Hari closed her eyes as the pain came again, should it be this sudden, wasn't there supposed to be a period of mild labour leading up slowly to the birth? Hari bit her lip, wanting only to be alone but Jenny was standing beside the bed, a look of indecision on her face.

'Mrs Crocker's good, mind,' she volunteered more gently 'and she only lives about five streets away. Looks as if you haven't got time to wait for the doctor to come.'

'Go get the midwife, then, Jenny.' Hari said through her teeth, 'Tell her to come straight away.'

Jenny disappeared and Hari could hear her running down the stairs. She sank back against the pillows as the pain eased and wondered that, in between times, she felt almost exhilarated and completely in charge of the situation.

It was a strange experience, this childbirth, when the pains came they made her feel so vulnerable, pinned to her bed, made her a creature of the earth with nerve endings and sensations rather than a rational human being who had successfully run a business. Then they eased and she was herself again.

It was a relief to see Jenny return after only a few minutes with the midwife. Mrs Crocker looked very capable, wearing a starched white apron over a plain skirt and blouse. Her sleeves were already rolled up in preparation for the work she would do.

'Fetch plenty of hot water, Jenny,' she said, 'that's the first thing we need and hurry, girl, by the look of it there's not much time.'

She bent over the bed and carefully placed her hands on Hari's swollen stomach. 'Yes, a good strong pain is coming, I can feel the tightening, that means your baby is going to be here before too long.'

Hari gritted her teeth hearing the small moaning sounds she made and yet unable to help herself. She was aware of Jenny bustling about the room and then she smelled the acrid scent of the rough soap as the midwife rubbed it over her hands and forearms.

'Like to be clean and fresh to handle new babies, I do,' Mrs Crocker said conversationally. 'Not the practice of all midwives, mind, but it is my practice and there's not many babies I lose.'

It was reassuring to hear the woman's confident tones and Hari relaxed for a moment, gathering her strength for the next bout of pain.

Edward returned with the doctor who summed up the

situation at once. 'I think your wife is in very good hands,' he said quietly, 'Mrs Crocker is one of the best midwives in the district, you won't go far wrong with her.'

'But you'll stay, doctor?' Edward sounded panic stricken and Hari longed to comfort him but she was too swamped with her own struggle to give birth and the hand she had raised dropped back to the bed as she gave up the effort to talk.

It seemed interminable, the pains were getting stronger and lasting longer until Hari felt that she couldn't go on. Her strength was ebbing fast, she wanted so badly to sink into an unconscious sleep, to get away from the turmoil that was taking place in her body.

And then, the pains seemed to change, she was suddenly invigorated.

'That's my girl, bear down now nice and strong, good girl, keep at it, it'll all be over soon.'

Hari heard low noises coming from her throat, her voice was hoarse and yet she knew, with a sense of triumph, that the ordeal was almost over.

'There's a good mother!' The midwife was triumphant, 'Your baby's nearly born, one more push will do it, good girl, that's it!'

Hari felt suddenly released, she closed her eyes and rested gratefully for a moment and then the sharp sound of the baby's cry roused her.

'And here he is, Mrs Morris, congratulations, you have a fine strong boy.'

Hari sighed with relief, the moment was one of exquisite happiness. She lifted her head and saw that the midwife was bent over the bed attending to the baby.

'Is he all right?' Hari heard her voice without recognizing it, it was thin and thread-like and she sank back on to the pillow feeling immeasurably weary.

'He's a strong hearty child,' the midwife said, 'no dainty

317

doll-like creature this but cut out for a navvy, he is. And such dark hair, not like his dad. Here take him. Mrs Morris, say hello to your son.'

He was surprisingly heavy in her arms and Hari, as she looked down at the crumpled little face, felt tears brim in her eyes.

'He's just perfect,' she said in awe, 'just look at his fingers, aren't they beautiful?'

The midwife was smiling in a proprietary way. 'Of course,' she said, 'all new babies are lovely to their mams, it wouldn't be right otherwise.' She moved closer to the bed, 'Now give the boy to his father to hold so that I can put you tidy.'

Hari became aware of Edward hovering at the foot of the bed and a heavy feeling of guilt swamped her. Edward came towards her and tentatively held out his arms and, reluctantly, Hari handed him her baby.

'Look doctor,' Edward said eagerly, 'I have a son, isn't it wonderful?'

The doctor made the appropriate noises and then moved to the door. 'Congratulations to you, Mrs Morris,' he said, 'I will come to see both of you in a few days' time.'

The midwife spent a while longer bustling around the bed but when at last she was satisfied that Hari was comfortable she washed in the bowl of fresh hot water Jenny had brought.

'I'll be back tomorrow,' Mrs Crocker said, 'and every day for as long as you need me.' She moved to the door. 'I advise that you are attended for at least two weeks.'

Hari sighed, glad to have Mrs Crocker's support. It was Edward who spoke.

'You keep coming for as long as you see fit,' he said, 'and you will be well rewarded.' He was smiling broadly, still cradling the baby and Hari closed her eyes against the pain of the guilt that seared her.

And yet, lurking behind the guilt was the overriding wish that Craig could be standing there, proudly holding their son, smiling his delight at the birth of the boy.

Hari held out her arms and Edward carefully returned the baby to her. He sat on the bed and moving the sheet from the baby's face peered down, smiling.

'What shall we call him?' he said. 'We haven't thought of a name yet.'

Hari was silent, she didn't know what to say, she stared down at her son knowing only that she loved him with every fibre of her being.

'What about Joseph Morris after my father?' Edward said thoughtfully.

'No!' The word burst from Hari's lips before she could restrain herself. She forced herself to smile. 'I thought it would be a tribute to my father if I called my first son after him, let the boy be David which is the English for Dewi,' she said quickly.

'Of course,' Edward smiled understandingly, 'I'm sorry, if that's what you want that's what it shall be.'

She put out her hand and rested it on his arm, 'It's me who should be sorry, I didn't mean to bite your head off.'

'It's only to be expected after what you've been through these last few hours. Just put the baby in the crib and I'll watch over him. Tomorrow we'll employ a nursemaid to look after him but for now you must try to get all the rest you can so that you'll regain your strength all the sooner.'

And in spite of the way her thoughts ran in turmoil around her head, Hari did eventually fall into an exhausted sleep only to dream of Craig bending over the crib, smiling down at the son who was the spit out of his mouth.

As the days passed and Hari grew stronger, she realized just how like Craig the baby was. His features were strong, his hair thick and dark and yet Edward totally failed to see it.

He doted on the boy, crooning over him whenever he had the chance which was often. Of late Edward had taken to delegating his work to the young man he had employed to help him in the office after his first bout of sickness.

It irked Hari to have him there all the time, she seemed to have no moments of privacy with her baby and sometimes she was hard pressed to control her impatience.

It was almost ten days after the birth of her son that Edward came into the bedroom, a broad smile on his face.

'We have a visitor,' he said. 'Craig is very anxious to see this fine boy of ours, can he come in?'

Hari drew a sharp breath and held the baby closer. 'Yes, I suppose so,' Hari said, feeling a deep resentment as Craig entered the room and moved towards the bed.

'I'll go and organize Jenny to bring us all some refreshment,' Edward said and Hari almost called after him to stay but her lips remained closed, she couldn't show herself up like that.

Craig sat on the edge of the bed and stared down at Hari with concern in his dark eyes. 'Are you all right?' he asked and she nodded without speaking. 'And the baby?'

Reluctantly, she drew back the shawl and watched Craig's face soften as he stared down at the new-born child. He looked up and met her eyes.

'I love you, Hari,' he said, 'I only wish I'd recognized it earlier. Come away with me, we'll leave Swansea and the gossips behind, we'll be together as we should have been from the start if I'd had any sense.'

'Don't, Craig,' Hari said in a whisper. 'I can't do that and well you know it, it's impossible.'

'Why is it impossible?' Craig said persuasively, 'Can you live a lie with Edward? I don't think you can.'

Hari rubbed at her eyes wearily. 'Yes, I can and I will!

Edward's so happy now, please don't say any more, not now, Craig, it's far too late.'

'I know.' He took her face in his hands and gently kissed her mouth. 'You must get strong and then we'll talk again.'

'Yes,' Hari said, grateful that he was not pursuing the matter. Her every nerve cried out for him, it would be wonderful to be with him, for the three of them to be a united family. But that was only a dream that would never come true.

Edward returned with Jenny close behind him carrying a tray. 'Here's my best port,' Edward said, 'you must have some, Hari, it's good for the blood and we shall all drink to my son.'

Craig got to his feet and towered above Edward who looked slight and pale beside him and very vulnerable. Craig lifted his glass.

'To the baby,' he said softly. Then putting down his untouched glass of port, he left the room without another word.

Hari lingered in bed for longer than she needed, afraid that once she was on her feet, Craig would come to torment her with his talk of love. It was Mrs Crocker who at last chastised her and roused her out of bed, bullying Hari into dressing herself.

'Take the baby for a walk in the park, for goodness sake!' she said, pretending to be cross. 'You're a fit healthy young woman and both you and the boy need some good fresh air in your lungs.'

It was several days later when Emily called to see Hari, bringing a gift for the baby.

'Thank you, Emily.' Hari opened the parcel and took out a silver christening cup. 'It's lovely, you shouldn't have.'

'He's a fine boy,' Emily said a little enviously, 'and you look blooming, Hari, motherhood suits you.'

'I feel very well,' Hari agreed and she did. Physically

she had recovered fully from the birth, she should be the happiest woman in the world and yet guilt hung over her like a cloud.

'You are looking happy and content enough,' Hari said taking in the bloom of Emily's skin and the shine of her chestnut hair. 'Your marriage must be a happy one.'

Emily laughed shortly. 'You sound quite envious, Hari, but yes, in spite of the gossiping tongues, John and I are making a go of things together.'

'I'm glad,' Hari said softly. 'Isn't it strange the way our lives have changed?'

Emily nodded. 'Our lives have changed all right, I was all set to marry Craig, to be Mrs Grenfell and to gloat over the combined wealth of both families and now all that seems so trivial and shallow.'

She leaned forward and smiled. 'And here are you, respectably married to Edward and with a fine son, you are a very lucky woman, Hari.'

Suddenly Hari knew she had to talk to Emily, ask her advice, share with someone the guilt that plagued her.

'Close the door, Emily,' she said softly, 'I must talk to you.'

Surprised though she was, Emily did as she was bid and returned to sit beside Hari. 'What's wrong? You look so worried, is it Edward or the baby?'

Hari shook her head. 'It's me, everything is all my fault, the whole sorry mess.' She took a deep breath. 'David is Craig's son, not Edward's, and I can't bring myself to tell my husband the truth, it would hurt him so much.'

If Emily was shocked, there was no sign of it. She placed her hand over Hari's and bit her lip thoughtfully.

'Does Craig know about this?' she said softly.

'Oh, yes, he knows, he wants me to go away with him, but how can I hurt Edward when he's been so good to me?'

'What do *you* really want?' Emily asked gently and Hari rubbed her eyes.

'I would like to be with Craig for ever, to have him bring up the baby with me but then I would be taking my happiness at Edward's expense.' She paused and struggled against the weak tears that rose to her eyes.

'I didn't know about the baby when I married Edward,' she said. 'If only I'd known I'd have been honest with Edward from the start.'

Emily shrugged. 'I can't advise you, Hari, I feel so inadequate.' She shrugged. 'The values I used to hold dear seem a little irrelevant now.' She smiled ruefully. 'Who would have thought that I would marry a man from what I used to think of as the "lower orders"?'

Emily rose to her feet. 'I have to go but I'll be there if ever you need me, Hari, there will always be room for you in my house.'

When Emily had left, Hari sat with the baby in her arms and stared out into the small garden where the leaves of the apple trees were falling to the ground leaving the branches bare.

Edward appeared in the doorway, he was smiling fondly at the sight of her holding the baby. 'You look like a little madonna there,' he said softly.

'I'm not a saint,' Hari said shortly, 'I'm a flesh and blood woman, Edward, and don't put me on a pedestal, please.'

He came and sat beside her and took her hands in his. 'Can I help it if I worship you?' he said reasonably.

In that moment Hari almost hated him, Edward was binding her to him with words and tangling her in his emotions so that she would never be free.

Hari decided in the next few days that she must start living her life as she'd done before the baby was born. If she got out a little more, she might find a sense of perspective and the strength to face her life with Edward.

Edward was more than a little put out when Hari told him she was taking the baby to the theatre in Goat Street.

'Why are you going over there?' he asked. 'I don't think a dusty smoky theatre is a very good atmosphere for the baby to be in.'

'I'll be back stage, Edward.' Hari said impatiently, 'In any case, Meg is in town and I promised her she would be godmother to David.'

Edward's colour rose. 'I don't really like the sound of that,' he said. 'I thought you would have chosen someone more suitable, Emily Grenfell perhaps with Craig as godfather.'

'Emily is no longer a Grenfell,' Hari pointed out, 'she's Mrs Miller now. And I'm having Charles as godfather, *Sir* Charles, that should please the snobbish streak in you, Edward.'

She realized her words were harsh but she wanted to strike out and hurt him. 'In any case, I won't be dictated to about my son's future, get that clear here and now, Edward.'

'David is *my* son too, Hari, or have you forgotten?' Edward said gently. Hari's first instinct was to lash out at Edward, to tell him he was *not* David's father, he had nothing to do with the baby but she bit her lip and looked away.

'In this, I have made up my mind,' she said firmly, and to her relief, Edward said no more on the subject.

Her greeting from Charles was as effusive as ever. 'Hari, my dear little lady, how wonderful to see you looking so well and this is your new offspring, let me have a look.'

To Hari's surprise, Charles took the baby and held him with easy confidence as though he had been used to babies

324

all his life. 'He is a wonderfully handsome child, cut out for a life in the theatre I dare say.' He smiled. 'Come and sit down, let me make you a nice cup of tea while we wait for Meg to return.'

'Return?' Hari asked, 'Is she gone out then?' She hid her disappointment and followed Charles from the foyer of the theatre along the corridors towards the shabby dressing-rooms.

'She will be back shortly,' he said, 'she has gone to the shops to buy some new fripperies.' He turned and smiled. 'And I imagine there will be some little surprise for the new baby.'

Hari smiled. 'Is it my imagination or are you looking just a little bit smug? Come on, Charles, what's going on.'

'All in good time, dear lady,' Charles said enigmatically, 'all in good time, but I will say this, you couldn't have visited us on a more auspicious occasion.'

The dressing-room was empty but on the table stood a bottle cooling in an ice bucket.

'I'd love to know what you are up to.' Hari said smiling, 'Won't you even give me the tiniest clue, Charles?'

'You must contain yourself in patience, my dear, Angharad,' Charles said. 'Now sit down and take this infant from me, he weighs a ton!'

The sudden sound of high heels clip clopping along the corridor alerted both of them. Hari looked up smiling as Meg came into the dressing-room, her arms full of packages. When she saw Hari, Meg unceremoniously dumped the parcels on the table and kissed Hari's cheeks soundly before peering down at the baby.

'What a sweet, dear little thing,' she enthused but when Hari asked her did she want to hold David she shied away in horror.

'Oh dear me, no, I'd drop the poor mite!' she said hastily. 'Why do you think I took up the stage? Precisely because I was not the kind to want a brood of children around my skirts.'

Charles put his arm around Meg and took her hand, holding it out so that Hari could see the huge ruby sparkling against a setting of diamonds.

'Meg has agreed to be my wife,' he said for once dispensing with his flowery mode of speech. 'We are going to be married at Christmas time, here in Swansea and you of course, Hari, will be the first one invited to the ceremony.'

He moved towards the table. 'And now,' he boomed with a return to his usual flamboyant style, 'you, my dear friend, will enjoy with us a glass of this heady brew to celebrate our betrothal.'

Hari smiled in delight. '*Duw*, there's happy I am for both of you, though why you haven't done it before I don't know.'

Meg pushed back her fluffy hair and smiled coquettishly. 'I think it took the appearance of a rival to push Charlie into making his move,' she said. She hugged Charles's arm. 'Not that *anyone* could truly rival you, my darling.'

She took the glass from Charles and smiled up into his eyes. 'You know, Hari's right, we should have done this a long time ago.'

'Anticipation is half the delight of any experience,' Charles said smiling, 'and I look forward with great anticipation to making you my wife.'

'I don't know if I'll ever get used to being Lady Briant,' Meg said thoughtfully, 'what *will* my dear father say?'

She turned to Hari, her butterfly mind already on other matters. 'You will make me some very special shoes, won't you? I want something different, design me a pair of shoes that no-one has seen the like of before.'

'I'll start working on them the minute I get home,' Hari

promised, her thoughts already whirling, her mind toying with ideas for pearl bedecked slippers in white satin and finest calf.

It was with a mixed feeling that Hari left the theatre and made her way back home, it seemed as though everyone was happily in love except for herself.

Emily had her John whom she adored and now Meg and Charlie were shining with happiness. Even Will had taken to creeping out at nights, an expectant look on his face. Was she destined never to be with the man she truly loved?

The baby was fast asleep in her arms and, as she looked down at his tiny, peaceful face, she knew that in spite of everything, she was the most fortunate woman in the whole world.

25

Working on the slippers for Meg's wedding to Charles gave Hari a renewed interest in the business and while she had been recovering from the birth of her son, orders had continued to come in from all parts of the country and now there was a backlog of work needing her attention.

Lewis and Ben had done their best to accommodate the customers and Will had been more than adequate on the more delicate side of the shoemaking but there was still a great demand for Hari Morris's individual touch.

'The first thing to do, is to employ some more cobblers,' Hari said to Will. 'The business is expanding and unless we honour our agreements the customers will go elsewhere.'

'Aye, you're right,' Will said sighing heavily. 'I've been trying to tell you that for weeks but you wouldn't listen, Hari.'

She put her hand on his arm. 'I'm sorry, Will, I've been a bit preoccupied with the baby, I realize that, but Edward's employed a young nurse to take care of David, just for a few weeks so I'll be able to spend more time seeing to things around here.'

'Look at this, Hari,' Lewis loomed over her, big and reassuring, 'I haven't done a pattern quite like this before.'

Hari took the small boot and examined it in silence for a moment. 'It's for a child with a bad leg, is it?' she asked seeing the way the heel was built up.

'Aye, one of Cleg the Coal's little boys had an accident,

fell under a cart and now the poor little boy has one leg shorter than the other. I've tried them on him and they don't seem to fit.'

Hari felt suddenly ashamed, she was neglecting all her old friends, she'd not even known about the accident, so selfishly engrossed in her own life she'd become.

'*Duw*, there's sorry I am to hear that.' She bit her lip and turned the boot over.

'I don't think it's balanced right, Lewis,' she said at last, 'see the sole here isn't level with the heel and the instep shaped like this won't give enough support.'

She looked down at the slipper she was shaping and then, with an air of determination, took off her leather apron.

'I'll go to see Cleg, measure the boy's foot myself.' She smiled at Lewis, resting her hand on his arm. 'I'm sorry. I've been leaving it all to you men instead of doing my bit but all that is going to change in future.' And her future was here, in the shoe business, that and being a good wife and mother must be her prime consideration.

When Hari arrived at the small cottage, Cleg was seated at the table eating his dinner of bread and cheese. '*Shw mae*, Hari, there's a stranger you are these days.'

'Morning Cleg, I've been a bit busy having a baby, mind,' she said laughing as she seated herself at the table.

Beatie came in from the kitchen, her face flushed, her sleeves rolled up above her plump elbows. 'Oh, it's you, Hari Morgan, slumming it today, are you?'

'Now Beatie don't take on like that,' Cleg said reasonably, 'as Hari rightly says, she's been laid up with the baby and all, you know what it's like looking after a child.'

'Are you getting a dig in at me, Cleg Jones?' Beatie's face grew redder, 'It wasn't me that let our boy run out into the roadway, mind.'

Cleg rose swiftly from the table and put his hand on his

wife's shoulder. 'Sit down, *cariad*, you're overdoing it with all that washing.'

Hari bit her lip, how different was the atmosphere in Cleg's house to the usual one of happy-go-lucky laughter.

'How is your son?' she asked Beatie and the woman looked at her with dull eyes.

'Our Billy's all right considering a cart rolled over him.' Her voice was hard.

'Still upset she is,' Cleg explained, 'though it all happened a good few months ago now.'

Hari was guiltily aware that she should have visited the family sooner, she had been so selfishly concerned with her own needs she was forgetting those of other people.

'I've come to measure Billy's feet,' Hari said forcing a note of cheerfulness into her voice. 'The boots I'll make will set him up fine, you'll see.'

'How do you know?' Beatie sounded belligerent. 'I don't see how boots can help a little boy to walk properly.'

'I've got a good friend,' Hari said, 'a man who walked with a very bad limp all his life. Now, with specially designed boots, he walks like everyone else.'

Beatie relented. 'All right, Cleg, fetch Billy from his bed, let Hari see him.'

She turned to Hari. 'Want a cup of tea, do you?' It was a gesture of conciliation and Hari knew it.

'Yes, please,' she said quickly, 'I'm gasping.' It was the right thing to say and Beatie almost smiled as she pushed the kettle on the hob.

'How's your baby then?' she said grudgingly and Hari thought over her words carefully before she replied, it wouldn't do to extol the virtues of her son, not with Beatie so distressed over Billy's accident.

'Well enough,' she said cautiously, 'though he was born early which worried me a bit.'

'Don't do them no harm to come early,' Beatie said swirling the water round and round in the brown china teapot without really seeing it. 'Worse if they go overdue, they grow too big then and it's harder giving birth.'

Cleg returned to the room carrying the little boy in his arms. 'Here's our Billy,' he said and the pride in his voice brought a constriction to Hari's throat.

The child was pale and thin and when Cleg put him down on to the floor, Billy leaned badly to one side.

'Can I draw a picture round your foot, Billy?' Hari said softly. She placed the paper on the floor and gently placed the small foot on it. 'I won't tickle you, I promise,' she said smiling.

The small foot was not damaged but the ankle still bore a deep scar and Hari tried not to show her distress. The child must have suffered a great deal, no wonder Beatie was so bitter.

There was silence as she worked and Hari was aware of the tension in the room. So was Billy because he put his hands to his eyes and began to cry.

'There, it's all right, I've finished now,' Hari said standing up quickly. 'You've been a good brave boy.'

'Lewis did the exact same thing, mind,' Cleg said, watching Hari fold away the paper carefully and put it in her bag. 'And still the boots weren't any good.'

'I know,' Hari said, 'Lewis is an excellent cobbler but he's not used to this sort of work and I am.' She spoke with more confidence than she felt.

'You can do something for our Billy then?' Beatie's voice was eager.

'I'm pretty sure I can make Billy a comfortable pair of boots that will lift his foot just enough so that he won't have to limp. And I'll put some soft calf at the top of the boot so that his bad ankle won't be chafed.'

Beatie poured the tea and smiled for the first time.

'Sit down Hari, I'm sorry I was such a grump to you when you first came in.'

'I understand,' Hari said softly, 'having my own son has made a difference, I can tell you. I don't think I'll ever be so wrapped up in myself as I used to be.'

'Aye, having a babby changes you all right, wait till you got a family like me, then you'll realize just how tired you can get and still carry on,' Beatie said ruefully.

Cleg rose to his feet. 'Well, I got work to do,' he said. 'Can't sit down drinking tea all day like you women.' He winked at Hari, 'Got a wonderful life you have, don't know why you're grumbling.'

'Get out before I throw the teapot at you, man,' Beatie said but there was a note of indulgence in her voice.

'Cleg,' Hari said, 'before you go, can I ask you to keep a look out for cobblers wanting work?' She smiled. 'Your Ben is doing well and so are the others, but I need more workers so keep your ears open.'

'I'll do that,' he said. 'I'll spread the word, tell anybody who is interested to come to your place, shall I?'

'Yes, please, Cleg,' Hari said and watched as Cleg kissed his wife and son and then, heaving his leather jerkin on to his shoulders, he left the house.

'Good man is my Cleg,' Beatie sighed, 'and I shouldn't blame him for the accident.' Her hands shook as she refilled her cup almost absent-mindedly. 'Left the door open a minute, that's all Cleg did and our Billy was out in the street before any of us could stop him.'

Hari could think of nothing to say, words were so trite, so inadequate when a woman was hurting as much as Beatie was.

Hari tried to imagine her own grief if anything should happen to David but the thought was too painful and she pushed it away from her quickly.

'Don't worry, Beatie,' she said, 'I'll make sure Billy

has the finest pair of boots this side of the Bristol Channel.'

Beatie smiled. 'I know you'll do your best, Hari, you always did care about others.'

She saw Hari to the door. 'How long will the boots take do you think?'

'I'll get working on them straightaway,' Hari said. 'Shouldn't be more than a day or two.'

'Right then, see you soon.' Beatie lifted her hand in farewell and then retreated back into the kitchen, closing the door after her.

Hari stood for a moment in the familiar street not seeing anything but the pale face of the small boy whose life had been blighted almost before it had begun.

But Hari would do her best for him, she was determined. She felt invigorated, filled with a new determination, she would make the boots a priority and everything else must wait.

But what about Meg's wedding slippers? She'd forgotten them. Well, she would just have to work all the harder for the next few days, that's all.

William stood near the back entrance of Emily's Emporium, his arm around Sarah's waist. 'Come on,' he whispered softly, 'come down the park with me tonight, you know how much I love you and isn't it normal for a man to want a woman then?'

'Oh hush, Will!' Sarah reproved, 'Sometimes I think you only want one thing from me.'

'You are a beautiful woman, Sarah, naturally I want to hold you and kiss you and make love to you.'

'Have you no shame and broad daylight too!' Sarah pushed him away but she was smiling. Will leaned good-naturedly against the back door of the shop and looked down at Sarah indulgently.

'You mean it will be all right for me to kiss and hold you and make love to you when it's dark then?' he said softly.

'Don't be daft,' Sarah said, 'and hush your talking, someone might hear, my dad might hear then you'd cop it.'

'I'm not afraid of your dad,' Will said and Sarah laughed up at him.

'I know you're not but I told you that you're daft, didn't I? My dad was champion boxer, mind.'

Will reached out and caught her arm. 'Are you coming out with me tonight? That's all I want to know.'

'Aye, all right then, if saying yes will give me a bit of peace, then so be it.'

'Saying yes will give you more than you bargained for, my lovely,' Will said wickedly. 'See you tonight down by the park gates then.'

'I'll think about it,' Sarah said but her wide generous mouth was curved into a smile.

Will whistled as he strode back to the workshop in the High Street, things were looking up lately, he had Sarah in the palm of his hand and work was improving too.

Hari was back at the helm infusing her workforce with her own enthusiasm and three more cobblers had been taken on making the workload lighter, but Hari herself was working extra hard trying to get some special orders completed.

She sometimes brought the baby into the workshop, good as gold the boy was too, and, in spite of Will's fears, Hari's health seemed not to have suffered at all by the birth, not like that of his poor old mam.

But then Will's mother had given birth to too many babies, childbirth had drained her so that when the sickness came she had no resistance to it.

Will would never forget Hari's kindness to him then, she had been a tower of strength, supporting the family, and in the end when there was no family left, taking Will away from the empty house.

'William!' Hari was sitting at the bench, the baby in the crib beside her, when he entered the workshop. 'Just the man I wanted to see.'

'Hey, not giving me more work to do, are you?' Will said smiling, 'Slave driver you are, everyone should have a day off, mind.'

'Just a tiny bit of a job,' Hari coaxed, 'I want some of these pearls sewn on to Meg's slippers, there's only me and you can do it and I want to get these boots done for Cleg's boy, I've been on them longer than I thought as it is.'

'Aye, all right,' Will said good-naturedly. He bent over the crib and tickled the baby's chin. '*Duw*, you're a lovely little boy then, aren't you?' he said and he heard Hari chuckle.

'Keep talking long enough and David will answer you,' she said, 'he's only a few weeks old, remember.'

'Never mind,' Will said, 'I've had brothers and sisters myself and they like it if you talk to them, there, see, David's smiling at me.'

'Got wind more like it,' Hari said good-naturedly.

Will sat quietly sewing the pearl beads to the satin-lined slippers with delicate stitches. 'Fair play to you, Hari,' he said at last, 'these shoes are lovely, I bet Meg will fall in love with them.'

'I know,' Hari said slowly and held up one of the small boots, 'and yet these give me more pleasure to work on because I know they'll make such a big difference to the way Billy stands and walks. See this extra piece of calf in the ankle, it's pliable and soft and yet it will support him where he's got a weakness.'

Will admired Hari as well as loving her like the elder sister she'd become. He wished he had the words to tell her his feelings, feelings that should be spoken, not kept

335

hidden as they'd been in his own family. Then suddenly, it had been too late for words.

'You are looking a bit down in the mouth,' Hari's voice cut into his thoughts, 'not quarrelled with Sarah, have you?'

'*Duw*, you're nosy!' Will said playfully. 'No, I haven't quarrelled with her, I'm seeing her tonight if it's any of your business.'

'Cheek,' Hari flipped at him with her fingers, 'remember you're only a beginner in life, you don't know it all by any means.'

She leaned forward and kissed his cheek. 'And why don't you trim that baby moustache of yours and shave the bum fluff off your chin?'

Will knew she was teasing him. 'All right, then, once I've finished this sewing, I'll go and make myself all beautiful, enjoy what's left of my day off.'

'Seriously, Will,' Hari said, 'don't rush into anything, with Sarah I mean. You've got a good future before you and I wouldn't want you to saddle yourself with too much responsibility too soon.'

Will had no intention of doing any such thing, he loved Sarah well enough but he did not yet want a wife.

'All right, Hari,' he said soberly, 'I won't do anything silly, promise.'

'Silly things just happen when you're young and in love,' she said.

'Is that what happened to you, Hari?' Will asked quietly, 'Is that why you don't seem happy any more?'

Hari gave him a quick look and Will did not miss the tell-tale flush that rose to her cheeks.

'I wasn't talking about myself. How are those slippers looking, beads all sewn on are they?'

Will rose from the bench in one easy movement. 'All done. Now can I get myself something to eat and make myself beautiful for my night out?' he said, smiling.

'All right, go on with you then.' Hari looked up at him, 'And thanks for the help, Will.'

He moved towards the door of the workshop, smelling the familiar scents of leather mingled with the soft milky scent of the baby. On an impulse, he glanced back.

'Don't work too hard, Hari, I don't want you falling sick, mind.'

He left her, then at once his thoughts were with Sarah, her soft womanliness, the sweetness of her lips when he kissed her and he sighed. Hari was right, it was all too easy to do something silly.

'Are you going out then?' Edward was seated in a chair near the fire, a glass of port in his hand. He seemed pale and restless but Hari had other things on her mind.

'I won't be long, I promised these boots for young Billy, don't worry, the nurse can look after David till I get back.'

'I'm well aware of the girl's capabilities,' Edward sounded fractious, 'but I do think you should be with our son more often.'

'But Edward, I've had David with me in the workshop all the afternoon,' Hari said in surprise. 'I'm not neglecting him, I promise you.' She kissed Edward's forehead, 'and I'll be back before you know it, you'll see.'

'All right,' he said grudgingly, 'but try to ease up, Hari, I worry about you working so hard.'

She let herself out into the cool of the evening air and drew her good woollen shawl close around her shoulders. Edward hated that shawl, he thought it more suitable for her to have a good woollen coat but Hari had no intention of conforming to anyone else's ideas of how she should look. She had worn Welsh wool for as long as she could remember and she was not about to change now. Sometimes she tucked David up in the folds of the shawl snug as a baby bird in a nest he was, held close and safe against her, she sighed, she really was a very lucky woman.

The boots were finished now, nestling in the basket hanging from her arm, strong and light they were, tiny boots, carefully fashioned and hopefully the answer to little Billy's needs.

'Hari!' The strong masculine voice stopped her in her tracks. 'I haven't seen you for days, you've always been busy in the workshop when I've called at Chapel Street.'

'I know,' Hari hardly dared look up, she felt Craig's nearness and resisted the urge to throw herself into his arms. 'I've been so busy, Craig, I didn't know if I was coming or going. There's been Meg's wedding slippers and Cleg the Coal's son's boots and I . . .' Her voice trailed away as Craig touched her cheeks briefly.

'You don't have to make excuses, Hari, I know that your life is with Edward now, I do understand.'

'I must go,' Hari said, glancing around uneasily. 'Why don't you walk to Cleg's house with me, that's if you're not expected anywhere else, mind.'

'I'm not expected anywhere else.' He fell into step beside her. 'I hear you've taken on new men.'

'That's right, I'm building up the business,' she said softly. 'I want to give my son a fine inheritance when he grows up.'

'I want to give *our* son just as much as you do,' Craig said, 'and I will, Hari, if you will only let me.'

'Your offer comes too late,' Hari said gently. 'The answer has to be no.' At the corner of the road where Cleg lived, she stopped walking. 'Don't come any further,' she said pleadingly, 'I don't want any gossip.'

She watched as he swung away along the street, a tall handsome man, well set and with a proud carriage, and she felt herself dissolve with love for him.

Briskly, she turned the corner and moved quickly along

338

the street full of cottages with windows curtained against the fading light. From within, she could just see the glimmer of lamp light and suddenly she felt lonely.

It was Beatie who opened the door to her. 'So you've come at last,' she said ungraciously, 'I thought you'd forgotten all about us.'

'No, I hadn't forgotten,' Hari said, 'it's just that the job took longer than I thought it would, that's all.'

'Well come in, though I was just going to put Billy to bed, the youngest one's gone already.'

'Hello Hari, gel.' Cleg smiled widely at her, looking unfamiliarly clean and scrubbed with little sign of his occupation as coal man. His dark hair was still wet from washing and clung to his broad forehead in small tufts.

'I've made the boots,' Hari said standing in the doorway of the kitchen, the basket held out before her. 'I hope they are going to be all right.'

'*Duw*, I'm sure nobody could do a better job than you, Hari, sit down and let's have a look at these boots then.'

He took them out of the basket one by one, turning them soles up and examining them carefully.

'Looks all right,' he said dubiously, 'though there's not much difference between left and right is there?'

'Just enough to make Billy walk straight, I hope,' Hari said anxiously.

Beatie pushed aside the remains of a meal and lifted Billy up to sit on the table. 'Let's have your good foot first, boyo,' she said gently to her son. It was easy slipping the boot into place and tying it up and all the time, Billy stared at his mother curiously, it was a long time since he'd worn boots.

'Now for the bad one,' Beatie said, 'that's going to be the test.'

'The boot opens up quite a good way down the uppers,'

339

Hari said, 'so you don't have to hurt the boy getting it on.'

'Aye, good idea,' Beatie said grudgingly. 'But what about when he stands up, that's what I want to know.'

She fastened the boot securely and then, taking a deep breath, lifted Billy to the floor. For a moment, the child stood uncertainly looking about him not knowing what was expected of him. It was Hari who held out her hand.

'Come by here, Billy,' she said coaxingly, 'let me see your lovely shiny new boots.'

He took a tentative step towards her and then another and then, more confidently, he stepped out quickly crossing the room to her side.

'*Duw*, will you look at that!' Cleg said, 'he's walking almost straight, it's a damn near miracle!'

Hari looked towards Beatie who was standing with her hands clasped over her mouth, her eyes filling with tears.

It was several moments before Beatie could speak but she came to Hari and, taking her hands, kissed them. 'Thank you, Hari Morgan, from the bottom of my heart,' she whispered, her face still running with tears. 'You've given my boy the chance to lead a normal life and I'll never forget you.'

Hari found her own eyes were moist. 'It's all right,' she said softly, 'it's all right.'

Cleg moved to the tea tin high on the shelf and poured out coins of various denominations. 'There's our savings, Hari, you take just what you want out of that, we can never repay you for what you've done.'

Hari forced a laugh. 'The boots didn't cost one quarter of that, Cleg, in any case I want some coal delivered so we'll call it quits.'

As Hari made her way back home, she felt as though she was walking on air herself, from now on she would make this sort of work her main objective, it was far more rewarding than anything she'd ever done.

As she entered the house in Chapel Street, she became aware that something was wrong. The nursemaid was in the hall with the baby in her arms and the doctor was just coming down the stairs.

'Mrs Morris,' he said in some relief. 'Thank goodness you're home, your husband has been asking for you.'

'What is it?' Hari asked, her mouth dry. The doctor drew her to one side.

'From first appearances, it would seem that Mr Morris has a severe lung condition,' he said quietly, 'I fear he is going to need a great deal of bed rest and some careful nursing, I trust you will be able to cope?'

'Yes,' said Hari dully, 'of course I will cope, Edward's my husband and while he needs me, I'll be at his side.' Hari drew in a deep breath and began resolutely to make her way up the stairs. Life was again flinging her a challenge and she would face it with whatever courage she could muster.

26

Emily found that being married to John Miller was the most wonderful thing that had ever happened to her. He was kind and considerate and it was clear from the very beginning that he worshipped the ground she walked on.

She lay in the warmth of the bed aware that he was not beside her but then, by the time she awoke, he had usually been working for some hours.

John was extremely good at figures she'd found and he could work out the monthly accounts much more efficiently than she'd ever done. Apart from which, he more than pulled his weight in the workshop. She laughed softly to herself, none of that really mattered, she loved him and that was enough, everything she had was his.

She ate a desultory breakfast and then dressed in her everyday working clothes, a skirt of dark worsted and a thick cotton blouse covered by a workman-like jacket. She knew her appearance was not at all in keeping with what fashions demanded but she'd found that fussy crinolines were not conducive to quick movement or to bending over, trying shoes on indecisive customers.

Sarah was in the shop and already had some of the less senior girls dusting the shelves and arranging new displays of boots and shoes to the best advantage.

'Morning, Miss Emily,' she said respectfully for it had been tacitly agreed that in working hours some degree of formality was necessary even though Emily was now the girl's stepmother.

'Morning, Sarah, morning, girls, keeping busy I see?' Emily smiled pleasantly though she felt she had lost face in the eyes of her staff by marrying a man they considered was 'beneath her'.

'Miss Emily,' Sarah said, 'there's a little bit of a problem, some of the boots and shoes are just not selling. My dad thinks they are out of date and perhaps we should have a sale to shift them before new stock is brought in.'

'That sounds a very good idea,' Emily said concealing the chagrin she felt that John had discussed the matter with his daughter before consulting her.

She moved through to the workshop though she seldom invaded what she saw as John's domain. His face lit up when he saw her and he came to her side immediately.

'I understand we need new stock?' She spoke a little coldly and John was aware of her tone at once.

'Yes, I think so,' he replied, smiling easily. 'Is anything wrong?'

'No,' Emily said quietly, 'but I would prefer to be consulted about such matters before you speak to Sarah or anybody else on the subject.'

John drew her outside the door and the coldness of the early spring air stung Emily's face.

'Am I to be treated as simply an employee without initiative then, Emily, or can I be allowed to do what I feel is my job without applying to you for permission every time?'

'Of course you don't have to ask my permission.' Emily was flustered, 'But I would like you to talk to me about any changes you wish to make.'

John bowed his head. 'So be it, Emily, I will make no decisions without referring to you first.'

'No, John!' Emily protested, 'I didn't mean that, oh, heavens, I don't know what I mean.'

But John had disappeared into the workshop and Emily stood for a moment debating whether to go after him or not. What did she want? she asked herself, was John her husband and naturally in charge now of their financial affairs or did she want to keep a stranglehold upon him questioning every move as if he were a child?

She returned to the shop and forced a smile. 'Prepare to have a sale immediately,' she said to Sarah, 'I'll leave it to your father to decide the new prices, perhaps you will talk to him about it.'

She turned as the door swung open and her smile became fixed as she saw Lady Caroline enter the shop, her daughter Elizabeth in her wake. Both of them wore billowing gowns under good topcoats and it was so clear to see how Elizabeth would look in years to come that, in spite of herself, Emily almost laughed.

'My little girl wants some new boots,' Lady Caroline gushed, 'something strong but not too heavy, she has tiny feet as you know.'

Emily wondered why Lady Caroline was patronizing her ready-made shoes when she had made such a fuss about her daughter's delicate feet requiring specialized fitting. She did not have to wait long to find out.

'Poor Hari Morris, you must have heard about her problems.' Lady Caroline draped herself in a chair and waved a gloved hand to one of the girls.

'A cup of mint tea and make sure it's hot,' she ordered. She returned her attention to Emily. 'Mr Morris has been taken poorly,' she lowered her voice and glanced around furtively, 'his lungs, I think. Very sad.'

Emily was concerned. 'I hadn't heard, is it very bad then?'

Lady Caroline adjusted her full skirts. 'I should think so, these lung sicknesses are usually fatal. In any event there have been no new designs forthcoming lately though

of course the workshop continues to turn out the old ones.'
She smiled disparagingly.

'The trouble with such individually made shoes is that
you can only wear them on a few occasions because once
seen they are not forgotten.'

Emily murmured a suitable response but she was thinking about Hari, how painful it must be for her to nurse a
sick husband and with a young baby to take care of too.

'My Elizabeth must have some of your best boots,' Lady
Caroline was off on another tack, 'nothing cheap, mind.'
She looked up archly, 'You know she is walking out with
Craig Grenfell, don't you?'

'Is she?' Emily said noncommittally. 'I'm so glad for
her.'

'Isn't life strange?' Lady Caroline remarked staring at
her gloves intently. 'I did think that you and Craig would
have made an ideal couple but there, life takes strange
turns and one person's loss is another's gain.'

Emily gritted her teeth resenting the implication that
she had been the one to lose, but then Lady Caroline was a
shallow woman, not given to fine sensibilities.

'I hope they will be very happy,' she said, glancing
across to where Sarah was kneeling before Lisa, trying on
a high-laced boot that rested snugly around the girl's small
ankle.

Elizabeth was a nice enough girl, somewhat over-
shadowed by her mother, but sometimes with a glint of
amusement in her eyes that revealed another side to her
nature, a side that Emily rather liked.

She hoped the girl had spirit, she would need it if she
was to cope with a man like Craig who was headstrong and
used to getting his own way.

Lisa, it seemed, had made up her mind on a pair of dark
leather boots and some indoor slippers, a speciality of
Clark's of Street.

'They are so warm and comfortable, mother,' she said enthusiastically, 'why don't you have some too?'

'Why not indeed?' Lady Caroline said smiling. 'I'll take half a dozen pairs.'

'But mother,' Elizabeth protested, 'they are stout enough for indoor use and will last you simply ages, what do you want so many pairs for?'

'It pays to order in bulk, my dear.' Lady Caroline took the tea that Sarah held towards her and settled back in her chair, 'I know that dear Emily will give me a special price for buying so much at one time, after all that's just what Hari Morris would do.'

Emily resisted the temptation to refuse quite baldly and forced a smile. 'I'm sure we can come to some arrangement,' she said.

'Right, then send my dear husband the bill as usual, and have the shoes packed up and delivered as soon as possible.'

Sarah followed Emily to the desk and smiled up at her understandingly. 'Not going to charge the old bat the full price, are you?' she asked laughing. 'Those were the things that were going to be in the sale.'

'Exactly,' Emily said, 'and it serves "the old bat", as you call her, right, doesn't it?'

'Aye, I couldn't agree more,' Sarah said, hand over her mouth to stifle the giggles.

'Send one of the girls to bring some more tea, Sarah, and I'll go and talk to the old . . . Lady Caroline, I can give her prior information about the sale, but be sure not to put the slippers out on show just yet, mind.'

Emily moved back to where Lady Caroline was sitting and smiled questioningly. 'Have you finished your shopping, if so we could go to the tea rooms for more refreshments. I'd like to tell you about our coming sale, I'll be reducing some of the stock tomorrow and of course you must have prior notice seeing that you are such a valued customer.'

Emily was aware of a quick ironic look cast in her direction by Elizabeth who was standing next to her mother's chair.

'Oh, dear me, no,' Lady Caroline shuddered, 'I don't want *sale* goods, what would people say?'

'Well, if you choose now, no-one will know.' Emily said reasonably, 'I haven't yet put up the new prices.'

'Go on mother,' Elizabeth urged, 'we could get in a stock of things as you usually do and save daddy some money into the bargain.'

Her eyes met Emily's and they were filled with laughter. Lady Caroline considered this and then inclined her head.

'You could be right, darling, well then, let's have a look if it's what you wish.'

She handed her cup to Emily and rose regally from her chair. 'Come along then, Elizabeth, I shan't have more tea, we haven't all day.'

Emily gestured for Sarah to come over. 'Make up some prices, use your initiative but don't take too much off, all right?'

'Right.' Sarah winked like a conspirator and led the women to the shelves with an air of servility that Emily knew from experience was totally false.

She moved upstairs and placed the used cups in the kitchen and then sat at the table, chin resting on her hands. She would take John to Somerset, no, she corrected herself, she would *ask* John to go to Somerset with her and choose some shoes from Mr Clark's stock.

It was high time she made her husband feel that he really was part of the business. She could see now that she had never been willing to relinquish the reins. If she'd wished to stay in charge of her own business so entirely then she should never have got married in the first place.

As it was, John was entitled to take complete charge of the business if he wished but he simply was not the sort to wield his marital rights like some stick to beat her with.

It was later in the day when John came upstairs and, as Emily breathed in the familiar scent of leather that clung to all shoemakers, she felt love for her husband flow through her anew.

'John,' she held out her hand to him, 'please John forgive me.'

'What for, love?' he said good-naturedly, he had obviously forgotten her attitude earlier that morning.

'For trying to be bossy and for acting as though you were an employee not my husband.'

He bent and kissed her forehead. 'I knew what you were like when I married you and I wouldn't want you to change, well not too much anyway.' He smiled. 'I love your independent nature, Emm, and I know how hard you have worked to build up this business and I have no right to dictate to you at this stage.'

'You have every right, John, you are my legal husband and therefore everything I have is yours.'

'I know.' John drew her to her feet and took her in his arms. 'But I'll never think of Emily's Emporium as mine, it's yours and all I want to do is to help you run it in the best way possible.'

'John,' Emily took his face in her hands, 'I have an idea, why don't we go down to Somerset, stay the night, perhaps several nights and then when we feel like it, choose some new stock for the shop?'

John kissed her mouth. 'To be alone, just the two of us, *duw*, it sounds too good to be true.'

'You agree then?' Emily said eagerly. 'We'll travel by train, it's so much quicker than by road and I'll book us in to . . .'

John put his hand over her mouth. 'Don't rush

things, Emm, let me do something towards this trip, will you?'

Emily laughed. 'All right, I won't say another word, I'll leave it all to you.'

John kissed her again and this time, his lips lingered on hers for a long time. Emily clung to him, loving him so much that it hurt. She was so lucky, so very lucky to have him and she must never again make the mistake of treating him as anything less than her husband.

Hari sat in the bedroom window staring out into the garden of the house in Chapel Street. The early spring weather was bringing out the crocuses and here and there a few hardy snowdrops still remained white droplets against the earth.

In the bed behind her, Edward was asleep, his breathing uneven and ragged. He was no better than when the doctor had first seen him, not even Hari's oft-applied herbal remedies seemed to help.

From the next room, Hari heard the faint cry of the baby and she rose quickly, not wishing to disturb Edward's sleep. It was the nursemaid's day off and from the way the girl kept making more and more complaints and excuses, Hari felt instinctively she would not be coming back.

Hari knew that the maid feared that Edward's sickness might be catching even though the doctor assured everyone that it was not.

'Come on then, David, my boy, I think you want changing, you've soaked yourself, haven't you?'

David smiled and held out chubby fists towards her, he was almost four months old now and a bright, happy baby who gave very little trouble.

When he was comfortable, Hari held him to her breast where he nuzzled his dark head contentedly against her.

349

Edward had wanted to employ a wet nurse but Hari would not hear of it.

'My kind feed their own children,' she'd said, fiercely protective of her rights and in his usual calm way Edward had smiled and given in to her.

But it was a long time since she had seen Edward smile, when he was awake, he simply stared up from his pillow listlessly compliant when Hari gave him food or medicine but making no effort to rouse himself except when he was forced to.

It was almost as though he had lost the will to live and Hari wondered guiltily if he could have possibly guessed the truth about David. But she shook the thought away, Edward hardly saw the boy these days and, when he did, it was only briefly.

Hari heard a knocking on the door and then it was opened and the voice of the maid was answered by a lower, masculine voice, one Hari could not mistake.

She sat David up and rubbed his back and then quickly buttoned up her bodice as she heard footsteps on the stairs.

'Craig, there's kind of you to come to see Edward.' She looked up, unwillingly meeting his eyes. Craig, it was rumoured, was to be seen more and more in the company of Lady Caroline's daughter, Elizabeth.

Craig smiled down at her, drinking in the sight of Hari with the baby in her arms.

'How is Edward?' he asked gently and Hari bit her lip, not knowing what to say.

'About the same,' she replied at last, 'I'm so worried about him!' The words burst from her lips, 'I don't know what to do to help him. I've tried all my herbal remedies and the doctor has given us several different medicines to try but nothing seems to do any good.'

'I'll go through and talk to him,' Craig said gently. He

looked longingly at David. 'The baby, he's well?' he asked, his voice thick.

'Strong as an ox,' Hari answered quickly, 'there's nothing to worry about where David is concerned, thank God.'

She put him in his bed and the baby waved his small fists in the air, obviously content.

'I'm lucky he's such a good child,' she said, 'especially as I don't think the nursemaid will be coming back.'

'Why not?' Craig asked in surprise. 'I thought you were happy with her.'

'I don't think she's happy with us,' Hari replied ruefully, 'she's afraid she'll catch whatever it is that Edward is suffering from.'

'Shall I see what I can do?' Craig said. 'I may be able to ask around and find you someone else.'

'No,' Hari said quickly, 'I don't think that would be a very good idea.'

Craig nodded and then moved quietly across the landing and into Edward's room. Hari stood for a moment, her hands over her face, giving herself a few moments to gain the strength to cope with whatever mood she might find Edward in when he was awakened.

Sometimes he would be so hopeless, so weary and defeated that she found it difficult to cheer his spirits.

But when she entered the room, Edward seemed to be making an effort to converse with Craig and she felt a slight lifting of her spirits.

'Isn't it good of my old friend to come round?' Edward made an effort to smile but his skin was stretched taut across his bones and his eyes seemed more sunken than ever. But perhaps she was seeing her husband through Craig's eyes for, although he tried to hide it, it was clear that Craig was shocked by the deterioration in Edward's condition.

351

'I've brought you a bottle of your favourite port,' Craig said, 'I've left it downstairs, perhaps Hari will give you some after your supper.'

'That's kind of you, Craig,' Edward's voice was weak and the effort to speak made him go into a spasm of coughing. Hari moved towards him and rubbed her hand gently over his thin spine.

'I'll get you some elixir, now, Eddie,' she said, 'I won't be a minute.'

She knew it was a useless gesture, the elixir did nothing to ease the pain Edward was feeling, but at least it gave him the impression that something was being done.

On an impulse, Hari put a large measure of port into the glass and carried it up to her husband. If it didn't cure what ailed Edward at least the drink might make him feel temporarily better.

It seemed to work for, after a moment, Edward pushed away the glass and smiled. 'I don't know what that new medicine is, Hari,' he said weakly, 'but it's damned fine stuff.'

'Here, have some more,' Hari held the glass to his lips and Edward drank eagerly. He sighed softly and allowed Hari to set him back against the pillows.

'I'm sorry, Craig, old fellow,' he said, 'but I feel very tired, I think I'll just have a little doze.'

Hari covered Edward over and led the way from the bedroom. Craig followed her silently down the stairs and then into the sitting-room and he carefully closed the door after them.

'Hari, Edward is very sick but then I don't need to tell you that. What I'm worried about is have you discussed Edward's financial affairs with him, I think it is something you are going to have to think about.'

Hari shook her head. 'No, I can't not while he is so ill, Craig.'

Craig strode towards the window, his hands thrust into his pockets. 'It grieves me to see Edward in such a state,' he said softly, 'but now you have to consider yourself, Hari. If anything should happen to Edward where would you stand?'

'I don't know,' Hari said, tears brimming in her eyes. 'How can I begin to think of things like that when he lies up there suffering?'

'Your business, how is it doing?' Craig persisted. 'Would you be solvent in the event that the very worst should happen?'

'I would not be rich,' Hari said softly. 'I've allowed things to slide while Eddie's been sick but I would survive on my own as I've always done.'

'Look,' Craig said, 'I've got to go away, to Bristol on business, I will be gone for about a week but when I come back I will talk to Edward, matters of finance must be discussed, it's no good ignoring the issues.'

Hari took a deep breath. 'It's good of you to be concerned, Craig, but it really is not for you to worry about. I can look after myself and David too.'

Craig moved across the room and took her by the shoulders. 'Can you, Hari? You don't see what I do, a young woman worn out with caring for a baby and a sick husband. You are only human, you can't do everything alone, you must realize that.'

He paused, 'Hari, let me at least talk to Edward, I won't upset him, I promise you, I'll be careful to let him think that my questions are asked as a general business move on my part.'

'All right, Craig,' Hari said at last, 'but not now, let him rest, you can see how exhausted Edward is.'

'As soon as I come back then.' Craig smiled suddenly and Hari felt her heart move within her. 'I love you, Hari,' he said softly.

She held up her hands as though to ward him off.

'Please don't say that, my feelings of guilt are hard enough to bear as it is. Anyway,' she forced a note of lightness into her voice, 'didn't I hear that you are still walking out with Lady Caroline's daughter?'

Craig's hands dropped to his sides. 'She's a friend, nothing more, she could never be anything more to me than that, Hari, she understands that even if her mother doesn't.'

Hari moved away from him and stood with the table between them, staring out into the garden but without seeing the flowers or the neat railings that surrounded the house, or the street beyond but seeing Craig's smile, the smile she saw every day on the face of her son.

'Please go, Craig,' she said gently, 'I'll see you when you get back from Bristol.'

He moved to the door. 'Look after yourself, Hari,' he said gently. 'It will do no-one any good if you allow yourself to fall ill.'

'I'll do my best to avoid that,' she said without turning. But she watched as he let himself out of the gate and as he strode away along the street, a tall handsome man, the father of her son, the man she loved and somehow she felt as if he was walking out of her life.

But her duty was here in this house with her sick husband, Edward needed her and she would give the last ounce of her strength to make life comfortable for him.

She thought with a sense of disquiet about Craig's words of warning about their financial position. Did he think Edward so sick then that he couldn't deal with them himself?

Quietly, Hari crept up the stairs, she passed the room where David was playing in his bed, gurgling cheerfully, watching his fists waving in the air.

Edward was asleep, a slight figure beneath the bed-clothes. Hari moved closer and stared down at her

354

husband, his breathing seemed a little easier and, silently, she walked on tiptoe away from the bed.

It was almost dark when Hari returned to Edward's bedroom. She held a lamp in her hand and, as she set it down on the bedside table, Edward stirred.

'Hello, Hari.' His voice was threadlike but he was smiling.

'Hari, forgive me, my love,' he said in a whisper, raising his hand towards her, 'I haven't been a good husband, I'm sorry . . .' His voice trailed into silence as Hari clasped his hand.

'You've been a wonderful husband, Eddie, don't say such things.'

'I'm sorry, I love you, Hari, and our boy but I . . .'

Those were the last words he ever spoke. His hand fell back on to the bed and his eyes were closed.

'Eddie!' Hari said urgently, 'Eddie!' But even as she touched his shoulder, she knew it was a vain gesture, Edward had given up the fight, he had gone from her for ever.

She knelt by the bed and rested her head on the thin, unmoving chest. 'My poor Eddie,' she whispered, 'you never knew that Davie wasn't your son, at least, you died happy and now at last you can rest.'

355

27

The spring weather was bright but still cold when Emily and John made their way along the road to the Clark's factory in Street.

'Somerset is a very beautiful place, John,' Emily said softly, her arm through his, 'in the summer time the roses are plentiful and fragrant.'

'Aye, it's a fertile place all right,' John agreed, 'but give me the ruggedness of Wales every time.'

Emily shook his arm. 'You are a home bird, aren't you? Isn't there any adventure in your soul?'

John looked down at her and smiled. 'Being with a woman as unpredictable as you is adventure enough for a plain man like me,' he said ruefully. 'Who'd have thought I'd have upped and left Swansea on a steaming monster of a train and come all this way to England and at my time of life too?'

'Go on with you, John!' Emily reproved him. 'Anyone would think you were old.' Her face became grave.

'I can't stop thinking about Hari so alone now that Edward has been taken from her. I saw her face at the graveside and she looked so pale and wan that I wanted to put my arms around her.'

'You did all you could, Emm,' John said softly, 'you went to see Hari and found that her friends from the theatre were handling the funeral arrangements so try not to worry too much, she has her child after all.'

'Yes,' Emily said wistfully. 'She has her child. Ah,

we're here, see there's the factory, isn't it impressive?'

Emily and John were shown into the factory by the machine-room foreman and it was clear that John was enchanted by the place at once.

'*Duw*, will you look at those machines!' He moved around the room asking questions of the women who worked the treadles and Emily knew by the look on his face that John was storing the information away for future reference.

John was particularly interested in the America Blade machines that had been adapted for sewing uppers to soles with waxed threads.

'See this, Emm?' John said enthusiastically. 'With this sort of machine boots can be made to keep out the worst of the weather, I've never seen such stout strong boots in my life.'

'Would you like a machine of this sort, John?' Emily asked innocently and John smiled at her.

'I think you have just read my mind, Mrs Miller.' He put his arm around her shoulder, 'I think it's about time,' he said quietly, 'that we had our own factory and made our own stock instead of having it imported from down here.'

'Don't let Mr Clark or his foreman hear you talking like that,' Emily said softly. 'I think they value the trade we give them very much.'

'I don't doubt it,' John replied, 'but, quite truthfully, we are a flea bite to this sort of factory, they must export to many countries.'

'We do that, Mr Miller.' John Keats came up behind them and Emily smiled up at the foreman warmly.

'We'd like to order some new stock,' she said. 'What are your latest designs in ladies' and men's fashions?'

'Well there's a ladies' Lorne Lace boot, that's very nice, I'll show you if you like. For little girls we've got a dress

357

anklet in black enamel seal which was first made in 1856 but is still very popular. Come and see for yourself.'

Emily took an immediate fancy to the Lorne Lace, it was a side-fastening boot with a small heel and a pointed toe and with a neat ankle line that would fit comfortably on most women.

'I think we'll have some of these and shall we order some more of the Gentlemen's Osborne boots, John?' Emily asked. 'They seem to sell very well.'

'Aye, I think so.' John was looking at a low-backed Prince of Wales shoe with interest. 'I like this,' he said, 'see the inlet at the side and the clever cut of the heel, I think we'll take some of these as well.'

Emily enjoyed seeing John so enthusiastic, he was a good cobbler and knew about leather so she was content to let him choose whatever stock he thought they required.

She remembered with sadness the shoes Hari used to make, so distinctive and different to anything that could be bought from the big manufacturers.

She felt tired when at last she left the factory with John at her side enthusing over all he'd seen.

'It would be fine if we could start our own factory, Emily,' he said. 'With machines like those the Clarks have we would soon make a profit.'

'If that's what you think, John, that's what we'll do,' Emily said decisively. 'I'm sure the initial outlay will soon be recouped.'

She bit her lip thoughtfully, she would need to risk a great deal to buy the machines but then she had faith in John, he was a sensible man with his head screwed on the right way and, as he said, they would soon begin to make a profit.

For a start there would not be the expense of bringing the stock up to Wales from Somerset or the high charges that Clarks made for their boots and shoes. On the other hand, as well as the machines there would have to be operators who could use them.

But surely sewing leather could not be so much different to sewing ordinary material, at any rate the treadles looked very much the same to Emily.

'Perhaps we could persuade Mr Clark to lend us one of his machinists for a few weeks,' she said. 'How do you think your Sarah would take to sewing leather?'

'I watched the girls on the Crispin sewing-machines very carefully,' John said. 'When you were in the office talking to the foreman I even got one of them to let me have a try of the Blake, it's like magic, I don't think we'll need anybody else, my love.'

Emily hugged his arm. 'I've got a very clever husband,' she said, 'and if I sound smug, it's because I am smug.'

They ate at the tiny inn where they were to stay the night and John drank moderately of the drink made from apples and found it was both heady and refreshing.

'Try some,' he said, 'only not too much or it'll knock your pretty block off!'

They went to bed at last and as Emily curled up beside John she sighed with happiness. He turned and took her in his arms and kissed her passionately. He was a strong virile man and Emily never failed to respond to his ardour.

As he parted her lips with his own and his work roughened hands began to caress her, Emily closed her eyes in pleasure. Tonight, she was sure, she would conceive the child she wanted so badly, a son for John.

'When are we going to get married?' Sarah's voice was faintly petulant and it grated a little on William as he rested beside her on the bed in her room at the back of the premises in Wind Street.

'It's impossible right now,' Will said. 'How can I leave Hari when she has just buried her husband. She is like a poor lost soul there. She looked after me when I needed her and so I am bound to stay with her at least until she's over her grief.'

'That's all very well and good,' Sarah said, 'but what if I have a baby? My father would kill me, you too.'

'You won't have a baby, trust me.' He was growing tired of the same old arguments, Sarah was a sweet girl but she was making demands on him that he was not prepared to meet.

He rose from the bed in a swift, impatient movement and began to dress.

'Don't go, Will,' Sarah protested. 'You always leave when I talk about serious things.'

'Well, you know the answer then, don't you?' Will said abruptly.

'Look,' Sarah's voice took on a wheedling tone, 'with dad away you could even stay the night, the other girls won't say anything, you needn't worry about that.'

Will didn't reply, Sarah was tightening the net around him and the more she pulled the more he struggled.

'I have other admirers, mind,' she said glancing up at him through curling eyelashes. 'You are not the only one to set his cap at me.' When Will didn't reply, she changed her tactics. 'Please stay,' she tugged at his jacket, 'there's no reason for you to go home.'

'There's every reason,' Will said. 'I can't leave Hari alone in that house in Chapel Street, can I?'

Sarah sighed, 'Hari, it's always Hari, anybody would think it was Hari you went to bed with.'

Will turned on her angrily. 'Shut your mouth, Sarah, there's no call to speak about her like that.'

'Well, she's no saint, is she?' Sarah spoke with a strength that halted Will in his move to the door.

'What do you mean?' he said quietly, standing quite still and Sarah, unaware of his anger, rushed on.

'Well, there's talk the baby is not her husband's, came *early*, so they say, not even nine months after the wedding,' she wrapped her arms around her knees. 'And the baby looks the spitting image of Craig Grenfell and we all know that he used to be living in World's End with Hari, mind.'

Will caught her by the shoulder. 'Keep your suspicions to yourself,' he said shaking her roughly, 'or you'll have me to answer to.'

'Don't be like that, Will,' Sarah knew she'd gone too far, 'it's only what people are saying, after all.'

'Well, you needn't spread the rumours any further, need you?' He slammed out and hurried from the building into the night. That's all Hari needed now was to be the subject of malicious gossip.

Poor Hari, she'd had enough to contend with, she had been stoical and patient during Edward's sickness and then she seemed to have gone to pieces after his very sudden death. It was only when she held her child in her arms that she seemed to be at all animated.

The theatre folk had been marvellous, Charles and Meg had stepped in and taken over and Will suspected that Charlie had paid for the funeral out of his own pocket.

Suddenly Will became aware of footsteps and, from the pounding of booted feet against the cobbles, it was clear that there was more than one man behind him.

Without knowing why, Will began to run, he darted down one of the lanes and concealed himself in a shadowed doorway. He saw the men rush past, three of them and they seemed to be carrying stout branches in their hands.

The sound of their footsteps died away at last and Will cautiously ventured back into the street, wondering who could possibly be chasing him. Were they simply footpads looking for easy pickings or could Sarah have been telling the truth and he had a jealous rival? Whatever the truth was, he was careful as he made his way towards Chapel Street.

He was turning the corner near home when he was suddenly confronted with the three men. They stood in silence, their very stance threatening.

Will took stock of the situation, he could turn and run or stay and fight. He glanced behind him, the street was long and empty and the chances were he would easily be caught.

He launched himself forward and caught one of the men unawares. William recognized him at once, he would never forget that sneering face, it was Sam Payton the thief who had stolen Edward Morris's boots all those years ago.

Taking the gnarled branch of a tree from Payton's hand, Will swung it round and the other two men backed away uncertainly.

'Get him!' Payton was scrambling to his feet and, even as he spoke, he thrust himself forward and caught Will around the ankles.

Will crashed to the ground, losing his stick, his head hitting the cobbles. He felt a stunning blow on the back of his head and then a boot crashed into his chest and Will gasped for air, even in his pain knowing he was in for a real beating.

He tried to rise but another blow felled him, the gas light above him wavered and dimmed just as he felt a fist crashing into his face. Slowly, he toppled forward, trying feebly to remain conscious but the darkness pressed in on him as he slumped senseless to the ground.

Hari looked at the constable uncomprehendingly, he rubbed at his chin and repeated his words.

'I'm sorry to bother you at a time like this, Mrs Morris, but we have a young man down at the hospital and from what little we can make out he is a cobbler at this establishment. Does the name Will Davies mean anything to you?'

Hari felt as though she was living in a nightmare, only a week had passed since Edward's death and now this man was telling her that Will was very sick.

'I'll get my shawl,' she said, her voice dulled with fear. She took Davie and wrapped him in the Welsh shawl and returned to where the constable stood in the hallway.

Nothing seemed real as she walked with the constable down the roadway to the hospital. Hari was unaware of the curious stares from people she passed and kept her mind blank, unwilling to think of Will so sick that a constable had been sent to fetch her.

The smell of the hospital brought a new wave of fear as Hari reluctantly handed the baby over to one of the nurses.

The room where Will was lying was quiet and still and smelled of soda.

'Is this Will Davies?' the constable asked kindly. Hari moved forward and stared down at the figure in the bed, fighting the waves of nausea that threatened to overwhelm her.

It was only by the tufts of bright hair that she could recognize him, his face was like raw meat, the eyes closed and swollen. His jaw seemed to be twice its normal size and Hari thought for a moment she might faint clean away.

She took one of his hands and kissed it tenderly. 'That's Will,' she said softly. 'What's happened to him, how bad is he?'

'You'll have to speak to the doctor, Mrs Morris,' the constable said gently. Even as he spoke, the doctor entered the room and lifting Will's wrist felt his pulse.

'What are his chances?' Hari said, looking the young bearded man directly in the eye. He shook his head.

'Not very good,' he said. 'But he's a young strong man, he may survive.'

Hari sank into a chair and leaned forward. 'Will, don't you leave me too,' she said softly, 'I can't manage without you.'

The doctor put his hand on her shoulder. 'He can't hear you, Mrs Morris,' he said, 'he's deeply unconscious.'

'Will!' Hari persisted, 'you must get well, we need you, David and me.'

The doctor drew her out of the room and smiled in sympathy. 'I suggest you come back in a day or two, we'll know more then.'

Hari walked home, not seeing the streets she passed through, she fought the tears that threatened to spill over until she was safely indoors.

Crying bitterly, she put David down in the bed where he immediately fell asleep. She stared around her at the emptiness of the house in Chapel Street and wondered why it was her life was falling apart.

There had been the shock of Edward's death, followed by the devastating knowledge that there was no money, not even enough to bury him. It seemed Edward, though good with other people's money, had not put his own affairs in order.

She rubbed at her eyes, it was only by the goodness of Charlie and Meg that the funeral had been able to take place and now she must pay them both back even if it meant selling everything she possessed.

And what did she possess? Not very much when she added it up. A few pairs of boots and shoes and some left-over leather and a few lasts. As for the workshop, it was rented, and there was no money for rent.

'Craig,' she said softly, covering her eyes with her hands, 'why aren't you here to help me through this ordeal? You promised you'd be back in a week, I need you Craig.'

But her words hung in the silence and Hari felt more alone than ever.

Craig stood outside the door of the office and seeing the door was locked sighed heavily. 'Damn!' He forced down his feeling of frustration; there was still no sign of the owner of the leather store.

It was imperative that, while he was in Bristol, Craig should see Mr Meyer. He was a good customer and Craig badly needed to move some of his stocks of leather.

Craig moved away from the office resigned to waiting another day. He was very conscious of his promise to Hari to be back in Swansea within the week but wait he must.

Reluctantly, he left the premises and stared along the street, wondering desperately how he could get in touch with Meyer. He went into the hotel next door and asked the elderly man behind the desk if he knew when Mr Meyer would be back.

'He's gone away,' the man said and Craig hid his impatience.

'I know that,' he said, 'but do you know when will he be returning?' The man scratched his grizzled hair.

'No, don't know that, sir, them offices been shut up all week.'

Craig was thoughtful as he walked back to the inn where he had a room. He would give Mr Meyer until the weekend and if there was no sign of him by then, Craig would go back home.

In his room, he consulted his notebook, he still had four customers to visit, most of them in or around the Bristol area, but Mr Meyer was always ready to buy a big stock of leather, especially if it was French calf which he didn't want the trouble of importing himself.

Craig threw himself on the bed and clasped his hands behind his head, thinking worriedly about Hari. She had looked so pale and desperate last time he'd seen her. She was just a little bit of a thing and the birth of the baby had taken the stuffing out of her.

At the thought of the boy, his face softened, David was fine and bonny, strong limbed and with a mop of dark hair, even Craig could see how much the boy resembled himself.

He sighed, it was a good thing that Hari had never told Edward the truth, especially now that he was so ill. He'd looked dreadful last time Craig had seen him. Edward had never been a robust man but the amount of weight he had lost had left him looking as though a puff of wind would blow him away.

Craig closed his eyes. Why hadn't he married Hari himself a long time ago and then none of this mess would have happened. He could have brought Hari and the baby on the trip with him, turned it into a holiday for the three of them, a family outing. Craig doubted he would ever have a family now.

He thought of Elizabeth with a wry smile, they had both known from the start that nothing would ever come of their relationship even though Lady Caroline hinted enough times that they should be married. The only one he wanted to marry was Hari.

Craig became impatient with the way his thoughts kept returning to Hari and rose from the bed in one easy movement, he would go downstairs, enjoy a drink, forget all about his private life and even about the elusive Mr Meyer.

The room was full of cheerful voices and smoke drifted across the room and the fragrant smell of pipe tobacco mingled with the rich fruity smell of cider.

Craig sat at a table alone and after a time a woman came towards him, smiling a welcome. 'Would you like a nice mug of cider and a bite to eat, sir?' She was younger than

Craig had first thought, her small face framed with curling hair, her mouth curved into a merry smile. The bodice of her dress was cut low to reveal full young breasts and Craig suddenly felt desire burn in his belly.

'Just the cider,' he said, leaning back in his chair. Her eyes looked him over with becoming impudence and then, turning, she moved gracefully away, fully aware that she was being watched.

She returned shortly with the cider and bent over him so that he could smell the fragrance of her. 'Strong stuff this cider, sir,' she said, 'especially on an empty stomach.'

'I feel like drowning my sorrows.' Craig smiled at her and handed her some coins. 'Make sure my mug is full so long as I need it.'

The cider tasted innocuous but, after a time, Craig began to feel the effects. The girl came towards him once more and smiled down at him.

'Are you sure there's nothing else I could give you that would bring you pleasure, sir?' she asked cheekily. 'My name is Berta, I'm telling you in case you want something brought to your room.'

'Thank you, Berta,' he said, 'I'll let you know.'

He put down the mug of cider half finished and knew it was time he went to bed. His head felt light like thistledown and he was having trouble focusing his gaze on the narrow staircase that led to the upper floor and his room.

Craig stood for a moment, staring out of the window, he was in a strange town among strangers and suddenly he felt the need to be home in Swansea. Tomorrow, he decided, he would pack up and leave, to hell with Meyer.

He stripped off his clothes and dropped them where he stood wanting only to fall into bed and find oblivion in sleep. The bed was hard but the bedclothes were clean and the room smelled sweet and yet, as he lay tossing and turning in the bed, sleep refused to come.

Craig was suddenly aware of the door opening and then he felt a warm naked body creeping into bed beside him. He reached out his hand and touched a bare breast and, instantly, he was aflame with desire.

'It's Berta, sir.' The voice had the softness of the Bristol brogue and as warm arms entwined around his neck, Craig sighed softly, it seemed so long since he'd held a woman in his arms and though it was Hari he wanted, she was married to his best friend and out of reach.

'Berta,' he said thickly, 'you are very beautiful.' He buried his face in the warmth of her neck. She wriggled close to him and her hands upon his body were practised.

'Have you had many men, Berta?' he asked softly and she put a small hand over his mouth.

'None as handsome as you, sir,' she whispered in his ear.

Craig's last feelings of reservation vanished, Berta was no shy virgin, she was a woman used to men and together they would fill each other's needs, with no recriminations when the morning light filtered into the room. And, at this moment, that was all Craig wanted.

28

Hari sat in the silent kitchen, the papers spread out on the table before her like an unspoken threat. Accounts, Edward's accounts detailing his income and expenditure over the past year.

Hari's first shock had been to learn that the house in Chapel Street was rented not owned by Edward as he had led her to believe. Then, as she'd worked through his papers, she'd come to realize that there was very little money to spare, certainly not enough to cover the rent for any lengthy period of time.

The first bout of blind panic had subsided days ago when she had first brought herself to open Edward's desk and go through his things. It had dawned on her only gradually that, once she had paid outstanding bills, she would not be able to afford to live in Chapel Street.

And yet, like the business woman she was, Hari had come to a decision, she would cut her losses, leave the house as soon as possible and move into suitable lodgings. At least in that way her own expenditure would be cut dramatically and she would survive until she sorted out her business once more.

Hari rose from her chair and moved to the window, clasping her hands together. She felt friendless for William, who was usually a tower of strength, was still lying near to death in the hospital. It all seemed like a terrible nightmare.

Hari sighed, she had already given the servants notice, the maids had left at once, once paid, they saw no reason to delay. And in her heart Hari could not blame them, they too needed the security of a roof over their heads.

Hari wondered now at her complete lack of foresight, Craig had tried to warn her about sorting out her affairs. Why hadn't she discussed finances with Edward before he was sick? She would have realized then that Edward had nothing but the wages he earned at work.

She wished she could confide in someone, talk out her problems but Charlie and Meg were out of town, gone back to Ireland where Meg had been born to visit her family. In any case, they had done more than enough for her, helping her with the funeral.

Well, she would solve nothing waiting here in the house that was no longer her home, she must get out, find new, cheap lodgings with the small amount of money she had left.

David was awake in his bed, Hari lifted him in her arms and held him close, his hair silky against her chin. She closed her eyes, in spite of everything, the shock of Edward's death, the impending loss of her home, she still had her son and for his sake she would rebuild her life.

She wondered briefly and painfully about Craig's absence, then she pushed the thought aside. He had not come to her as he had promised which must mean he had more important things to do with his life.

It was Cleg the Coal who told Hari of the rooms that were going vacant. She called there to deliver his boots, they had taken such hard wear that they needed tapping again.

'*Duw*, come in Hari, there's good it is to see you, sit down by here and have a cup of tea.' Cleg blackened by coal ushered her into the kitchen. 'Beatie, get this girl a cup of tea she looks fair washed out.'

Beatie quickly poured tea from the huge brown pot and set it before Hari. 'Cleg's right, you look awful.' She sat down beside Hari. 'There's sorry I was to hear about your hubby, sudden like, was it?'

Hari nodded, touched by the gestures of kindness. She drank the tea thirstily and felt a little better.

'I'm looking for rooms,' Hari said. 'I need to leave Chapel Street as soon as possible, the house would be too expensive for me to keep up.'

'I may know of somewhere,' Cleg said, 'I've got one more load of coal to deliver, Hari, but I'll see you when I get back, right?' He nodded to his wife. 'See you later, love.'

Beatie cut a slice of bread and placed it with a portion of cheese on a plate in front of Hari. She returned to the hob and ladled some warm porridge into a bowl.

'There, the little one will like that, my boys do.' She looked down at Hari in sympathy.

The women chatted about everything and nothing and it was a relief to Hari to forget her problems if only for a short time.

Cleg returned to the house with a slamming of the door. 'Thank the Lord that's my work over for the day.' He smiled at Hari.

'The rooms I told you about, they are still vacant. Not posh, mind.'

'Tell me more,' Hari said, 'so long as the place is clean and respectable I'll take it.'

'It's in the house of a customer of mine, Hetty Blake, she lets out rooms not far from your old place where you was brought up. Nice woman she is, but the place she's living in got a bad name.'

Hari smiled. 'Can't have a worse name than World's End, I don't think.'

'*Duw*,' Beatie broke in, 'Hetty is a friend of mine, why

371

didn't you say who you had in mind Cleg? Do anything for me would Hetty. Mind, there's wicked women down there in them bad houses, you know.' Beatie glanced at her sons playing in the doorway and lowered her voice. 'They have men in all times of the night and day. But I know Hetty isn't like that, mind, she's good and respectable, takes in washing she does as well as letting rooms, hard working is Hetty.'

'I'm sure I'll be all right there,' Hari said positively. David, satisfied with his bowl of porridge, had fallen asleep. 'I'm feeling more cheerful already,' Hari said smiling.

'Well me and Cleg, we owe you a favour, we haven't forgotten how kind you were making those special boots for our eldest.' She glanced at her husband.

'Shall I take Hari round to Salthouse Passage then, Cleg?' She glanced at Hari, 'You'd best see the place right away in case the rooms get let to someone else.

'Look after the boys for us,' Beatie said, 'little David is fasto and I promise I won't be long, just there and back.'

'Aye, I've heard that before,' Cleg said smiling, 'you'll have a cup of tea with Hetty then another one and a few hours will pass before you know it. Aw all right, go on then.'

Beatie flashed him a look, 'I'll be out of there before dark, boyo,' she said firmly, 'have no worries on that score.'

Cleg laughed, 'I don't know, why don't you make a few bob while you are down there.' He pinched her cheek playfully, 'but then, I suppose you wouldn't get many customers!'

'I'll ignore that,' Beatie said haughtily but her eyes were full of laughter. 'Come on Hari, take no notice of this big oaf of mine.'

Together, they walked down the street and Hari felt a sense of unreality, she was taking a step backwards and yet it was only a temporary setback, she would make sure of that.

'How far is Salthouse Passage?' she asked and Beatie glanced at her.

'Not far, feet killing you are they?' she added sympathetically.

Hari smiled, 'As a shoemaker, I shouldn't admit it but I think I've got a hole coming in one of my soles.'

'For shame, Hari!' Beatie said jovially, 'but at least you can tap it yourself.'

'Yes, I can, can't I?' Hari suddenly felt more hopeful, she still had the skill of the shoemaker at her fingertips and a last and some leather was all she needed to make a living mending soles and heels.

The roads grew meaner, the houses, cramped together in tiny courts and passages, were tall and dark and depressing. Salthouse Passage was no different to the others except that outside one of the buildings a woman, painted and powdered, advertised her trade. Somehow, it all looked strangely familiar to Hari though she couldn't imagine she'd been here before for any reason.

Hetty was a large, imposing woman with a round, scrubbed honest face. Hari liked her at once.

'Hari is a friend of mine,' Beatie said at once as the woman led the way through a long dark passage into the kitchen where a cheerful fire burned in the grate. 'She's looking for a room, I think my Cleg asked you about it?'

Hetty took in Hari's good if unpretentious clothes and, after a moment, she nodded.

'Aye, he did. Got a babby though, haven't you?' She didn't wait for a reply but carried on speaking. 'Had none of my own, mind,' she said seating herself in an armchair, plump legs spread to the blaze of the fire forming a huge lap of her knees.

'But I was a nursemaid for many years when I was younger, always did have a way with babies, me.'

Beatie sighed. 'You can have a way with my rips any time you like!'

'I'll mind them for you whenever you like, you know that,' Hetty said, smiling. 'Get up off your backside and make us all a cuppa while I talk business with your friend.'

Beatie sighed. 'Put on by all my friends, I am, too good-natured by half, that's me.' She pushed the kettle on the flames and, as Hari watched her, she was on edge, wondering if there was a room available for her in Hetty's house or not.

Hetty seemed to read her thought. 'Parlour,' she said, 'you and the baby can have that. I've just let the middle room or you could have had that too.' She glanced at Beatie, 'Take Hari to see the parlour, there's a good girl, the kettle isn't boiling yet and it's no good standing over it, it won't boil any quicker.'

Beatie shrugged, 'See how this friend of mine treats me, like an idiot, I don't know why I bother with her.' But she rested her hand on Hetty's plump shoulder for a moment before leading the way back along the passage.

'Here we are.' She flung open the door and Hari was pleasantly surprised to see that the room was quite large and spacious, the window looking out into the street but hung with good thick curtains. 'Hetty likes you,' Beatie said softly, 'she's never offered anyone the parlour before.'

Hari moved into the room that was filled with small tables and a variety of odd chairs as well as a scrolled back sofa.

'Don't worry,' Beatie said, 'Hetty will have this place ready for you in a tick, you'll see.'

Hari was doubtful but she was grateful that at least she had a roof over her head. 'Thank you for helping me,' she said, smiling warmly.

'Well, Cleg and me will always be grateful to you for what you did for our Billy,' Beatie said. 'And now you've got a new friend in Hetty, you'll see. Once she takes to you she's loyal to the last.'

Suddenly, Hari, who had not shed a tear since Edward's funeral, began to cry. Great sobs shook her body and she put her hands over her face, embarrassed by her own show of emotion.

'There, there, Hari, cry it all out, it's only natural like.' Beatie comforted, putting her arm around Hari's shoulder and guiding her back towards the kitchen. 'The poor girl is worn out,' she explained to Hetty, 'just lost her husband, see it's all been too much for her.'

'Well, she's got Hetty to look out for her now.' The big woman rose to her feet. 'Here I made the tea, it's all poured out, get it down the girl while I see to her room.'

Hari wiped away the tears but they came afresh, she could not seem to stop crying now she'd started. From upstairs, she heard Hetty's voice talking loudly, then there was a series of bumps and Beatie leaned forward touching Hari's arm.

'Don't cry any more, you got a good home now, see how Hetty's got her other lodgers organized, they're doing your room for you right away, you can move in as soon as you like. I told you she liked you, didn't I? Well, you'll be as snug as a flea in this house.'

Hari was on her third cup of tea when Hetty returned flushed but smiling to the kitchen. 'All done, you got your room, girl, and nothing more to worry about.'

'The rent?' Hari asked wiping her eyes and Hetty waved a big arm. 'I'll ask no more than you can afford, don't worry.'

Beatie was pulling on her shawl. 'I'll say good night then, Hetty,' she said, 'and I expect I'll see you soon.'

Hari followed Beatie along the passageway and stopped near the front door. The parlour had undergone a transformation, all the small furniture had gone except for an easy chair and one small table.

A bed stood against the wall farthest from the window over which the heavy curtains were closed, giving an intimate atmosphere to the room. A cheerful fire burning in the blackened grate threw out a comforting warmth.

'I'll be back tomorrow with my things, and thank you Hetty,' she said, her voice husky.

Cleg saw her back to Chapel Street, carrying the still-sleeping David in his huge arms.

'Now if you want my cart to take any of your furniture to Hetty's let me know,' he said, as he stopped outside her door.

'I won't be taking any furniture, Cleg,' she said, 'just a few possessions but thank you all the same.'

As Hari undressed and crawled into bed beside her son, she felt an immense sadness fall over her. She looked at the empty space that Edward had once occupied and reached out a hand to touch the pillow. Poor Edward, he didn't deserve to die so young.

She turned resolutely towards the small figure of her son and her arm wound protectively around him. Tomorrow, she would shut the door on her old life for ever and begin to work for a better future.

Craig had found Mr Meyer back in the office the next day but, to his dismay, the business had taken some time to sort out. The man had numerous problems, not the least of them being he didn't know if he had enough capital spare to pay for more stock of French calf.

'I will have to speak to my accountant about it,' he said,

'I must have some time, you realize these things can not be rushed.'

Craig longed to take the man by the collar and shake him into action but he swallowed his impatience and forced a smile.

'I can spare you two days, Mr Meyer,' he said, 'and then I'm afraid I must get back to Swansea, I have pressing business there.'

'I'll do my best,' Meyer said but his tone carried little conviction.

It had in fact taken more like another week with Craig urging and cajoling the man to make up his mind. At last Craig had issued an ultimatum. 'I leave tomorrow,' he said, 'while I've been waiting for you, I've managed to see the rest of my customers and now there's nothing more to keep me in the Bristol area.'

Grudgingly, Meyer had given him an order but it was a large one which compensated in some way for the delay. It was with a sigh of relief that Craig made his way to the station and began the first stage of his journey.

During the journey Craig thought of little else but Hari, wondering how she was coping and if Edward's condition had improved at all. He must have slept some of the time but at last, after what seemed endless hours, he finally arrived home in Swansea.

Summer Lodge smelled of beeswax, bright fires gleamed in the rooms in spite of the pale sunshine shining outside.

As soon as he had washed and shaved and eaten a hasty meal, Craig took a cab to Chapel Street and stood for a moment, staring up at the whitewashed house surrounded by neat railings.

In some way that he couldn't fathom, the place looked different. He walked up the path and pushed at the door, it was locked.

He moved around the back and a strange woman looked up at him curiously. She was bent over a scrubbing board, her sleeves rolled high above rounded elbows.

'Is Mrs Morris at home?' Craig asked with a sense of growing apprehension.

'Who?' the woman asked. 'There's no-one of that name here sir,' she added, taking in the cut of his clothes and the elegance of his boots.

'But that's absurd!' Craig said. 'I left Mr and Mrs Morris in this house when I went away a few weeks ago, there must be some mistake.'

'Doctor Grayham lives here now at any rate,' the woman said, 'I does for him, washing and such, perhaps you'd like to speak to him?'

'Yes,' Craig said, 'I would.' He strode into the house ignoring the woman's look of outrage and stared around him. The furniture was the same, the drapes and decorations were the same and the same pictures hung on the walls but there was a strangeness about the house, it was almost as though Craig had never been there before.

'Can I help you, sir?' The voice was young and friendly but with an air of authority in it that couldn't be ignored. Craig spun round to face a man in his early thirties dressed casually and with a pipe in his hand.

'I'm sorry if I'm intruding,' Craig said, 'I came to see a friend of mine, Edward Morris, he was living here – until a few weeks ago anyway. Do you know where he is now?'

'Come into the study,' the man said and there was a kindliness in his tone that told Craig something was very wrong.

'I'm Doctor Grayham,' the man indicated the port on the table, 'would you like some, I think you might need it?'

'Thank you.' Craig took the seat the doctor indicated and watched him pouring a good measure of the ruby liquid.

'I'm afraid it's bad news,' the doctor said taking a seat opposite Craig. 'Mr Morris succumbed to his illness and died. I'm sorry to be the one to give you the bad news.'

Craig felt a sense of shock, he'd realized Edward was sick but he hadn't realized how sick.

God, how had Hari coped with it alone? He should have been beside her, comforting her, helping her with the funeral arrangements.

'Hari, Mrs Morris, why did she leave the house?' Craig was bewildered, even if Hari didn't want to remain in the house where Edward had died, how could she have disposed of the property so quickly. 'Did she rent the house to you?'

The doctor shook his head. 'No, as I understand it, the Morrises were merely renting it themselves, they didn't own it.'

'I didn't know,' Craig said. 'Do you happen to know where Mrs Morris went?' he asked and was dismayed when the doctor shook his head.

'She was gone days before I moved in.' Doctor Grayham poured another drink. 'I don't think she had any choice, apparently there was rent owing and the landlord is a tough old stick, he wouldn't be the sort to be amiable about such things.'

Craig shook his head when the doctor proffered the bottle. 'No, thank you, I'd better go.'

'I'm very sorry I couldn't be of more help,' the doctor said as he showed Craig to the door.

Craig turned. 'Could you give me the name and address of the landlord, perhaps he would know something.'

'Most certainly, I'll fetch it for you.' The doctor disappeared into the study to emerge a few minutes later with a piece of paper in his hand. 'Here, and the best of luck in your search.'

Craig looked at the address, it was a house near Summer

379

Lodge. He hailed a cab and gave the man directions before climbing inside the coach.

How Hari must have suffered, losing Edward so suddenly and then being thrown out of her home. And where could she have gone? He thought suddenly of the theatre, Hari had friends there, someone would surely know where she was.

He called to the driver giving him new directions and the coach bounced along the cobbled roads towards Goat Street.

The lights were shining from the doorway and a queue of people stood waiting to enter the foyer, it seemed a performance was just about to begin.

Craig hurried to the back of the theatre and made his way along the passages that led to the tiny dressing-rooms. He was looking for the flamboyant figure of Charles Briant, but he was nowhere to be seen.

A girl in a gaudy costume was coming towards him and he stopped before her.

'Do you know where Charles Briant is?' he asked and the girl smiled up at him, long eyelashes fluttering.

'He's gone away with Meg, his new bride,' she said moving closer to him. 'Can I help?'

'When will he be back?' Craig said desperately and the girl shrugged bare shoulders, pouting at his lack of interest.

'Don't know, they haven't long been married, mind. Visiting her folks in Ireland they are, didn't leave any address, didn't want to be disturbed.'

Craig left the theatre and looked round for a cab, the street was empty now, the crowd had moved into the theatre. Impatiently, Craig set out on foot in the direction of Summer Lodge.

The landlord of the Chapel Street house lived only a stone's throw from the lodge and Craig knocked on the door loudly, waiting with a growing sense of frustration for it to be opened. He knew instinctively that he would get no help from the landlord and as it turned out he was right.

'Don't know where Mrs Morris is gone.' The man was elderly with a sour turn to his lips and a greying beard that hung untidily over his waistcoat. 'If I did I'd be after her for three months' rent,' he continued in a whining voice that grated on Craig's ears.

'Send the bill for the rent to me, Craig Grenfell at Summer Lodge,' he said impatiently. 'Are you sure you don't know anything about Mrs Morris, anything at all?'

'Well,' the man hesitated, 'I don't know if it's any use to you, but the young man who used to live at Chapel Street with the Morrises, it seems he had some sort of an accident and was taken to the hospital.'

Hope blazed within Craig as he digested the information. If anyone knew where Hari was, it would be William Davies.

'Thank you,' he said abruptly and then he was striding down the drive and towards the town once more. William must know where Hari was, he was like a brother to her, they were inseparable.

His step light, he covered the ground quickly. It was growing dark, the moon was reflected in the sea and the wash of the waves reached his ears as he drew nearer the beach.

The nurse was most sympathetic. 'Are you a relative of the patient?' she asked and Craig shook his head.

'No, but I must speak to him, it's urgent,' he said. The nurse frowned.

'I don't think you quite understand, sir, but come with me.'

He followed her into the silent room where William was lying asleep, a bandage swathed around his head.

'The young man is holding his own, but I'm afraid he's not regained consciousness since being badly beaten by some thugs. Dreadful things are happening on our streets these days,' she added.

Craig looked down at Will and pity rose within him, the boy was so still, his skin patterned with deep bruising beneath his eyes. After a moment, Craig turned and left the room, there was nothing he could do by being there.

Out in the darkness once more, he stared up at the stars. 'I'll find you, Hari,' he said softly. 'I'll find you if I have to search every house in Swansea.'

He turned then and, with slow footsteps, he left the hospital behind and made his way back to the empty house he called home.

29

'I love it, John.' Emily clung to her husband's arm as she stared up at the large, well-proportioned house that stood facing the sea on the outskirts of Swansea. 'I'm sure I could be happy here.'

'Well, it's the third time we've come to look at it and if you really are sure, I think we should go ahead and buy it before anyone else snaps it up.'

Emily laughed. 'At the price it's going for, there won't be any rush I don't think. But we can well afford it what with the machines installed in the workshop and production so good.'

'What are we waiting for then?' John leaned down and kissed her, 'This is the perfect place for us to start that family you are always talking about.'

Emily felt a shadow fall over her happiness, the longed for baby had not materialized and she knew that the fault must lie with her. She could not forget the doctor telling her, some time ago, that she might not be able to conceive a child. In any case, John had Sarah as living proof that there was nothing wrong with him.

'Let's go inside,' she said quickly. 'I love looking out over the bay, did you know you can see a storm coming over the rocks of Mumbles Head long before it reaches Swansea?'

'No. I didn't know that but I will watch out for it now that you have told me.' John tweaked her nose playfully.

'To be more practical, what about the kitchens? They are so large you must have staff to run things.'

Emily smiled, everything she possessed was now the property of her husband but he still deferred to her in all matters of importance.

'Oh, I will,' Emily said, 'I'll be too busy with the business to bother with domestic matters.' She moved inside the large entrance and regarded the empty, sunlit rooms thoughtfully. 'The drawing-room is a good size, isn't it, John?' She stared around her at the long windows leading out to a lawned garden and then moved to the elegant marble fireplace, touching the cold stone with the tips of her fingers.

'It looks enormous to me,' John said, 'but then I was brought up in a humble cottage, remember.' He put his arm around her shoulder. 'You do realize, Emily, that I would be happy anywhere with you, I don't need a grand house and all the trappings of riches, I only want a wife and a family to make me happy.'

She turned into his arms and kissed his mouth. 'I know and I love you for it but there is a need, deep inside me, to replace Summer Lodge in my life otherwise I won't feel I'm really a success as a business woman or as a person.'

John kissed her. 'If you will be happy here, Emily, so will I.' He said softly, 'Let's go and choose our bedroom.'

Laughing, they hurried up the broad staircase to the minstrels' gallery above. 'We shall naturally have the master bedroom,' Emily said, flinging open the tall, heavy doors and moving inside with a flourish of her hand.

The room was well proportioned with large windows that looked out over the golden five-mile curve of Swansea Bay towards the outcrop of rocks beyond the village of Mumbles.

'Isn't it beautiful?' Emily asked sighing softly. 'Imagine

it furnished and with good drapes, it will be so warm and cosy.'

'Cosy isn't the word I'd use,' John said, 'grand, luxurious, splendid, certainly.'

Emily came to him and rested her head against his chest, 'I love you, John, none of it would be worth anything without you, you know that, don't you?'

'You keep telling me so and I must believe it, difficult though it is to know what you see in an oaf like me.'

He smoothed back her hair and then held her away from him, looking down at her frowning a little. 'I must confess that I'm rather worried about Sarah,' he said, 'do you think it's a good idea to let her sleep up at the shop alone?'

'She isn't going to be alone,' Emily said forcefully, 'that's why I've employed Mrs Grinter as housekeeper, she'll keep an eye on all the shop girls, they are living in now don't forget, your Sarah will be fine.'

John frowned and shook his head. 'I don't know what to make of my daughter these days, she professed herself so much in love with young William Davies but now that he's laid up in the hospital she's walking out with Sam Payton.'

John paused. 'This Payton boy works as a cobbler, too, not with Hari Morris but with some master up in Carmarthen Road, I suppose the lad is all right and yet there's something about him I don't like.'

'Sarah can take care of herself,' Emily said briskly, 'she's young yet, she needn't make up her mind to marry anyone until she's ready.'

Emily rubbed at her forehead. 'It's poor Hari I'm worried about. She went into lodgings when her husband died and I haven't seen much of her since.'

'She's had enough to put up with lately,' John said in his slow way. 'Being widowed so suddenly and then having young William in hospital. And she's still trying to earn a living, mind.

'I saw her once,' John continued, 'didn't I tell you? It was when I went to the hospital with Sarah. We were visiting young William at the time.' He shrugged, 'But Sarah's visits are getting less and less, I think she's giving up hope of the boy ever recovering.'

'You are right as usual, my love,' Emily said. 'Hari has a lot to contend with and I would like to help her if I could.'

'Look,' John said gently, 'if Hari has dropped out of sight it's because she wants to be left alone, she could have come to you if she'd needed anything, couldn't she?'

'You don't know her,' Emily replied ruefully, 'she's very proud, she would never ask for *anything* especially not from me.'

'Well, for now there's nothing you can do about Hari and her problems,' John said practically, 'so don't worry about it. She'll be all right, just give her time.'

Together they left the house and, at the large wrought-iron gates, Emily looked back. The big white house called *Ty Gwynne* in Welsh seemed to beckon her, there, she felt sure, she and John would conceive the child they wanted so badly. Doctors could be wrong, indeed they often were.

When Emily returned to the shop, she saw that it was more crowded than ever, the new stock, the very latest in fashion, had been manufactured on her own premises, the outbuildings at the back having been utilized for housing the new machines.

The premises were not ideal, all that had been done was to whitewash the walls and clean up the buildings but they served a purpose for the moment. If business continued to expand Emily felt she would be able to look about for a proper factory building, something as elegant as those owned by Mr Clark of Street in Somerset.

'We'll have to take on more staff.' Sarah approached Emily, her face was flushed, her hair escaping from its bows, 'Me and the girls can't keep up with the customers who all want personal attention, mind.'

'I'll see to it,' Emily said, 'by the end of the week we'll have a fully qualified staff, don't worry.'

'Another thing,' Sarah sounded truculent, 'as senior saleslady I think I should have more money than the others, it's only fair.'

'You're right, Sarah,' Emily said and meant it, but it was a great pity that John's daughter seemed to have none of his charm. 'We'll discuss it later.'

John had gone to the outbuildings, he never did see the sharp, almost arrogant side of his daughter Emily mused, but then Sarah could be so changeable.

Emily touched Sarah's arm. 'How is young Will Davies coming along, are there any signs of improvement?'

'None that I can see.' Sarah's mouth trembled and even though she quickly turned away, her distress was evident and Emily suddenly felt sorry for her.

'When did you last see him?' Emily asked gently and then she became aware that the girl's shoulders were shaking. 'Please don't worry,' Emily added quickly, 'I'm sure William will be all right given time.'

'I can't bear to see anyone sick,' Sarah's voice was muffled, 'especially Will who was so strong and healthy, it just turns my stomach.' She glanced almost defiantly at Emily. 'I did think I loved him but I can't live with an invalid, I just can't.'

Emily put her arm around Sarah. 'It's all right,' she said, 'no-one can make you go to see William if you don't want to.'

She found Sarah's attitude difficult to understand, wild horses wouldn't keep her away from John if he was sick. But Sarah was obviously in distress and she needed to be comforted.

'He's all right at the hospital, he'll be well cared for, you can be sure of that.' She said firmly, 'And William won't be released until the doctors are sure he's well enough.'

It wasn't strictly true, the boy would need somewhere to go to recuperate when and if he regained consciousness. Still, that wasn't Sarah's problem or Emily's come to that. And yet she felt that she owed Will something, if only for old times' sake.

On the other hand, there was little doubt that Hari would have everything arranged; once Will was released he would probably go to live with Hari as he'd always done.

Emily sighed heavily, she was such a fortunate woman, she had a flourishing business and the most wonderful husband in the world. What did she care if she was no longer invited to the At Homes given by people like Lady Caroline or that she was scorned socially by the very women who were first in line to buy her fashionable footwear? She had everything she wanted in life, everything, that is, except a child to call her own.

Hari stared down at Will's pale face as he rested against the hospital pillows, the bruising was fading now and the swelling around his eyes had disappeared, he looked almost normal except for the stillness of his emaciated body.

It was a miracle that he was still alive, it must only be his tremendous strength of will that kept the spark of life aglow in him.

Silently she rose and leaning forward pushed the shock of bright hair away from his forehead. Tears misted her eyes, she loved Will dearly, he was like her own flesh and blood, she could not, must not lose him. Everything dear to her suddenly seemed to be slipping away from her grasp.

Hari covered her face with her hands. Why wasn't Craig

here at her side? He had let her down all along the line, his word simply wasn't to be trusted. He said he'd come back to her and there had been no sign of him, not when Edward had died, nor since.

Hari left the infirmary and made her way towards the mean streets surrounding Salthouse Passage, knowing it would soon be time to feed her son. David was a healthy boy and growing more like his father every day. Longing for Craig washed over Hari but she pushed the feelings aside, Craig had not meant the things he'd said, he did not want her, otherwise he would have come back for her.

The grimy houses seemed more dismal than ever, the windows staring blankly at her like hostile eyes. Hari drew her shawl around her shoulders, shivering for the sun did not penetrate the slight gaps between tall buildings.

Suddenly, a woman with heavily rouged cheeks stepped into her path and stood arms akimbo. 'Don't remember me, do you Miss High and Mighty? But I remember you right enough, threatened to set the bobbies on me, didn't you?'

Hari looked at her blankly. 'I don't know what you are talking about, let me pass if you don't mind.'

'Aye, short memories are handy enough when you wants to forget something unpleasant.'

The woman moved closer and pointed to her garishly painted mouth. 'Remember I told you I got a big gob that would see you paid back one day? Well now, Maria Payton have paid you back or at least made a start at it.'

Hari remembered then. 'You are the one who stole a pair of boots from Will all those years ago!' Hari realized suddenly why the area had always seemed strangely familiar to her. 'It's a wonder you want to remember such a dirty trick yourself,' Hari added hotly.

'Dirty trick indeed!' The woman put her hands on her hips. 'We all got to live somehow as you have found out by the look of it.' She sneered, 'Living down by here isn't no fun, is it?'

'At least I don't rob from people as bad off as myself,' Hari said angrily. She made to move past but Maria Payton deliberately barred her way. 'You are not goin' anywhere till I've finished with you.' She pushed Hari roughly and Hari stumbled against the wall grazing her elbow. She felt a sudden surge of fear, this woman meant to hurt her and, if she succeeded, what about David left at home with Hetty?

'This is silly!' She tried to speak reasonably, 'What on earth is the point in making a fuss about something that happened such a long time ago? Anyway, you stole boots from young Will and we got them back, surely that's fair enough?'

'Life isn't fair or haven't you noticed?' The woman pushed her again and Hari began to feel desperate. 'You made a fool out of me and now my boys have had their revenge.' She nodded her head in satisfaction.

'What do you mean your boys have had their revenge?' Hari's voice was suddenly quiet. The woman lifted her chin defiantly.

'That William Davies is in the hospital, isn't he?' She spoke with an air of triumph, her eyes glittering beneath powdered lids and Hari felt the searing heat of anger run through her like wine. She thought of Will, so battered and bruised and still lying unconscious and suddenly all she had endured during the past weeks seemed to crowd in on her.

Hari's fear was replaced instantly by a choking, blinding rage. At that moment the woman chose to push her again. Suddenly, without conscious effort on her part Hari moved swiftly forward and pinned Maria Payton against the wall.

'You are an evil woman!' Hari didn't recognize her own

voice. Without thinking, she held the woman tightly by her throat, not realizing the strength that years of shoemaking had given to her wrists.

'Leave me alone, you're mad!' The woman tried to struggle but her efforts were futile against the strength of Hari's anger.

'Let me go!' Maria Payton croaked, 'you're going to kill me.'

'Isn't that what you and your sons tried to do to William?' Hari's grip tightened and the woman moaned, all her bluster gone. 'Give us a chance, for Gawd's sake.'

'Like the chance you gave William, is it?' Hari said fiercely.

'Go on misses, pulverize her, she deserves it!' a voice called from behind her. Suddenly, Hari's rage receded, she released the woman who fell back against the cobbles, gasping for breath.

'Get out of my sight before I really do kill you.' Hari rose and picked up her shawl from the roadway, aware that a crowd of curious onlookers had gathered. She felt ashamed of herself brawling in the street like a common bawd.

She stepped over the woman who was rubbing her throat where angry wheals were beginning to form.

'In future, keep away from me and mine,' Hari said harshly, 'or sons or no sons I'll come looking for you as sure as God made the earth. Understand?'

The woman glared at her but she was too afraid to speak, she shrank against the wall as Hari moved past her.

When she arrived home, Hari was trembling. She threw off her tangled, mud-stained shawl and sank down into one of Hetty's kitchen chairs.

'*Duw*, what's wrong with you, girl?' Hetty said in concern, 'you look like you seen a ghost.'

'No, not a ghost,' Hari said ruefully, 'I met an old enemy, Maria Payton, do you know her?'

'Aye, I know her, a real bad lot she is and them boys of hers too, wouldn't put nothing past that family.'

'It was the Payton boys who hurt William,' Hari rubbed at her eyes. 'Boasted about it to my face the woman did.' She sighed heavily, 'Perhaps I should have left her to the constables?'

'Not on your life!' Hetty said at once. 'Folks round here don't do that kind of thing, we sorts out our own bothers we do.' She pushed the big black kettle on to the flames. 'Have a cuppa while that baby of yours is still asleep and forget Maria Payton. Tell me about work, did you make any fine new shoes today?'

'Aye, I did some repairs for the theatre people but my heart wasn't in it so I went to see Will.' Hari watched in silence as Hetty bustled about the kitchen, her big hands surprisingly deft, her feet in the shabby shoes hardly seeming to touch the floor. At last, the tea poured, Hetty sat down opposite Hari.

'The bobbies wouldn't do nothing if you did report the Payton boys to them,' she said softly. 'You should know that coming from a place like this yourself.'

Hari sighed, 'I suppose you are right, but I'm worried that, if Will recovers, the boys will go after him again.'

'Look on the bright side,' Hetty advised, 'let's hope they've had their revenge and will leave it at that, honour satisfied, so to speak.'

Hari remembered the look in Maria Payton's face as she'd cowered against the wall. 'I doubt that,' she said, 'I just gave their mother the fright of her life.'

'Well, when you make an enemy of that one, you make an enemy for life, I'd watch out for yourself, mind, Maria is cunning and vicious and I wouldn't trust her further than I could throw Cleg the Coal and his horse and cart.'

The lull in the conversation was broken by a sudden cry from Davie. Hari rose to her feet. 'He's hungry,' she said softly, lifting him from the makeshift crib. 'I'll take him into the parlour and feed him, I expect you'll want to get on with your work.'

At the door, she turned. 'Thank you, Hetty,' she said 'for everything.'

It was almost a week later when Hari, sitting at Will's bedside, saw a small movement of his fingers. First, his little finger lifted slightly with the lightness of a butterfly wing. Then his eyelashes, dark and thick and far more curly than it was any man's right to possess, fluttered against gaunt cheeks.

'Will!' Hari leaned closer, breathing his name, 'Will, can you hear me?'

His eyes opened slowly, as though he was very tired and Will was looking at her.

'William, *cariad*, it's me, Hari.' She touched his face with her fingertips, very lightly, fearing to startle him.

'How are you feeling, my lovely?' she asked, her voice hoarse with emotion.

Will's lips moved but there was no sound. Hari leaned closer. She could barely catch the whispered words but she felt that, weak though he was, Will was speaking with conviction.

'I'm all right.' A tiny smile turned up the corners of his mouth. Hari took Will's hand, rubbing her fingers over his skin as if to infuse some of her own strength into him.

'You'd better be, my boy, you know I can't manage without you.' Hari spoke through her tears, choking them back not wanting to upset Will. 'We've got a business to run,' she said firmly, 'and you've got a lot of work waiting for you when you are well, mind.'

Will's eyes were closing, it was as though the lids were weighted and were too heavy for him. But his fingers were warm in hers and the faint smile still lingered on his lips.

Carefully, Hari eased her fingers away from him and hurried out into the corridor. 'Nurse!' she called and the sister appeared at her side as if she had been waiting for the summons.

'What is it, Mrs Morris?' she asked and, shakily, Hari pointed to the small annexe where Will slept.

'He's better,' she said, 'he opened his eyes, Will *spoke* to me.'

The sister put a hand on Hari's arm. 'Now don't get your hopes too high,' she said carefully, 'there is often a period of improvement just before the end.' She turned away. 'But I shall get a doctor to look at the boy right away. Come back in about ten to fifteen minutes and perhaps we shall be able to tell you something.'

Hari wandered outside the infirmary and sank down on one of the hard benches that faced the sea. She closed her eyes against the hot tears, Will would be all right, he'd told her so and Will never lied to her. She knew she was being irrational. How could William be expected to know about his condition when he had been unconscious for so long? And yet he had spoken with such conviction that she had to believe him.

She looked up at the sky and the grey racing clouds made her feel small and insignificant and so alone.

She clenched her hands together, willing herself not to cry, tears would not help one little bit.

After a time, she rose and returned to the long echoing corridors of the infirmary. As she neared Will's room, the sister came out of her office. Hari held her breath, fearing the worst but then the sister allowed a glimmer of a smile to warm her eyes.

'You were right, Mrs Morris,' she said softly, 'William is going to be all right.'

30

Craig made his way to the infirmary with eager steps, he had just learned from Doctor Grayham that William Davies had regained consciousness. Now, at last Craig would be able to find out where Hari had gone into hiding.

He had searched in vain the sprawling, dismal streets of World's End, asking endless questions receiving nothing in return but suspicion and hostility. It was clear that if anyone had known where Hari was living, Craig with his fine clothes would be the last one they would tell.

Even at her shop he'd been met with a wall of silence, the cobblers unwilling to talk to him, suspicious to the last man. He supposed they were only being loyal, protecting Hari, or so they thought.

He cursed himself for staying away so long and while he'd been dallying with the sweet Berta in Bristol, Hari had faced her troubles alone. Now, it seemed she wanted nothing to do with him and he couldn't really blame her. He'd let her down badly and just when she most needed him.

Craig had stayed in Bristol for longer than he'd intended and though it was true that the prospect of more business was a strong reason to stay, Berta with her soft yielding body and ready arms was even more of an incentive.

The sea washed shoreward, the gentle waves sucking at the sea shells on the ebb so that they chattered like the voices of children at play. Craig hurried towards the building near the beach, impatient to talk to young William.

The nurse who stood in the doorway of the boy's room was reluctant to let him in. 'The patient is still very weak, mind,' she said sternly, the folds of the white hat fluttering around her head like a pair of doves.

'I appreciate that,' Craig said persuasively, 'and I promise not to tire him.' He moved into the bare room and the figure in the bed seemed very still and small. Craig moved closer and saw that Will's face was still pale and drawn, he must have been well and truly beaten to have suffered so much damage and Craig felt a sense of anger rise within him.

'William,' he said softly. 'William, can you hear me?' He sat beside the bed and watched as the boy's eyes fluttered open.

'William, I need to know where Hari is staying, I can't find out where she is.'

William looked at him doubtfully and, when he spoke, his voice was very weak. 'If you can't find her, perhaps Hari doesn't want to be found.'

Craig shook his head, 'I realize that but I can explain why I was away so long if only I can talk to her.'

He moved closer to the bed. 'I didn't know about Edward's death until I returned from my business trip or about your injuries, I wish to God I had, I'd have been home like a shot.'

'I'm sorry, I can't help you,' Will said, his voice fading.

'It doesn't matter.' Craig rose to his feet decisively, 'I shouldn't have come.'

He made his way out of the hospital cursing himself for his stupidity, all that he had achieved was to upset William.

Craig returned home, the sun was sinking down behind the hills and, as Craig led the horse to the stables, he vowed that he would go back to Hari's shop and wait there all day if necessary, he must talk to Hari.

When he entered Summer Lodge it was to find his mother had moved Spencer into the guest room.

'I looked after Spencer while you were away,' she said querulously, 'but you must take care of your brother from now on Craig.' Her voice was trembling, 'I can't afford nurses' fees any longer, it's your turn to give a helping hand.'

Craig cursed beneath his breath, he had enough to do without looking after his brother.

'Mother, you always favoured Spencer, why don't you keep him with you, I'll pay for a nurse gladly.'

His mother moved to the door. 'We'll see but at least I deserve a rest, you must see that.'

It irked Craig that his time was taken up, trying to sort out his brother's problems. Spencer was highly strung these days, given to moods of blackness. Craig saw his mother home in her carriage and then returned on foot to Summer Lodge.

'Craig, my dear boy.' He was stopped near the wrought-iron gates of the grounds next door to his house by Lady Caroline who had just alighted from a cab. She rested her hand on his arm and stared up at him in what she imagined was a flirtatious manner. 'My little girl has been missing you so much, haven't you darling?'

Lisa, stepping into the driveway, raised her eyebrows at Craig and he smiled.

'We're having a Grand Ball, dear boy,' Lady Caroline continued, 'we would love you to come.'

Craig nodded without replying and Lady Caroline gushed on. 'We've just been to Hari Morgan's place to ask her to make some shoes but we didn't get to see her only one of her rough cobbler fellows.'

Lady Caroline paused and stared up at Craig through

arched eyebrows. 'Do you know, even though her shop is still smart and fashionable, apparently the way that woman is living is appalling.'

'Where is she living?' Craig asked, his senses suddenly alert.

'Salubrious Passage, my dear, salubrious being the last thing I'd call it. Hari Morris occupies just one room there in the ugliest house you could ever imagine. What a shame her husband dying and leaving her without a roof over her head like that.'

'Excuse me.' Craig held his hand out to attract the attention of a cab driver. 'Sorry,' he directed his remark to Lisa, 'I have to go.'

He climbed into the cab, a feeling of elation gripping him. 'Salubrious Passage, please,' he said.

'I think you mean Salthouse Passage, sir,' said the cabbie.

There were several houses in the row and Craig knocked at the doors of three before he learned that Hetty Blake ran a boarding house.

He raised the gleaming brass knocker and stood tensely waiting as he heard light footsteps coming along the passageway.

The door opened and Hari stood there much thinner and more desolate than he'd ever seen her look.

He reached and touched her arm. 'Hari! Thank God I've found you,' he said softly.

For a moment she looked startled, her soft mouth pale like a crushed rose petal. Then her lips were suddenly set into a hard line.

'What do *you* want?' she demanded and impatiently she dragged herself away from his hand.

'Hari, let me talk to you, I know I should have come back sooner but I . . .' He stopped talking as Hari stared up at him, he could not lie baldly to her, not when she was looking through him with that direct look of hers.

'I wish I could have been here sooner but I was delayed,' he ended lamely.

'Delayed? Well, I think I know the reason for the delay. You see, a letter came to my shop for you, the "lady" said she'd found the address on a card in her room after you'd left. Wanted to know when you'd be back again. Berta her name was.'

'I'm sorry, Hari, I can't make any excuses except that I was there on business and I . . .'

Hari interrupted him abruptly. 'I suppose that sort of business was more important to you than the death of your friend.' Her voice was bitter and filled with sarcasm.

'I didn't know about Edward,' Craig said softly, 'and I'm so sorry that you had to face it all alone. I would have come at once had I known.'

'Would you?' Hari said scornfully and made to close the door. Craig caught her arm once more.

'Hari, you must believe me. Nothing would have kept me away from you had I suspected that Edward was so ill.'

'That's enough!' Hari said fiercely. 'You are not fit to speak Edward's name. Just clear off and leave me alone.'

'Look,' Craig began again, 'I should have stayed with you, I realize that now, I suspected that things were not right financially, I shouldn't have gone away.'

'Well, you did, and you enjoyed your stay so much that you forgot to come back. That says it all, now I really know how little I mean to you.'

'We are getting nowhere,' Craig said. 'Let's talk things out quietly, ask me in at least.'

'There's nothing to talk about,' Hari's voice was calm. 'You didn't keep your promise to come to me, that's all there is to it.'

Craig felt pain wash over him as he tried to take Hari in

his arms. He loved her so much and she was right, he had failed her when she most needed him.

'Hari, please listen!' he said softly. She pushed him away, then she had closed the door with a click of finality.

He leaned against the wall filled suddenly with a sense of determination, he wouldn't give in, he would wait outside until she had calmed down, then he would try to talk to her again.

And yet he knew by the set of Hari's chin, it would be a long time before she would find it in her heart to forgive him.

It was about an hour later when Hari emerged from the house, her shawl pulled well around her thin shoulders, her basket over her arm. She was too small to carry the burdens of widowhood as well as homelessness, he thought angrily. Craig knew that he must somehow persuade Hari to let him take care of her though it would not be easy.

He followed her, staying well behind her and Hari paused for a moment, adjusting her shawl.

The roads narrowed into small passages and dingy courts and Craig fell further back, not wanting to be seen. He looked around at the dismal buildings and wondered how Hari could bear to live in such surroundings. And his son, he did not want his son to know this miserable sort of existence.

A young boy darted suddenly from one of the houses and, before Hari could turn, he had snatched the shawl from her shoulders. He held it up tauntingly and, after a moment, Hari shrugged disconsolately and went on her way.

Incensed, Craig moved swiftly towards the boy and took the shawl from his hands.

'Hey, mister, what you think you're doing?' The boy was older than Craig had first imagined, he was small, undernourished, his face pinched and pale.

At the sound of his voice, a woman came out of the house her face heavily rouged, a smile spreading over her full lips when she saw him. She gave the boy a push.

'Get out of here, Tim, let decent folks get about their business.'

'But, mam, you said . . .' The boy's voice faded as the woman gave him a threatening look.

'Can I do anything for you, sir?' The woman raised her eyebrows meaningfully and Craig, looking desperately past her, saw that Hari was now out of sight.

'It's Maria,' the woman continued, 'all my customers speak highly of me, mind.' She peered at him intently, 'Don't I know you, sir?'

Craig shook his head. 'No.' He moved away unaware that the woman was staring at him with narrowed eyes and made his way through the maze of narrow streets and knew, with a sense of despair, that he had lost sight of Hari, he wouldn't find her now.

Reluctantly, he turned back, it was growing dark, he would not find her tonight and the thought of her tramping the streets, delivering her repairs, made him feel so angry and helpless.

But tomorrow, he would return to Salthouse Passage, Hari made it clear she didn't want him but he wouldn't give up, he would make her listen to him.

He was beginning to learn about Hari, she was fiercely independent and so very proud, perhaps that's why he loved her so much. And yet, he had the uncomfortable feeling she'd see him in hell before she would forgive him.

31

If Hari felt a great bitterness against Craig for his betrayal of her, she also felt a great sense of loss. And there was a feeling of disbelief that he could so casually take a strange woman to his bed, spending time with her when Hari needed him so badly.

Hari felt as though life was out to defeat her, dealing her blow after blow. Edward had been taken from her so suddenly, William had been near to death in hospital and all the time Craig had been carelessly going his own way, without a thought for Hari. And yet the desire to be in his arms and to have his love and support was sometimes overwhelming.

But people like Craig Grenfell were not to be trusted, hadn't she learned that much by now? These toffs were all the same. Just look at Emily, cocooned in her own little world of happiness, surrounded by all the trappings of affluence, she had not bothered to seek out Hari to see if she needed any help.

Emily had done well for herself, she now owned a productive manufactory as well as the successful Emily's Emporium and she was a very busy woman.

To be fair, Hari mused, if she saw fit to approach her, Emily would probably have given her all the help she needed.

Hari sat in her room nursing David in her arms, he was a fine child, growing stronger and lustier by the day. And it was obvious to anyone who saw him that he was a Grenfell through and through.

Hari changed the baby and slicked down his thick sprouting of hair with her fingers. 'You must look fine and handsome,' she said softly, 'if Hetty is to mind you for me to go to see Will.'

Hetty was sitting near the fire when Hari entered the kitchen, her skirt was above her knees as she warmed herself at the blaze.

'Got a touch of the bone ache today, I have,' she explained rubbing at her legs, 'must be the weather. Here, give me the boy, let me have a cuddle of him before he falls asleep.'

David snuggled contentedly against Hetty's ample bosom, his eyes already closing.

'Bless his little heart,' Hetty said, 'he's no trouble at all, this son of yours, I think the angels themselves must have brought him.' She kissed David's head and then smiled up at Hari.

'Give my best to Will and, remember, he'll have a room here when he's well.' She paused. 'By the way, we've got a new lodger for the back bedroom,' Hetty said. 'Nice sort of chap, good hearted and strong, he'll give me a hand when I want a bit of coal brought in or some logs chopped. You can always tell. Paid the rent on the nail, too, I think you'll like him.'

Hari smiled ruefully. 'I hope you are not thinking of matchmaking, mind, I don't want any man, I'll take care of myself.'

'Huh!' Hetty scoffed, 'a pretty young thing like you needs a man, after a decent time of mourning is past of course. Anyway, off you go to see that William. If I keep nattering to you, you'll never get away.'

Hari left the cheerful room with reluctance, it was a cold night and she'd have liked nothing better than to stay and talk to Hetty.

The passageway was long and shadowed, lit only by a solitary gas lamp. A tall figure appeared from the doorway to the middle room and stood before her.

'Hari, there's good to see you again, sorry I've had to take so much time off work lately.' The voice was strong and masculine and Hari peered through the gloom.

'Lewis! It is you, isn't it?' She reached out her hand and it was held in a firm grasp. 'You've taken lodgings here, does that mean your mam . . . ?' Her words faded away as Lewis held her hand more tightly.

'Mam passed on,' he said. 'It was a shock, mind, even though she was bad these last weeks. Anyway, I'll be back at work now that the funeral is over and I've got a chance to pull myself together again. How are you managing, Hari?'

'I'm all right,' Hari said, 'Hetty is a very good landlady, she gave me the parlour, the best room in the house.' She forced a note of cheerfulness in her voice. 'If you're as lucky as me, you'll be happy here.' Her eyes were growing accustomed to the gloom, she could see that Lewis had grown a beard which made him look much older.

'I'll be glad to see you back at work, we've been quite busy in the shop mostly doing work for the theatre people. I must say I haven't put a lot of effort into specialized shoes lately but then business in that direction is a bit slow.'

'I blame those Grenfells myself,' Lewis said. 'They use your talents when it suits them and then ignore you when they feel like it.'

'I've got to go,' Hari said, choking back the pain his words brought her, he had put into plain speaking the thoughts she'd tried to suppress. 'I'm late as it is.' She made to move past Lewis, but he caught her arm.

'You are not going out alone? It's almost dark and the streets around here are not safe, mind.'

'I've got to visit Will, he's in the hospital, he's expecting me, he'll only worry if I don't go.'

'Then I'll come with you,' Lewis said decisively. 'I'll just get my coat.'

Before Hari could protest, Lewis had hurried upstairs to his room. Hari moved to the door and peered out into the gloom. It had been raining and the cobbles had taken on a sheen that glowed gold under the lamplight.

The buildings rose tall and somehow menacing, most of them shrouded in darkness with only an occasional light to dispel the darkness. Hari shivered, suddenly glad that Lewis was going with her.

It was the first time she'd visited Will in the evening but she had been busy all day and she knew he would worry if he didn't see her at all. He must be wondering too what would happen to him once he was released from hospital. Hari smiled, she would set his mind at rest, tell him there was a home waiting for him in Salthouse Passage when he was well.

'Here I am, ready and willing.' Lewis was beside her smiling down and, feeling cheered, Hari stepped out with him into the street. They walked in silence for a time and Hari was grateful for Lewis's presence as they passed a public bar full of drunken men singing a bawdy song.

As the streets thinned out, the solitary notes of a flute could be heard clearly on the still air playing a haunting melody that unaccountably brought tears to Hari's eyes.

In the music lay the feeling of dreams lost and love destroyed but perhaps that was all in her imagination.

'Are you doing any design work at all, Hari?' Lewis's voice broke into her thoughts.

'Aye, a bit of drawing now and then but mostly I've been tapping boots, making new heels, that sort of thing,' Hari said, aware that her meagre takings were diminishing daily and feeling a sudden sense of panic.

'Perhaps we can drum up some business between us,' Lewis said eagerly, 'you always have come up with a solution, Hari.'

'Emily's ready-made boots and shoes seem to be all that the folks of Swansea need, at the moment,' Hari said quietly.

'Don't talk soft now!' Lewis sounded indignant, 'What about fine hand-made shoes, Emily's Emporium can't provide those remember.'

It was true but Hari had little energy these days, her inspiration seemed to have died when Edward did. Lewis had no idea of the time and effort it took to make individual designs and carry them forward into production.

'It's not like you to give up so easily,' Lewis said as though reading her thoughts. 'Just think about it, Hari, get that imagination of yours working.'

'Yes, I will try,' Hari said but there was little conviction in her voice.

Will was sitting up against the pillows, he was very pale but there was a light in his eyes that had not been there for some time. The reason was not difficult to see, Sarah was sitting near the bed, holding his hand.

'Will, you're looking much better!' Hari kissed his cheek. 'Hello, Sarah, there's pretty you look, that red coat suits you very well.'

Sarah smiled but didn't speak. Will took Hari's hand and frowned his disapproval.

'What are you doing out alone in the darkness? Both you and Sarah should be more careful, I don't like to think of the risks you're taking.'

'Lewis came with me,' Hari said, 'he's waiting outside, he'll walk both me and Sarah home, I'm sure.'

'Lewis?' Will asked. 'Is he back at work? He was home looking after his mam when I was . . . was taken sick.'

Hari brushed aside a curl of hair that had fallen over Will's forehead.

'Yes, he's back at work but don't worry about all that, what you have to do is to get well and come home to me, there'll be a good meal and a warm fire waiting for you, you can be sure of that.'

'Where are you living now, Mrs Morris?' Sarah asked archly. 'With Lewis, is it?'

Will looked at the girl sharply. 'What do you mean? Will someone please tell me what's going on?' He fell back against the pillows, a look of weariness on his face.

Hari could have slapped Sarah but now there was nothing left to do but to tell Will the truth.

'Will, poor Eddie didn't get over the sickness, I didn't want you to know, not until you were well again.'

'*Duw*, there's sorry I am, Mrs Morris,' Sarah said quickly, 'I didn't think . . .' As her words trailed away Will touched the girl's hand.

'That's all right, love, I don't want anything kept from me.' He turned to Hari. 'What else?' he asked. 'I can see there's more.'

'The house wasn't Edward's,' Hari said, 'it was just rented, I had to get out. But I'm all right, I've got rooms with a very nice lady, there's a room for you too when you get out of here and then you, me and Lewis will work at the business, make it flourish again, we'll pull ourselves up by our boot straps just as we've always done.'

'Hari,' Will touched her cheek, 'just when you needed me, I wasn't any use to you, I'm sorry.'

'Don't be silly,' Hari said, 'you couldn't help being sick.'

'Being set upon by a gang of thugs you mean,' Will said bitterly, 'if I ever get my hands on the ones who put me in by here, I swear I'll half kill them!'

Sarah rose to her feet. 'Well, I'd better be going or

my dad will have something to say to me.'

'Aw, stay a bit longer,' Will coaxed, 'your dad won't know what time you get in, will he?'

'Oh yes he will, that Mrs Grinter is a dragon, she reports back to dad and Emily on everything that happens in the shop.'

'Why not wait for me?' Hari said quickly. 'Lewis won't mind walking you back to the emporium.'

'No thanks, don't want to put you to any trouble, don't want to be no gooseberry either!' Sarah giggled and Hari felt an angry flush rise to her cheeks.

'There's no need to talk like that,' she said, 'I have only just lost my husband remember.'

'Sorry, only joking.' Sarah blew William a kiss and hurried from the room.

'Take no notice,' Will said but it was clear he felt uncomfortable. 'Sarah speaks without thinking, you mustn't mind her.'

'Yes, you're right,' Hari said, 'there's silly of me to take offence where I'm sure none was intended.' But she wasn't sure at all, Sarah had always been a difficult person to understand.

'What about work?' Will changed the subject. 'What sort of orders have we got?'

Hari smiled, 'I haven't sorted the orders yet, Will, it's wrong of me to wallow in gloom I know but I'll get round to it.'

Hari suddenly felt a new sense of purpose, there were people depending on her to help them make a living and she would do her best to justify their faith in her.

'Enough talking for tonight, Will,' Hari said touching his cheek, 'you need to rest, you're still not well, mind.'

'All right, if you say so.' Will smiled, watching as she moved across the room. When she reached the door, his voice halted her.

'Hari, you're sure you are all right? I mean to think of making a success of a business after life has played such mean tricks on you takes a lot of fire in the belly.'

'I'm sure.' Hari said firmly, 'You and me are going to do all right for ourselves, you'll see.'

Lewis was waiting outside for her, leaning against the wall of the hospital. He pushed himself upright when he saw her and peered at her in the darkness as though trying to read her expression.

'Will all right?' he asked. 'Only I saw that girlfriend of his flying out of here like a bat out of hell, wondered if the boy had taken sick again.'

'No, Will is well on the way to recovery,' Hari said, 'he still seems a bit weak and he's very tired right now but he's going to be all right.'

They walked in silence for a few minutes and then Lewis paused, staring down at Hari, clearing his throat nervously.

'I know this is a bit soon and perhaps I should wait a bit like but I want you to know you can always count on me, Hari.'

She looked up at him in surprise. 'I know I can, Lewis,' she said quietly, 'I've always been able to depend on you.'

'But more than that,' Lewis continued, 'I have always held you in the highest regard. I'm not putting this very well, Hari, but what I mean is, have I a chance with you once you are over your grief, your period of mourning?'

Hari looked up at Lewis, tall and handsome in the moonlight, his hands, big strong cobbler's hands hanging at his sides as though he wasn't sure what to do with them and felt a rush of affection for him, but it wasn't love.

'I'm sorry, Lewis,' she began, 'but though I like and

admire you very much, I can't say, hand on heart, that I feel love for you.'

If only she could love him, share her life with Lewis, build a business with him and more, build a stable family life in which David could grow up in a healthy normal background it would be wonderful.

'Love can grow, mind,' Lewis said, 'and I would be good to you and the boy.' He thrust his hands into his pockets. 'I know I've got nothing much to offer you now but I can work hard, you know that, Hari, and I would always be faithful to you.'

Hari remained silent, she could think of nothing to say and, in any case, tears formed a hard knot in her throat. Lewis stared down at her, not touching her.

'Don't answer now, it's too soon, I shouldn't have spoken yet of such things but remember this, Hari, I love you.' He sighed. 'I always have loved you ever since the first time we met but then you were always so far above me, I could never pluck up the courage to tell you how I felt in case you thought I was after your money.' He cleared his throat nervously.

'Then you got married and you were even further away from me than before. I've loved and wanted you for so long, do you think I found rooms in Hetty's house by chance?'

Hari began to walk towards Salthouse Passage and Lewis fell into step beside her. 'You sly boots.' She laughed a little self-consciously. 'But you're right,' she said, not wanting to hurt him. 'It is too soon for me to think about taking another husband but I am honoured, Lewis, that you think well of me.'

As they neared the house, Hari heard the sounds of voices raised in anger. With a shock, she realized that one of them belonged to Sarah Miller, what on earth was she doing in this area during the night time? She must be out of her mind.

'Just listen to me, Sam,' Sarah was saying, 'I went to the hospital because I felt sorry for Will, you didn't have to hurt him so bad, did you?'

'You come straight from him and then run sniffing round here after me, well, you can just go back to him, understand?'

Lewis looked down questioningly as Hari held his arm, putting her fingers to her lips in a warning gesture.

'Sam, I'm sorry!' Sarah was saying, 'I won't do it again, I promise you.'

'You won't get a chance!' Sam said angrily. 'I don't want no two timer for my girl.'

Hari could just make out the two figures in the doorway of the house where Maria Payton lived and the boy talking to Sarah was obviously Sam Payton.

Hari's first impulse was to rush forward and confront the two of them, to tell Sarah what a traitor she was going out with another man behind Will's back and the very one who had been responsible for putting Will in the hospital in the first place, but Sarah was shrieking at the boy now, her voice rising hysterically.

'And what am I supposed to do about the baby I'm carrying, your baby?' she cried.

'My baby is it,' the boy's voice was low with scorn, 'and how do I know that?' He gave a short laugh. 'It might be the work of that scum you slept with before, have you thought of that? You did sleep with him, didn't you?'

'The baby is yours!' Sarah was protesting. 'Will has been sick for too long, the baby definitely isn't his.'

'Then you'll have to convince him different won't you?' Sam Payton laughed, 'Just think, that fool bringing up my bastard, that should be a laugh.'

'You can't mean it!' Sarah was crying now, 'you said you loved me, told me that you wanted to marry me, how can you be like this to me, how could you have told me such lies?'

'A man will say anything when he wants something from a girl, haven't you learned that much by now?' There was the sound of the door being opened and then Sam spoke again.

'This is where we part company, goodbye, Sarah.'

The door was slammed and then Sarah fell against it sobbing bitterly. 'Oh *duw*, what am I going to do?' Her words were muffled in her fingers as Sarah stood crying her heart out in the darkness.

Impulsively, Hari moved towards her, out of the darkness and touched the girl's shoulder lightly. 'Sarah, it's all right, don't cry. Come on, me and Lewis will walk you home.'

'It's none of your business!' Sarah turned on Hari, her eyes burning, 'I suppose you heard everything, spying on me you were, creeping up on me like that!'

'We were just making our way home, Sarah,' Hari said reasonably. 'Why on earth should I want to spy on you?'

'Because you don't think I'm good enough for your precious William, that's why! Well, you can just keep your nose out of my affairs and if you tell Will any of this I'll deny it, mind.'

'I think it's up to you to tell Will,' Hari said softly. 'Come on home now, you're upset, you'll feel better after a good night's sleep.'

'Leave me alone!' Sarah spun on Hari, eyes blazing, 'And don't pretend to be so holy and good when everyone in Swansea knows that your baby is a bastard!'

'Hold your tongue!' It was Lewis who moved forward and stood close to Sarah, his face set and angry. 'Don't you go talking like that, do you hear?'

'Oh, get out of my way all of you and just leave me alone!'

Sarah darted past Lewis and disappeared into the darkness. Lewis shrugged, 'Let her go, she deserves everything she gets does that one, talking about you like that and you respectably married when you had your son.'

Hari walked beside Lewis in silence for a moment. 'She was right though,' she said at last, 'at least in a way.'

'I don't understand,' Lewis said slowly, 'the boy is your husband's son, isn't he?'

'No, Lewis,' Hari said softly, 'David is Craig Grenfell's child. I was expecting when I married Edward.'

Lewis was silent and Hari felt forced to explain. 'I didn't know I was with child at first and, when I found out, I wanted to tell Eddie but then he fell sick. I suppose I am just like Sarah when you think of it.'

'No!' Lewis said, the word bursting from his lips. 'That man took advantage of you, just as the gentry have always taken advantage of our sort, I could kill him for the hurt he's caused you.'

'Craig Grenfell has caused me pain,' Hari agreed, not seeing the look of bitter anger on Lewis's face, 'but I have my son and I love him.' She touched Lewis's arm gently. 'Thank you, Lewis, you don't know how much it means to have the loyalty of friends.'

'You'd have me by your side for ever if you'd only say the word, Hari,' Lewis said. 'You need the protection of a strong man, that's what I think.'

Hari sighed, 'You are right enough, Lewis, but let's not talk about it any more now.'

It was good to return to the warmth of Hetty's kitchen and find David asleep and Hetty just brewing a fresh cup of tea.

If she was surprised to see Hari and Lewis come in together Hetty didn't show it. She believed in minding her own business and letting other folks mind theirs. In any case, Hari Morris was a respectable lady, anybody could see that, there would be no funny business where she was concerned.

'Will is looking much better,' Hari was smiling as she took off her shawl, 'I shouldn't wonder if he's allowed home soon.' Hari took a seat near the fire accepting the cup of tea that Hetty handed her gratefully.

'Well,' Hetty said, 'his room in the attic will be ready and waiting for him, you can tell him that from me.'

Hari sipped the hot tea enjoying the strong sweetness of it. 'Do you realize, Hetty,' she said, 'you'll have three cobblers staying under your roof then, no need to ever go without stout shoes on your feet.'

'Aye,' Hetty said, 'Lewis here told me he was a cobbler, like you he was sent to me by Cleg the Coal's wife, owe Cleg and Beatie a debt of gratitude, I do.'

'So do I,' Hari said gently. 'I couldn't have found better lodgings if I'd searched the whole of Swansea.'

'Lewis!' she said, 'Come over here, your tea is getting cold.'

'*Duw*, tea is tea, hot or cold,' Lewis said but he came to sit near the table, his big arms resting on the scrubbed surface. 'I used to work for Hari, mind,' he said smiling at Hetty, 'she might seem a quiet little soul but she gets the work done, believe me.'

Hari forced a smile. 'I'm going to do my best anyway,' she said, 'try to get back most of my old trade, people who have gone for Emily's ready-made shoes, I'm sure it can be done.'

'Well, you've got a nursemaid for the boy, he can stay by here with me every day while you're at work,' Hetty said in her slow thoughtful way. 'Be happy to do my old job again I would.'

Events seemed to be moving too fast, almost as if they were being taken out of Hari's hands and when, later, she

414

lay in the bed in the parlour of the house in Salthouse
Passage she was unable to sleep, she tossed and turned in
her bed, watching the coals in the fire die one by one and
she was filled with fears of what the future might bring.

32

Emily moved along the row of machines, watching with admiration the speed with which the boots and shoes could now be cut and sewn. In only a few weeks, the emporium could be supplied with a new stock of footwear, it was little short of miraculous.

Business was so good that Emily had been able to expand and, soon, the new premises in the Strand would be ready for occupation; extra sewing and cutting machines would be installed and more workers would be taken on. Everything in Emily's world was wonderful except for one thing, she had still not conceived John's child.

He constantly reassured her that he was happy the way things were, that she was everything in the world that he desired and yet she knew that to have a son would bring him the ultimate joy.

She left the outbuildings and made her way back to the emporium, she had left Sarah in charge and yet she doubted about the girl's ability to cope with the responsibility.

Over the last few weeks, Sarah had been edgy, her temper uncertain and Emily was finding it difficult to deal with the girl's tantrums.

Emily wondered if she should have a word with John about Sarah's strange behaviour but she was reluctant to make trouble between father and daughter.

Lady Caroline was sitting in the shop with her daughter, an array of shoes spread around her, it was clear that Lady

Caroline was being her usual over-fussy self.

Sarah was bending over Elizabeth, helping her to try on a dainty evening shoe, and there was a look of impatience about Sarah's attitude that was easy to read.

'Why don't you go and have your coffee, Sarah?' Emily said warmly, 'I can see to the customers.'

Sarah looked up at her, eyes hard and angry. 'What's wrong, don't you think I'm capable of selling a pair of shoes now?'

Emily forced herself to remain calm. 'I just thought you would like a break, that's all.'

Sarah straightened and deliberately dropped the shoe she was holding on to the floor. 'Right then, please yourself.' She flounced away, head high and Emily made an effort not to let her anger show, but this sort of behaviour really couldn't be allowed to go on.

'What was it you were looking for, Lisa?' Emily smiled apologetically. 'Something for the evening was it?'

Before Elizabeth could reply, Lady Caroline was on her feet. 'Come along, Elizabeth, I really don't wish to patronize an establishment where a junior salesgirl can get away with such arrant rudeness.'

Caroline swept to the door, her daughter in her wake, leaving a variety of shoes cluttering the floor. Emily summoned one of the girls to restore order to the shop and made her way purposefully upstairs to the living quarters.

'Morning, Mrs Grinter,' she said to the elderly house-keeper who appeared to be listening at the door of Sarah's room.

'*Bore da*, Mrs Miller.' The woman appeared flustered. 'Could I talk to you in confidence?'

'Yes, of course but can't it wait? I have something to say to Sarah.'

'There's strange, it's about Sarah I want a word.' Mrs Grinter kept her voice low. She moved towards the table and stood staring down at it as though looking for inspiration.

'Well, what is it?' Emily asked puzzled by the woman's attitude. 'Please say what's on your mind.'

'Right, then, I think Sarah is with child.' The words fell into a stunned silence and Emily stared at the older woman in horror. Emily sank down into a chair and rubbed at her eyes distractedly.

'What makes you think that?' she asked slowly knowing that the older woman was shrewd and must have good reason for what she was saying.

'She's missed her courses,' Mrs Grinter said, 'I do the washing for these girls, mind. Apart from that, she's been retching every morning and anyway,' she ended firmly 'it's something about the eyes, you can always tell.'

Emily bit her lip, not knowing what to think, could it be true? It would certainly explain Sarah's strange bouts of temper.

'Who could be the father?' Emily said desperately. 'The only young man she's been in company with is William Davies and he's been sick for some weeks.'

'I don't know nothing about that,' Mrs Grinter said firmly. 'I only know there's been no followers allowed in these premises. What the girls do outside is beyond my control.'

'That's all right, no-one is blaming you,' Emily said quickly.

The woman bristled, 'I should think not, indeed!' She rubbed at the table with a duster almost absent-mindedly. 'Do you want me to speak to Sarah?' she asked. Emily shook her head.

'No, leave it to me.' She rose and went towards Sarah's room and at the door turned and regarded the housekeeper steadily. 'Perhaps you would like to go to the kitchen and make us all a nice cup of tea.'

Sarah failed to respond to the repeated knocking on her door so, after a few minutes, Emily entered the room uninvited.

'Sarah,' she said softly, 'I must talk to you.' She sat on the bed forcing down her irritation as the girl deliberately turned her back to her.

'I didn't appreciate that show of bad manners in the shop just now,' she began, 'I came up here to tell you to mend your ways or I'd be forced to dispense with your services but, first, I want to ask you if anything's wrong?'

Sarah didn't reply but her hunched shoulders and the curve of her spine revealed her vulnerability and suddenly Emily's irritation vanished.

'You are going to have a child, aren't you?' Emily asked and Sarah stiffened perceptibly. 'It's something you can't hide for ever,' Emily spoke softly, 'and if you are in trouble, I want to help you.'

Sarah began to sob, desperate, harsh sobs that shook her body. Emily hesitated for a moment and then took the girl in her arms, cradling her as though she was a child.

'There, there, everything will be all right,' Emily said soothingly, 'your father and I will take care of you.'

She rocked Sarah gently and, after a time, the girl's harsh sobbing ceased. 'I'm so unhappy.' Sarah scrubbed at her eyes, 'The baby's father hates me, he doesn't want me any more, my life is ruined and I wish I was dead!'

'No, you mustn't say that, you are young, you will get over this, we'll see to that.' Sarah sat up and dried her eyes with sharp angry movements and Emily knew she must be feeling betrayed and rejected by the man she loved.

'Was it Will Davies?' Emily asked and Sarah stared at her for a moment in silence, even now, Emily thought, the girl did not want to blame her lover.

'Yes,' Sarah said at last, 'Will is the only boy I've ever walked out with.'

'He must be made to face up to his responsibilities,' Emily said firmly. 'I know he's been sick but he's well on the road to recovery now, isn't he?'

Sarah nodded, 'He's well enough, that's why I went to see him but I don't want anyone else speaking to him, perhaps when he's home from the hospital I can talk to him again, perhaps he'll see reason then.'

Emily rose from the bed. 'Right, you must rest now, don't come back to the shop until you feel ready to face it.' At the door, Emily paused.

'Do you want me to speak to your father or will you tell him yourself?'

Sarah shook back her hair. 'Leave it!' she said sharply. 'I'll wait until I've spoken to Will,' she added more gently.

Emily returned to the shop, still overcome by what had happened. Into her bewilderment crept a slight feeling of envy, why should Sarah have a child when she obviously loathed the very idea and Emily be deprived of the joy a child would bring?

How she got through the rest of the day, Emily didn't know, she was becoming obsessed with the thought of Sarah's baby. If Sarah didn't want the child then perhaps she would allow Emily to bring it up, it was, after all, blood of John's blood. But of course Sarah would want it, once she held the baby in her arms, how could she help but love it?

As she closed the doors of the emporium for the night, Emily found that she was exhausted and her head ached intolerably. She wished she could talk openly to John but she must wait until Sarah had made up her mind what to do for the best. Perhaps William would agree to marry Sarah and, if he did, her problems would be over.

Emily stared out at the darkening sky and wondered why, having everything, success, wealth, a beautiful home and a fine husband, she suddenly felt that she had nothing.

The afternoon was fine but chilly and Sarah drew her coat closer around her as she made her way towards Salthouse Passage. William was home from the hospital now and she must try to persuade him to marry her, it was the only way out of her desperate situation.

Sarah was aware that Hari had overheard her quarrelling with Sam, knew the child she was carrying was his but who could prove anything? Many a woman had mistaken her dates, it was easily done.

In any case, she didn't think Hari would say anything to William about what she'd overheard, Hari was the sort who kept her nose out of other folks' business.

Sarah stopped at the end of the row of tall, depressing houses that made up Salthouse Passage and her heart sank, she didn't want to live in such awful surroundings but she needed a husband, a father for her child.

She thought of her lovely rooms above the emporium and her footsteps faltered, how could she live in this dingy street after the comfort she'd become used to? She had been a fool, she had allowed her natural desire to be loved to lead her astray.

Sarah sighed heavily, her father no longer wanted her, he had his precious Emily now. In any case, she had never really been close to her father, they were so different in every way. And Sarah had always felt that dad blamed her somehow for the death of her mother.

She leaned against one of the grimy walls, she could not help being born, could she? And she could not help it that she'd been unlucky enough to fall for a baby, a baby she really didn't want.

Sarah moved forward listlessly and knocked on the door of the house where Will was lodging. It was true she had hated visiting him when he was really sick, but she could not help her nature could she?

And now Will was himself again, a strong handsome young man, he would make a fine father, a better father than Sam Payton would ever make.

A tall old lady opened the door and Sarah looked up at her questioningly. 'This is where Will Davies lives, isn't it?' she asked politely.

'Aye,' the woman smiled, 'are you a friend of his then?'

'I'm walking out with him, my name is Sarah Miller.'

'And I'm Hetty,' the woman stepped aside, 'go on up, Will's room is in the attic but leave the door open, mind, we don't want to cause any misunderstanding, do we?'

Sarah forced a smile and then made her way up the gloomy staircase, her spirits sinking lower with each step. This was no way to live or to bring up a baby.

'Sarah!' Will was sitting in a chair, a last between his knees, a piece of leather in his hands. At least he was working again and he would do better in the future surely? Once he was really well he would go back to work for Hari Morris.

In any case, Sarah thought, with a sudden surge of anger, once she and Will were married, dad and Emily would have to help set them up nicely, they would just have to.

Will came to her and took her in his arms, holding her close. 'I'm glad you came, I wanted so much to see you but the fussy old doctor told me to take things easy for a few more days.'

Sarah put her ams around him and hugged him. 'You're awful thin, Will, you need feeding up,' she said gently. 'I want to look after you, my boy, make you strong again, you are going to need all your strength when I tell you what's happened.'

422

Will held her away from him. 'What is it, Sarah, what's wrong?' His face was full of concern and Sarah felt guilt sear her. But Will had been the one who had first taken her innocence, he'd had his fun with her and he must pay.

'I'm with child, Will,' she said softly, 'I'm sorry to shock you this way but I couldn't say anything before with you so ill.'

Sarah held her breath as Will stared at her in silence for what seemed an eternity, would he swallow it?

'My poor little love!' he said at last. 'You must have been half out of your mind with worry.' He held her close and kissed the top of her head. 'I'll take care of everything, we'll get married as soon as possible, you are to leave everything to me.'

Sarah felt a great sweep of relief as she relaxed against him, tears came to her eyes as she pressed her cheek against the thinness of his chest, he was a good man worth ten Sam Paytons, so why did she wish it was Sam holding her close?

But she would never stray from the straight and narrow again, she vowed silently, she would be faithful to Will always.

'Come on, sit down,' Will said smiling, 'I'll get you a nice hot cup of tea in a minute but, first, I've got to tell Hari the good news.'

'Wait!' Sarah said. 'Couldn't it just be our secret, at least until we're married?'

'Don't be silly, Hari's not one to stand in judgement and she's the nearest to family I've got, I must tell her.'

He called urgently down the stairs and Hari came immediately, her eyes anxious as they rested on Will. When she saw Sarah, Hari's expression was suddenly guarded.

'Hari,' Will took her hands in his, 'Sarah and me, we're getting married, we're going to have a baby.'

'Oh? . . .' Hari looked at Sarah and frowned but then the words she was about to speak died on her lips.

'Aren't you pleased for us, Hari?' Will asked abruptly, his voice questioning.

'Are you sure this is what you want – both of you?' Hari's eyes were on Sarah and she felt her colour rise. She lifted her head defiantly but didn't speak.

'Of course it's what we want,' Will said impatiently, 'I don't understand you, I thought you'd be happy for us.'

'I'm just concerned,' Hari said softly, 'you are both so young to be married, to have the responsibilities of a baby.'

'What would you suggest then?' Will said. 'That Sarah be left to cope on her own?'

'She wouldn't be alone, Will,' Hari said gently, 'she's got her dad and Emily. It's just that you've been in the hospital for quite some time and how far gone are you, Sarah?'

'I don't know exactly,' Sarah felt suddenly triumphant, it was clear that Hari didn't have the nerve to come right out with it and tell the truth about what she'd heard.

'What difference does it make anyway?' Will obviously couldn't see what Hari was hinting at. 'Sarah is going to have my baby and we'll be married as soon as possible, that's all there is to it.'

'I see,' Hari said softly, 'well then, I can only wish you every happiness.' She kissed William warmly. 'I want only the best for you, you know that.'

'I know,' William said, 'and there's no need to worry, we'll make a great success of our life together, Sarah and me.'

Sarah smiled, knowing she had won, the moment of danger was past, Hari would hold her peace.

33

Hari stood outside the old premises in the crowded, dingy backstreets of World's End where once her father had run a successful shoemaking business, and mused on how her world seemed to have turned full circle. Here she was, back at her roots and hoping to make a new beginning.

She could no longer afford to rent the premises in the centre of town, trade had not been too good which was perhaps her own fault for being so idle after Edward's death.

Business was picking up now but Hari reckoned that if her overheads were lower, she would feel more secure. She peered in through the grimy windows; the place seemed unoccupied and that at least was reassuring.

Hari moved resolutely into the back yard and stood outside the rear entrance to the tall house where she had spent her childhood, here she had learned her trade and here she had seen both her parents die. And here, said a small voice inside her head, she had first met Craig Grenfell.

She had tried hard to forget that Craig ever existed but it was difficult when she ached to be with him, longed to hear his voice, feel the touch of his hand. And her son, Craig's son, looked so much like him.

Craig had tried to talk to her several times but she had turned him away, angry at him still for dallying with another woman down in Bristol while she was grieving over both Edward's death and Will's illness.

She sighed heavily, Will would be married soon and naturally Sarah would be his first concern. At least Hari had David and he was a fine strong child with a shock of dark hair and the well-defined features of the Grenfells.

It was for David's sake that she must make something of her life, Hari felt that she must drag herself up from her mood of apathy and earn back the reputation she once had.

Her customers had made allowances knowing that she had been bereaved but if she wasn't careful they would all grow accustomed to buying the ready-made boots and shoes that Emily offered in great quantities.

She sighed, it was pointless standing here in the street, that would achieve nothing. She must speak to Mr Fisher who collected the rents for the landlord, he might be able to help her.

Mr Fisher lived in one of the neat, respectable houses close to Chapel Street and as Hari walked past the house where she had lived with Edward, tears brimmed in her eyes.

She had not been in love with Eddie and yet she had grown fond of him, he had been a good and kind protector, a buffer between Hari and the world. And yet his illness had taken all his strength and hers too, she thought ruefully.

Mr Fisher was sitting in his study, bent over a ledger, when the maid showed Hari into the room. He did not look up immediately but continued to write for a few minutes. Hari felt a sense of anger and frustration building up within her, as Hari Morris, respected designer of footwear, she had never been treated like this.

'Excuse me, Mr Fisher,' she said and her voice was polite but firm, 'I might have come to ask you a favour but I am not a beggar or a debtor so I would appreciate a little courtesy.'

He looked up slowly, his eyebrows raised, it was clear that he recognized her by the way his face lit up.

'Hari Morgan, there's pleased I am to see you looking so prosperous.' He pushed back his chair and stood up, smiling.

'I'm Mrs Morris,' she said, 'I used to live with my husband in Chapel Street.'

Mr Fisher offered her a chair. 'I do apologize,' he said, 'I thought you were one of the tenants come to make excuses about not keeping up with the rent, we get a lot of that, mind.'

He resumed his seat behind the desk and waited for her to speak.

'I want to rent a property from you,' Hari said. 'The workshop at the back of the house in World's End.'

Mr Fisher rubbed at his beard. 'Just the workshop?' he asked doubtfully. 'The landlord usually lets out the whole place at one rental.'

'It's all vacant now and has been for some time by the look of it,' Hari said reasonably, 'surely it's better to have rent for part of the place rather than none at all. Later, I might wish to take on the entire building.'

Mr Fisher looked doubtful. 'I don't think so, Mrs Morris, it's either the whole thing or nothing.' He shrugged, 'I wouldn't know how to split the rent, you see and anyway no-one is going to take the house with the workshop occupied, you must see that.' He paused. 'The rent for the whole building is very reasonable you know.'

'All right,' Hari said, 'I'll take the whole building then.' As soon as she spoke, she felt panic begin to build within her, where was she going to get the money to pay for it?

'It will be one month in advance of course,' Mr Fisher said and Hari frowned.

'I suggest that you waive the first month's rent to defray

427

the cost of tidying the place up,' she said with far more confidence than she felt. 'It really does look a sight even for that area. Just think, if I refurbish the place, even if I left after one month, you are taking no risks.'

'How do you make that out, Mrs Morris?' Mr Fisher was almost smiling, no doubt amused at her audacity.

'The property would look more appealing for a start,' Hari said, 'and I would light fires in all the rooms so that the house would be free of damp.'

Hari smiled confidently. 'I am a business woman, Mr Fisher, I intend to make a profit while occupying the building and, if I succeed, you will have a permanent tenant, isn't that worth risking one paltry month's rent for?'

Mr Fisher appraised Hari's good clothes and the well-polished shoes she wore and, after a moment, he nodded.

'Very well, I shall give you one month's free rental on condition that if you leave at the end of the first month, you *will* be liable for it.'

Hari rose to her feet. 'Thank you, Mr Fisher, it was a pleasure doing business with you.'

Hari felt exultant as she walked along the street, the keys to the house and workshop in her hand, now would come the hard part, how to raise the money to pay for her extravagant gesture.

The place needed a thorough cleaning, the walls must be painted and some curtains and mats would have to be bought to brighten the place up.

After the premises were brought up to scratch, she would have to buy in a good supply of leather for shoes she intended to make, she would have to work at full stretch to make enough sales in the first month to keep her going.

Hari knew she could count on Will to work with her now he was well again, he would need all the money he could get if he was to be married.

She still had Lewis and Ben to work at the cobbling but

it was the new designs that would make the money, she was still taking a very big chance and she knew it.

A sense that she was attempting to do the impossible filled her and when Hari walked into the house in Salthouse Passage, her mood was picked up at once by Hetty.

'I just put Davie down, he's fasto so we can have a quiet talk,' she said. 'I suppose you didn't get anywhere with Mr Fisher then?' Hetty deftly placed another cup on the table for Hari.

'Wrong, I got the whole of the premises!' Hari smiled ruefully. 'To get the workshop I had to take on the house as well and though I bluffed Mr Fisher into letting me have the place rent free for a month, I don't know how I'm going to pay for it.'

'Do the same as me, of course,' Hetty said, 'let out the rooms to boarders. Don't worry about leaving me, I've got a married couple who want to come here as soon as I have room.'

She poured more tea. 'I suggest you go and live in the house in World's End and take Lewis with you for a start, he's a very good boarder, pays on the nail, he does.'

Hari looked at Hetty with gratitude. 'There's a good idea!' Hari said. 'There are two bedrooms and the parlour I could let and me and the baby could use the attic.'

'That's the spirit,' Hetty smiled. 'And don't forget, if you take in a married couple you charge more for the room, mind.'

Hari rose from her chair and, on an impulse, hugged the older woman. 'You are so good to me, Hetty,' she said, 'I don't know what I'd do without you.'

'Hush now!' Hetty scolded, 'there's soft you do talk.' In spite of her words, Hetty was wiping her eyes with the corner of her apron.

'Now then,' she said, sniffing, 'we must see what bedding I can let you have, there are some curtains I can spare as well. You'll need beds, mind, but I know where you can pick up some old ones very cheap.' She held up her hand as Hari made to protest.

'I want to help you get on your feet, girl, now just indulge an old woman because you are like the daughter I never had.'

'I can't thank you enough, Hetty.' Hari sighed, 'But I promise you this, you'll never go without a good pair of shoes while Hari Morris can hold a needle.'

Doing up the old building proved to be an exciting project, everyone at Hetty's house down to the old man who lived in the attic next to Will gave a hand. Soon the building glowed with cleanliness and the faded but clean curtains hung at the windows gave the place a homely feel.

Cleg the Coal delivered a mountain of fuel and Beatie arrived with an armful of bed linen.

'Where on earth did you get all that?' Hari put down the whitewash brush she'd been using on the inside of the workshop and stared at Beatie open mouthed.

'I went round the big houses,' Beatie said complacently, 'told them I wanted the stuff for charity, don't know if they believed me or not but most of them gave me something!'

Hari put her hands on her hips. 'You are a cheeky devil, Beatie the Coal, but I could kiss you!'

She put down the brush. 'Come and have a cup of tea in my bright new kitchen.' Hari led the way indoors and felt a twinge of pride as Beatie clucked her tongue in appreciation.

'*Duw*, will you look at that grate, gleaming all lovely and black it is and the brass around it so bright you can see your face in it.'

'I got the chairs and table from the pawn shop,' Hari said, 'and to tell you the truth, I don't recognize the place now it's done up.' She sighed. 'It's hard to believe I was born and reared in this house.'

'You'll do well here.' Beatie said confidently, 'I can feel great happiness coming to you so don't you fret, Hari love.'

There was a knocking on the kitchen door and Will moved into the room, a smile on his face. 'I've got you a married couple for one of your rooms.' He sat near Hari and took her hand in his, 'I hope you'll be happy for me, Hari, Sarah and me, we're going to get married in just a few weeks.'

Hari felt her spirits sink, Will was going to get married to a girl who was carrying someone else's child. But guilt flowed over her, even as she opened her mouth to speak, because wasn't that exactly what she herself had done, married Edward while carrying Craig's baby?

'So long as you are happy, then so am I, Will. Come here, let me give you a big kiss.' She held Will close for a moment, grateful that he was well and strong again and hoping against hope that he was not making a mistake.

'Don't worry about the rent,' Will said proudly, 'the shoes I've been working on since I came out of hospital have brought in a little bit of money and Sarah has savings, between us we'll manage.'

'I hope you'll be working for me again, Will,' Hari said at once, 'I've got these premises for a month rent free. We'll achieve great things here, Will, I'm sure of it.'

'I know we will, you are so talented Hari, you're bound to succeed again once you put your mind to it,' Will said cheerfully.

'That's just what I said too!' Beatie rose to her feet. 'Well, I'd better be getting back to my brood but when you need the laundry washing, let me know, Hari, because you won't have time to wash bedding and make shoes, will you?'

Hari smiled, with such a lot of good will around her how could she fail?

Spencer Grenfell looked up at his brother and hate burned within him, all Craig seemed to think about was that Hari Morris and the brat she'd given birth to.

Whenever Spencer needed anything, he had to crawl and beg and yet this woman from the lower orders could have had anything she asked for.

'I need some money.' Spencer said, 'I'm tired of sitting in this house doing nothing all day, I *have* to get out or I'll go mad.'

Craig reluctantly reached in his pocket and took out some notes. 'See that you don't get into any trouble, then,' he said and, though he kept his tone light, Spencer knew there was a hidden threat behind the words.

Spencer left the house and made his way quickly down the hill, looking neither to the right nor the left of him. He knew where he was going, to the mean streets around Salthouse Passage where Maria Payton, for a consideration, would give him a warm welcome.

There had been a great deal of interesting talk in Maria's house lately, Sam Payton and his mother gossiping about Hari Morris, the slut Craig was in love with and that brat she'd borne. Perhaps the time had come to have vengeance on his brother, Spencer thought, and in the bargain extract from Craig some of the money that was rightfully his.

Hari took up residence in the house in World's End once again and though it was strange and sad leaving her room under the protection of the kindly Hetty, it felt good to have her own home again.

Lewis had moved his stuff in days ago and he had built a cheerful fire in the grate ready for Hari's arrival, he even had the kettle boiling on the flames as she came through the door. She put the baby down on the rug with a sigh of relief.

'That boy is getting heavy,' she said and then she stood for a moment looking round her.

'There's kind of you to get the fire going, Lewis, it's nice to come into a warm kitchen.'

'It's nothing,' Lewis smiled. 'I'm off out now but I've been doing a bit of talking to my mates in the public bars, reminding them what a good shoemaker you are.' He moved to the door.

'You are good to me, Lewis,' Hari said gratefully.

'I could be *very* good to you if you'd let me, mind.' Lewis's face was wistful and Hari sighed heavily.

'Go to the public, Lewis, I haven't got time to think of anything but making a success of the business.' She smiled to soften her words, 'I'll have a good meal for you when you come home and then I'm going to ask you to tap a pair of boots for me, big heavy working boots they are, need a man's hands to do them justice, I promised them for tomorrow.'

'It's as good as done.' Lewis paused a moment longer in the doorway and then went out and Hari breathed a sigh of relief. Perhaps it hadn't been such a good idea having Lewis as a lodger after all. It wouldn't do to give him any false hopes.

'Ah well, David,' she said, ruffling the baby's hair, 'I'll settle you down for a little sleep and then I'd better get some work started.'

Charles and Meg had sent quite a lot of work Hari's way and had intensified their efforts so that even more customers who wanted repairs for specialized shoes done were patronizing her shop in World's End but Hari knew that the real money was in new and unique designs.

Still, she must settle her mind to making her way back to her former productiveness slowly, the work would build up as it had done before and the orders would come in regularly, she was sure of it.

Hetty still cared for David most days but sometimes she seemed in need of a rest and then Hari kept David at home.

He was a good child and David slept late in the morning and then Hari spent her time running between the workbench and the kitchen, constantly checking that her son was all right.

One morning Hari called on Hetty only to find that she had not been very well. Hetty had barely slept all night and Hari decided she needed a rest.

In spite of Hetty's protest, Hari took David back home and put him to sleep in the deep cushions of the old sofa she'd bought and he seemed to like it well enough. At any rate he didn't stir when she entered the kitchen to check on him.

Throughout the morning, Hari had a string of customers, some of them just curious but others with genuine jobs for her to do. One or two of her old customers came back and Hari soon found herself surrounded by boots and shoes in all states of disrepair.

She ate a midday meal of fresh bread and cheese and then holding David she fed him on potato mashed with butter and milk. She was so relieved that now he was weaned, it made life much easier.

There was a knock on the door and instinctively Hari called out for the visitor to come in. She glanced up and the breath seemed to leave her body as she saw the tall figure of Craig Grenfell standing in the doorway.

'Hari,' he said softly, 'I must talk to you, don't turn me away again, surely you can find a little charity in your heart?'

The colour rose to her cheeks even as she stared at him coldly.

434

'We have nothing to say to each other.' She spoke quickly, and, rising, she put David down on the sofa.

Craig moved to look at his son and then held out his hand and touched Hari's shoulder. The warmth of his fingers seemed to scorch her skin even through the thick material of her bodice and, angry though she still was, she somehow couldn't move away from him.

'Hari, I'm asking you to forget our differences,' he said gently, 'we love each other so why keep up this barrier between us?'

He slowly drew her closer and she looked up into his face. His lips were very close to hers and Hari felt that she would like nothing better than to melt into his arms. Why was she being so stiff necked and proud?

And yet, reason told her, Craig had failed her when she most needed him, putting business and even another woman before what he called his love for her. And yet should she hold that against him for ever?

She moved away from him abruptly, she couldn't think, not with him so close to her.

'Look at my son,' Craig said softly, 'lying on an old sofa in a dingy house in the slums of Swansea. Why should he have to when I could give him the best of everything?'

Hari felt hurt to the core, couldn't Craig see beyond material things, wasn't she trying to do the best for her son?

'Could you give him the best of everything?' she challenged. 'Or could you just teach David to value material possessions above all else?'

'I'm sorry, Hari,' Craig said swiftly. 'That was insensitive of me, I can see you are trying your best but you don't have to work yourself to death when I can take care of you.' He came closer again. 'Please, Hari, I'm not an ogre, I love you, can't you just accept that?'

'No, I can't.' Hari said obstinately, 'I don't trust you,

Craig, you never seem to be there when I need you.' Her anger was rising.

'You even put a common bawd before me, I could never trust you again, can't you understand that?'

'I can't excuse myself for that, Hari, I regret it bitterly but I'm only human too, don't you think I want the comfort of warm arms around me?'

'I see, you'd want me to be just a doll in a doll's house, a pair of "warm arms". Well, I'm a person in my own right and if I work myself to death in an effort to succeed then it's my business and no-one else's.'

She opened the door. 'Please leave, Craig, and try to understand me as I really am, not as you would like me to be. I need success, I need to map out my own future, be a woman in my own right.'

Craig moved towards her and paused looking down at her. 'I wouldn't stop you working,' he said, 'but I could give you the security of marriage.'

'I've had that,' she said flatly, 'and it was all a dream, there is no security except what a person makes for themselves. Goodbye Craig.'

She closed the door quickly, afraid she would soften under the appeal in his eyes. Craig was not for her, perhaps she was not meant for marriage at all but was a lone woman who would carve out her own destiny.

And yet, as she sank down into a chair and stared down at her son, her eyes were moist with tears.

Later that evening Will came over to World's End and Hari hugged him warmly. 'Got some jobs for you,' she said, 'I've had a few pairs of boots in today and Lewis has promised to put in an hour or two. He's out the back washing ready for supper.'

She moved to the fire and stirred the pot of stew so that the aroma of meat and vegetables drifted invitingly round the kitchen.

'You'll have a bite to eat with us, Will?' she asked, already putting out the dishes.

Will sat at the table and smiled up at her. 'Hetty sends her love and asks can she mind Davie for you tomorrow?' He winked. 'She says she's feeling better now. I think the old lady is missing having you and the baby under her roof much more than she'll admit.'

Lewis entered the kitchen just as Hari was ladling out the stew and he sniffed appreciatively. '*Duw*, that *cawl* smells nice.'

Lewis sat next to Will and thumped his shoulder heartily with a few jugs of ale inside him. 'Hello there old butty, going to give me a hand with some boots later on?'

'Aye, I suppose so,' Will said, picking up a piece of bread from the plate, 'won't hear the end of it if I don't.'

'When are you moving in here then?' Lewis asked between mouthfuls of stew and Will shrugged.

'As soon as me and Sarah get hitched, I suppose, and I'm working on that, we want to wed as soon as possible.'

Lewis stopped eating and stared at Will in disbelief. 'You're not really going to marry her, are you?' he asked failing to see Hari's warning glance.

'Yes, I am, any objections?' Will's voice was cool and Hari nudged Lewis with her elbow.

'Eat up your stew,' she said in agitation, 'there's plenty more there, mind.'

'The boy's got to be told the truth,' Lewis said quietly. 'Don't fret, Hari, it's for the best.'

He turned to Will. 'Look, it's like this, me and Hari heard the girl rowing with Sam Payton, he's the one who put you in hospital and he's the one who put Sarah in the family way.'

Will was suddenly pale. He turned to Hari, his eyes full of pain. 'Is this true?' he asked.

Hari bit her lip. 'Yes, Will, it is, I'm sorry you had to find out like this but perhaps as Lewis said, it's for the best.'

'For the best,' Will repeated the words blankly, 'what a blind fool I've been.' He rose to his feet and rubbed his hand through his hair.

'I think I could forgive her anything, the deceit and the lies all of it except that she consorted with that *scum*!'

'Will, don't think too harshly of her, these things happen to us women even though we don't mean them to.' Hari couldn't bear the look of pain in Will's face.

Will turned and looked at Hari and, after a moment, he shook his head. 'I can't believe it. You are *sure* aren't you, Hari, there can be no doubt?'

It was Lewis who answered. 'We both heard the girl; pleading with Payton, she was, shouting at him that she was carrying his child. The man just shut the door in her face and told her more or less to go to hell.'

'I'm sorry, Will,' Hari said, 'there's no doubt about what we heard.'

'And you weren't going to tell me the truth, Hari?' Will asked slowly.

'No, Will, I wanted Sarah to be the one to tell you but I suppose she was afraid.'

Will moved to the door. 'I'm sorry, Hari, I won't be able to work tonight after all, perhaps tomorrow all right?'

'Will!' Hari was on her feet. 'Now don't do anything silly.'

'I'm a man now, Hari,' he said, 'I must make my own decisions.'

He went out and closed the door and Hari looked at Lewis appealingly. He rose and picked up his jacket.

'Don't worry,' he said, 'I'll make sure he comes to no harm.' Lewis paused for a moment and stared at Hari. 'Will had the right to know the truth, mind,' he said gently. 'He had to be told.'

When the door closed behind Lewis, Hari rose to her feet and began to clear up the remains of the meal. She put the bread back in the pantry and then, suddenly, she sank down into a chair and put her head in her hands.

But she couldn't cry for a rage was burning within her, against whom she didn't know. All that was clear was that, in this life, it seemed that the wrong people were the ones getting hurt.

After a while, she rose and pushed the kettle on to the flames, she would wash the dishes and then make a nice cup of tea and perhaps by that time Lewis would be back with some news.

But the minutes stretched into hours and all Hari could hear as she sat in the silence was the soft breathing of her baby and the occasional shifting of coals in the grate.

34

Hari sat in the kitchen and stared across at Hetty who was dressing David in his outdoor clothes.

'I'm so worried about Will,' Hari said softly, 'I don't know if Lewis was right to tell him about Sarah or not.'

'These things are always meant,' Hetty said sagely. 'It's all been taken out of your hands so there's no good going on about it.'

She buttoned up David's coat and pulled a woollen hat over his dark curls. 'I'll take him over to my house for the day, right love?' Hetty stared at Hari, 'And don't you go over doing it; worrying about all and sundry like you do doesn't make life any easier for you.'

'I can't help worrying when there's so much to fret about,' Hari said. 'There's been no word from Will since he walked out of here last week, how can I not worry?'

'I know,' Hetty smiled, 'you take the weight of the world on your shoulders and you only a little bit of a thing too.'

Hetty deftly wrapped the Welsh shawl around herself and the baby, tucking under the ends so as to support David's weight.

'At any rate, you know the boy will be fine with me so you needn't fret about *him*, all right?'

Hari returned the older woman's smile. 'All right,' she agreed, 'David couldn't be in better hands.'

Hari waited in the doorway, watching until Hetty had

disappeared along the street, then she returned to the kitchen and began to clear the table. Hetty was right, time spent worrying was time wasted, Hari had work to do.

In the shop, sitting at the bench surrounded by the tools of her trade, Hari felt a surge of pride, the way the work was coming in she would have more than enough money to pay the month's rent and to buy herself more leather.

She had begun to make a pair of evening slippers, working in a new design of soft kid and blue, shiny satin. She intended to decorate the slippers with blue glass beads given to her by Hetty. Soon, she would have a window display that would catch the eye of anyone passing and, in spite of the poverty of the neighbourhood, it was a thoroughfare much used by the gentry.

The door of the workshop opened and the bell jangled noisily. Hari looked up and was somewhat surprised as she saw Emily enter the shop.

'Hello, Hari.' Emily came up to the counter and her gaze went immediately to the half-made slipper on the last.

'What can I do for you?' Hari said, deliberately dropping a cloth over the slipper. 'It's ages since I saw you, everything all right is it?'

'I don't want to intrude,' Emily said apologetically, 'but I wanted to talk to you about Sarah.' Emily paused finding it difficult to go on.

'She's most distressed that Will has not been to see her for some days now, is anything wrong?'

'I'm sorry,' Hari said, 'but I have no control over Will, he's a man now and comes and goes as he likes.' Hari bit her lip, she could hardly tell Emily the truth about her stepdaughter.

'He has responsibilities.' There was an edge to Emily's voice, 'He can't be allowed to desert the girl after taking advantage of her. I know you are bound to support Will

441

but, in the circumstances, you must at least believe in fair play.'

'You don't know all the facts,' Hari said slowly. 'Please Emily, leave well alone, keep right out of it, that's my advice.'

'Naturally you are on Will's side but you can be thankful that it's me standing here and not Sarah's father.' Emily brushed back a stray curl of hair in agitation.

'John is very angry indeed about the way William is behaving.'

Hari sighed heavily. 'Please listen to me, Emily,' she said. 'You don't know the half of the story and here you are throwing your weight around as usual.'

'Look,' Emily said, 'we may no longer be close friends and a great deal of that is my fault, I admit, but we can at least act in a civilized manner. Can't you at least invite me in to where we can talk in private?'

'Yes, of course.' Hari rose to her feet. 'Come on through to the kitchen, have a cup of tea.'

'I don't want to trouble you for any tea,' Emily said, as she followed Hari into the warmth of the kitchen, 'just tell me where I can find William and I'll say my piece and be on my way.'

Hari felt anger building up within her. 'I don't know where Will is,' she said quickly, 'I only wish I did.'

'Don't help the boy wriggle out of his obligations, Hari,' Emily said reasonably, 'he's got Sarah in trouble and the poor girl is heart broken.'

'Rubbish!' The word exploded from Hari's lips. 'The child Sarah is carrying isn't even Will's, Sarah has been playing around with Sam Payton if you must know and since William learned the truth, he hasn't been seen. If it's anyone who is heartbroken, it's William.'

'I don't believe you!' Emily said, her cheeks suddenly red. 'Why are you trying to blacken Sarah's name, is it out of some sense of misguided loyalty to William?'

'The child's father is a man called Sam Payton,' Hari repeated, ignoring Emily's remarks. 'He lives near Salthouse Passage and he is the one who with some other hooligans hurt Will so badly that he ended up in hospital.'

She paused, 'Why do you think he beat Will up? Because of Sarah, of course.'

Emily had lost her colour and was now very pale. 'I think I will have that cup of tea if you don't mind,' she said shakily.

Hari quickly pushed the kettle on to the flames. 'Sit down, Emily,' she said more gently. Hari put out the cups aware of the sudden silence and she watched in sympathy as Emily sat down as though her legs were refusing to hold her.

Hari swiftly poured boiling water into the teapot. 'I'm sorry to break the bad news to you,' she said, 'but you had to find out sooner or later.'

Emily remained silent as Hari put out the cups. 'Drink it up,' Hari said pushing the cup forward, 'it'll make you feel better.'

Emily obediently sipped the tea. 'How do you know about this man, Sam Payton?' she asked and Hari sighed.

'It was when I was still living in Salthouse Passage, Lewis and I were walking home and we heard Sarah rowing with this man. It all came out then about the baby and everything.' Hari paused and stared down at her tea.

'Lewis felt it only right that Will be told the truth, Will walked out and, since then, I haven't seen him.'

'Oh heavens, this is all much worse than I'd imagined,' Emily said quietly. 'You *are* absolutely sure aren't you, Hari?'

'All I'm sure about is that Sarah has been a silly girl,' Hari said, 'and I don't think she should be judged too harshly for that.'

'How am I going to explain this to John?' Emily said almost to herself.

'As I said, I would keep out of it and let Sarah do the explaining,' Hari said drily.

'What a mess.' Emily rose to her feet. 'Well, thank you for the tea.' She sighed, 'And I'm sorry for my aggressive attitude, Hari.' She moved to the door and then paused.

'I don't know if this is the time to raise the issue but I've had a request for a pair of child's boots,' she began but Hari held up her hand at once.

'I don't need any handouts from you,' she said quickly, 'and I'm far too busy to take on anything extra.'

'Too busy to make a crippled boy a pair of special boots?' Emily asked quietly.

'Oh, that's different, I suppose.' Hari spoke reluctantly. 'What exactly is needed?'

'I'm not sure, perhaps I can send the child's mother to you?' Emily replied.

'I suppose that will be all right.' Hari moved to open the door and Emily stared down at her and sighed.

'I'm so sorry that we seem to have lost the close friendship we once shared,' she said softly. 'I realize now how I miss your sound common sense and I miss your honesty, I always knew where I was with you.'

Hari smiled ruefully. 'Then you were lucky,' she replied, 'I never did know what was going through your mind, Emily.'

Emily looked away quickly and Hari wondered if she had been a little hard. But she had only spoken the truth and Emily had made no great effort to keep in touch these last months.

With people like Emily, it was much better to keep at a safe distance. Closeness with Emily's kind only brought betrayal and disappointment.

As Hari closed the door, she saw Emily climbing into the cab that had obviously been waiting for her, it was clear that no expense was being spared, Emily was now a very rich woman.

Hari straightened her shoulders and returned to her work with fresh determination, she too would prosper, she owed it to her son to make a success of her life and to herself.

Emily sat back in the seat of the cab, satisfied that the driver knew of both Salthouse Passage and the man Sam Payton. What good it would do her to see him she wasn't quite sure but speak with him she would, somehow she would learn the truth about Sarah's baby.

The streets were mean and narrowing into nothing more than cobbled courts which provided just enough room for the cab to drive through. When the cab came to a halt, Emily stared around her for a moment wondering at the wisdom of being alone in such a place.

The driver coughed impatiently and Emily lifted her skirts and climbed down into the roadway.

'I can't wait here long, misses,' the driver said holding out his hand for money, 'I've got other things to do, mind.'

'I will only be a few minutes,' Emily said, 'and I will make the wait worthwhile so don't worry.'

The door of the house was open and Emily could see a long dark passageway leading into a kitchen. A woman with a shawl around her shoulders stood, arms akimbo, looking out at her.

'What you gawping at?' The woman's voice carried the length of the passage. 'This isn't no peepshow, mind.'

'I'm looking for Sam Payton,' Emily called. 'Does he live here?'

Startled, Emily felt a hand on her shoulder. 'I'm Sam Payton and yes I live here. Who's asking?'

She turned to see a handsome if surly man staring down at her.

'I'm Emily Miller,' she said quickly, 'Sarah is my stepdaughter.'

'Is she indeed?' The man's narrowed eyes appraised her good clothes and then he turned to the driver of the cab and jerked his head.

'Clear off, we don't need you nosing round here.'

'I haven't been paid yet,' the man protested and drew back startled as Sam Payton lunged towards him.

'Clear off right now if you don't want to go home with your head in a basket,' he snarled.

Without another word, the driver whipped the horse into a trot and disappeared around the corner.

'You'd better come in.' Sam Payton took Emily's arm none too gently and almost pushed her into the kitchen.

'Look, mam, a toff come to see us, now what do you make of that?'

He sat down and put his booted feet up on one of the chairs, looking Emily over with undisguised insolence. 'Not a bad looker for a toff and a bit young to be Sarah's stepmammy.' He smiled unpleasantly, 'Perhaps you'd better tell me what you're here for.'

'I just wanted to know one thing.' Emily paused, the interview wasn't going at all as she'd planned, she had meant to be in complete charge of the situation.

'I've been to see Hari Morris, she told me about you and I want to know the truth. Are you the father of Sarah's child?'

'So that bitch sent you, did she? She's always been trouble that one but the answer is yes, I suppose I could be the father,' Sam said, 'it's all according to what's in it for me?'

Emily was taken aback, she'd expected a denial, anything but this sneering acceptance.

'There's nothing in it for you,' Emily said with more strength than she felt, 'why should there be?'

'Well,' Sam Payton paused, 'I reckon if I make an honest woman of the slut I should be paid to take her off your hands, to save you the embarrassment of having a bastard in the family.'

Emily made a move towards the door, 'I see I've made a mistake in coming here,' she said coldly.

Sam Payton was on his feet in a minute and stood blocking her way. 'It's not polite to walk out, mind, not when mam is making you a cup of tea.'

Emily looked at the heavily rouged woman who stood near the fire, a cracked teapot in her hands and suppressed a shudder.

'I don't want any tea, thank you,' she said. 'I really must be going, my husband will be worried.'

'Wait, you haven't told me how dear Sarah is doing, keeping well, is she?' Sam Payton was standing uncomfortably close and for the first time Emily felt threatened.

'Yes, she's well, now if you'll excuse me, I'd better be getting home.'

Sam Payton didn't move. 'You know, mam,' he said smiling at the heavily rouged woman, 'I should marry into this family, I've heard all about them from Sarah. This lady is none other than one of them rich Grenfells, *you* know the Grenfells, at least one of them *very* well.'

He gave a mocking touch to his forelock, 'And this lady who is kind enough to make you some nice, very expensive tea is my mother, Maria,' he said. 'So please to sit down and enjoy it, don't let good tea go to waste.' He touched her hair lightly with his fingertips and then his hand slipped down to her shoulder. 'I'm sure you could afford to let me have just a little of all that wealth.'

Suddenly, Emily was very angry. 'Let me pass!' she said loudly, 'or I'll have the constable on you. Trying to get

447

money by threats is against the law and I think Sarah has had a lucky break by not marrying you!'

'Let her go, Sam,' his mother warned, 'it don't do to pick on her kind.'

After a moment's hesitation, Sam Payton stepped aside. 'Lucky for you my mam is here,' he said roughly. Emily hurried down the passageway hearing his voice behind her.

'And you can tell Sarah to keep away from me,' he called. 'She's nothing but a whore! And as for that meddling shoemaker's daughter, she'd better stop trying to make trouble for me or she'll learn what real trouble is!'

Once Emily was out of the mean court, she began to run. She wanted to put as much space between herself and the man's threats as possible for Sam Payton was dangerous. He meant nothing but trouble and Emily shivered, wondering if she'd inadvertently stirred up a hornet's nest.

At least now she knew the truth, Sarah's troubles were not all the fault of William Davies but were more of her own making.

Emily sighed, how, she wondered, could she break the news to John that his daughter was not the wronged innocent he believed? It would not be easy but it was something that had to be done.

Hari had been right, it would have been better if Emily had minded her own business and kept right out of the affair altogether. But it was too late for that, far too late.

35

Meg stared up at the building in World's End and saw that it was well kept and the windows sparkled with cleanliness and were draped with fresh curtains. She had come to see Hari, they hadn't been together much since Meg's marriage to Charles.

She knocked on the front door and it was opened by a tall handsome man who stared down at her with open curiosity.

'Good-day,' Meg said politely, 'I'm looking for Hari, is she at home?'

'She's working, as usual.' He spoke reasonably, as if she should have known that Hari wouldn't be receiving visitors at this time of morning.

'Oh, I see, how is the business doing? I'm afraid I've neglected Hari a little these last few weeks.'

'Hari is managing quite well,' the man replied, 'building the business up little by little but she needs all the help she can get.' He smiled. 'I'm Lewis, I work for Hari, I'm just having a break, would you like to come in and I can call her from the workshop then?'

Meg stepped inside. 'No, don't call her, I'll go round and see her myself now but only if I won't be disturbing her.'

Lewis shrugged, 'Hari works like a slave making and repairing boots and shoes but it's tough enough to meet the monthly rent on this place so she lets out rooms as well, didn't you know about it?'

Meg was speechless, she simply hadn't stopped to think about how Hari was managing these days, so wrapped up had Meg become in her marriage to Charles that she supposed she'd not been all that much help to Hari in her latest venture.

'You used to get work for Hari,' Lewis stood at the kitchen table looking large and out of place as he put out the cups and saucers. 'Those theatre people pay well for special footwear, don't they? Can't you get in some more orders, it would make a difference, see.'

Lewis glanced at the kettle, steam was beginning to issue from the spout. 'Can you make a cup of tea, *merchi*?' he said.

As though galvanized into action, Meg rose to her feet and picked up the china pot, staring at it as though she had never seen its like before.

'Just tip in some water to warm the teapot and I'll get the box of tea,' Lewis said kindly.

Meg made the tea and then sank down into the chair and lifted the cup to her lips. She never had been domesticated, she'd always worked in the theatre and these days Charlie saw to it that she had servants to cater to her every whim.

'Hari is a wonderful person,' she said with a rush of emotion, realizing that tears were very near to the surface. Why had she been so selfishly engrossed in her own life when Hari was obviously finding life very difficult?

'She is that.' Lewis rose from his chair. 'Well, I've got to get back to work, otherwise Hari will have my head on a plate. Shall I tell Hari you are here?'

'No, there's really no need to disturb her, I'll see her another time.'

Slowly, Meg took up the cups she and Lewis had been using, it was about time she gave Hari a helping hand and she might as well start straight away.

Emily sat opposite John and, staring at his white face, felt pity for him wash over her.

'You had to know the truth, my dear,' she said softly, 'we can't go on blaming William when the baby probably isn't his.'

'I know.' John rubbed his eyes wearily, 'What am I to do with the girl, Emily, she has changed beyond all recognition from the sweet daughter I once knew.'

'She has grown up,' Emily said gently, 'she has become a woman with all the problems that can bring.'

John smiled at her, warmth illuminating his tired face. 'You are a good wife to me, Emily, I don't know what I've ever done to deserve someone so wonderful.'

'Nonsense!' Emily protested but love for her husband overwhelmed her. 'Anyone would do the same thing in my place.'

Emily rose to her feet. 'We'll go to see Sarah right away, shall we?' She held out her hand to John and he rose and came towards her.

'We'll offer to help her in any way we can, set her up in a house on her own if that's what she wants. One thing is clear, she can't stay at the shop much longer, it's not at all a suitable place for a girl who is expecting a baby to live, all those stairs to climb, it can't be doing her any good.'

As Emily sat in the coach beside John, she clung on to his hand knowing she was dreading the coming interview with Sarah. As the girl's pregnancy had advanced, she had become moody and irritable which was only to be expected given the circumstances.

It was late afternoon and the shop was still busy, customers nodded and smiled in Emily's direction and she absent-mindedly responded to their greetings.

Upstairs, Mrs Grinter was sitting near the window sewing a tiny garment and, when she saw Emily enter the room with John beside her, she pushed it quickly to one side.

'Sarah's in her room, resting,' she said. 'I told her not to work today, you don't mind, do you, Mrs Miller?'

'You did the right thing,' Emily said gently. 'I wouldn't want Sarah falling sick. Put the kettle on will you Mrs Grinter, make us all a nice cup of tea.'

It was John who knocked on the door of Sarah's room and John who was first to enter. Emily followed him and saw that Sarah looked a little pale and there were circles of darkness beneath her eyes. John took his daughter's hand.

'My poor little girl,' he said gently, 'we've come to see what we can do to make you more comfortable, Emily feels you can't live here like this, it's not at all suitable for you.'

'What do you expect me to do then, live in a poky room on my own somewhere?' Sarah said truculently.

'Not at all!' Emily said quickly. 'If you want your own house, you can have it and enough staff to care for you and the baby when it comes.'

'I'd rather come to live with you,' Sarah said quickly. 'I don't want to be on my own.'

'Of course you can live with us,' John said at once. 'We wouldn't dream of leaving you on your own, if you don't want to be, would we Emily?'

Emily felt dismayed at the turn the conversation was taking, she didn't want Sarah's disruptive influence to spoil the harmony she shared with John, but how could she put that into words without sounding selfish?

'We can take you home with us right now if that's what you want,' John said but Sarah shook her head.

'No, dad, I don't feel like moving today, there's plenty of time, the baby isn't due for a couple of months yet.'

Emily was ashamed of the feeling of relief that swamped her, at least there would be a short reprieve, time perhaps for her to get used to the idea of sharing her home with John's daughter.

John patted Sarah's shoulder. 'There will be every comfort for your baby when it arrives,' he said jovially, 'Emily will see to that, won't you love?'

'Of course.' Emily felt like an outsider looking in on a scene that had nothing to do with her. 'I'll go and see how that cup of tea is coming on.'

Mrs Grinter was setting the tray and Emily sank into a chair, pushing back a stray curl. She took the cup the housekeeper handed her and sipped the hot, sweet liquid gratefully.

'I'll have mine out here,' she said, 'give them a little time to talk.'

'Aye,' Mrs Grinter said darkly, 'there's a lot to talk about.'

'What do you mean?' Emily asked and Mrs Grinter set the tray back on to the table.

'That girl has got her dates wrong,' she said quietly. 'She's further on than we all thought, sooner you get her out of here the better, I'll be pleased. I've seen a few babies into the world but I'm no midwife, mind.'

Emily was silent, if Sarah's dates were wrong, she'd better be settled somewhere fast. Mrs Grinter was still grumbling.

'I'm worried in case she goes into labour, I couldn't take the responsibility of all that.'

'Mr Miller has already asked Sarah to come and live with us,' Emily said reassuringly, 'it will all be sorted out, don't worry.'

But would it? Would she ever get to the truth of whose child Sarah was carrying?

Meg's determination to do something for Hari had been growing ever since she'd spoken to Lewis about the problems Hari faced. She and Charles had talked it over and had decided to surprise Hari with the gift of premises inside the theatre itself, that way any artists appearing there would be tempted by Hari's skill as a shoemaker.

Hari had put up all sorts of arguments about independence and not wanting charity until Meg begged to be allowed to help.

'Please darling Hari, let me do this one thing, just think how it will draw in the crowds for our productions! We will all benefit, you must see that. In any case, my Charlie feels he has never repaid his debt to you for making him those special boots. Hush now, we will hear no more about it.'

At last, Hari had been persuaded, providing she kept on the place in World's End as well, and now the work on the premises was complete and the opening would take place within the week.

Hari stood in the evening sunshine with Meg beside her and gazed at the large, newly fitted window to the side of the theatre entrance feeling the excitement of a challenge burning within her. She had wanted to expand and now Meg and Charlie had given her a wonderful chance to do just that.

The window was dressed in Hari's traditional stark style with swathes of silk and only three pairs of shoes and one pair of fashionable boots on display.

'I can't help thinking of the opening occasion of the other shop,' Hari said, 'Emily and me, we had such dreams and *duw*, for her at least they've come true.'

'Charlie brought me to the champagne party,' Meg said smiling, 'what a long time ago it all seems.'

'Well, I'd better get off home now, I have a lot to do,' Hari said, touching Meg's arm.

Meg nodded her agreement. 'I can understand that you want to get back to that son of yours, I don't suppose you like to leave David with Hetty for too long, do you?'

'Well, I'm always afraid of putting on Hetty, she's so good-natured,' Hari said. She paused and pushed back a stray curl.

'I know it's silly but I keep hoping every time I go to Hetty's house that William will have returned, I'm so worried about him, Meg.'

'He's a man now,' Meg said, 'try not to worry about him, he'll come home when he's sorted himself out.'

Hari made her way back to World's End at a brisk pace and, as she entered the house, she felt relieved to be back indoors. Hari suddenly felt her elation vanish, she was suddenly tired and dispirited, she was making a success of things and yet her life seemed hollow and empty without Craig and without William; the two men who were so dear to her had gone from her life perhaps for ever.

Emily looked up from her books and her gaze was drawn to where Sarah sat next to her father on the huge leather sofa. The girl was pouting and John was trying to talk sense into her.

'I don't want you going out alone, not in your condition,' John said reasonably, 'goodness knows what could happen.'

'But I'm beginning to feel like a prisoner,' Sarah said hotly, 'I can't do this, I can't do that, I'm not a child you know.'

'It's only because I care about you, *cariad*.' John rested his hand lightly on Sarah's but she pulled away and rose awkwardly to her feet.

'I've got to get out or I'll suffocate!' She moved to the door and Emily folded away her books.

'What if we go for a walk?' she suggested though it was the last thing she wanted to do. 'A breath of fresh air might do both of us good.'

'Aye, all right.' Sarah spoke reluctantly and Emily knew

that the girl had agreed only because it was a way of getting out of the house.

Sarah had caused chaos ever since she'd moved in with John and Emily, her behaviour had been that of a sulky child and she seemed to take great delight in baiting John. More than once Emily had bitten back the angry words that rose to her lips.

It was a fine afternoon and Emily felt her spirits rise, perhaps the walk would do them both good. She glanced at Sarah who had pulled a shawl over her swollen body and looked very pretty indeed now that the frown had disappeared from between her eyes.

'Shall we go on to the beach?' Emily asked and Sarah shrugged.

'I don't mind.' She gazed ahead not meeting Emily's eyes. 'I suppose it's too much to ask that you let me be on my own for a little while?'

Emily sighed. 'All right, if that's what you really want but meet me back here in half an hour.' She watched as Sarah moved away and then followed her at a discreet distance. Emily felt she owed it to John to keep an eye on his daughter whether Sarah liked it or not.

The girl moved purposefully now towards the streets around Salthouse Passage. It was clear that she intended to make a visit and Emily bit her lip guessing that Sarah was making her way towards the home of Sam Payton.

She was not wrong, she saw Sarah knocking on the door of one of the shabby houses and, after a short wait, the man came to the entrance and leaned insolently against the door jamb.

'What do *you* want?' he asked briskly and Sarah clutched the shawl close around her.

'I want to be with you, Sam,' Sarah said and from where she stood hidden in one of the doorways Emily heard the quiver in Sarah's voice.

'What do I want with a baby hanging round my neck?' Sam said scornfully. 'Look, Sarah, we had fun once but I'm not the fatherly kind, see.'

'But Sam, I won't be like this for ever,' Sarah said desperately, 'once I've had the baby we could have great times together again.'

'I'll think about it if you get rid of the child,' Sam said shortly and, without another word, he closed the door in Sarah's white face.

Emily felt anger boil up within her, how could the man treat Sarah in such a callous way? Not wanting Sarah to know she had witnessed her humiliation, Emily moved quickly along the road towards the spot where she and Sarah had agreed to meet.

Sarah, when she came, was almost in tears, and was holding her shawl close as if for comfort. 'I want to go home,' she said, 'I feel really bad.'

Emily led Sarah back towards the house feeling sorry for her, no-one deserved to be so badly treated.

'I'm going to bed,' Sarah said once they reached the house, 'I've got such awful pains in my stomach, I can hardly stand.'

Emily fussed around Sarah, helping her get undressed and into bed. 'Do you think your labour pains have started?' she asked anxiously as Sarah winced.

'I don't know,' Sarah said. 'I've never had the misfortune to have a baby before, have I?'

Misfortune? How Emily would love to be in Sarah's place right now. 'I'll call the doctor to look at you just in case,' she said reassuringly.

John was concerned by the look on Emily's face. 'What is it?' he asked, taking her by the shoulders.

'I don't know but it looks as though the baby is coming, can you fetch the doctor, love?'

Time seemed to drag while they were waiting for the

doctor to come and, all the time, Sarah's pains were getting worse.

'I can't stand this!' she said to Emily, 'I don't even want the baby so why should I have to go through all this?'

'It won't be for long,' Emily said gently, 'look how many women have babies every day, you'll be fine don't you worry.'

'It's all right for you to talk,' Sarah said, 'you are not the one in pain.'

Emily was relieved when the doctor arrived, his voice calm and unemotional as he examined Sarah.

'A very healthy young woman,' he pronounced. 'I don't anticipate any problems here.' He looked at Emily. 'Can I rely on your assistance, Mrs Miller?'

'Yes, of course.' Emily spoke with more assurance than she felt. She fetched an apron from the cook's room and wrapped it around herself, her hands trembling. She was so excited, anyone would think it was her own baby coming into the world.

The doctor proved to be right, Sarah's confinement proceeded very smoothly and his attitude throughout was almost unconcerned though to Emily it was the most wonderful thing she had ever witnessed.

When, at last, the child was born, the doctor handed her to Emily with a few terse instructions.

'It's a girl, Sarah!' Emily said breathlessly, 'a beautiful little girl.' She would have given Sarah the child but Sarah turned her face away and would not even look at her baby.

The doctor shook his head. 'Don't worry, it takes some new mothers a little time to adjust,' he explained and Emily held the baby close as though the little one might sense her mother's rejection.

Looking at the crushed and reddened features of the

baby, Emily felt she had never seen anything so beautiful.

'Don't worry, little love,' she whispered, 'I'll look after you.'

In the days that followed the birth of the baby, Emily tried all she knew to make Sarah take an interest in her daughter. But Sarah refused point blank to even hold the child, let alone feed her. At last, Emily was forced to get in a wet nurse for fear the baby would starve.

It was about two weeks after the baby was born when Emily went into Sarah's room and found the baby alone in her crib. The cupboards were empty and not even one of her possessions was left to show she had ever been in the house, Sarah had vanished.

Emily, holding the baby close, felt a dart of pure happiness. 'You are mine now,' she said in a whisper, 'all mine.'

36

Hetty stared ahead of her wondering why the tall buildings and dingy windows with faded curtains hanging askew were wavering before her eyes.

She hoisted David up higher in her arms telling herself that he really was getting far too heavy for an old woman like her to carry. She had felt strange earlier that day and she knew she should not have gone over for David, she should have stayed in bed.

And yet today was the opening of Hari's new shop at the theatre, all the gawpers would be there, folks come out of sheer curiosity but who might stay to buy.

Hetty's head began to ache and she felt so sick and dizzy that she paused for a moment, leaning against a wall, trying to pull herself together. She was not far from Salthouse Passage, only a few more yards and she would be home. She could put David down for a nap and then she too could sleep. Sleep, it seemed such a wonderful idea, why was she so very tired in the middle of the afternoon?

By the time she reached the doorway of her house, Hetty knew there was something badly wrong. Her arms felt weak and Hetty was forced to put David down on the mat where he wobbled precariously before gaining his balance. He pointed up at her and Hetty tried to speak to him, to comfort him but the words would not come.

Hetty looked about her, trying to see through the haze

that shrouded her eyes, if only someone would come to help her, where were all her boarders? Of course, they'd gone to the theatre in Goat Street, eager to see what Hari had achieved.

She suddenly felt a blackness pressing in on her, she fell to her knees and slumped against the wall, staring around her desperately.

And then, it was as though her prayers were answered, a young couple were coming down the passage towards her, she tried to force herself to concentrate, held up her hand but she could not speak.

'What's this? It looks as though the woman's drunk!' the man said. 'Well, it makes things a bit easier for us.'

Hetty tried to protest that she was not drunk but sick and yet the mist before her eyes was growing thicker. Dimly she recognized that the girl was Sarah Miller, she would help surely?

Hetty saw the young man pick David up and stare at him. 'So this is Hari Morris's bastard is it?' he said. 'Son of the high and mighty Craig Grenfell?'

'That's right.' Sarah looked around nervously, 'Come on, Sam, let's get out of here.'

'Here's my chance to get even with that bitch of a shoemaker and to earn myself a tidy packet at the same time,' Sam said. 'Sod Spencer Grenfell, it might have been his idea to take the kid but I'm the one taking all the risk.'

He moved to the door and Hetty tried to call out but her head was spinning.

'I'm going to take this kid somewhere where no-one will find him.' Sam Payton paused thoughtfully. 'I know, up on the workings above Cwmbwrla, the very place.' He smiled. 'And I'm going to ask a fancy price for returning the brat unharmed.'

Hetty could see the mouths moving but she could no

longer hear the words the two young people were speaking.

Hetty's eyes closed as she lapsed into unconsciousness and when she opened them again, she was alone, the young couple had gone and so had David.

She tried to call out but it was useless, her voice was little more than a feeble croak. Hetty felt her senses reel and then a full obliterating darkness overcame her.

Hari looked round the shop with a rising sense of triumph, the crowds of people who had come to attend the opening exceeded her expectation, it was going to be all right, no, it would be more than just 'all right', the new shop would be a great success.

Charlie's Fine Leather Store as she had decided to call the shop, would soon be an integral part of Swansea, as well established as Emily's Emporium and serving the public not with machine-made stock but with the fine individual designs for which Hari had become known.

'It seems to be going well.' Meg came to stand beside Hari, watching as Lewis moved among the crowds, elegant in his new suit bought for the occasion, an order book in his hand.

'Your idea of having a young man to serve the ladies seems to be working,' Hari said softly, 'and see, even the men who are looking for boots are more comfortable talking to Lewis.'

'He's a good cobbler and a good friend,' Hari agreed and Meg smiled warmly. 'I must admit that I like Lewis very much and I have complete trust in his judgement.'

'He's always been very kind,' Hari said, 'I think he more than deserves his position of overseer in the shop and what's more he knows a good piece of leather work when he sees it.'

'This is a great day for all of us, Hari,' Meg said gently,

'Charlie's in his oils, see how he's greeting the visitors as if they are the most important people in the world? He's very good at that.'

Hari heard the pride in Meg's voice and smiled. Meg looked directly at her catching Hari unawares.

'I know you're pleased with the shop, Hari,' she said gently, 'and yet you are not really happy, are you?'

Hari raised her hand to her hair in a self-conscious gesture. 'I've a few things on my mind, that's all. I wish William was here for one thing.'

Hari looked down at her hands knowing that Will wasn't the only man on her mind, she was thinking of Craig and his apparent rejection of her. She had forced herself to go to his office to buy some French calf, but he had not attended to her personally but had sent his foreman to deal with her order. Perhaps he had given up on her and who could blame him?

Now that her business was beginning to improve again and she could hold up her head, Hari felt the time had come to talk. Craig obviously didn't feel the same.

'Can you stay here all day, or do you have to get back for the baby?' Meg asked and Hari, startled from her thoughts, looked up.

'Oh, I expect Hetty'll keep David until supper time,' she said. 'I know Hetty wants me to enjoy the opening of the new shop to the full.'

Hari sighed, 'Thank goodness Hetty is so good with David, he loves her dearly, I'm very lucky, really.'

'Luck has very little to do with it,' Meg said forcefully. 'You are talented as well as enterprising, you have got only what you've worked for.'

'If you say so.' Hari smiled, 'Oh dear, there's Lady Caroline with Elizabeth in tow, I'd better go and do a bit of bowing and scraping, Lady Caroline is very extravagant when it comes to buying shoes!'

Lady Caroline regarded Hari with curiosity, looking down at her through the pince-nez that Hari felt sure were an affectation more than a necessity.

'I hear you've opened up this place with the help of an *actress*?' Lady Caroline's tone implied that to be an actress was only one step removed from being a street walker.

'Meg was an actress,' Hari agreed smoothly, 'that was before she married Sir Charles Briant, of course.'

'I see.' Lady Caroline digested this information in silence and, behind her back, Elizabeth made a wry face.

'No matter,' Lady Caroline said at last, 'I need some special footwear, I'm tired of seeing the same slippers on all my friends, I want to be different.'

'That's what we're here for, Lady Caroline,' Hari said evenly. 'Shall I have Lewis bring you some of my designs?'

'No, that would not be suitable, my daughter is after all an unmarried lady, it's not fitting to have any young man taking her foot measurements and looking at her ankles.'

Meg appeared at Hari's side, 'Perhaps I can be of some help,' she said quietly. She turned to Hari. 'One of the assistants says that someone is asking for you,' she said quietly, 'apparently he's waiting in the foyer.'

Hari excused herself, her heart was beating swiftly, as she moved between the crowds of people, was it possible Craig had come to see her?

But it was not Craig waiting for her in the foyer. 'William!' Hari hurried towards him, frowning with concern. William was thinner and a little pale but otherwise he seemed all right. Relief flooded over her as she flung her arms around him.

'Will! You've come back, oh *cariad*, you don't know how glad I am to see you. I had such a fright when you went off without a word.'

William held her close for a moment and then looked down at her, his face grim.

'I know and I'm sorry it's taken me so long to come home.' He moved away from her, his hands thrust into his pockets.

'What's wrong?' Hari said, feeling a prickling of apprehension.

'There's bad news,' he said gently, 'I went back to the house in Salthouse Passage and . . .' He paused, 'It's Hetty, she's in the hospital.'

Hari felt an iciness wash over her, fear was almost a tangible taste in her mouth.

'What happened, was there an accident?' she asked, her voice was thin and indistinct.

'I'm sorry to be the one to tell you this,' Will said, 'but I found Hetty lying in the kitchen, she was unconscious, she must have been taken ill quite suddenly. One of her boarders came in, the old man from upstairs, told me about the shop so I knew where to find you.'

A new dread washed over Hari, 'Davie,' she whispered, 'is he all right?'

Will frowned, 'Davie? He wasn't there, there was no-one there, except the old man.'

'Oh, my God!' Hari slumped against the wall, she didn't dare imagine what might have happened to her son, had he wandered off alone and was lost and crying for her or had he fallen beneath the wheels of a cart and been killed?

'My baby,' she whispered, 'where are you?'

A feeling of sheer blind panic swamped her and then Hari made an effort to pull herself together. She must be methodical, she must start at Hetty's house, find out if David had been left there asleep perhaps. Even now, he might be safely tucked up in bed.

'Will, come with me,' she said more calmly. 'I must look for my son.'

Suddenly Meg was at her side. 'What is it, Hari?' she asked anxiously.

Hari explained briefly and then shook her head. 'It's best if you stay here for now,' she said. 'William and I will go and see what's happened.'

The journey to Salthouse Passage was interminable. Fear beat at Hari like dark wings and everything seemed unreal, a dreadful nightmare from which she must soon wake.

The house at Salthouse Passage was empty, the door stood open. Though Hari and William searched all the rooms, Davie was nowhere to be found.

Hari forced back her tears. 'We'll go to the hospital,' she decided. 'Perhaps Hetty has regained consciousness by now, she might have left Davie with someone.'

A feeling of guilt washed over her, in her worry for her child she was forgetting that Hetty might be very sick, near to death even.

At the hospital, the nurse shook her head when Hari asked after Hetty but she allowed them to go into the ward to stand by the bedside for a few minutes.

'Poor Hetty, what's happened to you?' Hari whispered aghast at the sight of Hetty's white face with her mouth dragged down on one side.

'It's some sort of seizure,' the nurse explained, 'it happens sometimes particularly with the elderly.'

Strange, Hari mused, she had not thought of Hetty as elderly. Hetty seemed to shudder and then her eyes opened.

'The baby,' her voice was slurred, 'they've taken Davie. I'm sorry, Hari, I let you down.' Hari swallowed hard, her world was turning upside down and there seemed nothing she could do to stop it.

'No Hetty, you could never let me down, I love you, Hetty. Tell me who has taken Davie, do you know Hetty?'

Hetty shook her head and tried to speak again but the words would not come.

'Don't worry,' Hari said, 'we'll get Davie back, it will be all right.'

Hetty made a supreme effort to speak. 'Go and find the boy, Hari, you go.'

She turned to William and stared up at him imploringly. 'I'm going to die, aren't I?'

'Don't talk like that, Hetty,' Will clung to her hand, 'you'll get well again, you'll see.'

Hetty tried to smile but her twisted mouth was contorted. 'I wouldn't want to live not like this, I've had enough of the world but I want company while I'm leaving it.' Her voice faded to a whisper and her eyes closed with weariness.

Hari bit her lip, she wanted to stay with Hetty but she couldn't, she *must* go on searching for Davie.

'You stay here, Will,' she whispered. 'I'll be all right, I promise you.'

Will looked doubtfully at Hari and then his gaze fell on Hetty who was still clinging to his hand and he nodded.

'All right, go on you, I'll come as soon as I can.'

At first sight, the house at World's End was as Hari had left it that morning. Upstairs, her boarders went about their business, none of them having seen anything out of the ordinary.

Hari moved around the house, searching for she knew not what, something, anything that would give her news of her son. And over everything hung the cloud of Hetty's awful sickness.

Hari went into the workshop and suddenly she saw it, a note was pinned to the bench, with a message scrawled in large untidy handwriting.

Hari took up the note and read the ill-printed words out loud.

'If you want to see your kid alive you'd best start collecting money, a heap of it.'

Hari sank down on to the stool and stared at the note as if it could tell her where her son was.

'What does it mean?' she said aloud, her voice trembling, 'what does it *mean*?'

She straightened her shoulders. 'It means,' she told herself, 'that Davie is alive, and that's what counts.'

37

'I hate it here!' Sarah Miller stared out through the window of the shed that stood on the slopes of the hill, built against an outcrop of solid rock situated above the valley of Cwmbwrla. 'I can't stand all that booming noise, are you sure the workmen won't be blasting down by here?'

'Don't talk soft girl!' Sam Payton's voice was rough. 'If they was going to blast here would they put up a shed on the land?'

'I suppose not.' Sarah looked round at the empty shed with just a solitary mug lying on the floor and then she glanced at the child sleeping on a bundle of rags.

'Well, I'm not staying here long, mind, I don't want a kid around my skirts that's why I upped and left home.' She pouted at Sam.

'Emily wanted a baby, well she can have mine, I don't want it.'

'Aye, lot of noise and trouble they are right enough.' Sam rose to his feet. 'Well, my second note is ready, think a thousand pounds is enough to ask?'

Sarah looked up at him, Sam was not all that bright, she decided.

'It's about all Hari could raise I should think,' she said, 'that sort of money won't be lying about the place, mind.'

'Well, don't be clever, I know that much myself,' Sam said. 'But Grenfell must be worth ten times that at least.'

'Yes, why not go to him direct then?' Sarah said placatingly. 'Just let's get what we can quickly, is it? If we ask for more, they might just get the constables in.'

Sam looked at her scornfully, 'I think there's more chance of getting the money if *she* goes begging to Grenfell, anyway, I want to punish her, don't I?'

He moved to the door. 'Right, I won't be long,' he smiled, 'I'll stop for some food for us on the way back, righto?'

Sarah nodded and went to the small window of the shed to watch as Sam disappeared from sight. She sighed, he was bound to stop for a mug of ale too if she knew him. Aye and she had got to know him the last day or two and he wasn't the man she'd believed him to be. Still, she'd cast her lot in with him now, there was no going back. Once they had the money they would shake the dust of Swansea from their shoes for ever.

Hari spent all night sitting at Hetty's bed side with William, forcing back the bitter tears, her arms aching for her son. She wondered distractedly if whoever had him was taking good care of him. She had tortured herself with thoughts of going to the constables but she was afraid that, if she did, Davie might be harmed.

It was about five o'clock in the morning when Hetty opened her eyes. 'God bless you both,' she said softly and clearly and then she died.

Hari stared at Hetty's face, peaceful now in death, and the tears came. William put his head on his hands and Hari knew that he too was overcome with emotion.

'Go home, you,' Will said at last, 'I'll stay and see to things here.'

Hari touched his shoulder lightly and then left the hospital feeling as though the fates were against her.

The note was pinned to the door and, with a trembling

hand, Hari took it down. The demand was for a thousand pounds in exchange for the safe return of her son. A thousand pounds, the one who had abducted Davie might as well ask for the moon.

It was then that Hari knew she must go to Craig. She left the house in the first dawn light, carrying the note in her hand as though it was a link between her and Davie. As she walked, anger burned in her and a pure hatred for whoever had taken her child but, as she drew nearer to Summer Lodge, she knew that she just wanted her son back whatever the cost.

Summer Lodge had a sleepy look about it, as though no-one was yet up and about behind the richly curtained windows. And yet Hari knew that the servants would have been at work for some time, lighting fires, fetching hot water to the master of the house and seeing to all his needs.

The maid who answered the door looked at Hari's good clothes and unable to make up her mind about the early visitor pressed her mouth into a straight line.

'The master isn't receiving callers, yet,' she said primly and moved towards the door as if to close it against Hari.

Hari didn't hesitate, she pushed the girl aside and went purposefully towards the stairs, hurrying upwards ignoring the maid's shouted protests.

Craig was in his dressing-room doing up his shirt cuffs. He took one look at Hari's white face and came towards her.

'Something's wrong, what is it?' he asked, holding out his arms instinctively.

Hari went to him and he held her close, smoothing back her hair.

She closed her eyes, knowing somehow that Craig would make everything right.

'Read this,' she said, her voice thick with tears. 'Somebody has got Davie.'

Craig crumpled the note in his clenched fist, his face white. 'You did the right thing coming to me,' he said. He finished dressing quickly and led the way downstairs.

'Have you any idea who would have taken our son?' he asked and Hari shook her head desperately.

'Now sit down and think rationally,' Craig said, 'tell me all you know.'

Craig's presence had a calming effect on Hari, she told him quickly how William had found Hetty unconscious in her kitchen and of how Hetty had regained consciousness at the hospital and talked incoherently about someone taking Davie away.

'Is there anyone living around Salthouse Passage who bears a grudge against you?' Craig asked.

'Well, there's Maria Payton and her son, Sam,' Hari said, 'they've never liked me, not since Sam was a child. Never liked William either, that's how Will ended up in hospital.'

'Maria Payton, that name sounds familiar,' Craig said, his brow furrowed.

Hari looked up at Craig desperately. 'I think we've found the one person in Swansea who hates me enough to do such a thing! Craig, can we go round to the house right away?'

'Take it easy, now,' Craig said softly, 'let me do a bit of searching around on my own, we can't just accuse these people without proof. They'll be in touch again with directions where we are to leave the money and then we'll have them.'

He took Hari in his arms and held her close. 'Trust me, I'll get our son back whatever it takes,' he said softly.

Spencer was sitting in his bedroom, drinking port and reading a newspaper when Craig entered his room.

'What do you know about Maria Payton and her son?'

His voice was dangerously quiet. 'I know you go to the woman for certain services.' Craig caught Spencer by the lapels of his jacket and shook him.

'This woman is a whore and I know you've been visiting her, so don't deny it!'

'You're mad!' Spencer blustered, 'I don't know anything about her or Sam.'

Craig shook him again. 'I didn't mention her son's name, you just gave yourself away and if you don't tell me at once where they've taken my son, I'll kill you!'

'Somewhere above Cwmbwrla.' Spencer was frightened, he believed his brother meant every word he said, he had never seen Craig so angry. 'A shed, I think, Sam Payton had some idea of getting a ransom for the boy but I had nothing to do with it.'

Craig flung him back into the chair. 'I'm going now and when I come back you are to be out of here. If I set eyes on you again I won't be responsible for my actions.'

'But where can I go?' Spencer said seeing his comfortable way of life vanishing.

'Go back to our dear mother or go to hell but just get out of my house and out of my life.' Craig's voice was suddenly deathly quiet and Spencer knew he meant every word.

Craig left the room then and Spencer looked around him desperately, if Payton harmed the boy there would be hell to pay, he'd better leave Craig's house before anything happened.

Spencer picked up a bag and started quickly to pack his clothes.

The sound came from the vicinity of the workshop, it was slight and yet Hari, senses alert, heard it at once. She hurried through the yard and found the door of the workshop was just swinging shut.

She pushed it open and looked outside just in time to see the figure of Sam Payton climbing over the wall. As Hari watched he disappeared along the narrow court and she could scarcely breathe, her worst fears were confirmed. Sam Payton was the thug who was holding her Davie captive.

Hari returned to the workshop and, as she expected, the note was there staring menacingly up at her from the bench. She read the words at first with a sense of apprehension, she was to take the money to the foot of the workings above Cwmbwrla and leave it there in a bag.

Her mind was racing even while she told herself to be calm, there was blasting going on up on the hill, a new road was being hewn out of the rocks, it was a dangerous place to be.

She looked down at the note again, the hillside was isolated except for a few roughly erected sheds. To a man like Sam Payton, it would be the perfect place to hide a stolen baby. Without waiting to pick up her shawl, Hari hurried from the workshop and into the street.

The foreman of the gang stood looking down at the plans stretched out across the table in the makeshift shed set up on the hill.

'We'll be blastin' lower down today, Taffee,' he said pointing at the plan.

'How much lower down, boss?' Taffee was a young man, with thick sprouting eyebrows and a full beard of which he was very proud.

'About where the old shed was put up, I'd say.' The foreman folded up the papers, he was tired of working, tired of the noise of blasting, he was getting old and his bones ached from being constantly out in all weathers.

'Hey, there's some good timber in that shed, boss, can't I go and get some of it for my chicken pen?'

'The wood is rotten.' The foreman looked at Taffee with derision in his weather-beaten face. 'Why do you think we abandoned it?'

'Looks all right to me,' Taffee said gloomily. 'Must be some good pieces of wood there. I think there must be a lamb trapped in there too, I could swear I heard it, like a baby crying it was.'

'You keep away from there, my boy.' There was a warning in the foreman's voice. 'Dangerous place to be right now because all the blasting above it has made the land unstable. All we want is a good shower of rain and the whole hill could slide and cover that shed.'

The foreman went back to his plans, it was time he made up his mind where he was going to place his next charge and, in case Taffee had the daft idea of trying to salvage some of the timber, it had better be on the site of that old shed.

As Hari hurried through the streets, past Salthouse Passage, a fierce anger gripped her, was Davie being left alone in the shed, frightened and cold and crying out for her? She felt she could readily kill Sam Payton for what he had done.

Hari didn't look back as she made her way up Carmarthen Road towards Cwmbwrla but she wished that Craig was here at her side, he would give Sam Payton the hiding of his life if he laid hands on him.

She was breathless by the time she reached the foot of the hill rising up from the valley of Cwmbwrla and Hari's heart was pumping furiously.

She could see the rise of scarred land where the blasting had taken place and, on one of the ridges, a band of workmen were standing. Hari hurried towards them, her feet slipping in the mud.

'Hey, where are you going misses?' A man with a

weather-beaten face came towards her, arms outstretched as though to hold her back. 'You can't go up there, *cariad*,' he said, 'the place is going to be blasted in a few minutes, the charges are all ready.'

'No!' Hari's voice was low with fear. 'My baby is somewhere up here.'

'That's impossible,' the man said, barring her way, 'no-one is up there, believe me.'

Another man stepped forward, his full beard at odds with the youthfulness of his face.

'Don't you remember, boss?' he said. 'I told you I heard a sound like a baby crying coming from the old shed.'

'Aye, I remember, Taffee,' the older man shook his head, 'but there won't be time to stop Ben from blasting, we'd never get up to the top of the hill in time.'

Hari heard a shout and she turned to see Craig manhandling Sam Payton, both men slipping on the loose earth of the hillside. In fear Hari cried out to Craig but he was too far away to hear her.

The figures of the two men seemed to fall and then they disappeared from sight behind the hill.

Hari ran forward, her feet slipping on the muddy ground, dimly she heard the foreman calling out from behind her but his words were drowned by a sudden blast of noise from above.

Hari felt rather than heard herself scream. The very hill seemed to lift and hover in the air and a cloud of dust rushed over the group of people standing below.

Then Hari was picking herself up from the earth, spitting out dust and slipping over the loose soil, upwards to where the shed had once stood.

Dust flew everywhere blinding her and Hari slipped again, grovelling in the dirt to find footing. She was aware of a couple running past her hand in hand and through the dust recognized Sarah clinging to Sam Payton, her face covered in earth. But where were Craig and Davie?

Planks protruded like broken teeth through the torn earth and Hari forced herself to go on running, dragging air into her desperate lungs, she forced herself upward.

A second explosion ripped through the air and Hari was thrown to the ground like a rag doll. Tears of fear pouring down her face, dust swirled around her chokingly as she struggled to rise.

'Craig!' she cried his name, her throat aching with the effort as she stood hopelessly, trying to see through the clouds of debris.

'Look out!' She heard the voice of the foreman dimly, 'The whole hillside is going to come down.'

She didn't move, if Craig and the baby died then she might as well die too.

And then, through the dust a figure emerged. He was covered in earth, his face and hair spattered with mud.

'Craig!' Hari stumbled towards him, her heart pounding, and, as he drew nearer, she saw that in his arms, he carried their son.

She ran then as though in a dream, her feet dragging through the muddy ground and it seemed she would never reach them. She was aware of the sobs tearing at her throat as she tried to force herself forward.

'Thank God!' She found herself clinging to them, her baby and the man she loved. He was real flesh and blood and in Craig's arms her baby was safe.

They clung together for what must have been only moments but it seemed like an eternity. 'I love you, Craig, I love you more than I can ever tell you.' Hari heard her own voice as though it didn't belong to her.

'Come on, my love,' Craig said gently, 'I'm taking you home.' They descended the hill, clinging to each other, his arm firm around her waist, both her arms holding him tightly.

As they emerged through the clouds of swirling dust, a great cheer went up from the crowd of workmen at the foot of the hill, voices ringing out against the now-silent land, hands clapping, applauding the bravery of the man who had saved the life of the small child.

Hari swallowed her tears, they were together now, a family and nothing would ever separate them again. Hari glanced back at the scene of destruction behind her and the ragged hillside suddenly seemed the most beautiful place in all the world and Hari knew she would not have to look back ever again but would go onward now to a new and better life.

THE END

THE OYSTER CATCHERS
by Iris Gower

Emmeline Powell had been born a country girl, in a small, whitwashed cottage on Honey's Farm. When her father died, Emmeline, bereft and lonely, married Joe Harries, a man much older than herself and one of the fishermen of Oystermouth.

The wives of the oyster catchers were sturdy, stoic women, used to helping their men with the catch, and they didn't like the frail outsider who had married into their community. Nina Parks especially didn't like her – Nina was a widow who thought Joe Harries should have been hers. Emmeline – Eline – grew more isolated, more unhappy, trapped into an ill-matched marriage without friends to help her. And then she met Will Davies.

Will was to open to new worlds to her, worlds of personal achievement, the unfolding of a talent she never knew she possessed, and the realisation that she knew how to love. As tragedy and passionate feuding began to erupt in the oyster village, so Eline clung to her integrity, her ability to work, and her hopes for the future.

The Oyster Catchers is the second book in Iris Gower's enthralling series, *The Cordwainers*.

0 552 13688 3

A SELECTED LIST OF FINE NOVELS
AVAILABLE FROM CORGI BOOKS

THE PRICES SHOWN BELOW WERE CORRECT AT THE TIME OF GOING TO PRESS. HOWEVER TRANSWORLD PUBLISHERS RESERVE THE RIGHT TO SHOW NEW RETAIL PRICES ON COVERS WHICH MAY DIFFER FROM THOSE PREVIOUSLY ADVERTISED IN THE TEXT OR ELSEWHERE.

☐	14060 0	**MERSEY BLUES**	*Lyn Andrews*	£5.99
☐	13915 7	**WHEN NIGHT CLOSES IN**	*Iris Gower*	£5.99
☐	13631 X	**THE LOVES OF CATRIN**	*Iris Gower*	£5.99
☐	13688 3	**THE OYSTER CATCHERS**	*Iris Gower*	£5.99
☐	13687 5	**HONEY'S FARM**	*Iris Gower*	£5.99
☐	14095 3	**ARIAN**	*Iris Gower*	£5.99
☐	14097 X	**SEA MISTRESS**	*Iris Gower*	£5.99
☐	14096 1	**THE WILD SEED**	*Iris Gower*	£5.99
☐	14447 9	**FIREBIRD**	*Iris Gower*	£5.99
☐	14448 7	**DREAM CATCHER**	*Iris Gower*	£5.99
☐	14537 8	**APPLE BLOSSOM TIME**	*Kathryn Haig*	£5.99
☐	14566 1	**THE DREAM SELLERS**	*Ruth Hamilton*	£5.99
☐	14567 X	**THE CORNER HOUSE**	*Ruth Hamilton*	£5.99
☐	14686 2	**CITY OF GEMS**	*Caroline Harvey*	£5.99
☐	14692 7	**THE PARADISE GARDEN**	*Joan Hessayon*	£5.99
☐	14603 X	**THE SHADOW CHILD**	*Judith Lennox*	£5.99
☐	14492 4	**THE CREW**	*Margaret Mayhew*	£5.99
☐	14693 5	**THE LITTLE SHIP**	*Margaret Mayhew*	£5.99
☐	14499 1	**THESE FOOLISH THINGS**	*Imogen Parker*	£5.99
☐	14658 7	**THE MEN IN HER LIFE**	*Imogen Parker*	£5.99
☐	14752 4	**WITHOUT CHARITY**	*Michelle Paver*	£5.99
☐	10375 6	**CSARDAS**	*Diane Pearson*	£5.99
☐	14577 7	**PORTRAIT OF CHLOE**	*Elvi Rhodes*	£5.99
☐	14655 2	**SPRING MUSIC**	*Elvi Rhodes*	£5.99
☐	14636 6	**COME RAIN OR SHINE**	*Susan Sallis*	£5.99
☐	14671 4	**THE KEYS TO THE GARDEN**	*Susan Sallis*	£5.99
☐	14708 7	**BRIGHT DAY, DARK NIGHT**	*Mary Jane Staples*	£5.99
☐	14744 3	**TOMORROW IS ANOTHER DAY**	*Mary Jane Staples*	£5.99
☐	14640 4	**THE ROMANY GIRL**	*Valerie Wood*	£5.99
☐	14740 0	**EMILY**	*Valerie Wood*	£5.99

All Transworld titles are available by post from:

Bookpost, P.O. Box 29, Douglas, Isle of Man IM99 1BQ

Credit cards accepted. Please telephone 01624 836000, fax 01624 837033, Internet http://www.bookpost.co.uk or e-mail: bookshop@enterprise.net for details.

Free postage and packing in the UK. Overseas customers allow £1 per book (paperbacks) and £3 per book (hardbacks).